Craig Cliff was born in Palmerston North, studied in Wellington and worked in Australia and Scotland before settling back in New Zealand. He has published essays, reviews and poetry, and wrote a column for *The Dominion Post* for four years about his double life as an author and public servant. His short stories have been widely published and anthologised, including in *Essential New Zealand Short Stories* (2009), and his collection, *A Man Melting*, won the 2011 Commonwealth Writers' Prize for Best First Book.

His first novel, *The Mannequin Makers* (2013), has sold editions in Australia, the US, the UK and Romania. *The New York Times* declared it 'a book that makes grand promises and delivers'.

Cliff participated in the University of Iowa's International Writing Program in 2013 — where he first became interested in Saint Joseph of Copertino — and was the Robert Burns Fellow at the University of Otago in 2017. He currently lives in Wellington with his young family.

NAILING DOWN THE SAINT

★ CRAIG CLIFF ★

VINTAGE

VINTAGE

UK | USA | Canada | Ireland | Australia
India | New Zealand | South Africa | China

Vintage is an imprint of the Penguin Random House group of companies,
whose addresses can be found at global.penguinrandomhouse.com.

Penguin
Random House
New Zealand

First published by Penguin Random House New Zealand, 2019

10 9 8 7 6 5 4 3 2 1

Cover and text design by Cat Taylor © Penguin Random House New Zealand
Cover photograph: *St Joseph of Cupertino in ectasy* by Felice Boscaratti, San Lorenzo
(Vicenza), taken by Didier Descouens, used under the Creative Commons Attribution-
Share Alike 4.0 International license (https://commons.wikimedia.org/wiki/File:Chiesa_
di_San_Lorenzo_a_Vicenza_-_Interno_-_San_Giuseppe_da_Copertino_in_estasi_di_
Felice_Boscaratti.jpg)
Author photograph by Darren Cliff, Splendid
Prepress by Image Centre Group
Printed and bound in Australia by Griffin Press,
an Accredited ISO AS/NZS 14001 Environmental Management Systems Printer

A catalogue record for this book is available from the National Library of New Zealand.

ISBN 978-0-14-377374-0
eISBN 978-0-14-377375-7

The assistance of Creative New Zealand towards the production
of this book is gratefully acknowledged by the publisher.

ARTS COUNCIL OF NEW ZEALAND TOI AOTEAROA

penguin.co.nz

MIX
Paper from
responsible sources
FSC
www.fsc.org   FSC® C009448

A portent . . . does not occur contrary to nature, but contrary to what is known of nature.
— Saint Augustine (354–430 AD)

I think that it is a different climate today. I do not think Oliver Stone gets JFK made today. Unless they can make JFK fly. If they can't make Malcolm X fly, with tights and a cape, it's not happening. It is a whole different ball game.
— Spike Lee (2012)

LA VITA DI
SAN GIUSEPPE DA COPERTINO

THE LIFE OF
SAINT JOSEPH OF COPERTINO

1603 — Giuseppe Maria Desa born to Felice and Franceschina Desa in Copertino (sometimes spelled *Cupertino* in English), in the southern Italian province of Puglia.

1614–19 — Bedridden and unable to attend school until he is healed by a hermit in Galatone.

1620 — Applies to join the Order of Friars Minor Conventual (aka Conventual Franciscans) at Grottella, near Copertino, but is rejected as a simpleton incapable of being educated. Joins the Capuchins at Martina Franca as a lay brother.

1621 — Asked to leave Capuchins after eight months. Returns to Copertino.

1625 — Finally accepted by the Conventual Franciscans at Grottella. Begins by tending the stable but is eventually allowed to study for the priesthood.

1628 — Ordained as a priest. His extraordinary feats — levitation, reading minds, predicting the future, being in two places at once, miraculous cures — become more frequent and widely known. These will continue, barring a few dry periods, until his death.

1634–35 — Forced to travel around Puglia with the Father Provincial. Accused in Giovinazzo of acting as another Messiah. Ecclesiastical tribunal in Rome begins looking into his case.

1638 — Appears before the Inquisition in Naples.

1639 — Rome declares Giuseppe's innocence, but orders him to live secluded from others in the Sacred Convent in Assisi. Despite orders forbidding it, an audience with Giuseppe is highly sought after among the nobility of Europe.

1653 — Sent to the Capuchins in Pietrarubbia, but lasts three months before his popularity forces another move, this time to Fossombrone.

1657 — Giuseppe's final move: to the Conventual Franciscans in Osimo.

1663 — Death of Giuseppe in Osimo.

1735 — Beatification.

1767 — Canonisation of San Giuseppe da Copertino.

PART ONE

MAY 2017

HOLLYWOOD/BABYLON

It might never have happened — the return of his flying dreams, the bursts of precognition, his entanglement with a cult of levitators — if Vilma Vegas hadn't stepped into his path as he carried a stack of leather-bound menus to the host's podium at Sforza's. 'After tonight,' she said, slipping a clear plastic sleeve on top of the menus, 'you might be interested in these.' He looked down. Headshots. Hers was an invented name, he was convinced, but both her waitress résumé and now these headshots said the same thing: Vilma Vegas. Total commitment to the role. Admirable.

'You can't—' he began.

'I know who you are, Duncan Blake.'

'I'm not hiding.'

'You're not exactly broadcasting it, either.'

For a moment Duncan wanted her to articulate *it*. What light was he concealing behind this stack of menus, beneath his company-issue black and white checked shirt? And how did she think he should broadcast whatever *it* was? Have his IMDb profile (KNOWN FOR: *FURY'S REACH* — PRODUCER; *CURIO BAY* — DIRECTOR; *MIST* (SHORT) — DIRECTOR) tattooed across his forehead? Tell everyone he served, every jobseeker he interviewed, every delivery person and observer from Corporate that the CIA's file on him was probably still open? That two years ago he was unceremoniously dumped from the director's chair of his first major motion picture after three days of principal photography and he hadn't made anything since? That Echo Park's parting gift — letting him retain a producer's credit, thus keeping his name forever associated with the train wreck that was *Fury's Reach* — now seemed their final cruelty?

He exhaled and nudged the sleeve of headshots with his chin. A deliberately awkward gesture that meant: *Must be getting on . . .*

Vilma didn't budge.

Ten seconds passed and they were still standing there in the aisle between the server station and the bar, Vilma trying to catch his eye, him staring at her name badge, thinking about how he must appear to her. A straight-laced assistant manager, tattooless, on the slight side of medium build, short black hair hinting at curls, his two-week beard greying at the chin. Vanilla, vanilla, vanilla. Perhaps she'd watched one too many episodes of *Undercover Boss* and thought this was a disguise. That surely someone with any talent couldn't look so ordinary, so at home with *Sforza's* embroidered on his left breast. That if she confronted him he would give up the ruse, pull off his hairpiece to reveal a Lynchian pompadour, grow six inches, and let out the corset that was concealing his true and imposing heft.

'I'm wasting my time, aren't I?' she said and reached for her headshots. 'At first, I thought: surely this is part of a plan. Your plan. At least research for a film. But now, that look, your eyes—' She held up her hands as if framing a close-up of his baby blues that were more like murky greys these days, each iris radiating tiny red bolts of parental sleep deprivation and service industry shit-taking. 'I can't see it.' She contracted her hands, two sudden implosions. 'I just can't see it. And it's such a fucking downer, man, to think LA, for you, has come to this. Fucking America, man.'

'Is this your break?' he asked, knowing her shift had only started ninety minutes ago. He could initiate an employee counselling session for this breach of the Staff Manual. Could cite any number of clauses. Conducting Personal Business. Solicitation and

Distribution of Literature. Throw the fucking book at her for this.

For *what*?

He rolled his head from side to side. To ease the tension from holding two dozen menus so long and so pointlessly. To keep from losing his religion in a Michael Stipean fit of elbow knocks and yelps. Nothing pissed him off more than people seeing his current situation as an apt metaphor for the state of the movie business, or the US, or the whole fucking world.

His dad did it on his last visit from New Zealand (and in every Skype call since).

His sister did it in her handmade cards for birthdays and wedding anniversaries.

Mack, his lone female friend from high school — the one who'd dropped out of his life until a fresh email ribbing him about the *Fury's Reach* debacle — seemed to do little else. 'You're a creative genius, babe, working in a restaurant franchise that never had a heart to begin with.'

But when his co-workers did it? That was the worst.

It was true that he had gone from directing a decently backed adaptation of the first book in a successful young adult trilogy to working at Sforza's North Hollywood in the space of nine weeks. And it was true that the chain of Sforza's Cucinas that had emerged over the last decade was — *no argument here* — heartless. According to online and fry-station scuttlebutt, the whole concept was dreamed up by GastroCorp's VP of Product Development rather than sprouting organically from a single successful Mom-and-Pop. Not that GastroCorp hadn't tried that route when its board commanded diversification of its fast-food-heavy portfolio. It's just that every two-bit restaurateur with a local following dreamed of franchising their concept to fuck and had over capitalised to the point they all proved impossible to fleece. Enter Sforza's, with its table service, tightly restricted bar and wholesome food *just like Nonna used to make*. Four Sforza's 'units', as restaurants were referred to by Corporate, appeared in LA in such quick succession that no one could remember which was the first. Each unit was engineered to be identical and timeless. The way the decor blurred the boundaries of kitsch and bland. The reproductions of Old Country monuments shot with Old Timey filters on every wall. The red and white tablecloths. The wax-drooling candles set in straw-wrapped Chianti bottles. The looping soundtrack of Frank Sinatra, Dean Martin, Louis Prima, Buddy Greco, Vic Damone and Jerry Vale. The prevalence of pretty servers in tight brown blouses because isn't that the kind of thing dads like? So yeah, no one was going to dispute that Sforza's, as a concept or a reality, wasn't deeply troubling and maybe even symptomatic of a wider malaise that the American people had wilfully ushered in by driving out to the nearest interstate for $7 baby back ribs on Wednesdays, constantly demanding more for less, preferring forced geniality over genuine interaction, and believing — still — as evidence to the contrary continued to gather in the periphery of their lives like a huddle of homeless people beneath an underpass, that all it took to succeed in America was the right work ethic and, come to think of it, good teeth. Yes, all right, that much Duncan was willing to lay at the many identical feet of Sforza's. But to bring him into it? As if his current lull was:

a) totally foreseeable,

b) somehow linked to the perils of late capitalism, and

c) he had no plan to get out of it?

C'mon!

'Well, when are you on a break?' Vilma asked with narrowed eyes, 'coz I got more to say.'

'Two,' he said.

'Out by the dumpsters?'

He gave a tiny nod, as if they were organising an illicit rendezvous.

Despite the fact Sforza's was genetically engineered to colonise every community with twenty-five thousand or more potential diners, GastroCorp's rush to bring the concept to market meant there had been oversights. The Staff Manual, for example, was pretty much a straight copy of an old Applebee's Employee Handbook, with identifying brands and phrases changed but slapdash pagination errors and flat-out inexplicable omissions. Like, somehow, the section forbidding visible tattoos or body piercing. The responsible drudge at Corporate was fired, no doubt, and the oversight amended in the second-tranche roll-out of twenty-five units across Arizona, Nevada and New Mexico, but by then Sforza's LA locations had become the refuge of recent arrivals with showbiz aspirations but too much ink. It lent the family restaurants an edginess that, against all logic, seemed to work. A slice of Portland inside a slice of Little Italy in the city on Earth most immune to irony or cognitive dissonance.

Vilma was new — a month or so into her year-long haul before she'd start accruing vacation leave and another year before she could take any of it — but she could have been Sforza's LA poster child. The big Mattel eyes. Her pinch-of-this, pinch-of-that ethnicity. The snakes, 'forties pinups and frangipani-blossom tattoos that emerged from every opening of her tight brown Sforza's shirt. Fun, flirty, a whiff of dissolution. She looked like the first girl to get it in a slasher flick, which is a role she'd absolutely take if given the opportunity. Even as he had this thought, Duncan cursed the ease with which he'd fallen back into this LA-induced cycle of chauvinism, misanthropy and — *here it comes* — apathy.

He spent the rest of the lunch service inside the giant carved-out melon that was his head concocting better versions of the day's dialogue, better ways to block each scene, while his autonomous vessel smiled, frowned, apologised and appeased until he found himself out on an upturned San Pellegrino crate between the cardboard dumpster and the food-waste dumpster. Vilma arrived a minute later, carrying her own plastic crate.

'You don't mind me saying *Fury's Reach* sucked hard, do you?'

Duncan closed his eyes.

Vilma continued, lighting a cigarette. 'I mean, it clearly wasn't your fault. Who knows what might have happened if they kept you on. But in the first place, the studio should have, you know? Why get someone with your eye for landscape, your less-than-mainstream leanings, to kick-off a franchise set entirely on a spaceship?'

That she had seen *Curio Bay*, his first feature, and maybe his shorts, took him aback, made him bite.

'Well,' he said, 'why would *I* accept the job?'

'You're not serious, right?' She took a drag from her cigarette and exhaled, going for something, some look. Maybe *Gilda*. Maybe *Basic Instinct*. 'After what I've been saying "yes" to in this town, and you feel sorry for yourself for signing on to make a movie for Echo Park?'

'What have you been saying "yes" to, Vilma?'

'Look. Maybe you blew it and that's that. *Finito*. But maybe you'll get another shot. I'm coming from a place of pure self-interest here. I don't know anyone else who's ever had that kinda bank behind them, even if it was for a nanosecond, even if they were using you. They were, weren't they?'

It was Duncan's turn to shrug.

'Because,' Vilma continued, 'maybe you will turn it around somehow, get on board something else. All I'm saying is, remember me. Maybe you'll write something—'

'I'm not writing at the moment.'

'When was the last time you got laid?'

'And that has got what to do with—'

'When?'

'I'm married.'

'I know that. You got a kid, too. I asked around. You're not hiding, remember? I wasn't propositioning you, Duncan Blake. This isn't that kind of intervention. You should fuck your wife. It'll do you both the world of good.'

'Her parents are staying.'

'Jesus. The insurmountables. Might as well curl up and die.'

'I don't know why you think you can read me, Vilma. That you can talk to me like this. As if you understand.'

'You're right. I don't get you. Do you even want it anymore? Is there *any* hunger left? Like —' she paused, pushed one hip higher than the other and rested her hand on it, a power pose ripped straight from a Beyoncé video — 'I saw you that time Frank Motta came in, my first week.' The way she said his name. Like a detonation. 'You greet him, you bring his ravioli—'

'Manicotti. Always the veal manicotti.'

'—and you don't drop a fucking hint you're this talented guy?'

'A talented Assistant Manager?'

'Stop. You shit on yourself and you're shitting on all of us too, white man. There ain't no one here that doesn't want to make movies, be in movies, do soundtracks for movies.'

He lifted his eyebrows to mean both *Whatever* and *Sorry*.

'You see that article in the *Reporter*?' she said, dialling down the fierce. 'Says that Motta's back in town?'

'Huh?'

She pulled her phone from her Sforza's-branded server's pouch, ignoring the Cellphones and Other Devices clause of the Manual that demanded phones remain in a server's locker until end of shift. 'Killian tweeted it this morning. Here—' She passed him her phone. It was a typical breadcrumb of a *Hollywood Reporter* article. Frank Motta was seen in LA yesterday and expects to be here till Wednesday. Word is *Tirami Sù*, his forever-delayed Saint Joseph of Copertino biopic, is back in pre-production. No actors are currently attached to the project. The article ended with a hyperlink to a longread about Motta's infamous, unfilmable passion project, which Duncan didn't need to click.

He handed Vilma back her phone.

'You think he'll come in tonight?' she asked.

'No.'

'Tomorrow night?'

He sighed. He was trying not to get his hopes up. If Motta was in town for more than a couple of days, he usually called into Sforza's for a plate of manicotti and a diet Coke. Sometimes it was Duncan's North Hollywood unit. Sometimes Bell Gardens or Reseda. When the famous director did appear — normally with his assistant, Uffy Golinko; once with two studio stiffs who struggled to conceal how sinking to Sforza's level made them feel — Duncan would take the opportunity to ask Motta how his meal was or deliver the check. Enough that his face was familiar, that they were establishing a rapport. The Staff Manual expressly forbade servers pressuring hosts or management to have 'a specific type of guest' seated in their section, or approaching a guest in another server's section, but placed no sanctions on Assistant Managers.

With middling power comes middling opportunity.

He and Motta had shared maybe six conversations over the last year, none lasting more than a minute. Duncan never once mentioned cinema, or his own last name. There was a chance Motta knew of him. They'd both been at the Toronto International Film Festival four years earlier. A remastered version of Motta's 1991 film, *The Book of Corners*, was screened as a Special Event, followed by a Q&A with the director. *Curio Bay* won the FIPRESCI Discovery Award, the first in a minor cascade for Duncan, which caught the attention of Second Wave, an eco-terrorist group, who used clips from his film in recruitment/ransom videos. All of this hubbub played its part in Echo Park Pictures (which bankrolled most of Motta's films) asking Duncan to take the helm of *Fury's Reach*. But, to the best of his knowledge, he'd never been in the same room as Motta until he clocked on in this red and white Rat Pack sepia ruins and toothpick shakers perdition that couldn't even muster the nerve to call itself a restaurant.

He knew the eyes and ears of every Sforza's crew member were fixed on him whenever Motta dined in. They gave him grief after each appearance for his reluctance, his false modesty. If he wasn't going to take the chance, at least let someone else. He could point to the Staff Manual, but knew that was weak sauce after the Bill Gobbins incident. Gobbins was Sforza's North Hollywood General Manager. Duncan's boss. He walked the floor maybe one dinner service a fortnight and still harboured dreams of adding to his IMDb profile (KNOWN FOR: *BAD LIEUTENANT* — POLICE OFFICER; *K-PAX* — TRANSIT OFFICER; *ARMY OF DARKNESS* — FAKE SHEMP). The one time his and Motta's orbits coincided, Gobbins had been reduced to a frothing, genuflecting stooge at the director's feet. Duncan had the same checked shirt, the same power, but refused to abuse it. They'd hate him, his crew, if they weren't so baffled.

Vilma had clearly picked up on all this. 'You gonna make your move on Motta one of these days?' she asked now. Duncan thought he remained perfectly still, his face expressionless, but she said, 'You fucking are! Look at that grin. Jesus. You've been playing the long game.'

If she could figure this out after four weeks and one proper conversation, how transparent would he be to Motta?

'Tell me,' she said. 'Tell me your grand plan.'

'No way. I never said I—'

'Enough of that shit, D.' No one at Sforza's called him D. 'I'm on your side. I want to ride your coattails. Okay, listen. What about I tell you something in exchange?' She got up from the plastic crate and stubbed out her cigarette on the side of the food-waste dumpster.

'Go on,' he said.

'So this was like two months ago, before I started here. I'd been in town a while and was, you know, broke as shit. No gainful employment. My friend, she says, "What about porn? I know a guy." I say, "No fucking way," but then two nights later I meet this guy in the club, and it's Eva's friend—'

'The pornographer.'

'Right.' Vilma pulled down her shirt, which was designed to ride up every time a server cleared a table or lifted a high-chair. 'So he's this fucking huge black guy. Not fat. Like, linebacker huge.'

'Vilma—'

'Fine, you don't wanna hear? This isn't your average Unsuspecting Jane Stumbles Into Porn story.' Duncan was looking at his black Oxfords. 'Meh, okay,' she said, 'but I asked you a question a minute ago and I *tried* to share. Your turn to pony up. What's. Your. Plan?'

'Look at the time,' he said, not even bothering to lift his wrist. 'Break's over. For both of us.'

'D,' she pleaded. 'I took this job because of you. My friend told me you worked here.'

'The same one who got you into porn?'

'It was just the once and it's a funny story, man. But I ain't telling that shit to you no more. And no, a different friend. Pinkie.'

'Oh, Pinkie. She's great. How's she getting on?'

She stuffed her phone back into her server's pouch. 'Break's over, D. For both of us.'

RETURN TO CASTLE WOLFENSTEIN

That night Duncan dreamed of flying. He was able to lift his body off the ground and breaststroke through the air. He was inside a house. It was somebody's home, their minimalist haven, unlike anywhere he'd ever lived. He had enough control not to bump into the ceiling, could ease under lintels in his hunt for something or someone.

It occurred to him, in this dream, as he passed from room to vacant room, that it was like a video game. *Wolfenstein* or *Doom*. Retracing his steps through an almost cleared level, poring over the sites of previous kills — the bodies of the zombies or Nazis having evaporated — in search of an overlooked key that would unlock the next level. He'd been there before. Both in these empty rooms and in this position, hovering five feet off the wooden floor.

He felt long-dormant muscles stretch and strain.

The memory of previous flights came back, not as individual scenes but as a collective wave. I've always been able to do this. Why did I forget?

I have special powers.

But how special was such a slow and pillowy form of flight? What use could it have? Surveillance? Burglary? No. No one is a villain in their own dream. If the key or whatever it was he searched for was not his to take, there'd be a good explanation. The theft would be justified by the game-logic of the dream.

But there was no quest.

He continued breaststroking from room to room, feeling more at home in his floating body. Only then did he pass into larger rooms with higher ceilings, more space to perfect his flight, to test its limits.

In the morning, he felt it in his pecs. All that dream-swimming.

And he felt it in his gut.

I have flown before.

In dreams, perhaps, but I have flown.

ADULT-FILM-ACTOR

'Kari tells me you're now working tonight?' Teresa said, placing a hand in the small of Duncan's back. He was at the kitchen sink, filling a glass of water for his son, Zeb.

'Uh-huh,' he said. 'Cindy, the other manager, her daughter's sick.' Teresa's blank expression told him to continue. 'I said, "Can't you get your mom to look after her? I got my folks staying from out of state." But Cindy was in a real bind.'

Teresa was a great mother-in-law in many respects. She'd spent time on a commune as a child — just how long, Duncan never got a fix — and there were hints of this in the cheerful, off-hand way she dressed, how she sat on the floor cross-legged in the company of adults or, as she had that afternoon, to play My First Carcassonne on the coffee table with Zeb. She liked to talk, to discuss things from the news, things that had occurred to her in the course of her day. An apparently able-bodied man parking in a handicapped space. How much immigration was too much? Conversations that could be like pulling teeth in the wrong hands, but she knew how to draw people in, help tease out their views, without ever seeming to judge which side of the moral dilemma they eventually came down on. What she could not abide, however, was prolonged shyness or reticence, which she read as iciness and hostility.

Since Duncan was family, she had particular demands. He must call her 'Mom' and, by extension, he must refer to all mothers, except his own mum, the American way. Teresa and David Sedlak were to be his 'folks', never his 'in-laws'. This troubled Duncan, the way it served to overwrite his own parents back in New Zealand. That his parents were divorced and living in different towns seemed to vex Teresa, as if the lingering chill in her not-so-new son's demeanour was the result of the failure of his genetic forebears to stick together. After six years with Kari, three of them in the US (and almost two of those dealing with Sforza's patrons flummoxed by anything other than American English), he made the many small but necessary linguistic tweaks — 'vacation' for 'holiday', 'drugstore' for 'chemist', the total abandonment of the metric system — almost automatically, though he often found himself gritting teeth at the end of sentences.

'Oh, that's too bad,' Teresa said, walking into the living room and finding Zeb had disappeared. 'I was looking forward to another game of *Catan*.' The Sedlaks were big on tabletop games. Talking to David, Duncan's American dad, you'd think board games were the big cultural phenomenon. That movies and video games were niche interests. Maybe such a universe would be preferable: more sedate, less sexualised, less violent — though not everyone could take a tabletop drubbing as well as David. He'd smile as you took one of his keepers in *Fluxx* and say, 'Nicely done,' or 'There's always next time.' That was as animated as he ever got. He was shorter than his wife, thinner too, but Duncan could always feel his quiet, steady presence in the room, like a cup of dust from a dwarf star that weighs more than a dozen Earths. Or maybe that was how all husbands felt about their fathers-in-law.

'The three of you can still play tonight,' Duncan said to Teresa, placing the glass of water on the only corner of the coffee table not covered by game tiles, 'once Zeb's asleep.'

'Yeah,' Teresa said. 'Won't be the same, will it David?'

David gave an untroubled shrug.

Kari came in carrying Zeb, who was almost four and too big to carry far. Something had upset him, though that wasn't saying much. He'd been on the cusp of tears — if not tears then catatonia — for weeks. Bad enough that one month felt like a lifetime. That the futures Duncan imagined for his son had begun to morph and contract, their colours drained.

Kari worked office hours as a graphic designer and handled evenings with Zeb while Duncan was at Sforza's. Duncan spent his Mondays and Tuesdays off with Zeb, putting on elaborate puppet shows and enjoying other people's dogs at nearby parks, though even the sight of a golden retriever puppy the other day had failed to elicit a smile. He worked shifts on Sundays and alternating Saturdays, which meant he and Kari and Zeb had only one day together a fortnight. Today, however, instead of the three of them knocking around home, it was five. Subtraction by addition. The plan, before Duncan had swapped shifts with Cindy, was to go out for dinner, a five-thirty booking at an unfranchised neighbourhood place so they could get Zeb to bed before eight. That could still happen, of course. It's just Duncan wouldn't be there. Subtraction by subtraction.

'There you are, Zebbie,' Teresa said. 'Fancy another game?'

Zeb started bawling.

'Hey,' Kari said. She placed him on the ground, where he lowered himself on to his stomach and lay flat on the sun-parched rug. 'He's tired.'

'It's two in the afternoon,' Teresa said.

'He normally has quiet time after lunch.'

'We had quiet time, didn't we, Zeb?'

The boy stopped for a moment to lift his head from the rug and wipe his nose with his forearm, then went back to sobbing.

'Playing a board game with a three-year-old isn't quiet time.'

'A kids' board game. We had fun!'

'Has he been drinking water?'

'I just got him a glass,' Duncan said, somehow entering the conversation for both the prosecution and the defence. Mother and daughter looked at him, betrayal on both faces.

'He probably wants to play outside,' Teresa said, 'with other kids.'

'He has friends,' Kari said. 'This is supposed to be family time.'

Duncan picked up Zeb and brushed the biscuit crumbs from his forehead, which bore tiny waffle patterns from the rug. 'You thirsty?' He stooped to pick up the water glass. 'Have a drink.'

Zeb held out a hand to say no.

'I'm just saying,' Teresa said.

'No, Mom,' Kari said, 'you're not saying it, but I read you loud and clear. It's not okay that he's an only child. That we live out here, so far from you and the umpteen cousins you have on tap in La Crosse. As if we could do what we do in La Crosse.'

'We have a Sforza's opening—'

'What if we were trying for a baby, Mom? What if there was something medical?'

'Are you? Is there?'

'How 'bout I fix you a snack?' Duncan said to Zeb, loud enough to stop the other conversation. 'Then I've got to start getting ready for work.'

He carried Zeb into the kitchen and placed him on the counter. He'd done this ever since his son could sit up straight. It helped that the kitchen was a small, galley-style affair so they were never more than an arm's length apart. Of course, Zeb was old enough now to look after himself, which meant he was too old to be sitting on the counter — as was Kari's stated opinion — but Duncan persisted, making a game of it with Zeb, who had to keep a lookout for his mom.

'Chopping board,' he told Zeb, who slid it from its nook beside the microwave. 'Knife.' Zeb splayed his legs and reached between them to open the cutlery drawer. Duncan, keeping an eye on him in case he toppled over, grabbed bread, Blue Bonnet and the last remaining jar of Marmite from the stash his dad had brought from New Zealand on his last visit. Duncan had encouraged his son to develop a taste for it to forge a link to his Kiwi heritage, a *taonga tuku iho* he could bestow/inflict as a father. His success in this endeavour, however, meant three jars had lasted less than two months and he had no clue where their next fix would come from.

Zeb sat quietly, watching his father make two sandwiches and cut them into quarters.

Duncan helped him down and handed him the chopping board with the sandwiches. 'To the table.'

'Is that a good idea?' Kari asked as Zeb exited the kitchen. Of late he was prone to knock over bowls of cereal, trip on his own feet. A side-effect of his sudden inward turn? A growth spurt? Perhaps the fact he'd never once slept through an entire night was finally catching up with him. There was no shortage of explanations, but it was easier to blame Duncan for placing the bowl too close to the edge of the table — *You know how he is at the moment!* — or selecting the wrong shoes.

Before Duncan could respond, Zeb had swooshed to the table and placed the board and its sandwiches on top without incident. Duncan and Kari exchanged *Fancy that* faces, and he took the chair next to Zeb.

'Here you go,' Teresa said, putting Zeb's water glass in front of him. 'That looks yummy.'

'You want one, Mom?' Duncan asked, teasing.

'You know, I think I'll pass. Maybe when you start drinking coffee. But you two enjoy your snack.' She pulled Kari into the kitchen.

He had told Cindy he needed some time away from his in-laws, and there was some truth to this, but it wasn't the main reason he'd asked to swap shifts. Frank Motta hadn't come into the restaurant the night before, which meant there was a chance of him appearing that evening and every subsequent one until he showed up or left town. Duncan wasn't convinced it was the right time to make his play, even after his conversation with Vilma, but he needed to be there. To have the opportunity and make that call.

Cindy was an actress (KNOWN FOR: BEETHOVEN'S 5TH —

Denise; Cars — Cindy Copter (voice); Deception (TV Series)
— Reporter) and would be pissed if she found out the real reason
for the swap, but she wouldn't have to know if Motta didn't show,
or if he did but Duncan continued to play it cool (or dumb, in
the eyes of Vilma). And if he did throw himself upon Motta's
mercy, chances are he'd be done with Sforza's, whichever way the
encounter went, and Cindy's wrath would have little chance of
reaching him.

Zeb: 'Something in it.'

'Yeah, bud,' Duncan said, buoyed by the sound of his son's
voice but not registering the words.

'There's something in it,' Zeb repeated, and started pulling the
pieces of bread apart. Duncan reached out to stop him — once he
started playing with his food it was all over — but he didn't pivot
at the waist, just made a heavy, bear-paw swat that clipped Zeb's
water glass — *of course it did!* — which rocked one way then the
other before dumping its contents on to the table and down into
Duncan's own lap.

He stood, instinctively.

His son looked up at him, stony faced, bone dry.

Teresa reappeared. 'What happened, Zebbie?' she asked, which
set him off.

'Daddy!' he cried.

'Dunk.' Kari sighed and turned back into the kitchen to grab tea
towels. 'You know how he is at the moment.'

'It was me, actually.' He looked at Teresa, who'd put the water
glass there, but why even get into that?

Zeb stood up on his chair, the hysterics escalating.

'God, no, don't do that,' Duncan said, but didn't pick him up
because he was still standing hopeless and frozen with his saturated
crotch. This gave Teresa her opening. She scooped up her grandson
and started mussing his fine sandy hair. 'Maybe me and Grandpa
can take you to the park?' she said softly. 'To the park with the
swings and the slides. With the kids and the people walking dogs.'

'*Aladdin*,' he said, still wailing.

'What's that, sweetie?'

'*Aladdin*!'

Teresa turned to Duncan.

'He wants to watch *Aladdin*,' he translated. 'We'll need to cast it from one of our phones.'

'But you watched that yesterday, Zebbie.'

And the day before that, and every day for the last three weeks. Duncan and Kari had fought this battle. Surely it wasn't healthy to watch the same thing over and over. They worried an obsessive streak was emerging.

'What is it about *Aladdin*?' Duncan had asked Zeb that first week, in a moment of calm between screaming fits.

'Flying carpets,' he'd replied.

Duncan had waited for him to expand, for the dam to break and all his son's contained thoughts and fears to pour out, but he'd lapsed back into silence.

'You know I would get you one,' Duncan had said, 'if such a thing existed.'

Zeb shrugged, but his two words, the merest gesture of engagement, had been enough to end thoughts of an *Aladdin* embargo. And wasn't studying one film in depth better than grazing from the never-ending buffet of newness? Wasn't that what Duncan had been doing with Motta's filmography, in preparation for his moment at Sforza's? For this night and everything that might come after?

'I'll get the movie going in a second,' Kari said, in triage mode now. She handed Duncan a kitchen towel for his crotch and started mopping up the water on the table with another.

'I might as well have my shower now,' he said.

'Did he get to eat anything?'

'Two quarters. One half.'

'Hey Zeb,' she said, 'I think Grandpa likes *Aladdin*. He might even know the songs.'

Duncan took off his t-shirt and jeans in the laundry and went to his bedroom in just his boxer shorts and sport socks. He gathered his Sforza's uniform while checking Twitter on his phone. Nothing about Motta's movements in LA, not that he could see. Instead it was the usual mix of pasted articles about the President, participation memes and carefully packaged confessions.

It's 2pm and I'm done being an adult for the day. Gonna pull my curtains and eat a box of Lucky Charms in bed.

Been living in Spain six months and my neighbor just told me I've been saying 'wank' when I mean 'bird' #yousaypajaro #isaypajero

He thought about how to handle Vilma when he saw her. She'd know the reason he'd swapped shifts — he suspected her intervention yesterday was, in part, to make sure he was around if Motta showed his face — but if the whole crew knew, the dinner service would be a shambles. The problem was: he knew next to nothing about her, had no leverage. Okay, he had his checked shirt and maybe the fact he might make another movie someday. But in conversation Vilma had him beat.

There were at least seven Vilma Vegases on Twitter, five with the default silhouette for an avatar, and the two with proper pictures didn't look anything like his Vilma. Either she was a lurker or used another name.

He looked on IMDb. There was a 'Vilma Vega' but no picture, no bio, no nothing.

He searched just for 'Vilma'. Five decent hits: a Hungarian, an Austrian, a Filipino, a Brit and an American (Vilma Ebsen, sister of Buddy Ebsen of *Beverly Hillbillies* fame). Further down the search results page for 'Vilma' was a list of keywords which began with 'Evil-man (1199 titles)' and 'devil-mask (11 titles)'. It took him a beat, but he saw how both terms squirrelled 'Vilma' inside them like a cryptic crossword clue. He clicked on Keywords and found more.

> *Evil-mark (9 titles)*
> *Evil-magician (19 titles)*
> *Civil-marriage (12 titles)*

The list continued, with phrases matching four out of five letters:

> *Film-adaptation (20 titles)*
> *Evil-mother-in-law (15 titles)*
> *Evil-meteorologist (1 title)*
> *Adult-film-actor (8 titles)*
> *Hail-mary-pass (1 title)*

There was something in this algorithm, something useful, a jumping-off point. The way it moved so swiftly from the search term and soon the term itself was disappearing, like an isotope in decay. It connected to the images in his first short films, this sense of randomness, decay, modification — but it was only text. What could he do with text?

Nothing.

He became aware that he was still in his damp underwear. Was sitting on his bed cyber-stalking, or attempting to, one of his colleagues. An attractive, ambitious, female colleague. His heart was beating fast. Had been even before he'd bumped into an idea, perhaps the memory of any idea. Before he'd read *Evil-mother-in-law* or *Adult-film-actor*.

He got up, grabbed his earbuds and went into the family bathroom. He dropped his clothes on the floor, locked the door, turned on the shower, but closed the glass door without getting in. On his phone's browser he opened up an incognito tab, summoned Pornhub and entered 'Vilma Vegas' into the search box.

1079 results, but only one perfect match.

Tattooed babe Vilma Vegas tries out a new toy

Total commitment to the role. Admirable.

This was not the first time he'd resorted to masturbating in the bathroom with the shower running, but it was the first time in many years he looked set to spank it over someone he knew. There'd been Kari, furiously in the murky, pre-smartphone days of friendship, then less and less often as their coupledom became cemented and his scenarios became too riddled with continuity errors to continue to green light. And before that? Was there anyone else since Tara and Deedee James?

The video started with Vilma entering what appeared to be a low-rent casting studio, or the porn approximation of one. She was the only person in the frame. Denim shorts and a black sleeveless top somewhere between a runner's tank and an evening-wear separate. He plugged the jack into his phone and one of the earbuds into an ear, leaving the other free to detect disturbances in the hall. A man's voice, the double-bogus casting director, was asking Vilma if she was nervous (she said she wasn't), what she did ('I'm a writer' — a writer?) and complimenting her body (she struck her Beyoncé power pose in thanks).

'Who's that?' the guy asked.

'Her?' Vilma said, lifting up a little more of her tank top with one hand and pulling her shorts down below her hip with the other to reveal a pin-up girl sitting on a diving board. 'Esther Williams: swim champ and business woman.'

'She hot. And the other?'

Vilma adjusted herself to reveal another pin-up occupying the same passage between hip and navel on the opposite side. 'Hedy Lamarr. She invented frequency-hopping spread-spectrum technology for missiles, without which we wouldn't have WiFi or Bluetooth today.'

'She hot, though.'

There was a lot of new information for Duncan to process. The fact Vilma said she was a writer. Her brand of hipster feminism. But he couldn't help thinking about the lighting, how it wasn't right. It was too bright, too direct, to be a real commercial building. It made Vilma's skin look leathery, her tattoos hard to see beneath her surface sheen.

His interest in film and his interest in sex had been entangled from the first.

Long before he came to Hollywood, before his first formal efforts at university or in 48-hour film contests, there was his father's Panasonic Palmcorder, heavy as a bag of coins, that recorded on to tapes the height and width of audio cassettes but three times as thick. His first film, so to speak, was recorded live on that brick, using the record button to cut from scene to scene. There was no editing beyond that. Not yet. No narrative either. Not in a traditional sense. He recorded his father hoeing his veggie garden, cut to his mother slicing beans in the kitchen, then to the wind billowing the net curtains in his second-storey bedroom and, in a slow tracking shot that was really just Duncan baby-stepping further into his room and up to the glass, his neighbour, Tara James, bouncing on her trampoline. He was twelve. She was thirteen — already too old, too outwardly sophisticated, to bounce on that trampoline. He'd captured her in a private moment. But at twelve he couldn't articulate the power this granted the shot, or distinguish its particular thrill from the more obvious, more urgent attraction of her breasts like clenched fists beneath her white school blouse.

Or her radiant legs.

Or her butt.

Or her always-perfect hair now wild, obscuring her stupidly happy face.

There were more films like this. Surveillance videos. Montages of moments of his life he felt were charged with energy. Some of it sexual. But also: there was something about his parents. The amount of time they spent alone. The glaze of preoccupation that had settled on their lives.

Around this time he learned to masturbate over the course of three days. Three showers. The first time he wasn't expecting to come, didn't know that was a thing, was so caught up in his toe-clenching climax that he missed the discharge. He still thought about this first burst of spunk from time to time. How it must've transformed into a stringy, noduled mess like spunk always does when it comes into contact with water. How some of it would've become clogged in the shower grate for the next semi-attentive user to find. But masturbation only took off when he connected this strange, instinctively shameful act with thoughts of Tara James bouncing on her trampoline, and then, one fateful day when he was left home alone, watching that scene over and over on the VCR he'd labelled 'NBA Action #2' and kept hidden under his bed.

Vilma Vegas had shed her tank top and denim shorts by this time. She was rifling through a gym bag that had been tossed to her by the guy behind the camera. This must be the linebacker-huge dude she'd mentioned yesterday. From the bag she pulled a curved chrome dildo. She held it away from her like a bathroom fitting — a shower nozzle or a door handle that had come away in her hand.

'Na-uh,' the guy said. 'Keep looking.'

She placed the dildo to one side and pulled out a pinkish latex one about the same length but two or three times the girth. *This?* her expression said.

'I'm thinking there might be something else a little more your speed.'

She shook her head, meaning *You're crazy, dude*, rather than *No, thanks*. Was she drunk? Just a little? Perhaps this was the same night she met the linebacker 'in the club'?

The next thing she pulled out of the bag was much smaller. What the heck was it? Duncan had been holding his phone sideways but hadn't yet maximised the video. He did this now, but it didn't help much. He waited a second for the dude with the camera to zoom in, but he didn't. Fucking amateur. Duncan went to pinch the screen to zoom in on the object that was resting on Vilma's open hand like a startled mouse, but instead of keying in on this thing the video froze, was replaced by text. He thought maybe this was part of the video, that it was a sort of *Punk'd* for the Pornhub Generation, then thought, what if this was all for him? What if the conversation yesterday wasn't meant to coax him into hitting up Frank Motta for a ride on his coat tails but to place the breadcrumbs that would lead him here? That the challenge when he got to work would not be keeping his intentions with Motta under wraps but maintaining plausible deniability with Vilma about having watched this video.

Pah!

Maybe it was having his heart rate elevated so long. Maybe it was transference from having Dwarf Star David embedded in the corner of his living room the last four days. He was being paranoid. He gathered himself. Read the text.

Casting to Chromecast — Sedlake Living Room

'Duncan?!'

It was Kari. Running down the hall.

He fumbled for the icon in the top right-hand corner of the screen to stop casting the video on to the TV in the other room. The TV on which Zeb and his grandparents had been watching *Aladdin*.

Oh fuck oh shit oh god.

'Duncan?' Kari beat on the bathroom door.

He noticed for the first time the amount of steam in the room. From the shower having run so hot for so long. He powered off his phone, slipped it into the pocket of his black Dockers that lay rumpled on the floor, eased open the shower door and slunk beneath the scalding stream.

MACK ATTACKS

'So what was it?' Mack asked. 'A Little Bird?'

'What, a bird? No.'

'Not a real bird. It's a kind of smart sex toy.'

'I don't know. I never got to— God, that's not the point.'

'Yeah, yeah, you're mortified. The lost hit points with the out-laws. The psychic damage to your son. Though it doesn't sound *that* bad. Hold on, let me look up the video myself. Gonna have to put you on speaker.'

'Mack, no.'

Duncan was pulled over on Vanowen, one block back from the Hollywood Burbank Airport, if that's what people were still calling it this week. He'd already driven past Sforza's, was killing time and tamping down his thoughts before his shift started, when his phone began to ring on the passenger seat. He'd leaned over to check the caller. Kari or Teresa, he'd have let it go to voicemail. But Mack? She had some knack. A sixth sense for when to stick the needle in.

Talking, though, had its attraction. Mack was one of the world's great masturbators, had shut herself in her room for two whole years after high school and, though she didn't discuss what happened in that blip and they'd never talked about porn as teenagers, she talked about it a lot these days. She claimed it had begun as a passing anthropological interest, surrounded as she was in her work by guys with sub-par social skills and having dated a few who'd been open about their habits. It was like finding a Rosetta stone for 49.2 percent of the population. Scratch the surface, she said, and you'll find a sludgy reservoir of porn that explained every dudely action or inaction. Her 'research' — you could hear the scare quotes over the phone — took her back to the days of video, for which she seemed almost nostalgic: the goofball humour; the muffage; the bespoke songs composed for the slow unbuttoning, only to fade out when the thrusting began. And, she'd declared, if you add The World According to Porn to the outsider complex, the frustrated entitlement, shared by the privileged white straight male geeks, it's hard to be surprised by any online horror that bleeds into the real world.

Another talk like this might help centre Duncan for Motta, if the guy showed. So he'd answered the call and, to bridge one of Mack's early silences, had hastily confessed.

'What do I search for?' Mack asked.

'No.'

'Come on, babe, play nice.' She'd called him 'babe' since forever. Had shown up at his high school calling everyone that, like some Hollywood producer posing as a fourteen-year-old schoolgirl, only she seemed to be doing it ironically. As if she'd ever turn Hollywood! She was real, belonged to the world of cellulite, not celluloid, could bend old language around new corners. It was as if every 'babe' had an implied, parenthetical retort, like the title of an unlikely pop hit.

(You're no picture yourself) Babe.

(Nothing you can do can get to me) Babe.

And then, as they became just-friends, the brackets dropped away and it was all Did you do the chem homework, babe? and I'm going to buy the new Tomb Raider after school, babe. Somehow, after more than a decade of silence, things had started back up in the same cosy groove and here they were, talking porn and babe-ing it up on either side of the Atlantic.

'You still in Latvia?' he asked.

'Estonia.'

'Close.'

'Actually, Estonia is closer in many ways, culturally, linguistically, to Finland.'

'You sound like a PBS travel show.'

'Sorry, babe. It's what you get from shoutcasting with a bunch of know-nothing dipshits. Hard to turn it off. They call them Mack Attacks.'

'They?'

'Fans. My fans. There's a montage on YouTube. Probably more than one. I'm not that into watching myself. And don't get me started on the comments. But this one I know for sure is there, it's called "Mack's Facts".'

'Totally sounds like PBS.'

'Yeah, well. This video, the one they forced me to watch, it actually made me think of you. You know those short films you used to make at school? How you'd just point the camera at me and get me talking, then you'd cut it up so that only the interesting bits were left.'

'Uh-huh.' Mack had never seen Duncan's first gonzo Palmcorder efforts, didn't know about his wankbank tape — a compilation of jackable moments he'd recorded from TV that had seen him through the worst of his adolescence. This openness about porn and masturbation was a feature of only the most recent incarnation of their friendship, one enabled, it seemed, by their being on other sides of the planet. Mack had come to LA once, almost two years ago, for a *DoTA* tournament at the Staples Centre and an awkward coffee with Duncan. She wanted to catch up with her old friend from school days, let him know how successful she was and razz him about how his great swerve into the mainstream had gone. Mack was a commentator, or 'shoutcaster' in gamer speak, mostly for European professional video-game tournaments. She was one of the few females in her field and enjoyed a certain fame, which meant she was wanted in the US on occasion. The couple of times Duncan had tried to check out Mack's work he'd felt so bombarded by the speed of the gameplay and the strange dialect Mack and her fellow shoutcasters spoke that he couldn't last more than five minutes. They sounded like aliens whose own language now borrowed the cadence and intonation of the endless stream of ESPN2 their scientists had managed to intercept. His not liking e-sports made him a bad friend and probably a bad choice to make films for Millennials or the real powerbrokers: the kids of Millennials.

'Why'd you call?' Duncan asked out there by the airport.

'A hunch. A tingle. It was either going to be a cold sore or you needed me. I'm glad it's not a cold sore. Motherfuckers.'

A jet roared overhead.

'What time is it there?' Duncan asked.

'Quarter to twelve.'

'At night?'

'At night.'

'Look, Mack, I gotta go. My shift starts in fifteen.'

'You like it there, don't you, babe? You're Sforza's through and through.'

'I fucking hate it, Mack.'

'And?'

He considered telling her about Motta. He'd never shared his plan to right his cinematic career with her. As if telling would somehow scupper his chances, the way you weren't supposed to talk about a screenplay you were working on until you'd cracked it. Kari knew, though they barely spoke about it now. She'd been against Sforza's in the particular, and could do with fewer nights alone with Zeb, but she was happy to have money coming in while he sorted himself out. Did she think he'd really be taken in by Motta? The protégé and the patron? It hadn't seemed so crazy when he put in his job application for Sforza's. There was a lot of heat, of the wrong kind, attached to him after he was jettisoned from *Fury's Reach*. The idea of disappearing in plain sight had been attractive. So too the vision of Motta's outstretched hand. Lightning had already struck once in his career with the offer to direct *Fury's Reach*, so surely if he committed to this role, pursued Motta, set his heart on it, good things would come. And, as of yesterday, Vilma was in on the secret too. Maybe it was time his best friend — sad as it was that this detached voice, a couple times a month, was his best friend — came inside the tent as well.

'I—' He stopped, still weighing the decision.

'Can I put forward a theory?'

'Surprise me.'

'*Fury's Reach*, getting pulled from the chair: total red herring. Having Zeb, becoming a parent. That's what spooked you. It just so happened you couldn't see where your next pay cheque would come from. You could have turned the *Fury's Reach* thing on its head, worn those creative differences as a badge of honour, gone back to making your thoughtful little art-house flicks, which I love by the way, babe, don't get me wrong, but no one's pulling out the chequebook for those. So you took the route of countless Where Are They Now? chumpsters and opted out. A meagre but steady income putting other people's food on the table.'

'Hey hey hey,' Duncan said. 'Stop. You trying to get me pissed? Screw you if you really think that, Mack. Scared? Confused — for a bit, sure. But that scenario you paint, it's so thin.'

'What was it then? What *is* it?'

'Why do I feel like you're gonna rat me out? Like you're, I dunno, fuck. I'm on this paranoid jag, so filter accordingly. But it's like you'll tell the Directors Guild on me, you fucking tattletale.' He laughed.

The other end of the line was quiet. So quiet it might be dead.

COLONISTA

Felicity MacKinnon had been the new kid in town halfway through the first year of high school. The rumours about her varied widely.

Her dad was in prison for drink-driving into a family of Japanese tourists.

Her family was Exclusive Brethren and she'd been kicked out for refusing to wear a headscarf.

Her mother was so hot it was, like, how'd *that* come from *there*.

It's true that she wasn't much to look at back then: a little chubby; her acne-ravaged skin raw, pebbledashed. She did herself no favours by insisting people call her Mack — *Do I look like a Felicity to you, babe?* — and being a terror on the hockey pitch.

The first time he really took any notice of her was when she did a history project on *Sid Meier's Colonization*, a game Duncan had been hooked on a few years before. They'd all been asked to read first-person accounts of new settlers, write a report and present it to the class. Instead, Mack treated Meier's game, which must've only been four or five years old at the time, as a kind of historical document. Turn-based strategy had been overtaken by real-time games like *Command and Conquer*, and she could see the significance of this shift. It was actually a decent piece of games scholarship, her report, as Duncan remembered it. But their teacher, Ms Rapana, interrupted her partway through.

'Felicity, this is not the task you were set.'

'Yes, it is. This game is an important document that allows contemporary youth to experience the challenges and moral dilemmas of colonisation first hand.'

'And an example of such a dilemma?'

She set down her report. 'Easy. How to deal with the Indians. I mean, on the face of it, the game is hideously racist. Only the Europeans can establish cities. Only they can turn the gold into anything useful: galleons, horses, trade goods. The player, whichever European nation she picks, is faced with the choice of playing nice with all the tribes, paying their tributes, maybe training some missionaries so you'll get converts to tend your crops, or just eradicating them. When you wipe out an Indian village, you get gold. You also free up more land for your own cities to harvest. You just know that Sioux village is sitting on top of a juicy tobacco leaf.'

'But?' Ms Rapana prompted.

'But shouldn't a game about colonisation be racist? Like, the Spanish get more gold than any of the other Europeans when they wipe out a local village, so the player is encouraged to follow the path history actually took, to act like the Conquistadors. That's effing genius — sorry, Miss, but it is. The game lures you into this moral dilemma. There's all this bounty. But someone else was there first. But you have muskets. And you can get mercenaries from Europe if things really go sour. The deck is stacked in your favour, and it's so much fun. The only time you stop and really think about anything is when your mum forces you to go outside.' This prompted sniggers from the third of the class who still believed Mrs MacKinnon was a MILF. 'That's when you realise,' she continued, 'you've been behaving like a genocidal monster. And you know what, Miss? The game isn't racist enough. There are no slaves. You've got to get Indians or white colonists to harvest your cotton. As if. The game pussyfoots around slavery. Which is nice, in that it doesn't make ten-year-olds get used to buying and selling black people and working them to death. But is that better than wiping

41

them from history altogether? And why's it okay to mistreat the Indians and not the blacks?'

'Okay, Felicity, that's quite enough.'

Duncan was floored. It was the greatest presentation he'd ever seen. The first time, certainly since his father had moved out, that anything anyone had said in class had spoken to him directly. The way Native Americans were treated in the game had bugged him. He preferred to play as the French, who didn't piss off the tribes as easily, or the English, who were able to get more converts to come and work his fields willingly. Never the Spanish. But he hadn't analysed it. Later, talking with Mack after class, she pointed out that it was kind of racist to make the Spanish perpetually incentivised to wipe out the locals. 'If another nation had made it to those Incan cities first, you're telling me they wouldn't have felt their trigger fingers itch?'

Duncan thought Mack would get an A, but instead she got detention.

TINSELTOWN IN THE RAIN

'Hey D,' Vilma said when he stepped into the dining area at Sforza's, 'I thought Cindy was on tonight?' A half smile.

'Any Motta sightings?'

Her smile broadened. 'Well, no, I can't say we've had any great filmmakers here today, present company excluded.'

'Ha. Well, maybe we'll get lucky tonight.'

'Will we?' She leaned into the 'we' with particular relish.

'You got your normal section?' He looked over her shoulder to the collection of tables, leaners and booths nearest the bar.

'You know it. Got a double-date on Six.' She pointed through her right shoulder. 'Three guys, one girl, all very nervous. Nine is two suits. Might be lovers, might be jilted business associates. Or, y'know, just fucking exhausted. Still on their first Morettis after an hour. And Ten, well, you can see Ten.'

Duncan tiptoed to spy a plump couple and their three gaunt and mortified teen and tween kids.

'Let me guess,' he said. 'The parents refused the offer of the WiFi password?'

'Rather be hated by their kids than ignored.'

'Looks like the kids don't need their phones to achieve both.'

'Fuck that phase, right?' Vilma said.

'Yeah,' he said, though he suspected they were looking at the scene from different sides of the table. She was closer in age to

43

the kids than the parents, and was probably projecting her own teenage cruelties on to their body language. He was the father/ the father was him with another decade of three-cheese lasagnas and disappointment under his belt. This ghost of Duncans Yet To Come must have felt his gaze: he raised his eyes from his polenta fries and, with the economy of movement of one wholly committed to idleness, signalled *come here* with a flick of his index finger.

Duncan put his hand on Vilma's shoulder. 'Daddy wants you.'

'He couldn't have heard me, right?'

Duncan pushed out his bottom lip, thinking already about how long he had until Zeb would hate him. Ten years? Or was the age at which kids hate their parents getting younger, the way girls were getting their periods earlier and earlier? All those hormones Big Farma were pumping into chickens, cows, pigs, turkeys, salmon — surely something also snagged the boys. He thought about Zeb at twelve, refusing to hold his hand. At eight. Five. The first time someone teased him about his name, if it hadn't happened already.

He needed to place his hand on the back of a chair to make sure he kept his feet.

Mack was right, kind of. Having a kid had fucked him up.

Exhibit A: He cried like a baby when he finally got around to seeing *Interstellar*. Those times Matthew McConaughey's character was forced to miss great chunks of his children's lives in a matter of minutes of his own biological time. He was saving humanity, but had he really thought about the consequences? Duncan had been sitting on the couch with Kari, watching a movie with her for what felt like the first time since Zeb was born, the previous twenty months one long constant wish for time to speed up, for the baby to sleep, for the Second Wave circus to end and the CIA to back the fuck up, to be granted the energy and the headspace to make the best possible fist of his debut major motion picture, but dammit to hell he was crying. Crying at the thought of missing his own son's first word (already overdue), or crappy daycare paintings numbers 150 through 200, or the phase when he's gonna hate his dad no matter what. But just to live it, as a father, had been suddenly unmissable.

The problem wasn't so much that Duncan had lost his nerve as a filmmaker, but that he'd lost any sense of taste even before Echo Park gave him the boot. He wept at $165 million blockbusters, for chrissakes. He was in no fit state to make anything himself.

On his floor walk Duncan noticed a new server, Lawson, with his hands plugged deep into his pockets. He and Cindy had interviewed the kid a couple of days ago. The lunch shift with Cindy would have been Lawson's first and, from his posture, he was wishing it had been his last. He was from Amarillo. Somewhere near Amarillo. *Friday Night Lights* country. He had quarterback looks — six-foot-something, square jaw, thick auburn bangs coaxed to attention with drugstore pomade — but the personality of a house-brand marshmallow. What was the best-looking boy in town supposed to do if it wasn't play varsity? Head to Hollywood, of course. He'd be crushed by the place in time, but Duncan saw no reason for it to happen all at once.

'Hey Lawson,' he called, 'how about you shadow me for the next little while?'

'You sure? I'd appreciate that, sir.'

Duncan waved off the boy's manners, slipped into his schmaltzy uncle role as if it were a freshly made bed. 'You want to be in movies, right?'

'Yes, sir. Action movies. Stunts and such.'

'You have the look. Well, this is *nothing* like making a movie. Family dining is ninety-five percent action, five percent downtime. It's more like directing traffic at a busy intersection. No one expects great things from an intersection. The best they can hope for is: quick and painless. Much the same with a dinner at Sforza's.'

(Duncan had, of course, cited his directorial chops in his Assistant Manager job application. His cover letter spoke of the 'lessons in leadership' and 'forward planning' that filmmaking had instilled. It was bullshit. Bill Gobbins, though. He ate it up.)

'My job,' he continued, 'done properly, is one of preventative maintenance.' He led Lawson towards the kitchen. 'Oiling the joints before they squeak. Replacing the tyres before the tread is all the way gone. Paving the way for the first hour of the dinner service, for that momentum to build, for the flow to develop that'll carry us all to closing time without incident.'

Lawson nodded. His eyes were wide and watery.

There was a time Duncan thought moments like this were training for his next directing gig. Playing the leader to lead the players. Now he just sounded like the worst kind of DVD commentary track and revelled in the awfulness.

'You've waited tables before, right? At your aunt's place?'

'Yes, sir,' Lawson said. 'This is just—' He sighed.

'Was Cindy rough on you?'

'No. I mean, I deserved it. I'm gonna do good tonight, though.'

Duncan led the kid around as he checked in with the other servers, Preeya, Dane, Barker, Yu-Wen, Liz — each new name seemed to cause Lawson physical pain — getting a read on energy levels, how the kitchen was faring, the status of yesterday's interpersonal spats. He explained how the host, Martina (KNOWN FOR: *AMERICAN IDOL* SEASON 11 — 4 EPISODES), set the tone for the service, choosing where to seat the walk-ins based on how long they might stay, how rowdy they might get and how well they might tip. How in the kitchen it was a search for rhythm, though with the constant turnover of staff not every search was fruitful. They had to keep the starters rolling out as fast as possible and then, with the help of Duncan and the servers, read the room. Some diners, the older ones especially, didn't like to wait between courses. Others didn't like to be rushed. All of them expected you to be telepathic. Families could be incredibly efficient or a total train wreck. But no one wanted a cold chicken parm.

'Okay,' Duncan said, 'that's enough of me rambling on about this place. Time for you to get to work.'

'Thank you, sir.'

'Enough of that "sir" carry-on. Have you seen where we are?'

They were both looking in the direction of Vilma's section. She was leaning to retrieve empties from a table of guys, their courtesies shelved or forgotten with the sight of Hedy Lamarr emerging from Vilma's waistline.

'Attaboy, Lawson,' he said, resisting the urge to muss his hair. 'Now go tell Martina you're ready to serve some guests.'

When Duncan got to the pass, Felix, the head chef, said, 'Why the fuck you holding Corn-fed's hand?'

'Him? He seemed rattled after Cyclone Cindy.'

Felix cinched his lips and lifted his chin so that the word tattooed in cursive across the front of his neck was legible, though Duncan wasn't sure what *Crucible* meant exactly. 'Fuck that guy,' Felix said.

'Look, we just got the twelve-top seated. The push is on its way.'

The chef turned back to the kitchen and took it out on the sauté cook.

Seven o'clock.

Eight o'clock.

Service continued with its usual slips and shudders but no disasters, no sign of Motta. The rush was passing. Martina had her pick of tables to seat any stragglers who arrived. Based on the coats they were bringing in with them, it had started to rain. The place would be dead by nine. No one in LA got wet if they could avoid it.

At 8.30 Vilma came up to him as he polished wine glasses behind the bar. 'All right if I take my meal break soon, boss?'

'I might join you,' he said. 'Can you put through a half JM and a Sprite?'

'Diet?'

'No.'

'Okay,' she said in a drawn-out *If you're sure?* way.

'I like to sit in Thirty-three. Meet you there in ten.'

He checked with Martina and they agreed the kitchen could close at nine. Sad for a Saturday and bad for GastroCorp's bottom line, but when it rains, it rains.

Vilma was already started on her honeymoon soup with turkey meatballs when he got to the booth. His half-order of Johnny Marzetti — a baked coronary of macaroni noodles, ground beef, red sauce and cheese — was next to her bowl. She slid it over to his side of the table.

'So,' she said, slicing a pale meatball in two with the side of her spoon, 'we do this all again tomorrow?'

'I guess. You rostered on?'

'What else am I gonna do?'

'Maybe you could write?'

He watched as she mentally read back through the transcripts of the last couple of days, her résumé, anything that might have given him the impression she wrote. No doubt she recalled their exchange between the dumpsters yesterday:

VILMA: *Maybe you'll write something—*

DUNCAN: *I'm not writing at the moment.*

The door had been opened. Why, if he knew she wrote, hadn't he told her to write something for herself then? Because he'd looked for, and found, her video. The one where she claimed to be a writer but played with sex toys for cash. He was confessing. He could see all of this, or thought he could, on her face. He was pleased to have a firmer footing in their exchanges, a say in how they might play out, but then she said, 'Like a script?' as if she was still back on what he'd said, like she hadn't caught on at all.

'You write, don't you?'

'Sure,' she said. 'I dabble. When I went to Australia, I put "Writer" down as my occupation on the Customs card, you know, as a joke.'

'You've been to Australia?'

'Just Sydney. It was with a boyfriend. An ex.'

'He was Australian?'

48

'He wasn't a Hemsworth, if that's what you're thinking.'

'It wasn't.'

Vilma looked down at her soup, lifted a spoonful of the broth up half an inch and tipped it back into the bowl.

'Maybe you could show me something you've written?' Duncan said.

'That would be a waste of time.'

'Let me be the judge.'

'I'm not a writer, okay, D? It's something I claim to be when I'm drunk, or high, or nervous.' He thought how she might have been all three in the video. 'I am a good actress, though. And you're a good filmmaker. Let's just keep it at that.'

'So when Motta comes, what do you want? What's the best outcome for Vilma Vegas?'

'I don't know. You're the *bobo* with a plan. I figure something good happens to you, it might trickle down to me. Maybe you become one of his ADs. Maybe you get involved in editing, you know, play to your strengths. And the next time you fat cats are having lunch somewhere a squintillion times classier than this shithole, and your bestie Frank Motta says he's looking for a tough-as-nails vamp that knows taekwondo, you drop my name. All right?'

'What belt are you?'

'Dark enough to kick your ass if you keep stepping on your own dick.'

'Okay.'

'What kind of prep work have you done?'

'For getting my ass kicked?'

'For Motta.'

'Oh, you know, three or four hours a day for the last two years.'

A different voice: 'Who's Motta?'

Lawson was standing at the edge of the booth.

'You don't know who Frank Motta is?' Vilma asked.

Lawson bit his bottom lip.

'You are going to get chewed up and—'

Duncan raised his hand to stop her. 'Easy. Why don't you just tell him who Frank Motta is, rather than jumping down his throat?'

'He can Google, can't he?'

'I didn't mean to—'

'I bet,' Vilma said, looking up at Lawson, 'you don't know who Duncan Blake is either?'

Lawson: blank stare.

'Fuck's sake.' She stood, pulled the kid a couple of feet away, and began to spell out Duncan's minor fame and major failure, and perhaps — Duncan couldn't really hear, but the longer this Vilmapedia entry went on, the less likely it was she was still talking about him — she gave an overview of Motta's career too. How he'd emerged from New York in the late seventies, early eighties. Same time, same place as Spike Lee and Jim Jarmusch — two more names likely lost on Lawson — though the only thing those three had in common was geography and age. How, of the three, Motta took the longest to be acknowledged as a singular filmmaker. At first he was lumped into the tradition of the great Italian American Directors, as if three-and-a-half directors makes a tradition. But his films never once featured a wiseguy. Violence was threatened but rarely delivered. Then, because his movies made money, he was 'commercial' and the Hollywood press tried to treat him like Spielberg or Lucas.

He heard Vilma say, '*Kid Gloves*?' Then, 'Theodore Hall?' her voice getting louder, clearer, more indignant. 'The youngest scientist working on the Manhattan Project? How he gave information to the Russians and the CIA totally knew but couldn't bring a case against him without exposing the fact they'd decoded this cache of Russian intelligence, so he's allowed to go to England and be this brilliant professor at Cambridge?'

Duncan leaned out the end of the booth to see Lawson nodding, receptive to the impromptu lesson. Vilma seemed to be enjoying the power.

'All right,' Duncan said, 'that's enough.'

Lawson inched back to the booth.

'But it's not just a biopic,' Vilma continued in a rush, one last motherly instruction before the line goes dead. '*Kid Gloves* is really about surveillance culture. And,' she said, sliding back in behind her honeymoon soup, 'he makes a film every year, pretty much. The man is bank.'

Duncan thought about *Tirami Sù*, whether it would really be Motta's next film. Talk of the proposed biopic of the seventeenth-century Franciscan friar and levitator, Saint Joseph of Copertino, first surfaced in the early eighties but it kept getting leap-frogged by other pictures. Motta always had a new starlet-muse he was helping to break through. Amazing scripts he couldn't turn down. Studio commitments he had to honour. All the while actors were attached to his passion project, only to distance themselves months later. Motta, or his minders, had used this picture so well throughout his career to balance the impression that he was a safe pair of hands — the kiss of death for a director's Oscar aspirations — and to deflect rumours of Motta's womanising and general impropriety. Was it Catholic guilt that drove the project, cynical image management or genuine artistic drive? Stick 'em all in a blender, Duncan thought, and you'd get closer to the truth. The film sounded like a bomb, though. Expensive. At risk of alienating the religious, angering the Vatican and completely passing the rest of the world by. But the fact Motta persisted with the project, nursing the script himself between its shifts with strung-out scriptwriters, lent him the air of a true artiste, the eccentric auteur, that his brand was missing.

To make the film at last promised to undo all of this.

But if it went ahead, and if Duncan got sucked into the slipstream, it could reboot his own career, even if the Saint Joe film flopped.

'Hold on,' Lawson said, back to standing at the edge of their booth, 'is this the guy that made *Who Wants to be the President*?'

'Yeah,' Vilma said without enthusiasm. Motta's 2004 film was set in an imagined 2016. When a major cable network buys the rights to all televised debates for the Republican and Democratic primaries, and the presidency itself, they turn the race into a 24-hour reality TV show, part *Who Wants To Be a Millionaire?*, part *Survivor*. It got a warm enough reception at the time, though some criticised the softness of its targets, but parallels with recent events meant it had garnered a new wave of attention and a much less nuanced response.

'What's your favourite Motta film, Vilma?' Duncan asked.

'*French Inhaler*,' she said without hesitation, and turned to Lawson. 'You should watch *French Inhaler*. It's the biography of the ultimate kiss-off song. A cross between a talking heads documentary and crime scene re-enactment.'

'Okay, sure,' Lawson said.

'What's yours, D?'

'I honestly can't say,' he said, toying with his Marzetti. 'I've watched each of them twenty, thirty times.'

'Wow,' said Lawson.

'Except maybe *Kid Gloves*, which hits too close to home after my own brush with the CIA.' He looked at Vilma to see that she knew this part of his story — the death threats against him and his family owing to his association with Second Wave, the CIA's suspicion he was fabricating said threats, that he was in bed with fucking eco-terrorists — which she seemed to, or she was too proud to let on she didn't. 'I've read the books, the biographies the films are based on. Watched all the peripheral documentaries. Read the criticism. Studied the FX he's used, is using. All those showreels are online,' he said as an aside to Lawson, then returned his gaze to the Marzetti. 'It's really subtle. You're not meant to notice. It's not about explosions and mythical creatures, but efficiency. Being able to shoot quickly and still make the final images match those in your head.' He turned back to Vilma. 'And then there's all the reading about Saint Joseph of Copertino.'

'I don't get why he's so hung up on that guy.'

'Motta's got a New Age streak. His minders help to keep it pretty well buried but it's there if you know where to look.'

'Like, he believes in levitation?'

'There was that thing on *Letterman* in the mid-nineties, before he took a break, remember? No? You're too young, I guess. He tried to lift Dave's coffee mug with his mind. The way I think about it, the Saint Joseph story, is: dudes can't fly. But there's hundreds of people who saw it first hand, basically swore affidavits. Princes and popes. How do you dismiss all that evidence? What other explanation is there?'

'Mass hallucination?' Vilma said.

'One of the rigs they use for those *Crouching Tiger* movies?' Lawson said, suddenly animated.

Vilma: 'Optical illusion.'

Lawson, crouching now, his eyes level with Duncan and Vilma: 'A wingsuit, like in *Point Break*?'

'Huh?'

'He's talking about the remake,' Duncan said, and turned to Lawson. 'This was in the 1600s, mate.'

'Church conspiracy,' Vilma said, thumping the table.

'Um,' Lawson said.

'There's no shortage of theories,' Duncan said. 'At minimum, I reckon Joseph must've been an undiagnosed epileptic. I don't know exactly how Motta would handle it. I mean, I have hunches, ideas. But it *is* interesting. Or it was, to begin with. But *Tirami Sù* is a jumble for me now. Like all his films. It's been two years, you know? I can't see *Hester* any more, or *Right Down the Line*, not properly. I just see everything that went into a film. I feel like I made them, in a way. I can't love them, can only see their flaws.'

He looked up. Vilma's eyes were cartoon wide.

'Damn, D,' she said. 'You're ready.'

'I'm gonna sound like a trainspotter.'

She furrowed her brow, confused by the reference, probably thinking about the Danny Boyle film and wondering how he might come off like a Scottish heroin addict. He didn't dare look at Lawson.

'A film obsessive,' he said. 'Some dweeb you humour until you can find an excuse to slip away.'

'Then don't be like that. You're normal, I think. Normal-ish.'

'Normal is bad too. Normal is forgettable.'

She reached out and stilled the hand that held his fork. 'Then be brilliant. Don't over-complicate it.'

'Fine, I'll just be brilliant tomorrow, or next month, or on October fifth. Meantime, I'll watch *French Inhaler* another twenty times.'

'Did I miss a memo?' Martina said, standing hard up against Lawson at the opening of the booth. 'The team meeting without me?'

Lawson stood up. Martina ignored him.

'I just seated a certain VIP at Table Six,' she said. 'Duncan, I'm gonna need you to tell the kitchen to put their do-rags back on.'

'Motta?'

Martina nodded.

'Alone?'

She nodded again.

He looked at Vilma, who was playing it cool. Lawson, though, looked spooked, as if this was all an elaborate way to expose his naivety.

'Okay,' Duncan said, sidling along the bench to exit the booth. 'I'll get them to whip up a Motta special, then pay my compliments.'

'I'm sure you will,' Martina said.

He stood, smoothing the front of his Dockers and shrugged at Vilma.

She looked down at her soup, surely cold by now, and took a slurp.

ERGO

'Sit down,' Motta said, before Duncan could say anything. 'I get depressed eating alone. Makes me feel old.'

Did he look old? Duncan knew Frank Motta was born in Queens in March 1954, was pretty much twice his own age, but those were just numbers. He looked as he always had, forever forty-five. An effect achieved, in part, thanks to the shaven head he'd sported since film school. Like Yul Brynner, he'd done it first for a role and decided to stick with it. 'I was losing it anyway,' he once told *Entertainment Tonight*. 'I couldn't bear the slow decline. I'm a control freak. Offer me the remote and you'll never get it back.' His eyes — so often remarked upon in hack profiles as 'penetrating' or 'knowing' — were a pale brown that glinted green and gold as they darted around the restaurant. He wore a white v-neck t-shirt under a dark-blue blazer: clothes unable to hide that he'd been working out seriously since September 11, 2001. 'I went into the gym in my building for the first time ever that day,' he'd told *The Atlantic* in 2006, 'and started pulling away at a rowing machine. I guess I was looking to exact some form of revenge. Some punishment.' As if his intellect and filmmaking prowess weren't enough, he could now make you cower with his idle strength.

Duncan sat and asked, 'Where's your assistant?' He knew her name, knew more than was socially acceptable about Ms Golinko, but thought better of being too forward too soon.

'Uffy's working, bless her.' He spoke fast, forever trying to get out of a speeding ticket. 'I said I'd get her a takeout sausage and pepper sandwich, hold the sausage.'

'I'll sort that for you.' Duncan pushed his chair back to stand.

'Wait,' Motta said, holding up his hand.

They were sitting in Preeya's section. Duncan waved her over. 'You're having your usual with us tonight, Mr Motta?'

'Yeah,' he said. 'But Duncan, call me Frank, all right?'

He wasn't surprised Motta used his name. People did it all the time, reading his name badge and dropping 'Duncan' into a sentence as if they'd just promised to put his kid through college. *I see you as a person, not as a nameless waitron.*

Duncan passed the order on to Preeya. Motta began talking as soon as they were alone again.

'People ask me — when I say people, I mean Uffy mostly — why I persist in coming to this place.' He pressed his hands together and leaned toward Duncan. 'I mean, this shtick, right? *Just like Nonna used to make.* Well, I can't speak for the rest of the menu, but your manicotti is. Maybe my Nonna was a lousy cook. I doubt it, but maybe she was. And whatever those guys are doing back there —' he jerked a thumb in the direction of the kitchen — 'probably microwaving the shit out if it, well, it reminds me of my Nonna, which reminds me of my mother and the boy I used to be. It's a useful wormhole, y'know? So I can look past all of this —' he smoothed the tablecloth — 'for a taste of that.'

Duncan nodded, unsure what to do with this. He'd looked into why Motta dined at Sforza's. For a time he'd thought maybe his parents or grandparents had owned a restaurant back in New York, but he'd come from a family of cobblers.

'You know,' Motta continued, 'I was really ticked off at Echo Park for what they did to you, Duncan.'

Now *there* was a lot to unpack. He knows who I am, Duncan thought. Later he would reflect on just how much insider knowledge Motta had about the way Echo Park had shafted him.

Had John Lever, a contemporary of Motta's with a reputation for saving projects, been waiting in the wings the whole time? Motta might know. But in the moment Duncan was able to put a lid on such thoughts and parry back.

'You're still making films for them, though,' he said. No hurt or surprise in his voice, at least to his ears.

Motta laughed and ran his tongue over his top teeth. 'Yes, yes I am. I'm sure the other production companies are just as bad. I said to Uffy, actually, when I heard what had happened with you and Echo Park, I said to her, "What can I do? Who do I talk to?" but she told me to just let it lie. She's the smart one, about that sort of thing at least. One thing I've learned from three decades in this business, it's this: you can't be smart about everything. Uffy says, "You're close, Frank. Next film, they gotta let you make your Saint Joe pic."'

'And they are? At last?'

'Meetings,' Motta said. 'Three days of meetings just to get back to where we were before we flew out here. We were supposed to go to Italy next week to scout locations, me and Uffy.'

'Aren't you a little high-powered to scout locations?'

'It's not location scouting, per se. The money men want me to film it in Mexico. Ergo, we *will* film in Mexico. I don't think I've ever said the word "ergo" in my life. Must've picked it up in a friggin' meeting. This Italian trip, it's about making sure I have the pictures right in my head. So I can get the sets right. Get the lighting right, the architecture, the sunsets, either on film or in post.'

'A lookbook?' Duncan said, but Motta ignored him.

'But we're behind on the edit for this thing we're working on now.' *Folding the River*, if IMDb was to be trusted, the story of the man who laid out the grid for Manhattan's streets and the rival surveyor who tried to rip him off. 'Two weeks in Italy? Go fuck yourself, Frank. Maybe I can get a weekend. I'm supposed to have an audience with the Pope, you know?'

'What does Uffy say?'

Motta smiled. 'She says, "Go clog your arteries while I make some calls."'

As if on cue, Preeya arrived with Motta's veal manicotti. 'We'll bring the sandwich with the check, sir.'

'Thank you, sweetie,' Motta said. 'You gonna eat with me, Duncan?'

'I just ate.'

'Really. Here? How was it?'

'Filling.'

Motta wrapped the table with his knuckles. 'You're funny, Duncan.'

'I guess.'

'No, that's a good thing. You need a sense of humour. You don't mind, I'm going to dig in.'

'Of course.'

There was a lull while Motta took the first bite of his meal and Duncan tried to get his bearings. Out of the corner of his eye he saw heads peeping over the brass rail of the server station, faces in the window to the kitchen. He looked over to the bar. Vilma and two other servers sat on stools, gawking. Vilma straightened her back, puffed up her chest, pulled her hands into line with the bottom of her rib cage. It looked like a breathing exercise she'd been taught in acting class: *Find your centre, Duncan.*

'Have you got a full crew for *Tirami Sù*?' Duncan asked.

'We're not calling it that anymore,' Motta said, waving the question away. 'You ever been to Venice?'

Venice? He knew Saint Joseph of Copertino had never been that far north. But Duncan had. 'Yes,' he said.

'What'd you think?'

Duncan, weighing his response, let out a long glottal 'Ah—' He and Kari had been to Venice in their second year as a couple. They'd almost left the city on separate trains towards separate lives. 'I— I hated it.'

Motta raised his eyebrows, two black carets.

'It was hot, muggy. We were there for the Biennale — my wife's an artist, a designer — and the place was just so frustrating.'

'It was built that way, of course,' Motta said as a school teacher might. 'To confuse invaders.'

'Yeah, I get it. But no one ever talks about Venice like this horrible, dirty, tacky labyrinth. It'd be okay if they did, but instead it's supposed to be this romantic place.'

'You been to Naples?'

Saint Joseph definitely had. He was scrutinised by the Inquisition there. If the script was anything like what Duncan had pieced together from incidental references in interviews over the years and his own reading of the saint's life, Naples could be an important part of the film's second act. But Duncan hadn't been there. His one and only trip to Italy had been to the north with Kari.

He stuck with honesty and shook his head.

'It's dirty and confusing, too,' Motta said. 'Dangerous, if you don't have your wits about you. But I don't think anyone could accuse it of being tacky.'

'What about Osimo?' Duncan asked. 'Assisi? Fossombrone? You must've been to them all before?'

Motta nodded. 'When you work on something as long as this,' he said, as if by way of apology. 'But long ago. The early nineties, maybe. Before my boys in the box could do what they can now.'

Motta meant visual effects artists, the way they could replace one building for another in post-production, or stitch together hundreds of individual shots of extras into a seamless crowd scene in some impossible locale. Duncan had learned the ins and outs in preparation for *Fury's Reach*, where computer graphics would play a big part in turning the small white interiors of the set into believable locations on a generation ship hurtling toward a fertile new home: displaying constellations through the hatches; creating the exterior shots of the *Fury*. More recently he'd learned how Motta was using VFX to cut costs on location while sticking as close to his original vision as possible.

'You've seen my film?' Duncan asked. '*Curio Bay*? At Toronto?'

'Did you show at Vancouver? No? Maybe it was Toronto, then.'

'And you know I didn't have any boys in the box then? No CG, just old-fashioned smoke and mirrors. It took a few days to get the shots of the dolphins, but when it's just you and a couple of mates you're paying in beer and compliments, you can afford to be patient.'

A shadow of disappointment, or something very like it, cast across Motta's face. What had Duncan said? Surely Motta didn't want him to be in charge of VFX. If offered, should he accept and risk another *Fury's Risk*-sized balls-up?

'I'm going to be straight with you, Duncan. I *did* just come here tonight for the manicotti. But seeing you, the way you always act so proud—' He held up his hand to stop any interjection. 'I'm sure it's no act. But I come in here, out of the rain, and this idea occurs to me. It's why this has slipped into some kinda job interview. And I can tell that's what you want as well. I can tell. But the more I let you talk, the more you might talk yourself out of a job. I like you — I *think* I like you — so this is what's going to happen: I'm going to put my proposal to you, I'll give you my card, and you can let me know your response tomorrow. Uffy's gonna kill me for this, by the way. But how about you get on the flight to Rome on Wednesday? You follow the itinerary Uffy has meticulously planned. You be my eyes. No, you be you. I want your eyes, fresh eyes. See, I'm still formulating this as I talk. Uffy, she'd be jumping in right now with all the reasons not to. But this is *my* project.' He let that comment sit for a moment, took one last bite of his manicotti, placed his cutlery on the plate, raised his eyebrows once more in childish delight and turned to retrieve his satchel from beside his chair. He placed it on a corner of the table and began to rummage through it. Duncan could see several scripts, some on white paper, some on pink, some on yellow, as well as the edge of a laptop inside the director's bag. Was he about to receive the script for *Tirami Sù* or whatever Motta's passion project was now called?

'Ah, got one,' Motta said. 'Here.' He held out a business card. 'Give me twelve hours to talk Uffy down from the ledge before you call or email, because it'll be her you're talking to.' He did up his satchel and placed it back down on the floor.

No script. Not yet.

Duncan: 'That's quite an offer.'

'Don't talk yourself out of this,' Motta repeated.

'Thank you.'

Duncan held the business card between thumb and forefinger of both hands, feeling the thickness of its stock, the solidity of this moment. Yet the words the card carried were a blur in the swirling world. It was as if he'd seen *Interstellar* again. Someone else in this moment wouldn't feel half of what he felt. This was what he had wanted. What he'd worked for, even if so little of his prep had been called upon. He'd just needed to sit there and let Frank Motta talk himself into this gift.

And then he saw it. Or felt it. A single pulse of knowledge that shot through his entire body, and which he was able to unfold and comprehend as two minutes of screen time. The death of Saint Joseph of Copertino in his tiny room in Osimo. The Vicar General and Father Silvestro Evangelisti standing over the fading miracle worker.

Inspiration or premonition, he felt sure of one thing: this movie was going to get made. And he was going to be involved.

He looked back up at Motta, who was already checking his phone. Over the director's shoulder: the goons from the kitchen were all out in the dining area, forming a line with the floor staff that stretched from the server station around to the bar. He held up the business card, but instead of the slow clap he might have received in a John Lever film he got a very Mottarian response: brutishly folded arms and shaking heads.

Fucking management.

Fucking patriarchy.

Fucking America, man.

OSIMO

It's September 1663 and Giuseppe Desa is dying. A life of pious-
ness, privation, mortification of the flesh and ecstasies — O! the
ecstasies — has exacted its toll. He has taken flight more times
than is seemly to recount. The Inquisition thought so, for a time.
Until he rose in ecstasy above the altar. Case dismissed.

The Vicar General and Father Silvestro Evangelisti are in
Giuseppe's small cell, little more than a timber box set inside the
stone and mortar convent. A bear skin sits atop the pallet bed,
a dying man atop the skin. The surgeon has just left, hefting his
calf-leather bag of cooling cautery irons down the hall in search
of others strong enough for his brand of palliation.

The Vicar General notices Silvestro's nostrils flare. 'You
might think the room would smell of grilled meat, might you not,
brother?'

'There is an odour, though.'

'Oh yes. Have you not yet placed it? It's the bitter greens our
brother has subsisted on since, well, you will know better than I.'

'Of course.'

'You knew him in Copertino?'

'Yes, when we were both much younger men. We have not
been much in the same place since then. It is a blessing I came
from Montefiascone when I did that I might see my friend on the
last stage of his journey.' Silvestro draws another breath through

his nose. 'Wormwood,' he says, smiling, 'that is what he would sprinkle on his supper that it might bring him no pleasure.' He sniffs again. 'But now there is a sweeter smell —' he pauses, raises his index finger as if testing the direction of the wind — 'like the warm crust of a pasticciotto.'

The Vicar General sniffs too, and chuckles. 'What fools we must seem.' He raises his eyes to the false ceiling of the cell. 'Drinking in the smells of a dying man. One of His favourites no less. Come, it is time to administer Extreme Unction.'

Silvestro reaches for the oil, and Giuseppe stirs. 'Oh, what sweetness of Paradise,' the dying man croaks.

'Are you with us, old friend?'

But Giuseppe is halfway to the Lord and does not respond. His skin is dry and cracked after weeks of fever. His grey beard is threadbare, reduced to half its former volume. His dark eyes are milky. Silvestro anoints Giuseppe's eyelids, ears, nostrils, lips, hands, feet and loins with oil, each time seeking the Lord's pardon for the sins of sight, hearing, smell, taste, touch, walking or carnal delight this particular organ might have committed. Giuseppe's body begins to glow. It cannot be the oil. Not the oil alone.

It is evening and the lamplight is low. Silvestro looks at the Vicar General. The older man's face is awash with buttery light. He smiles.

'Another miracle. Will he not let the scribe's hand rest?'

Silvestro is weeping. He feels the Vicar General's hand on his shoulder. Remembers Giuseppe as he first encountered him. *Pippi Boccaperta* — that's what the other lay brothers called him. All those times they'd found him open-mouthed before the sacred images of the church at Grottella. And what has he done for the rest of his life but leave the mouths of others gaping at his feats? The levitation, the scrutiny of hearts, the bilocation, the spontaneous healing. He was a mystic from an earlier brand of Christianity, unfit for the sober, guarded church of the

Counter-Reformation, though the attempts of Rome to hide him, to nail him to the floor, never worked for long. The people of Assisi, Pietrarubbia, Fossombrone and Osimo soon found there was a miracle maker in their midst and clung to him, this connection with the Divine, as they might to a rope offered by the heavens.

Giuseppe never asked for any of it. Indeed, Silvestro thinks, he actively prayed for the charisms to stop. To be left alone. 'I am unclean,' he would say. 'I am the least worthy of men. I do not deserve God's grace or the Virgin's love.' A kind of refrain. Perhaps this is what he is muttering now, though Silvestro and the Vicar General cannot decipher this new and final tongue of the saint, no matter how close they bring an ear to his now glistening lips. He is flush with the Spirit. Flush with death.

He has arrived.

PART TWO

MAY–JUNE 2017

OUT OF THE NOW

Duncan was wedged in economy — *Thanks for the downgrade, Uffy!* — between a young guy in a grey UC Davis hoodie and a fifty-something woman in the aisle seat. The guy was already slouched and turned toward the window, hood pulled over his bulky headphones. But the woman, biting her cuticles and smiling at every flight attendant who passed, she had TALKER written all over her.

She gasped, once, twice, as if about to plunge into icy water, and said, 'I've always wanted to go to Italy.'

They hadn't even started to taxi.

Duncan looked around, hoping for someone across the aisle — another lonely soul spoiling for conversation, a sucker with a surfeit of empathy, anyone who'd take her off his hands — but no one would meet his eyes.

'My husband,' she continued, gasping again, looking at her hands, 'doesn't travel.' She turned to him and gave a guilty smile. She was faintly freckled, springy haired, but her face was puffy, lumpen. A terrible word, but he'd thought it. Had she been crying? She reminded him of someone. Lea Thompson, maybe, when she was made-up to look thirty years older in *Back to the Future*? Was this unkind? Lea Thompson, at least, had aged much better in real life.

'He doesn't travel, but you know what? Now, I *do* travel. Italy!' She groaned and clutched the end of each armrest.

'Well,' he said, unable to hold his silence any longer, 'I'm sure you'll have a wonderful time.'

And she was off: explaining her itinerary (Rome, Amalfi Coast, Florence, Cinque Terre, Venice), how her husband had proposed to her (a new vanity plate on his Mustang that read PANDY, a merger of their names, long before people caught the Brangelina bug), and every joy and disappointment of life as a wife, mother and part-time realtor in Fresno.

When at last they were in the air and the seatbelt sign had been switched off, he retrieved his satchel — a semi-conscious echo of Motta — and got out his laptop.

'Work,' he said, making a *What can you do?* expression with face and hands.

'Of course,' she said. 'Of course. And maybe later you'll tell me about *your* family.' She nodded at the ring on his finger. It was something he never did, look for a ring on other people. Was it a generational thing? A guy/girl thing? Was she coming on to him?

He clicked to open a file of notes he'd prepared long before he'd known what type of job Motta would give him, when it was still a pipe dream. Over the keyboard he unfolded a paper version of the final itinerary from Uffy. It was eight pages thick, printed on both sides in small type. He'd tried to rework his notes before he left, tease out what was now important. But those three days between the offer and his departure had been so intense, and with the itinerary seeming to shift by the hour, his cut-and-pastes from biographies of Saint Joseph of Copertino and critical assessments of Motta's oeuvre had been impenetrable, another kind of commotion when what he needed was silence, calm. All he had was that unshakeable scene: Joseph's death in Osimo, as vivid as if he'd seen it in one of Motta's earlier movies, pored over it two dozen times, dissected it and put it back together. But what good was two minutes of certainty when another ninety remained in complete darkness? And now, en route to Rome, he felt the eyes of the woman in the aisle seat on him and his screen.

He brought up another document from his research folder, a selection of quotations from Motta that pertained, in some way, to his passion project.

> My next film will be a little different. *Hester* had a spiritual dimension, but I want to really delve into that. Wallow in it. [laughs]
> [*Playboy*, 1982]

> It's called *The Mystic*.
> [*Entertainment Weekly*, 1984]

> It's called *Tirami Sù*.
> [*New York Times*, 1986]

> You've got to take risks. You've got to attempt something difficult, something that hasn't been done before. But, and this is the most important thing, you've got to stick the landing.
> [*Variety*, 1989]

It was hard to reconcile this Motta, the one Duncan thought he'd known from his soundbites and cinematography, with the man he'd encountered at Sforza's on Saturday night. Each time he recalled their conversation, the director's words shifted and blurred. When he tried to pin down a statement, his hands passed through it like smoke.

It didn't help that so much had passed since their encounter. The torrent of emails from Uffy on Sunday afternoon, the meetings Monday and Tuesday with everyone but Motta, each time being promised a copy of the script for *Giuseppe* — as the project was now called — at the next meeting, only to receive another volley of excuses and revised non-disclosure agreements for his signature. He still didn't have a script when he checked in at LAX late Wednesday morning. He'd lingered outside the security check, waiting for a runner bearing a thick brown envelope.

A runner that never came.

He was scriptless but not completely in the dark. Uffy's itinerary, this final version, mapped out every hotel check-in time and local specialist's cellphone number he'd need for the next fifteen days. Every nave in every church that he needed to capture, logging its qualities — the light, the reverb, the birdsong through the stained glass — so that Motta's team could construct its likeness in Mexico or on the screens of FX maestros in Mapo-gu or Miramar.

Motta had an audience with Pope Francis on the morning of the seventh of June and in the afternoon it would be Duncan's turn to impress the director. Talk about a hard act to follow. And, not having seen Motta since that night in Sforza's, Duncan had to complete his metamorphosis — retromorphosis? — from Assistant Manager to Serious Filmmaker. Not only produce great content — his lookbook, his insight into the places Saint Joseph lived and levitated — but present himself as indispensable from then on out. One of the smart people Motta liked to surround himself with. Maybe that was the easy part. He had to get the content first.

He'd never scouted locations, not properly. *Curio Bay* fell into his lap. *Fury's Reach* was set on a spaceship and even then he'd had a team of professionals tee up the handful of on-world locations for flashbacks or dream sequences. What would one of these proper scouts think about his good fortune? An amateur being sent in a professional's stead. Maybe he was digging himself deeper yet again. His next *Fury's Reach*. A gift horse brimming with explosives. If only he'd given it the most cursory dental inspection. But no, he'd jumped in, headlong, again. The guild of location scouts, if such a thing existed, would rise up against him. Refuse to work on any of his future projects. Fuck them. He'd scout his own locations. How hard could it be? His path to success would have its detours, including this recent off-road stretch — *unconventional all the way!* — but he'd persist. He was persisting. Was working for Frank Motta. He'd take the best measurements, the greatest photos; his light readings would be terrific. The best. And what about how a piazza or a monastic cell made him feel? How much scope was there for him to shape the scenes that took place in each of his locations? Could he call them *his* locations? There must be some way to carve out a continuing role on the project. A way to prove his worth. His indispensability.

He had fourteen days until he saw Motta in the Vatican.

Fourteen days to find *it*.

It's called *The man who could fly*.
[*MovieMaker*, 1991]

It's called *Yonder flies your saint*.
[At Venice Film Festival, 1993]

—I can move things with my mind. Oh, totally. Telekinesis. Yeah! You don't believe me. I'll show you.
—Maybe after the show, Frank.
[*The Late Show with David Letterman*, 1995]

'TK!' the woman said, her face so close to his screen that her cheek almost brushed his upper arm.

'I'm sorry?'

'Telekinesis. Are you a writer?'

'No.'

She pursed her lips, trying to decide if he was joking. 'My yoga instructor,' she said, 'he gave me this book. It's really mind-opening stuff.'

'I work in film,' he said, as if answering her initial question would shut her up. As if working in film and opening your mind were mutually exclusive, which in Hollywood might even be the case.

'So much of what we think is impossible *can* be achieved,' she said. 'I met this woman in class who'd been diagnosed with non-Hodgkin lymphoma. It's often curable but they found it late. The doctors were pessimistic, so she beat it herself. *With her thoughts.*'

He was out of ways to stop her talking. Maybe there was a safe word, as if she were a dominatrix or a police dog? It was wrong to think about her in this way. She was just excited. Just scared. They weren't so different. Maybe if he just said her name, like in *Rumpelstiltskin*? Had she said it? He remembered the licence plate, PANDY. Had she said her husband's name? Her kids'? He hadn't listened well enough. She could be Paula or Pauline or Patricia and her husband Randy or Andy. Or he could be Paul or Patrick and she was Mandy or Sandy. And would she go by Amanda or Sandra these days? Was her boarding pass visible? Her name on her luggage?

She was still talking. 'You know we only use ten percent of our brain's capacity.'

'That's a myth,' Duncan said, trying a confrontational tack.

'Maybe it's twenty percent.'

'Even if that was true, which it isn't, who's to say it's not just, like, extra storage? Like, your phone has 32 gigs of memory and you're only using eight. Does that make your phone more powerful than you give it credit for, or does it mean you can just store a lot more photos of your cat?'

She looked excited. 'And what about the mind? Where do you think that resides?'

He tugged at the short hairs of his beard with both hands, as if he could pull the rest of his face with them, rip it clean off. Jesus. Would he be having conversations like this at every stop on his itinerary? Maybe it was good practice for how to shut down the claptrap so he could get on with the job, take his photos and hightail out of there.

She was looking at him, waiting for an answer.

'If the brain is like my phone, the mind is the internet,' he said, then added, 'maybe,' lest it sound as if he'd thought about this before, as if he enjoyed such conversations.

'Go on.'

He sighed. 'I need my brain to access my mind, but my mind is bigger.'

'Yes,' Paula or Mandy or Sandra said. 'Yes!'

'And when you're on a plane,' he said, wanting to add *Or you're a new age yoga nut* but stopped himself, 'you've got to switch off the connection and just live within your device.'

'Eat the food, watch the movie.'

'Go into hibernation.'

'Exactly.'

'Exactly,' he said, put his earbuds in and closed his eyes.

I give a lot of interviews but I'm no extrovert.
I just make a lot of movies.
[*Salon*, 1999]

If I couldn't make pictures anymore, I'd be a
house builder.
[*Charlie Rose*, 1999]

If I couldn't direct anymore, I'd get piano
lessons.
[At Hong Kong International Film Festival,
2000]

If I wasn't doing this, I'd be back in New York,
fixing stiletto heels.
[At the British Film Institute, 2002]

Kari's reactions when she first heard Motta had offered Duncan a trip to Italy, in chronological order:
  1.) Reserved.
  2.) Restrained.
  3.) Resigned.

The three Rs of marriage. Although, to be fair:
  1.) He had just woken her up.
  2.) The celebratory Sambuca shots he'd shared with Vilma were probably still on his breath.
  3.) They hadn't yet had a chance to discuss the incident with the Chromecast.
  4.) Duncan's good news meant she'd have to look after Zeb on her own for a fortnight after having him and her parents to share the load that last week.

But think of the big picture! No more Sforza's. 'If I do a good job in Italy,' he'd said, getting animated, 'who knows where it'll lead? I could be a special consultant during the shoot in Mexico. Maybe even manage the second unit. Direct all the crowd scenes, the landscape stuff, even if I am trying to make the Yucatán look like a half-dozen different parts of Italy. Even if Frank Motta is a bit of a bastard and his passion project is more than a little out there — a levitating friar! — this is my chance at redemption.'

In the morning, Kari still seemed stuck on the three Rs.

He rang Mack in search of a reaction more akin to his own excitement, and found it. She particularly liked the timing. She had a two-week gap between *DoTA* tournaments. Wouldn't it be cool to get together, road trip around Italy on Echo Park's dime? Why the heck not, right? Every fibre of Duncan's being said this was a BAD IDEA — not because there was a chance of anything romantic between the two of them; no, Mack had plenty of other ways to make things complicated without bringing sex into it — but he was still giddy from his Motta plan having kinda sorta worked, so he didn't stamp out the idea then and there. And so it came to pass: Mack was arriving from the Baltics a day after Duncan.

Mack the jetsetter.

Mack the minor celebrity.

He still wasn't used to it. Still couldn't shake the image of her as a shut-in.

You're being criticized against the fashion of the day. But fashions change. Who's to say what will last and what will resonate with your children or their children? My job, each and every time, is to cast out a boat that will float regardless of the tide. [*Interview Magazine*, 2003]

We're back to calling it *Tirami Sù*. The saga continues! [laughs] It translates as, 'Lift me up'. I wasn't sold on the title when David Birkett first proposed it. I couldn't get over the dessert. For one, I don't drink coffee. If you don't have the energy to get through a day without caffeine, you're in the wrong job. But then, as time went by, I kept coming back to this idea of being uplifted. How the film will layer these elements, despair, spiritual dryness, faith, ecstasy, the miraculous, and the result will be, *must* be, uplifting. [At Sundance, 2003]

I wish I'd made *Groundhog Day*. Sure, I could have said something old and foreign and revered. There are dozens, literally dozens, of those films I'd like to have made, too. But *Groundhog Day*. It's masterfully put together. That sequence where Bill Murray commits suicide three times in thirty seconds. Toaster in the bath, delivery truck, swan dive from the bell tower. The film goes dark. So dark. But the music, it's kinda hammy. It helps us read it all as cinema. Look at the way Murray pulses his hands as the truck's about to hit him and there are these two notes, perfectly in time, straight out of the shower scene in *Psycho*. What came first: the hand movements or the music? Neither! Neither, it's happening all together. It's cinema. You can tell I've really thought about this, right? It's an incredibly spiritual film. Buddhists, Catholics, lots of people have found what they're looking for in that picture.

[*The Tonight Show with Jay Leno*, 2005]

Dinner was served ninety minutes into the flight.

'Gotta feed the machine, right,' the travelling half of PANDY said, nudging him with her elbow.

The kid in the window seat tore off the tinfoil and started shovelling the beef with pizzaiola sauce into his mouth, head-phones still on, hood still up. To him, Duncan was as big a risk as Mrs Pandy. *What are you studying? Why are students from UC Davis called Aggies? What are you listening to? What's your favourite movie?* Not that he'd ask those questions, but he had to concede he looked like he might. He was thirty-two. Had spent the last two years taking college-aged kids with parental-hope-dashing aspirations under his wing, playing good cop to Cindy's bad cop. But he hadn't *really* thought about how the servers saw him, beyond hating him for not making his move on Motta sooner. Was Lawson sniggering behind that unwitting farmboy front? Was that his way of putting his headphones on and hood up and ploughing through his shift with as little effort as possible? What about Vilma? Surely not. She was the only one he could count on being real.

After that night with Motta, she'd started sending him WhatsApp messages, each a new theory to explain away Saint Joseph's levitations.

Sunday:

> *It was hypnosis, right?!* 👀
> *PS did you know there's a levitation emoji?* 🕴
> *Looks more like Michael Jackson in the Smooth Criminal video to me.*

Monday:

> *A monk's habit DOES seem well suited to concealing cables or steel supports . . . HT Lawson.*
> *And what about big ass magnets and the diamagnetic properties of water? (look it up)*
> *Maybe St Joe took a big drink beforehand?*
> *Or swallowed a chunk of Bismuth? LOOK IT UP!*

Tuesday:

> *So scientists were levitating nano-objects ten years ago using the Casimir force (here's a* link*, lazybones). Maybe Joe stumbled on the same thing slightly (!) earlier??*

Wednesday, as he headed to LAX:

> *Crystals! Or, y'know, the existence of a force which belongs to a non-material reality but manifests itself in the material world.*

She was — what? He took a deep breath, felt himself getting lighter in his seat, imagined lifting off, just an inch, restrained only by his belt.

'My husband wouldn't eat this,' Mrs Pandy was saying.

Over her words and the constant swoosh of the engines and A/C, he could make out a tinny beat from the Aggie's headphones. Kanye? Kendrick? The new Lil Yachty? Oh God, he really did want to ask what the kid was listening to.

★

I think about what that film [*Tirami Sù*] would have been if I'd actually made it in '82 or '83, whenever Jim [Sattler] and I finished the first attempt at a script. I think about it and I thank God. I'll make it one day. When the script is there, when I can do justice to the project.
[*The Movie Times*, 2006]

The language of cinema is the language of dreams. Most seem to have forgotten this.
[Essay, 'The Dreamer's Art', in the *New York Review of Books*, 2007]

I think about death a lot. [laughs] I do. Not in a morbid way, at least I don't think it is. When you make a picture, you try and capture the essential parts and leave off before you go too far. I like to leave my characters with a couple things left to do. Is death the end of everything, or just the end of the picture?
[At Tribeca Film Festival, 2007]

★

'You'll find time to Skype with Zeb,' Kari had said as they cleaned up after breakfast on Tuesday, 'won't you?'

He hadn't asked why she'd said Zeb, not her and Zeb, just replied, 'Of course.'

'What's the time difference?'

'They are nine hours ahead of us.'

'So that means . . .'

They both looked off into space, calculating. Zeb was in the living room, watching as Jafar sent the thief Gazeem into the Cave of Wonders — a scene that had scared Duncan when he was twice Zeb's age, but his son never flinched.

'Mornings are best, maybe?' Duncan said. 'Like, maybe now, which would be about dinnertime in Italy?'

'They eat later over there.'

'Even better. I can Skype you and Zeb from my hotel room.'

'Not every day.'

'I could probably manage it.'

'I mean, for Zeb. He might want — well, maybe he doesn't need reminding every day that you're not here.'

'So you think I'll just slip his mind?'

'No, obviously, he'll miss you. He'll ask for you every five minutes.'

They both were silent, considering how this might have been true even a month ago. But now? Would Zeb say anything at all? Would he just accept it, the way he accepted Gazeem being swallowed by the sand when the Cave of Wonders collapsed and disappeared?

'I'll let you be the judge,' Duncan said.

'And Mack will be with you,' Kari said.

'It'll be good to have an excuse to spend some time away from her.'

Kari made a face and leaned down to set the dishwasher.

'I forget you don't really know her,' Duncan said. 'You don't need to be worried.'

'I'm more worried about the girlfriend that fits into the palm of your hand.'

'Huh? Oh.' He looked down at his phone. 'Listen—'

'You ever wonder why Mack is the friend who came back into your life?'

'No. I mean—' He scratched his cheek. 'No.'

'Could you ever see yourself contacting an old friend out of the blue, like she did with you?'

'I've sent a few friend requests in my time.'

'You know what I mean.'

'She wanted to give me grief about *Fury's Reach*. That's how she is. That's how *we* are, together. She brings me down to her level pretty quick.'

'If you say so.'

'So you think I'm pretending I'll have a miserable time for your benefit?'

'No, I think you really believe you'll have a miserable time, in Italy, with your friend, on the road for two whole weeks.'

'It's work, though. First and foremost.'

'How much are they paying you?'

'It's complicated.'

'Uh-huh.'

'Expenses are covered. There's a per diem.'

'But you can't go back to Sforza's afterward.'

'I'm sure I could. But I didn't have enough leave for them to hold my job. Corporate Policy. Revolving door. You know how it is in hospitality. And anyway, weren't you the one who didn't want me working there in the first place?'

'That was two years ago, Duncan. You're telling me circumstances haven't changed?'

Had they? Was she pregnant again? Or was she referring to Zeb's condition? Had they started calling it a 'condition'? Perhaps she had stopped believing in him as a filmmaker.

'Come on, Zebbie,' she shouted. 'I'm pausing your movie

and you can watch again after daycare. Daddy's picking you up today.'

No 'Aw, Mom.'

No tears.

Zeb got up, switched the TV off at the set and went into the hall to put on his shoes. That was new. Duncan and Kari looked at each other.

'What you lose on the swings,' he said.

'Two steps forward,' she said.

There's a connection between religious miracles and magic. What we call magic now — stage performers, cutting a lady in half, all that — is highly, highly cynical. But what if the artistry was shackled to something else? I liked Chris Nolan's film, *The Prestige*. The way there was more to the magic. It was blood and flesh and electricity. Kooky, sure. But what if we didn't need Nikola Tesla to make real magic?

[*Deadline*, 2009]

Someone once wrote that my films demonstrated exceptional ambition and adequate talent. I'll take that. And I'll take this. Bless you. Thank you.

[Acceptance of Directors Guild of America Lifetime Achievement Award, 2009]

'So, Mr Film,' Mrs Pandy said, once the meal trays had been removed and the lighting lowered for the sleeping portion of the flight, 'any recommendations?' The screen on the headrest in front of her displayed the different categories.

'I haven't been through them yet,' he said.

'Anything I should look out for?'

'I mostly watch kids' movies at the moment.'

'Like Pixar?'

'Disne—' He stopped himself, knowing if she fired up *Aladdin* he'd have to bring the plane down. 'Yes, Pixar. But maybe there's a travel show about Italy?'

'I guess,' she said, a kind of disappointment in her manner that could have been put on, could have been real. Maybe all she wanted was to blow him in the toilets? No, that was his own sludgy reservoir of porn talking. He put the tips of two fingers into the soft flesh under his chin and blew his stupid brains out.

I was complaining the other day about this culture where everything is immediate and then discarded. It has absolutely infiltrated Hollywood. They're remaking *Spiderman*? Why in the name of all that is holy are they remaking *Spiderman*? Then someone pointed out I was onto my fourth wife and I had to shut up pretty quick.
[*The Playlist*, 2011]

I've no problem with using visual effects. I'll lie to your face, I don't care. So long as you believe me.
[*The Making of: Running Mates*, 2011]

Sometimes I think I'd like to make a film for $10,000. Me, a couple of friends and whatever

equipment I can carry. Then I think that's the best way to ruin a friendship.
[Screendaily.com, 2012]

★

Tuesday afternoon, the day before his departure. The lawyers had been and gone, and it was clear that the promise of one last meeting with Motta was not going to eventuate. It was just Duncan and Uffy left.

'Last order of business,' she said, handing him a green folder.

Over the preceding days he'd observed her closely, trying to figure out if she hated him or *really* hated him. She recognised him from Sforza's, the few times she had dined with Motta, and clearly felt it was nuts to send someone who hadn't been involved in the project, couldn't speak Italian and had limited experience scouting locations or working with VFX. But the best outcome for Motta, and thus for her, was to finish his current project, then get *Giuseppe* out of his system as quickly and as painlessly as possible. Rescheduling their location-scouting jaunt could derail everything.

Duncan had opened the folder to reveal a document headed up *Itinerary — Final Version*.

'For real this time?' he asked.

She shrugged. She was in her early thirties. The way she was dressed, made up, presented — hair dyed black and straightened, red-framed glasses, her outfit a literal power suit: the pin-stripes were lightning bolts when viewed up close — it was clear she would age better than him, if she wasn't outstripping him already. He knew they'd both studied in programmes better known for producing academics than filmmakers: him in New Zealand, her in New York. He hadn't been able to uncover anything she'd shot. No shorts. No student projects. Which was odd. But you could see the ambition burning inside her. It burst forth, cherry red, on her lips, her fingernails, in the corners of her eyes. It thrummed beneath her words. If he thought he'd been playing the long game, slumming it for two years at Sforza's until his chance with Motta, *she* had invented it. For a decade she'd been Motta's right hand, his other cheek, his spleen. And she was going to get hers. But now was not the time to make a play. Not with *Giuseppe*. This film couldn't fail, even if it seemed she had little faith in it succeeding.

'You call them convents,' he said, pointing at the itinerary, 'not monasteries. I noticed that during my research, too, reading Pastrovicchi and Parisciani —' he paused, waiting for a flicker of respect that never came — 'but I figured it was a translation thing. Aren't convents where nuns live?'

'If you're familiar with Frank's work,' she said, as if delivering a carefully worded rebuttal to a journalist, 'you'll know how particular he is with details of language. That applies to pre-production, too. *Laypeople*, in English —' another pause — 'do tend to think of "convent" and "monastery" as gendered terms. But the difference is more accurately tied to their relationship with society. A monastery is where the religious go to separate themselves from society. A convent is much more connected to the wider world. The mendicant orders, like the Franciscans, live in convents. This is all still clear in Italian, and to people in the Church. Frank would rather be right than easy.' Uffy readjusted her glasses and said, 'Maybe we need to go through this one more time.'

And they did, line by line, Uffy saying, 'Now, this is important,' with every new town. As if it was a highly complicated action sequence and he was in charge of the pyrotechnics: one error and the take would be blown, and with it an island nation's GDP worth of explosives. Except she'd gone into so much detail, had worked so hard to cover Motta's butt, had immersed herself in the world of the seventeenth-century levitator — the names of every village, every *convent*, rolled off her tongue — that he might as well have been one of those dogs they shot into space. He was merely the vessel through which her itinerary would be realised.

The few remaining times he had the courage to ask a question, she'd shrug, run her finger down the page and read out the answer. It wasn't indifference, her bearing, but a mixture of pride and disdain. She was proud of her work. But this was no longer the itinerary for Motta's final looksee before setting up camp in Mexico. It was now something else. A tchotchke. A party favour for a beleaguered member of the boys' club. Perhaps Duncan was — or might become — another Motta passion project, one nested within a larger, longer-gestating one. He'd hate himself, too, if he was in her shoes. He kind of did hate himself, or at least felt guilty about having skin the colour of old lace, a penis and a second chance.

All these movies about the world almost ending. Just once, I wish it would and we could move on to something else.
[*The AV Club*, 2013]

You might think a picture about a man who can fly, for example, is science fiction. Telekinesis: science fiction. Being in two places at once, reading minds, seeing the future. To me, that's not science and, in some cases, it's not fiction.
[*Entertainment Weekly*, 2013]

Zeb had stood on the cement edging of the park in Valley Glen, looking blankly at the sandpit, the slide, the unstable bridge.

'How about the swings?' Duncan said.

No response.

He picked up Zeb, who remained stiff, and carried him like a rifle in a military parade. He slotted his legs through the openings of the bucket-style swing seat and pushed him from the front, scrutinising the boy's face for a hint of his younger, freer self.

'I'm sorry you had to go to daycare today. I know it's a Tuesday, but I had to work. You know I have a new job, right?'

Zeb's eyes lowered.

'And I'll be going on a plane tomorrow. One day we'll go on a plane again back to New Zealand to see your Nana and Mike, and Grandad and Gina, and your aunty Bianca. That'll be fun, won't it?'

Three kids sprinted in from the south-west edge of the park, but stopped to climb the chain-link backstop of the softball diamond.

'Looks like we'll have company soon. Maybe some dogs will come, too? Eh? That'd be cool.'

Zeb said something, softly.

'What was that?'

'Higher.'

'Oh really?' Duncan asked, grabbing the front of the swing, pulling it up to his chest and holding Zeb there. The boy's eyes were level with his, though they looked straight through him. 'You want to go *higher*?'

'Higher,' Zeb said, passionless.

'You sure?'

'Higher.'

'Here goes— Wait, are you sure? Are you brave enough? Are you? Too late!' He let him go and gave a strong push at the end of his return journey. 'How's that? That high enough for you? Eh, Zebbie?'

Duncan got on the adult swing beside Zeb's and began to swing too, matching his son's degrading arc until they'd lost all momentum. He wanted Zeb to say something. To demand another push or to be let out. Any desire, however expressed, was welcome. But he just dandled in the breeze.

'This movie I'll be helping with, it's set a long, long time ago. When people believed in some fantastic things. Like being able to fly. Or being able to know what is about to happen. Or making people better just by touching them. This one guy, Joseph, he can do these things. A flock of sheep is struck dead by a hailstorm, but Joseph brings them all back to life. He flukes his exams and manages to become a priest, but the Church doesn't like that he does these things. Especially the flying. They think he's showing off. He really isn't. He's trying *not* to fly. And where's the power coming from, anyway? How can they be sure God's behind it and not, uh, someone else? So the Church keeps trying to hide him. They move him around Italy, from convent to convent. That's where I'm going. To visit the places Joseph went, to help this man, my boss, I guess, make a movie about him. What do you think about that? Maybe one day, when it's finished, we can watch the movie together? Eh? Wouldn't that be good?'

There were a dozen kids in the playground now. A girl in a denim dress and skinned knees stood looking at Duncan with her arms folded.

'Nearly done,' he said.

'You better be, you perv.'

'Come on. How old are you?'

'What's wrong with him?' she asked, pointing at Zeb, whose face had contorted as if he'd licked a battery.

'He's a good judge of character. C'mon Zeb, let's blow this joint.'

'*Aladdin*,' he whispered as his father lifted him from the swing.

I have my best ideas in the shower. Sometimes, when I'm working on a script, really tearing it down to build it back up again, I'll take four, five showers a day. People leave you alone in the shower. There's something about the rhythm of the water on your body, the sound just obliterating the normal voice in your head. I came up with the idea for my Saint Joseph pic that way. It wasn't a shower. It was a waterfall actually. How terrific, right? I was in Hawaii, on vacation with my first wife. This was just after I finished *Hester*, 1978 or '79. We go on this nature walk and I'm getting bitten by bugs and sweating and letting the whole world know about it. Ada convinced me to go for a swim — she was a very persuasive woman — and I get under the waterfall, the water is pounding down on my shoulders, and the pieces of this *thing* just come together. I knew the story of the saint's life. I was very popular with my Sunday School teachers. But for the first time I thought about Joseph as a man. Flesh and blood. A man who, through a process of devotion, unlocks something else, something physical. And I saw these moments in Joseph's life — being a bumbling novice, fluking his examinations, his first levitation — as cinema.

The challenge was, and still is, finding people who share this vision.

[*TimesTalks* video series, 2014]

After three episodes of *Passion for Italy*, Mrs Pandy finally drifted off to sleep and he was free to work without scrutiny.

It didn't happen.

He fired up his own in-flight entertainment. Under 'Classics', Alitalia boldly offered *Interstellar*, though he opted for recent Italian films, none of which brought him to tears or made him any more fluent in the language.

★

When you're young, you make films on this first burst of energy. You ride the wave and make five, six pictures in a row that tell the stories of the things in life you think are important. Then you look around and go, what next? But the truth is, you haven't said all you could, haven't covered nearly as much ground as you thought you did when you're, what? Thirty-five, thirty-six. Each new film becomes an effort to plug another gap in what you want to say. And then you turn sixty, and you go, 'Hold on. What's the basis of all of this? What underlies it? It's faith or spirituality or whatever you choose to call it. Can you build a house without building its foundation? Will my work stand up without a clear statement from me about faith? So I keep on at people, trying to get that picture made. [*The Director's Cut* podcast, 2016]

AN INCREDIBLE ROMANTIC

A bird's egg, Duncan thought as the Fiat Punto pulled up outside the terminal at Brindisi. Its blue-green colour. The lower half speckled with dust and road tar. And small enough, it seemed, that it could fit in his palm. That it might be crushed if not handled carefully.

Gianluca, his guide and driver for the next day and a half, opened his door and stood so that his head and chest were above the roof of the car. 'Duncan?'

'Yup,' he said, remaining motionless beside his luggage, still stuck on the bird's-egg analogy and the undercut expectations that were starting to accumulate. The itinerary had suggested he would be met at the gate. He'd pictured a guy in a suit holding a whiteboard with his name on it. But he was not Frank Motta. And he was whacked. Whacked by the flights but also his own disbelief at being whacked. He'd flown back and forth between California and New Zealand a bunch, was used to losing a day or gaining one. It never seemed to affect him. But here, now — the last four days (or was it five?), maybe they'd caught up with him.

Gianluca, as if finally cottoning on to the fact Duncan was lazy and entitled, slapped the roof of his car — the shell appeared to warp from the impact — and came around to collect the bags. He wore a white Ralph Lauren polo shirt, bright green chinos and purple Chucks. Everything a size too small. He wasn't fat, or ripped, just that middle ground you found outside LA; the body of someone who eats pasta and gelato but walks places, probably a couple miles every day, thanks to his job as a tour guide.

Those chinos though.

That green.

Is there such a colour as electric green?

Duncan slunk into the passenger seat, checked his phone and the answer was: YES.

The car ride began in silence, which suited Duncan just fine. One more time through the rushes from the last week: that should get his head straight.

Motta. Uffy. Kari. Vilma. Mack.

Kari. Motta. Vilma. Mack. Uffy.

Mack. Vilma. Uffy. Motta. Kari.

After half an hour on a forgettable highway, olive trees plugged into tinder-dry earth, the silence inside the blue-green Punto began to feel more oppressive. Had he done something to offend Gianluca? He should have put his own bags in the trunk. Perhaps Gianluca, as a Copertino local and Grottella specialist, was out of his element, all his English reserved for facts about Saint Joseph. Or perhaps he was used to foreigners being whacked after fourteen-hour journeys and knew to pick his moments.

As Duncan's thoughts returned to the present, he became aware of the tightness in his calves, the budding numbness in his butt.

Gianluca turned to him. 'You want to see Grottella first, yes?'

The bird's egg shivered as it was overtaken by a truck.

For all the time spent on the itinerary, Duncan's mind was now blank. The fact his Copertino guide was picking him up from the airport had lured him into a false sense of security. He knew that after two nights in the town of Saint Joseph's birth he was to drive himself north in an 'Alfa Romeo Giulietta or similar'. But what was he doing today? Perhaps he needed to check in at his hotel first? Pick up a parcel or a second expert? The itinerary was in his satchel, which was in the trunk.

Fuck it, he thought. 'Please,' he responded.

'Grottella tonight,' Gianluca said, 'then tomorrow the birth-place, his sanctuary and down to Galatone, right?'

'Right.'

'You will be with me tomorrow?' Duncan asked.

'Yes.' There was something sharp and pissy in his tone. 'All of tomorrow. For dinner, I know a place.'

'I have a friend joining me. Tomorrow evening.'

'I will make the reservation for three, yes? Or will the two of you want to be alone?'

'A reservation for three would be great,' Duncan said, then wished he'd clarified that his friend was just that, a friend, not a fly-in floozy or a local squeeze, but Gianluca chose that moment to lurch into the right-hand lane without indicating and took an exit that led on to a two-lane road lined by still more olive trees.

The olives gave way to skinny cypress, flagging fan palms, the occasional two-storey house, a petrol station, a lumber yard. So, these were the outskirts of Copertino. Duncan had pictured something lusher, darker, more mountainous. Perhaps it was the name of the church and convent where Saint Joseph had first found his footing as a man of the cloth — *Santa Maria della Grottella* — that had planted this erroneous seed. Over the last two years he had read plenty about Copertino, had studied paintings of Joseph's levitations, had watched Edward Dmytryk's *The Reluctant Saint* (1962) — the only other biopic of Giuseppe Desa — and Francesco Rosi's *More Than a Miracle* (1967), in which flying Brother Joseph makes a couple of fanciful cameos. He'd even managed to track down the script of Carmelo Bene's *A Boccaperta* from the seventies, which envisioned theatres placing a second screen above the first in order to show the saint's flights. To the surprise of no one, the script remained unproduced. But nothing had yet dislodged the echoes of 'grotty' and 'grotto' and the dingy, dilapidated picture they had assembled in Duncan's mind of the saint's hometown.

They passed a sign welcoming them to Copertino that appeared to show Joseph levitating, though the decal bearing his image had started to bubble and crack.

He felt the Punto slow as they passed a wide grassed area.

A glimpse of a bell tower and cupola on the other side of the park.

'Is that—?'

'I will get us closer,' Gianluca said.

They turned on to a street that ran along the right edge of the park, and headed toward an insipid yellow building, all right angles and defeat. *Hotel Grottella*, according to its large but faded sign. His hotel? It rang a bell. Perhaps he would have one of the rooms with a balcony that looked directly at the church?

Gianluca didn't take the turn toward the church. The paving deteriorated and they had to veer around a large pothole before turning left on to a narrow road pocked with puddles. Concrete-block walls were marred with fresh graffiti.

AUGURI AMICAAAA

sei un incredibile romantica

These words, the calligraphy, struck him as happy, good-natured, but he couldn't be sure. Happiness seemed a strange trigger for vandalism.

He got out his phone to translate this second phrase. According to Google: *you are an incredible romantic*. He suspected a gap remained between these words and the true sentiment — perhaps he was missing the sarcasm completely — but he felt a little less dense to be tackling the next fortnight with Google by his side.

He looked up and there was the church, its left flank, the forward part composed of sandy bricks, and the rear smooth, white-washed, bureaucratic. They came to a stop hard against the shin-high chain that surrounded the complex. Gianluca's Punto was the only vehicle in sight.

Duncan's phone told him it was 5 p.m. local time. The golden hour was approaching, though his body felt it should now be morning.

'Okay,' Gianluca said, and nodded at Duncan. He removed a pair of tortoiseshell sunglasses from the sun visor and slotted them into the neck of his polo shirt. 'Let's do this.'

Duncan oozed out of the car and noticed the statue just a few feet away of a man, Saint Joseph no doubt, clutching a ten-foot-tall crucifix. It was carved from white stone that had blackened along the top of the crossbar and the rippled bottom of Joseph's habit. The soles of his bare feet were white, perhaps recently cleaned, and raised six inches from the pedestal. But the way he clung to the cross. It made it look as if he was trying not to be blown away by a hurricane rather than lifting to the heavens in ecstasy.

From the trunk Duncan retrieved the XC model Canon that Uffy had entrusted to him: 'We need this back,' she'd said, self-important and dismissive, as if she was giving him the key to a gas-station bathroom, 'got it?' The camera seemed designed for a run-and-gun approach, able to shoot video in 4K while compact enough to take anywhere and slip beneath the notice of thieves and security guards. Perhaps he could make a film out of the next fortnight, a kind of shadow-world version of Motta's *Giuseppe*. Instead of following in the footsteps of a seventeenth-century levitator, he'd subject his audience to ninety minutes of him and Mack struggling with restaurant menus and sneaking around the back of churches for a glimpse of a priest removing his cassock through the ruby gloss of stained glass.

Or not.

He also grabbed the satchel containing his notebook, itinerary, laser distance measure, old-fashioned tape measure as backup, and a light meter. Light, there was a lot of it. Light and space.

Out front of the church everything was flat. The park was ringed by date palms that bled into a shaded area with tennis court, kids' playground, cafe. *Parco Grottella*, according to the sign. No overhangs, no crevices. Not the kind of image you'd find on the walls at Sforza's, and certainly not the Grottella he'd pictured when reading Pastrovicchi's life of the saint. Yes, he'd need to trash the scenes he'd concocted for the film's first act. Take the film and overexpose it. The early years of the saint's life would be bright and dry. His cell, his sanctuary from life in the heel of Italy, would be dim and damp. His self-inflicted punishment made clear through the contrast in light.

Good, he thought, this is why I came. Why Motta sent me. A script would only close down the possibilities.

He slung the camera strap and satchel over opposite shoulders. It was almost thrilling. An intrepid explorer about to leave his dugout canoe and set foot on the banks of an uncharted stretch of Amazon. Only: he was in Italy, standing beside a four-hundred-year-old building, about to be led around by a less-than-chipper tour guide. Mack would be merciless if she saw him. Eager and under-prepared. No better than Mrs Pandy.

'Come on, John Rambo,' Gianluca said, and pulled at his camera strap.

They walked to the edge of Parco Grottella to a new-looking wall composed of irregular-shaped rocks and — surprise, surprise — more cheerful graffiti scrawled in red:

Stupendo fino a qui . . . ♥

Google: *Gorgeous up to here . . .* ♥

Only this place wasn't gorgeous. Nor was it hideous, or imposing, or especially dirty. The old sat beside the new, but the place felt empty, lifeless. Like he was back inside a cleared level of Castle Wolfenstein. Back inside that dream of his. The excitement of moments ago had gone and was replaced with, what? Next to nothing. No, he was on the cusp of feeling something, seeing something that he didn't want to. The pointlessness? Sudden-onset homesickness?

Gianluca started talking. Duncan turned back to face the complex.

'The church was founded in 1543. To the left is the convent. There is an event on this evening in the courtyard. The winners of a competition for schoolchildren throughout Italy. You might like to go along.' He bobbed his head and turned out his palms as if to say, *I wouldn't be seen dead there, but you might enjoy it.* 'Construction on the convent began in 1618 and it is rumoured that among the unskilled labourers was a young man named —' he paused for effect — 'Joseph Desa. If not for Joseph, the man he later became, this complex may have closed in 1652.'

Duncan was surprised he'd said 'Joseph', not 'Saint Joseph' or 'San Giuseppe'. Perhaps he figured any slip into Italian would be wasted breath. But to leave off his saintliness?

'Even so,' Gianluca continued in the manner of someone speaking to a dozen rather than to one, 'it was left to decay during the periods of suppression of monastic orders in the nineteenth and twentieth centuries. During World War Two the building was seized by the Air Force and used as an ammunition store for airports in Leverano and Galatina. It is said that the Allies did not target this complex, however, because many of the pilots were Italian-Americans and were devoted to Joseph, the patron saint of aviators. A few years later the Conventual Franciscans regained possession and began renovations.'

'Are you not religious?' Duncan asked.

Gianluca lifted his sunglasses to look him in the eye. 'Why do you ask?'

'It's my job to ask questions.'

'I thought it was your job to take pictures and measurements?'

'That too.'

'Well,' he said, 'my job is to tell you about the complex, its history.'

Duncan knew he should ask about the exterior of the church — was it sandstone? He should ask what the surrounds would have looked like in Joseph's day. He should take a light reading — it really was bright — but instead he said, 'I just expected a believer. But you don't believe, do you?'

Gianluca started walking toward the church and gestured for Duncan to follow. 'I believe Joseph Desa lived, without a doubt.

He was born the same year King James of Scotland ascended to the English throne. It is not so long ago. And whatever you think about the Church, it keeps good records.' He stopped and put his hand on Duncan's shoulder. 'But you do not sound like an American?'

'I'm not. I mean, I live in LA but I'm from New Zealand.'

'New Zealand? *Che bello*. I thought you were an American.' Gianluca laughed. '*Mio Dio*. But you are working for Americans, yes? Columbia Pictures?'

'Echo Park, I guess, but yeah, same difference.'

Gianluca started walking again. 'I worked in Rome for many years. Hollywood people, Americans, they are the worst. But you are from New Zealand! Tell me, my friend: is it true they will film in Mexico?'

Duncan had thought this was insider knowledge but regathered himself and gave a disappointed shake of his head, meaning 'Yes.'

'Ah. *Vaffa*!' Gianluca made an obscene gesture back toward the car park where, presumably, if you travelled far enough you'd strike the Hollywood sign. 'What can I do to convince you that this is a terrible idea?'

'Me? I'm not— I mean, it wouldn't take much to convince me, but it wouldn't do any good. I only got this gig a couple of days ago. I'm not sure I'd be here if they could have gotten a refund on all the deposits they put down.'

'Ha.' Gianluca clapped once and wiped his hands as if they were covered in breadcrumbs. 'Okay. You and I are powerless. We are pawns, yes? Okay, I feel better.'

'Really?'

'I will no longer feel —' he rolled his hand over, scrolling through options to select the right word — 'complicit. I will say to anyone who listens, That film is a piece of shit. The director, he never came to Italy, he just sent a pawn to take some photos.'

'And ask some questions.'

'Yes, yes. And I will tell you this, my friend: I believe Joseph *believed*.' He made a fist and brought it close to his forehead, like the singer in a video for an eighties power ballad. 'Excessively, no doubt, but his heart was in the right place and he helped many people with his excessive belief. He helped others believe in more reasonable and helpful ways.' He brought his hands together, as if in prayer, and began to speak more softly. 'I believe in the capacity of the human mind to resolve a great deal of what ails the body. If it helps to believe a man or the relic of a saint is doing the healing, so be it.'

Duncan thought of Mrs Pandy and her friend with the fleeting non-Hodgkin lymphoma.

'The reason I have a job today, however,' Gianluca continued, 'is the fact this Joseph levitated. Flew eighty paces from the portal of the convent to a Calvary that was being erected on the road into town. I can show you the place. We can pace it out together. Gianluca stuffed his hands in the pockets of his parakeet pants. 'I believe such feats are overstated. I cannot help but explain them away with a sceptical mind, however lazy this may be. But I have earned my laziness. And I cannot deny it is the most interesting part of Joseph's story, these flights. Come,' he said, 'there are many flights inside the church to relate. Up to the pulpit, to the Holy Sepulchre, to the altar of Saint Francis, to our Lady of Grottella.'

Gianluca pulled open the door of the church and gestured for Duncan to enter.

TRINITY-LITE

'So, my friend,' Gianluca said, clamping a hand on Duncan's shoulder to mark his arrival in the vast, empty restaurant on the Hotel Grottella's ground floor, 'I enjoyed your movie.'

'You watched it?'

Gianluca took his seat and composed himself. Drawing out the time between Duncan's question and his response seemed to delight him. Made the tip of his tongue poke out from the corner of his mouth. 'Yes,' he replied at last. 'While you were having your nap. On here.' He held up his phone. 'I know, sorry, but I do not like to go home during the day. My wife—' he said, and waved off this thought.

'Streaming?' Duncan asked. Gianluca nodded. 'On Netflix? *Curio Bay* is on Netflix in Italy?'

'*Si*,' Gianluca said, drawing out the syllable as if he was in an opera and this was his only line.

Duncan's agent, Tanner Burge, had dropped him at the start of the year, but before that he'd been trying to sell the streaming rights in various territories. Duncan hadn't seen a eurocent in the way of royalties, but maybe it had taken this long to appear. Maybe other doors were about to open.

It was his second night in Italy. It might all have seemed magical to him a week ago — that he would sleep a stone's throw from where Saint Joseph of Copertino had slept for his first seventeen years as a Franciscan; that he was working for Frank Motta, building up a library of images and impressions to help this master bring his passion project to fruition at long last. The reality of this place and his task, however, left him feeling flat.

The church at Grottella had been expanded and refurbished so often since Joseph's time it was virtually useless for filming. Duncan spent longer than he needed inside the church so as not to offend Gianluca but, even then, when he made to leave his host suggested he spend another five minutes in there, alone. Duncan had handed over his notebook and camera and walked to the altar. Sparrows chirped from unseen ledges. One electronic votive candle flickered in an imagined breeze; the rest of its array remained unlit. He'd contemplated the small, crude Madonna and child at the back of the church that had caused such raptures for Saint Joseph. It wasn't quite as bad as the amateur restoration of the 'Ecce Homo' fresco in Spain, but it was in the same ballpark.

He'd willed himself to feel something. To lift, if only in spirit.

Alas.

The convent was now an information centre about the saint, and its courtyard had been overrun with preparations for the prizegiving. He'd spent his first evening out on the balcony of his hotel room, listening to the schoolkids singing the refrain:

Giuseppe volava!

Google: *Joseph was flying.*

Even these kids called him simply Giuseppe, not San Giuseppe. As if he really had lived among them. An uncle. A second cousin. But rather than the one who'd died in the war, or emigrated to Brazil, he was the relative who flew.

Now day two was in the books. His memory card contained all the images of Copertino and surrounds he'd ever get the chance to capture. The plan from here: grab a beer and wait for Mack, whose arrival depended on a series of planes, buses and private transfers. Then the three of them would head back into Copertino proper and the place Gianluca had chosen for dinner. It was 7.30, early doors for Italy. Still light outside, still warm. The only other person in the hotel's restaurant was the owner, a big man in a white t-shirt, standing behind the bar, reading something on his phone. With his build and his buzzcut he could have passed for a Polish plumber or a Belarussian wrestler. The only noise came from an anchorwoman, fierce and immaculate, jumping from item to item — something about the Pope, a meeting of leaders in the Middle East, the retirement of a footballer — on a TV screen inside a wall cabinet otherwise laden with sporting trophies. Or perhaps, Duncan reconsidered, they were religious items. Chalices, ciboria, a monstrance — words from the new vocabulary this trip was building.

'You really enjoyed it?' Duncan asked, gesturing at Gianluca's phone.

'I thought: I too would choose to save the life of a dolphin over a fucking tourist.' He laughed.

'An American tourist at least.'

'Of course. A New Zealander? No way.'

'I'm going to be just another fucking tourist without you tomorrow, Gianluca.'

'You'll be fine. Besides, you are not a tourist. You are a vexed Hollywood pawn, right? Echo Park must have other guides booked for you?'

'Not until Assisi.'

'Assisi? And you will go to Naples first?'

Duncan pulled the itinerary from his trouser pocket and unfolded it. 'Tomorrow, after picking up our rental car, we drive to Martina Franca.'

'Ah yes, Joseph's first failure with the Capuchins.'

'Then —' he paused to give his tongue time to attack the place names — 'Montescaglioso, Matera, Altamura—'

'Bang bang bang,' Gianluca said, accompanied by three claps.

'—and then across to Naples.'

'And you are okay with driving in Italy?'

'I'm used to driving on the right.'

'Yes, but in Italy we do not drive like other places. And our roads are not the same. We have many types of roads, many types of driving. And Napoli?!' He made a circle with thumb and forefinger and raised his other three fingers. Elsewhere this would have meant *A-OK*, but here, in this context, it was something like, *Good fucking luck.*

'I'm sure I'll be fine.'

'Okay,' he said, unconvinced. 'Confidence is good. Everyone else on the road will be confident, for sure. Your friend, has she arrived?'

'Not yet. Can I get you a drink?'

'Allow me,' Gianluca said, but didn't rise from his seat. Moments later the owner was over with two draught beers.

'*Grazie*,' Duncan said.

Gianluca took the owner's hand between both of his and said something Duncan didn't catch.

'They call this the heel of the boot?' rang out a voice, loud, cocky, familiar. The kind of voice that might belong to a street hawker or a maiden aunt. Duncan turned to see Mack in a long tan leather coat — if it was black she'd have looked like a stunt double from the set of *The Matrix* — over a tight-fitting seafoam-green dress. 'Looks like the arsehole to me!'

He turned back to the others. Gianluca smiled as if he'd just been tipped with a stack of coupons, the owner as if he'd been addressed by a visitor from the Horsehead Nebula.

'She's, uh, with me.' Duncan stood, went to take Mack's suitcase, but was swept into a hug and the dank microclimate of the leather coat. That she'd managed this was a surprise. He used to be taller than her, but then she never used to wear heels.

'You know it's almost summer, right?' he said, extracting himself from the embrace.

'It's Italian leather, babe.'

'Come, sit down,' he said. 'Gianluca, this is my buddy Mack.

Mack, this is Gianluca. He's been showing me around Copertino the last couple of days.'

'A pleasure,' Mack said, offering her hand like a duchess eager to dismount from a hansom cab.

Gianluca was wearing the same electric-green chinos and purple Chucks as yesterday, dressed up with a pink-sherbet shirt, the sleeves folded to his elbows. What would he make of Mack? She'd long ago lost the baby fat, beaten the zits, given up the hockey thrashings, but, to Duncan at least, she wasn't pulling off this glamour-girl look. Something about her posture. The emphasis on her breasts. The uncanny valley between how she thought she looked and what he saw. It was like one of those body-swap movies where the lousy womaniser gets zapped into the figure of his latest dumpee: that first morning he dresses in her sexiest clothes but can't manage five steps in her stilettos.

'Good trip?' Gianluca asked.

'Babe, it was terrible. I don't get why you lot have gone all in on Ryanair. So you're sick of bailing out Alitalia, I get that. But to get in bed with Ryanair? It's only one step up from sticking a label on your forehead and FedExing yourself someplace.'

'A drink, Mack?' Duncan asked.

'I wouldn't say no to a beer.'

Duncan held up one finger and mouthed, '*Un'altra.*'

The owner nodded and returned to the bar.

'So, Mack,' Gianluca asked as they sat, 'are you in the movie business too? An actress maybe?'

'I see my legend has not preceded me.'

'Duncan is not very forthcoming,' Gianluca said, smiling.

'That could go on his tombstone. *Duncan Blake, 1985 to*, hmm, *2070: Not very forthcoming.*'

'He will live that long?'

'Can we not start a sweep on how long I'm going to live?'

The owner brought over another beer, placed it next to the first two, which hadn't yet been touched. Mack reached over, took the fresh one, lifted it and waited for the others to pick up theirs before she began her toast. 'To old friends and new,' she said.

'*Salute!*' said Gianluca.

'*Salute*,' echoed Duncan, but Mack had already taken a gulp.

'Below-average drop,' she said. 'Refreshing at least.'

'So,' Duncan said, 'Gianluca was telling me *Curio Bay* is on Netflix here.'

'Dubbed?' she asked.

'Subtitles,' Gianluca said.

'Would be pretty quick to dub, I reckon. Only about three lines of dialogue, eh?'

'There's more than that,' Duncan said.

Mack drained the last of her beer and clunked the glass on the table. 'What's the plan, Stan? Do I have time to go two-for-one?'

'We're going into town for dinner,' Duncan said. 'Gianluca will take us in his car. How about you go drop your things off in the room while me and Gianluca finish our beers?' He slid the room key across the table.

'Oh, all right,' she said, as if stung by the suggestion. 'Room fourteen,' she said, reading the keyring. 'And that is?'

'Through that door, up the stairs, turn left at the landing. You'll probably need to turn the hallway lights on, or use your phone — this place is not exactly pumping. It'll be obvious which of the single beds is mine.'

'From the cum stains?'

Duncan gave her the finger but she'd already turned away.

'Your friend is quite—' Gianluca said, searching for the word.

'Abrasive?'

'Confident.'

'It might appear so,' Duncan said, and took a long sip of his beer.

'And you are friends?'

'For my sins. We went to high school together back in New Zealand. We've only seen each other in person once in the last, shit, fifteen years. Online, over the phone, she's easier to take somehow.'

'Bah,' Gianluca said. 'It is good to see someone not afraid to be themselves.'

Duncan took another sip of beer.

'*È una gran tentazione non avere tentazioni*,' Gianluca said. 'That's something your Saint Joseph used to say.'

'What does it mean?'

'It is a great temptation to have no temptation.'

DOWNSIZING

The restaurant in Copertino was, according to Gianluca, typical of the Salento region. Its long but narrow dining hall, with room for two columns of tables and a central aisle. Its vaulted brick ceiling reminiscent of the local churches, but without the whitewash and about an eighth of the height. It made the restaurant feel dark and close. Here, at last, was the grotto feel he had expected of Copertino.

'You can only think of it like traditional sports for so long before that starts to limit its possibilities.'

Mack, still draped in Italian leather, was explaining e-sports to Gianluca, who, it seemed, had not noticed the rise of video games as a spectator sport.

Duncan served himself the last of the ear-shaped pasta in its fresh tomato sauce, then forked up the final oversized slice of salami from the antipasto and pushed it into his mouth like a busted umbrella being thrust into a rubbish bin. How strong was the red wine? How much did each carafe contain? He hadn't seen a menu. Gianluca had told them they were going to be treated to a selection of dishes, local specialties, typical plates. There was that word again. *Typical*. He'd used it a few times when talking about church construction, paintings of saints, town planning. When it came from his mouth, it didn't carry the negative connotations it might in Duncan's world.

You forgot to transfer the clothes from the washing machine to the drier? Typical.

Another old white dude wins an Oscar? Typical.

He considered excusing himself to go Skype his family from the bathroom, but it was already too late. Zeb would be in daycare. Kari at her office, leaning over her giant tablet, sucking the end of her stylus, thinking creative thoughts, doing good work. She complained about it, of course. The way the decision-makers would say, 'Let's bring in the Creatives', as if they were sideshow freaks. As if keeping hold of a childhood passion for drawing, for clean lines and visual punch, cultivating it, working damn hard and following the thread until it led to an income — a stream of gigs, if not a stable career — as if that meant it was okay to marvel at them, treat them like volunteer labour and ogle their naivety. Didn't she know the only way to make money, have influence and enjoy life was to own things: magazines, shopping malls, football teams? New Zealand had softened her socialist tendencies, but LA and the general shitshow that was US politics had re-radicalised her, if only in her nightly unloading with her husband. But she was all talk. She'd actually been against him quitting Sforza's. No, she wouldn't ruffle feathers. She liked her work too much. Her family.

Zeb. He missed Zeb. He tried to field a logical defence: how could he miss this child who never said thank you anymore, who hardly ever spoke, and who dissolved into gloop before *Aladdin* just as his father was reduced by *Interstellar*? Duncan had learned it was never too early to feel guilty for ruining your kid's life. For the first six months, he'd regretted deeply the name he and Kari had chosen. Zebulon — after the dude who'd named Kari's hometown: Zebulon Pike. Now there was a name. Zebulon Blake had held a similar ring during the pregnancy. They liked the sci-fi edge to it, the folksy sound of the diminutive Zeb. But as soon as he was born and the documents were lodged, all Duncan could think about was his son's lifetime of doubletakes, playground taunts and muffed coffee orders. Every time a family member or acquaintance said what a cool name it was, it only made it worse. Better no one mentioned it, as if they'd called him John.

Or Jake.

Or Joseph.

But he was Zebulon. Zeb. Zebbie. The Zebster. To pull it off, he would need a big personality — a John Goodman presence, a Foghorn Leghorn bluster. Would the name bring it out of him? The way all Chads are destined to die in flaming wrecks and the lives of all Kylies converge at the point of single motherhood, sweatpants and too much eyeshadow. Or would Zeb's ill-fitting name further weigh him down?

Duncan looked back at the table. An unseen waiter had brought another round of food. A plate of grilled eggplant. Fried balls of crumbed mozzarella. Crispy meatballs. Thin, pale steaks swimming in a light, buttery gravy.

He stabbed a meatball with his fork.

'Is that pork?' Mack asked, pointing at the steaks with her knife.

'Veal,' Gianluca said.

'Ooh, yes please,' Duncan said, and reached over to serve himself a cutlet.

'And these?' Mack asked.

'*Polpette di cavallo*. Horse meatballs.'

'I see,' said Duncan, moving the meatball to the side of his plate and carving into the veal.

'Interesting,' said Mack.

'What?'

She had a way of playing with her hair, mussing up the back as if testing its volume, then bringing her hand back out and shaking her whole head. It was a tic she'd always had, if you could call something that elaborate a tic. 'You'll eat veal but not horse? You know what veal is, right?'

'Yeah. It's just—' He put a forkful of the veal into his mouth and chewed. 'I have a rule.'

'Go on.'

The meat wasn't as tender as he'd have liked, the sauce feeble, but he had chosen his side and had to follow through. 'It's just,' he said, 'I don't like to eat animals that were domesticated for a purpose other than for the table.'

'Right,' Mack said slowly. 'Gianni, did you follow that?'

'No,' Gianluca said. He didn't seem fazed by being called Gianni. Perhaps it was something others called him. Perhaps he let confident women call him anything.

'Horses, right,' Duncan said, 'were domesticated for transport, to help with ploughing, harvests. To then go and eat them seems a little ungrateful, don't you think?'

'How do you know they weren't domesticated to be eaten?' Mack asked. 'Have you looked that up?'

He hadn't. He'd concocted the rule the last time he was in Italy, his trip with Kari to the North: a time when looking something up meant waiting until he was in front of a computer screen, which ninety-five percent of the time meant the impulse was completely forgotten.

'I see what you're saying,' Gianluca said. 'Horses are beautiful creatures. But I think these ones —' he pointed at the plate of meatballs — 'were raised to be eaten.'

'Let me get this straight,' Mack said, her voice a notch louder. 'You think it's better to take a baby cow, stick it in a crate for a couple months and then kill it before its hooves have ever touched pasture, than to honour a horse that's lived a full and productive life by making more use of its earthly form than bulking up a fucking dogroll?'

'Yep.' Duncan took another sip of wine. 'I'm not saying it's perfectly logical. I mean, I could argue it's better to honour all the bobby calves that are produced by the dairy industry by putting them into a — what is this, saltimbocca? — than burning them on a pyre, but honestly, I don't want to eat a horse. Just as I wouldn't eat a cat or a dog.'

'What about sheep? Were they domesticated first for wool or for meat?'

'I eat lamb.'

'What about a wild animal? A boar?'

'Yep.'

'A bear?'

'Who eats bears?'

'Russians, Latvians, Estonians—'

'Actually,' he said, 'Estonia is a lot closer to Finland—'

'Babe.'

'No, I wouldn't eat a bear. Maybe I have another rule about carnivores. I'll get back to you.'

'Well,' Gianluca said, picking up a horse meatball with his fingers and biting into it, 'we have no bears on the menu. There will be fish.'

'Wild?' Mack asked.

'What do you mean wild? Of course wild.'

'You can farm fish. Salmon. And what are those fish they farm beneath their houses on the Mekong?'

'Pass,' Duncan said.

Gianluca looked lost again.

Mack looked up from her phone. 'Basa.'

The table fell silent. Duncan noticed three beads of sweat in a line across Mack's forehead. On cue, she began taking off her coat, a task complicated by the fact she was seated closest to the wall in a spot where the ceiling curved in to form an arch. At one point she had to place a hand on Gianluca's thigh while she shimmied her other arm out of its sleeve. Duncan could feel the eyes of the other diners on them.

When she had placed her coat over the back of her chair and sat back down, Duncan asked, 'And how many calves went into making that, do you think?'

'Babe, I'm not the one with dumb rules.' She turned to Gianluca. 'My rule is: Go for it.'

'Just do it,' Gianluca said, containing a laugh.

'Fill your boots,' she said, holding aloft a carafe of wine.

'Walk a mile in my shoes,' Gianluca said. The two of them were soon doubled over with laughter.

The waiter, a kid in his twenties with Andy Garcia hair, except it was swept left to right not front to back, delivered another round of plates without comment.

White fish drowning in olive oil. *Plonk.*

Something — more fish? — rolled up and stuck through with toothpicks. *Clunk.*

Five thin knobbly sausages, like franks knitted from brown wool, on a bed of arugula. *Thud.*

How would this waiter cope at Sforza's North Hollywood? He wouldn't last a single service with Cindy. Then again, how would Lawson do here? Or Vilma? Would she be ogled more or less in this place? Maybe that's why all the servers he'd seen so far were dudes. He looked back at Mack and Gianluca, slapping the table and snorting back more laughter. However nice Gianluca was, for all his canned professionalism, Duncan could see him getting a little handsy with the next female who was forced to enter his personal space.

Gianluca turned to him, wiping an eye. 'And this lovely lady will be travelling with you to Martina Franca?'

'Yes. All the way to Osimo and back to Rome.'

'Osimo?' he said, demonstrating with his emphasis of the first syllable and the hard 'z' how poor Duncan's pronunciation had been. 'And then Rome. In just two weeks?'

'Another twelve days, give or take.'

'And what will you do, Mack, when your friend is taking photos of churches and convents?'

'I guess I'll be there, too. I dunno. What is your job exactly, babe?'

'I'm going all the places Saint Joseph of Copertino lived, taking pictures and measurements so they can be recreated on film.'

'In Mexico,' Gianluca added.

'In Mexico,' Duncan said.

'When do I get to read the script?' Mack asked, rubbing her hands together.

'Never.'

'Come on, I can help. But I need to know what we're making here.'

'I can't give it to you because I don't have it.'

'What?'

'I signed a bunch of NDAs, then I never got it. I just have this itinerary,' he said, producing it, already a little foxed along the folds, from his trouser pocket.

'Setting you up to succeed, I see?'

'Maybe,' Duncan said. 'I mean, maybe I have scope to stamp my mark on the script? To say, *Pietrarubbia, now there's a place!* Show them how a scene there could do the work of three elsewhere.'

'But, like, how long does a church take to do?' she asked, her hand reaching for the back of her head again.

'It depends,' Duncan said. 'Today, we went to the Sanctuary of Saint Joseph in town, which was built over the stable where he was born—'

'Like Jesus?'

'And Saint Francis,' Gianluca said.

'It's a thing,' Duncan said. 'Joseph's dad was on the run from his debtors and his mother had to hide in the stable. The church there now has the saint's heart and a few other relics, but it was closed for renovations. Typical, eh?' He smiled. The other two exchanged *Was that funny?* glances. 'The structure was all built later, so it wouldn't have been much use anyway. His childhood home was just across from the church, but that too has been converted into a kind of shrine. So, all up, these two things on my To Do list took about forty-five minutes and yielded diddly squat.'

'But Grottella,' Gianluca said, half in protest, half in jest.

'Yeah, Grottella, next to our hotel, where Joseph lived. That took about, what? Two and a half hours? Three?'

'So plenty of time to extemporise,' Mack said. She rubbed her hands together again.

'Well, no, I don't think so. I mean, today we also went to Galatone, to the south of here, where Joseph was taken as a boy to be cured of this massive tumour that covered his lower back and butt.'

'Nice.'

'And we spent the rest of the afternoon driving around, getting the topography straight, looking for things to add to the lookbook for Motta — colours, trees, the faces of people.'

'Wank wank wank wank wank.'

'And,' Duncan said, slapping the itinerary against the table, 'there's plenty of driving coming up.'

'And you will drive too?' Gianluca asked Mack.

'I wish,' Duncan said. 'Mack here never learnt. She was too busy doing thumb crunches.' He held an imaginary PlayStation controller and flexed both thumbs.

'You will navigate, then?' Gianluca offered, placing a hand on her shoulder.

'Her phone will navigate,' Duncan said, not sure why he kept up this needling tone.

'GPS is fine,' Gianluca said, 'but when you get into the historic centre, sometimes it is better to — how do you say — follow your nose?'

'Did you say Mexico, babe?' Mack asked.

'That's where Echo Park is making Motta film it. I came here thinking that was wrong — artistically, practically, even ethically — and I know that's what you think, Gianluca. But there's not a lot to work with here either. Throw in the narrow streets and all those EU laws and regulations, maybe Mexico and a thousand person-hours fudging it in post is the better option?'

'Did you hear about the location scout for that TV show,

Cartel?' Mack asked. 'The one that got shot twenty-four times in Mexico City?'

'When was this?'

'Wandered up the wrong alley. You gotta have a fixer in a place like that.'

'When was this?' he insisted.

'Last week?' Mack said, unsure, reaching for her phone again.

'We are not Mexico,' Gianluca said, placing his hand on Mack's to stop her.

'I'm sure you can Google it,' Mack whispered to Duncan. She slid her hand from beneath Gianluca's, picked up one of the sausages and bit off a chunk with her molars, reminding Duncan of Bugs Bunny with a carrot. 'What's the deal with the levitation thing anyway?'

Gianluca looked at Duncan, as if to say, *Do you want me to take this one?* Duncan was still thinking about the murdered location scout.

'Well,' Gianluca began, 'in Joseph's case, the official line is that it was a charism, a gift from the Holy Spirit. For, let's say, his extreme devotion, he was rewarded with states of ecstasy that often included leaving the ground.'

'Toward heaven,' she said, as if processing the information. 'Like a magnet up there was pulling him a little harder than the magnet that keeps the rest of us on the ground.'

Gianluca shrugged. 'I guess.'

'And how many times?'

'Hundreds. Arcangelo Rosmi, a diarist who lived with Joseph for seven years, stopped recording after the seventieth levitation. He said, in so many words, "If this is not enough proof, then another three hundred will be meaningless."'

'And lots of others saw him do it?'

'Even the Pope,' Duncan said, fighting a fresh wave of exhaustion to participate.

'Pope Urban VIII,' Gianluca added, 'and all his cardinals. The inquisitors in Naples. The future King of Poland. The Duke of Brunswick. The Infanta Maria of Savoy.'

'How high?'

'Sometimes a metre or so,' Gianluca said. 'But sometimes to the top of an olive tree or a large crucifix, according to the testimonies.'

The restaurant now felt very dim. Duncan looked back at the plates of food on the table. They appeared grainy, unappetising, like stills shot on a crappy cellphone camera — the sort you might post on the TripAdvisor page of a rival restaurant (not that GastroCorp would put such directives in writing).

'According to the testimonies,' Mack repeated. 'So you're a sceptic?'

It was as if the other side of the table was the other side of a piazza and Duncan could only hear what was being said through a quirk in the acoustics and had no way of participating himself. Why now? Amid the kind of conversation he'd primed himself for with Motta, before he knew he'd be sent location scouting. Even yesterday, he'd stage-managed just such a conversation with Gianluca about belief. But now he felt removed from the action. Worse than a director, who always had the power to call 'Cut!' No, he was a hanger-on, a spectator, obliged to wait and join the second wave of grazers through the craft service table.

Second Wave.

He was the sap whose quiet, spare-change character study was co-opted by those ruthless eco-terrorists in their efforts to bomb, gas and ransom the general public into a new Gaia-centric consciousness.

But that wasn't what had dislodged him from the moment.

Was it the wine?

Was he tired?

Was he sick of the saint already?

He thought about the pages he'd seen plastered on walls leading away from Saint Joseph's birthplace earlier that day. White pages with black home-office inkjet text.

San Giuseppe, said one, *PREGA PER NOI*.

Google: *PRAY FOR US*.

Simple posters from the most recent feast day of the saint.

San Giuseppe, protect our young people, said another.

San Giuseppe, bless your parish

San Giuseppe, comfort our elders

RETURN San Giuseppe

And then, near this last one, he'd seen a message scrawled in English, or mostly English, in white crayon on a rusted door.

I want to RASCH you.

Google was as flummoxed by *RASCH* as he was.

It had troubled him in the moment. Perhaps this was what had returned to trouble him now.

Rash, rape, ravish.

In two days the only Italian who'd spoken willingly to him was Gianluca, and he was being paid, through Uffy, by Echo Park. In Copertino it felt as if there were eyes behind every shuttered window. Like he was an outlaw entering a Wild West town, about to call out the sheriff. And those walls, the devout posters and confounding graffiti, were the only way Copertino had of speaking to him. Warning him. He could see the bullet-riddled body of the location scout for *Cartel* slumped between dumpsters. Wrong alley at the wrong time. Those same beady eyes through the shutters. He'd been nervous all right, and now, thanks to a goddamn Mack's Fact, he had something concrete to fear. Not Mexican drug lords, perhaps, but bodily harm. The twixt-dumpster slump of the unlucky snooper.

'What did you study?' he heard Mack ask Gianluca.

'Theology and art history.'

'Theology? So you're steeped in this stuff?'

'That was a long time ago. I worked in the Vatican Museum for many years, as a guide, before I moved back home. I do many things down here. There is not so much demand for guides like me in Salento.'

'So you, like, what? Had a crisis of faith?'

'More like I think you call it "downsizing"? We don't move around so much here, but in America, say, you have a very big house, with many rooms, but then you get old and move somewhere smaller that is easier to look after yourself.'

'Yeah, downsizing.'

'There is a kind of faith that takes almost no effort at all. This is what most people have around here. They may or may not go to Mass. They may or may not go to confession. If they do, they don't think much about it. For them, it is like buying groceries. Like cutting fingernails. This is the faith I have now. The other faith, it is exhausting. It consumes you. Each question leads to another question and another. Like that very big house, you clean one room but then you have another and another, and now the first room is dirty again. Eventually, you need to stop and say that the rest of the way you will take on faith. But I went far. I had a big house. I thought I needed all of it. When my son died—' He held up his hand, anxious not to be interrupted. 'He was very young. Very small. He did not have a good time on this Earth. When he died, it was as if there was an elastic cord attached to my belt and I was snapped back, back through the hallway of my big house, through the deep thinking, the theological debates, the considered faith, the ability to believe in miracles, small and large, the belief in anything but a cold and distant God and a world of unceasing blindness. Can I bring myself to believe in Joseph's levitations? No, because I know what lies through the next door and the next. And it isn't happiness. It isn't contentment. Better to be here—' He rapped the table with his knuckles. 'Eat horse, drink wine, screw. Fill my boots.'

'Babe,' Mack said. 'That got real.' She leaned toward Gianluca, took his face between her hands as if about to kiss him, and said, 'No further questions, your honour.'

Duncan: 'I think I'm going to head back.'

'Oh, please,' said Gianluca, 'ignore me. We have dessert, coffee, *amaro*, all of this to come. And I have many more bad things to say about your Hollywood.'

'You two stay. I'll take a taxi. I'm whacked. Again. I don't know what it is. But I need to hit the hay.'

'You sure, babe?' Mack asked.

'Got a lot of driving to do tomorrow.'

'No taxis,' Gianluca said. 'I will drive you back. It is only five minutes. You wait here,' he said to Mack, 'okay?'

'Okay.'

'I will take you to Lecce in the morning,' Gianluca said, 'to collect your rental car, yes? It's not far.'

Duncan wasn't sure if he was merely repeating the itinerary or offering to go above and beyond.

'Thank you,' he said.

'It is nothing. Nothing.'

ABSOLUTE ELSEWHERE

Duncan was flying again. Scooping the air with his hands to move about the empty house — though maybe this time it was Gianluca's mansion, the one cleared of theological proofs, of gymnastic belief; maybe it had always been Gianluca's mansion? — when he came across one of those vibrating restaurant pagers that had been popular with al fresco places once upon a time, only it wasn't a restaurant pager, and he wasn't floating above the ground, he was lying on his stomach on a single bed. The buzzing continued. His phone. He picked it up. Mack.

'Uh.'

'You have the only key, babe.'

'What time is it?'

'Dunno. The sun is rising.'

'Hold on, I'll come down.'

He pulled on a t-shirt and jeans, went downstairs and out the more discreet of the hotel's two exits, the one by the car park.

'Mack,' he half-whispered, half-called.

'Coming.' She emerged from behind a dumpster, readjusting her dress, which looked almost white in the moonlight. Her coat was folded over the crook of her arm.

He led her inside. Back in the room, he left the light off, flopped on to his bed.

A metallic graunch, like the treads of a tank. He looked up.

Mack, using her cellphone as a torch, had found the pull-cord for the thick military-canvas blinds and begun to raise them.

'Mack!'

'Just want a little light.' She pulled once more. 'There.'

Duncan put a pillow over his head, then pulled it down below his chin in frustration. 'Have a good night, did you?'

'Yup. Babe, what's up with these power points?'

'Try the one in the bathroom. You going to be all right in the car in a couple of hours?'

'I'm not drunk.'

'That statement does not pass the sniff test.'

'What's with you?'

'I was asleep.'

'But at the restaurant? Have you always been a piker?'

'What did you and *Gianni* get up to, anyway?'

'He's cool. His sister has a place down the road, so we went there for an aperitif.'

'Uh-huh.'

'They're good people. Gianluca is a big teddy bear.'

He saw again Mack with her hand on Gianluca's thigh while trying to remove her coat. Her hands either side of his face.

'You know he's married, right?'

'I didn't get up to any funny business. I considered pashing his sister, but—'

'His sister?'

'What's so crazy about that?'

'Sorry,' he said. 'This— I just woke up. I think that wine—'

'Are *you* going to be all right in the car in a couple of hours?'

Duncan let out a froggy croak.

'I've slept with married guys before. Just two. A married woman just the once. It tends not to be four hours after meeting them, at their sister's house, but if those shitty years of high school taught me anything; if—' She stopped, changed course. 'It's easy to be timid and miserable, babe. It's hard to be timid and happy, maybe

119

impossible.' She lay down on her bed, her heels still on.

'And you figured this out while barricaded in your bedroom?'

'It helped.'

'I told you how I got this gig, right? All the work I put into studying Motta, his films. How easily it fell into my lap, in the end?'

She yawned. 'You did.'

'And you know all about *Fury's Reach*, at least as much as I know. I mean, maybe it was a genuine opportunity that I genuinely fucked up. Or maybe Echo Park always intended to fire me, to cash in twofold on my fifteen minutes of fame from *Curio Bay* and Second Wave, the buzz from hiring a notorious young director and firing him just as the shoot begins without having to really risk anything. Whatever Echo Park was playing at, I've gotta take at least some of the blame. I mean, I trusted Tanner Burge, for a start. Some agent he was. He *knew*. He must've known what was going on, who buttered his bread. But me? I should have known I couldn't leverage that Second Wave drama without being tarred. Boy, did I get tarred. And me, directing *that* film? Sci-fi? How could that pass the sniff test? It's amazing I actually got three days of footage in the can. And yet here I am, scouting locations for Frank Motta's passion project, a thing he's been dreaming about for thirty years, and I —' he started keeping count on his fingers — 'can't speak Italian; don't believe in God or levitation; wasn't raised a Catholic, and find all of the crossing yourself and dabbing holy water stuff utterly, utterly foreign; and I've only directed one proper movie, which everyone seems to have taken the wrong way. So, tell me, oh wise one, have I gone and done it again? Walked right into the next trap laid by the universe and over-extended myself? Mack? Babe?'

Duncan rubbed his eyes, shut them, lay back on his bed and listened to the soft rumble of his sleeping friend.

CURIO BAY

A man in his mid-fifties, rough edged and taciturn, rents a house overlooking a bay on New Zealand's south-eastern edge. It's rugged, sparsely populated. No cellphone signal, no WiFi. The nearest landline is at the campground, which is slowly emptying out as autumn takes hold.

The man cuts his fingernails, makes instant coffee, stands on the balcony of the holiday home. There's a pod of dolphins living in the bay. Hector's dolphins, the rarest and smallest kind. They chill outside the breaker line, scoot within metres of the shore, pull back to the centre of the bay. They are visible with the naked eye, as are the tourists who swim out to be among them — tiny, wrongheaded dots.

Another instant coffee, an unseen sunset, a vivid sunrise.

The man walks down the road, past the surf school hut, past the campground office, past a dozen signs instructing visitors not to approach the dolphins. He climbs to the point. To the north: his bay, the one with the dolphins. Calm, sheltered. To the south: a rocky shelf streaked with brown, the remnants of a petrified forest. The spray hangs in the air, attempts to shroud the violence of the waves.

He retrieves a long narrow case from his car. We see a dolphin up close, framed by a circular telescopic lens. The black rounded dorsal fin. Now fins, plural. Five, six, seven of them.

A dolphin arcs out of the water, almost sleepily.

Three dolphins, visible inside a bright, clear, cresting wave.

A woman, her hands held above her head, wades into the water. To her waist. To her armpits. To the point she has dorsal fins either side of her. She raises her feet to the surface, floats on her back as if crucified in the water.

A kid on a boogie board swims into frame, his yellow flippers slapping the top of the water.

The dorsal fins sink. The dolphins slink away.

The man seeks out the Department of Conservation rangers: a married couple who split their time between three or four tourist spots in the area. He's told to come back at three o'clock, nine the next morning, maybe they'll be here midday. The man at the campground store just shrugs.

He stands in front of an information board, reading, re-reading. He stops a couple who are headed down to the beach. She is blonde, German-looking. She wears a wetsuit that cuts off at the knees. Her partner wears board shorts. His chest is tanned but at the same time faintly pink, as if he has just been slapped, has been slapping himself. Have they read the information board? Do they understand it? They nod and hurry down the path.

The guy who runs the surf school is waxing a board, says he's always careful to give the dolphins plenty of space. But they can be curious, you know. Sometimes they'll initiate the contact.

The man trims his beard. Makes coffee. Opens a packet of biscuits. Super Wines.

Through the lens he watches the bay. There's a calf, a dark apostrophe, sticking close to its mother.

A couple enters the water, five metres apart. Maybe they are the Germans, back for another encounter. Maybe not.

We see him then, the watcher, lying on his stomach. Lying on the carpet of the living room of the holiday home, his eye to the sight of a hunting rifle. The ranchslider to the balcony is open. A cold breeze lifts the covers of the magazines on the coffee table, the map books and tourist brochures on top of the bookshelf.

He watches. Rises. Leaves the house, finally encounters the rangers. Maybe the information boards need to be translated. Beachgoers need to be monitored full time. It's not right.

He is thanked for his concern.

He buys milk from the campground store. The man behind the counter passes him a handwritten message. He asks to use the phone. He says little. His face gives nothing away.

Another hidden sunset. Beyond the white line of the breakers the colour temperature drops until the bay appears blighted by an oil slick.

Another sunrise, all pinks and purples.

He searches through the sight for dorsal fins. Bare water.

He changes his undershirt. Takes a piss. Inspects his teeth in the bathroom mirror.

Standing on the balcony, he watches the waves. To the left of the bay half a dozen people sit on their surfboards, listening to their instructor. To the right, at last, a cluster of dorsal fins. The sun is as high as it's going to get. People are walking along the beach. A family collecting shells. A woman walking her terrier.

Two kids, maybe twelve and ten, strip off to their togs and wade into the water, one boogie board between them.

TOÄD

Mack descended the steps from the Hotel Grottella a full twenty minutes late. She was wearing big Audrey Hepburn sunglasses, a screen-printed t-shirt knotted high on one side to flash a triangle of gym-membership flesh, and yoga pants with a Technicolor Day of the Dead motif leading down to bare ankles and white trainers.

Duncan and Gianluca were leaning against the Punto, having long ago chewed through all they felt like saying at that hour of the morning. They exchanged looks, shared a wavelength.

Duncan cleared his throat. 'You know we'll be going into a bunch of churches today?'

'And?'

'And, well, look at your t-shirt for starters. A burning skull, eating a— what? A surfboard?'

'Look closer, babe.'

He should have kept his mouth shut. At least she wasn't wearing that fucking coat. But there he was, hitting the marks, delivering the lines, just as she had scripted. There were three kinds of people, he thought. Those who dress for aesthetics, those who dress for comfort and those who dress to set up their own dumb jokes.

The t-shirt was standard heavy-metal fare, black with the word TOÄD — a band he'd never heard of, though he wasn't that into metal — in gothic font above the skull, but on closer inspection there was another line of text in a smaller, more angular font:

THE WET SPROCKET.

He laughed on cue.

'Right?' Mack said, smiling. 'I mean, how great to have a band so easily dismissed as limp nineties radio rock colliding with —' she ran fingers down from chest to navel — '*this*.'

'Only a handful of people would take the time to get it back in the States. But here? Do you get it?' he asked Gianluca, who pushed his hands forward to say, *Don't bring me into this*. 'In Italy,' Duncan continued, 'in a friggin' church, they're just going to see the red glowing eyes, the string of blood from the skull's mouth and think you're, I don't know, Satanic?'

'What about your outfit?'

He was wearing blue jeans and a white button-down shirt with faint grey stripes, the only flourish coming from one of the hand-tooled leather belts his grandfather used to wear.

Mack: 'I can't decide if you're going for too-old-to-be-an-intern intern, or Latter Day Saint.'

'I was going for respectful comfort.'

'Satanic?' She looked down at her t-shirt and made a *tsk* sound. 'Do you think the devout prefer Satanists to atheists? I mean, they have more in common with Satanists, on one level at least.'

Duncan wasn't sure if they were still on script or not, if he was winning or losing. 'Well, you might be able to ask them today if you, like, change your t-shirt. And maybe those leggings.'

'Fuck that. This is the start of our road trip.'

Duncan groaned. *Road trip*. Just the phrase made him feel a million miles from Motta.

'Here was I thinking you might be cool about this,' she said, 'for once in your life?'

'Like Toad The Wet Sprocket cool? Or Scandinavian Death Metal cool? Coz I'm getting mixed signals.'

Her expression. Was it seething? Had he won that round?

★

The silence in the Punto as it shivered toward Lecce wasn't awkward, just silence. Mack was immersed in her phone in the back seat. She and Gianluca were tired, no doubt. It felt odd to be leaving Giuseppe's birthplace already. What did he really have? A couple of gigabytes on a memory card. Two dozen pages of measurements and observations in his notebook. What had he learned? Plenty about Gianluca. And, perhaps, a glimpse of a different Mack. Footholds for a future heart to heart, if that's what the situation demanded. But Giuseppe? He'd decided, at least, to call him by his given name from here on out, rather than the Anglicised Joseph.

When in Rome.

Also, having been to Copertino, it now bugged him when it was changed to Cupertino in English, like the town in California, home of Apple's HQ. Such confusion was best avoided. And, besides, he was an Android guy.

Outside the rental-car outfit, hugs exchanged, luggage in hand, Gianluca turned back to Mack. 'It was a pleasure meeting you, Felicity.'

'Babe,' she said, grabbing for the back of her head.

'And Duncan,' he said, 'drive safe, okay, my friend?'

There were two clerks behind the counter, both with straight black hair and dark kohl-rimmed eyes. Strikingly similar but not identical, probably not even related. More like two celebrities who get mistaken for each other when they try to go incognito — Amy Adams and Isla Fisher, Margot Robbie and Jaime Pressley, Julia Roberts and Steven Tyler — a confusion that seemed to irk them equally and which they took out on their patrons. Between the two of them they spoke maybe a dozen words before Duncan was taken out back and shown the small silver Nissan Micra that was to be their car for the remainder of the trip.

Mack, who'd been glued to her phone the whole time in the office and during her zombie walk to the car, finally looked up. 'Jeez. It's like a starter car on *Gran Turismo*.' She cocked one eyebrow, then went back to what she'd been reading.

'Excuse me, this can't be right,' Duncan said, reaching into his satchel to find the piece of paper. 'It says here—'

'Compact,' the clerk replied.

'No, no, no,' he said. 'Hold on. *Alfa Romeo Giulietta or similar*, it says here. *Intermediate*, not, uh, *compact*.'

'That is an old version,' she said.

'Huh?' His first thought: this car was somehow an update of the Alfa. Another Italian icon that had been swallowed up by a multinational. Hadn't he seen something on a doco on Netflix about the guy who designed cars for Chrysler also being in charge of Alfa Romeos? But Nissan was a whole other automotive ecosystem.

'Your booking was changed,' the woman said. 'Two days ago.'

'Uffy!'

'Pardon?'

'Never mind.'

Mack, not looking up from her phone: 'What's up, babe?'

'Motta's assistant downgraded us.' He'd noticed one or two of the hotels had changed between the earliest version of the itinerary and the final one, and had assumed it was related to cost. But to have things being changed now, while he was on the ground. It felt treacherous. Uffy was becoming the Newman to his Jerry.

'A Nissan, though,' Mack said. 'Who drives a Japanese car in Italy?'

'It seems we do.'

Maybe Mack's my Newman, he thought. Can you have two Newmans?

'Is it automatic?' he asked.

'Manual,' the woman replied, not getting her tongue back far enough for the English 'u', plugging the Italian 'oo' in its place. Was it laziness or some physical barrier she'd failed to breach? Maybe this was the source of her bitterness, the blip in her English that kept her working in retail rather than delivering PowerPoints for some pharmapetrochemical hedge fund? He considered placing a hand on her shoulder, consoling her, even though he was the one who hadn't driven a stick for years. Maybe it was a good thing the car was small.

Once inside the Micra, he handed Mack a page with the various stops they would make along the way, but she was more interested in sorting out the music than plotting their route in Google Maps. The rental car woman stood watch, now joined by her lookalike colleague, there for a laugh. To see him stall or scrape the paintwork. Would he have been this anxious if Gianluca hadn't made such a big deal of driving in Italy? Perhaps this anxiety would benefit him on the road — a weary vigilance that would inoculate him from the needless, headlong lunacy of the locals?

'I need to know where to go when I get out of this car park, Felicity?'

'Don't you start. I've finally got my mother trained.'

'How is she?'

'Same old. Turn left.'

'But you don't even have Maps up.'

'Aha!' Mack said. Music began through the car's stereo. Toad The Wet Sprocket, Duncan thought. If not for the t-shirt, he might have said Gin Blossoms or Dishwalla — one of those bands he'd never thought or felt much about when they were current and he was growing up, but now, despite himself, could deliver a tingle of nostalgia.

He was crawling forward, conscious of the smirking sentries, the approaching car-park exit, the lack of reliable directions. He heard a knock, like a coffee mug being plonked on to a table. Mack's eyes went anime wide.

'You just clipped that pole,' she said.

'I can't have.'

'Your wing mirror.'

'It's fine.'

'Fucking eh. And you wanted a bigger car.' She turned to look at the rental-car clerks. 'We should get outta Dodge, pronto.'

'Directions?'

'Left,' Mack repeated.

Duncan sighed and rolled on to the road, accelerated, changed into second gear as he turned the wheel, and found his lane.

'You're doing it, man.'

'Shut up and tell me where I need to go.'

She sighed, pulled the page out from beneath her thigh and started typing into her phone. 'Oh,' she said.

'Oh what?'

'Pull a U-ey.'

THE ROAD

Giuseppe's walk of shame took place in the spring of 1621. The only points of continuity between then and now, as far as Duncan could see, having driven back toward Copertino before gunning it north, were the sky and the flat dry earth. As long as Giuseppe could find water and shade, had something on his feet and a morsel to quiet his belly every now and then, it couldn't have been that bad. But there were stories, weren't there? Being chased by a pack of wild dogs. A drifter who Giuseppe took for the devil himself. Being turned away by his uncle and beaten with a ladle by his mother when he finally made it home.

That dunce.

That screw-up.

If the audience could sympathise with his mother, it'd only make Giuseppe's ascension more dramatic.

Out the window: a countryside in transition. Rows of young grapevines a few inches tall, years from a decent vintage. Fields of solar panels, polytunnels, circular bales of hay. Shadows cast by power pylons, passing airplanes. All of it cut up and apportioned by sun-bleached roads with just the memory of road markings. Every outbuilding a ruin. Every worker an old man leaning over his hoe.

Inside the car: the retrograde musical stylings of Roachford ('Only to be with you'), Lisa Loeb ('I do') and Better than Ezra ('Desperately wanting').

Better than Steppenwolf, at least, he thought.

He'd never found the road movie a compelling genre. The too-neat overlay of physical and spiritual journeys. All that screen time devoted to angles wide and low: to tyre tread, road tar, cactus and canyon to make the pro forma English essay point that we human beings are small and shortlived. Whoop-dee-shit. Neither Motta nor Duncan had ever flirted with the genre. And yet there he was, at the wheel, retracing Giuseppe's walk of shame in reverse, with his plucky sidekick/soundtrack producer in the passenger seat, and another seven itinerary pages of Plot Coupons to collect from a stream of Adventure Towns before he could unlock access to the Boss Room in the Vatican, wherein Motta would reveal the true meaning of his Quest and open the door for a sequel.

It was intoxicating.

The incantatory power of the words 'road trip', uttered by Mack.

The fact he was now behind the wheel, rather than being driven.

Maybe, he thought, in the end we all get the genre we deserve.

But then, he'd already done his road trip — a cross-country trek with Kari and Zeb when they first moved to the States — and he hadn't felt the slightest tug from cinematic clichés. Kari's brother, Nate, had seized the opportunity to upgrade his ride by offering them his 2006 Chevy Impala, though they'd have to drive it from Wisconsin back to LA. But why not? They had three weeks before his *Fury's Reach* duties began, and they used every second to follow the Mississippi down to New Orleans before heading west through Texas, New Mexico and Arizona to the Golden State. Three thousand miles picked off in two nap-sized chunks a day, staying in whichever hotel could offer them a crib and buffet dining to try Zeb on a range of solid foods before a quick towel bath or basin dip and then lights out by 6.30, at which point either he or Kari could duck out and explore whatever podunk town or secondary city they were lodging in while the other listened to podcasts in the dark. Where was the romance? Where was the adventure? It was not to be found in the shuttered riverside towns or the bored desolation of the high plains, nor in the sight of the same chain restaurants whenever two interstates met.

And certainly not at the wheel of Nate's tan Chevy.

Perhaps if it had been an Impala from the sixties, a jet-black, soft-top sport coupe, and not that bad riff on a Japanese sedan, its underbelly already bubbling from winters of road salts (Duncan still owned the car, still loathed it).

Perhaps if they weren't so limited by Zeb's nap times.

Perhaps if they'd planned it better.

Perhaps if they'd planned it worse.

Alas.

They had carved their backward L through the same territory as *Easy Rider*; *Paris, Texas*; *Rain Man* and *Thelma and Louise* without incident, save a couple of burst diapers, an unfounded tornado warning and the twenty-four-hour stomach bug that forced them to stay an extra night in St Louis.

But now all of those films and their drossy offspring, the two-word, gross-out, brain-drainers of the last twenty years — *Road Trip, Sex Drive, Due Date* — had reared up and inflicted themselves on this day and the dozen that would follow, imposing their road-movie framing upon every sight, sound and aspect of pacing, despite the fact they would span no deserts, encounter no biker gangs or bestiality (touch wood), were just pottering halfway up Italy and popping into churches and convents along the way.

Perhaps it hadn't just started, this framing.

Perhaps these films had begun to act on him before he'd even left LA.

Perhaps that was why he hadn't stopped Mack from coming. A subconscious gesture of genre fulfilment.

She was what his journey from La Crosse to LA had lacked. Someone to test him. To conjure obstacles from cloudless skies. That much was clear from the moment she descended the steps from the hotel that morning. Drama in white sneakers.

And then there was Uffy, unravelling things back in the States.

Mack and Uffy. Harley Quinn and Poison Ivy.

Which would make him— What? Batman? He was hardly a super-hero. And if there was one genre more done to death than the road movie, it was that one.

Duncan stopped twenty minutes into their journey to record the landscape, despite misgivings about the usefulness of the images he recorded; drove for another twenty, stopped, drove again. Such was the pace of an Italian road movie. Any faster and you'd cross a border before the next sunrise. Maybe there were proper Italian road movies, but he could only recall Antonioni's *L'Avventura*, full of blasé overgrown kids, the occasional boat or train, but devoid of real adventure, and Fellini's *La Strada*, where the horse-power displayed was more literal than one might expect from the home of Lamborghini, Ferrari and Alfa Romeo.

And the adopted home of the mighty Nissan Micra.

Returning to the car after a half-hour reconnoitre of Avetrana and its Chiesa Madre, he found Mack engrossed in her phone again, plugged the rest of the route into Maps on his own phone and placed it in one of the cup holders in front of the gear stick.

'So Giuseppe, right,' he said, as he pulled away from the curb, answering one of Mack's questions from the previous stint of driving, 'was this simple kid. He was bedridden for a couple of years and sucked at school when he did go. But he really loved the Church and all his uncles were involved, pretty high up in the local ranks of the Franciscans, so it seemed natural, right? Only, when he tried to enter as a lay brother in Copertino, his uncle said no. Eventually he got accepted by the Capuchins, which are a different monastic order, in Martina Franca.'

'What's the difference?'

'Between Franciscans and Capuchins? I'm pretty sure they wear different coloured robes.'

'Deep.' She held up her phone to her mouth. 'What's the

difference between Franciscans and Capuchins? Huh,' she said, looking at the results. 'Seems Capuchins are a type of Franciscans, founded in the sixteenth century as —' she put on her reading voice — '"an attempt to recapture the contemplative vision of Francis and to share the fruits of that contemplation with the poor and the other forgotten members of our society."'

'Yeah, but what colour habit do they wear?'

'I'm seeing both black and brown.'

'What were you reading about before?'

'What?'

'You've been transfixed by your phone since we left the hotel.'

'That's levitation, Holmes,' she said, slicing her hands through the air with her Jack Black passenger-seat karate.

'So you might actually be useful?'

'Gianni told me some things after you bailed last night.'

'Like what?'

'You probably know it all already. Like, there are plenty more levitators out there besides Joseph.'

'Road-trip rule,' he said, giving in to the pull, 'we only call him Giuseppe, or San Giuseppe da Copertino, from now on.'

'Not just other Catholics. Buddhists, Hindus—'

'Street magicians.'

'Did you know—'

'Hold on, let me find the button for the *Mack's Facts* sting.' He jabbed at the car stereo, shutting it off.

'—on a bus trip in Death Valley, Charles Manson is said to have levitated the bus over a creek crag.'

'And the Manson family just scream reliable testimony.'

'What do you think?'

'About levitation in general? No. It's not possible.'

'Really?'

'You sound so surprised.'

'What about Jo— I mean, Giuseppe? You think that's all made up? A vast conspiracy? You said he was simple.'

134

'So the story goes. There's one guy who reckons Giuseppe was essentially a gymnast and his levitations were just big leaps. The way he always let out a scream before taking to the air. How he is said often, but not always, to have flown to the top of something — a tree, a crucifix. Maybe he was a seventeenth-century Michael Jordan?'

Mack began to hum 'I believe I can fly'.

He could show her the WhatsApp messages from Vilma, all her theories to explain Giuseppe's flights, but decided instead to use the one he'd received that morning without attribution. 'There's another school of thought that says it's all some mass hallucination caused by eating spoiled rye bread. It makes you trip, but also can cause seizures and spasms. So, like, maybe Giuseppe was the way he was because of bad bread, and somehow everyone who came into contact with him got just enough of that juju to think this spasming wreck was being blessed by God above.'

'Presumably Motta doesn't believe this theory?'

'It's more of an M. Night Shyamalan twist.'

'O-ho, 'twas the bad bread all along, Brother Joseph. We need to find a bakery.'

Duncan didn't bite.

'So,' Mack said, shifting her weight, 'you really don't believe in levitation? In telekinesis?'

Silence.

'Do you know about the Thousand Flowers?'

'Is that a band?'

'It's more of an intentional community.'

'Like a commune?'

'They believe in levitation.'

'Oh, a cult,' he said.

'More than believe. They train people to actually levitate.'

'Is this like, what's it called? Yogic flying? This isn't a branch of those crazies who did the sarin gas attack in Tokyo? I'm not consorting with terrorists.'

'Since when?'

'Since ever.'

Mack made a fake cough, said, 'Second Wave', and coughed again.

'I never wanted that—'

'Why do you hate the planet, Duncan?'

'I don't.'

'Then why do you hate human beings?'

'Sorry, I mean, *gee*! Whatever happened to those swell guys and gals in the hooded gas masks? In jail, I suppose. Or hiding in a cave somewhere, eating twigs and berries.'

'*Anyway*,' Mack said, 'there are so many of these intentional communities—'

'Just say cults.'

'—when you start to look. And I've been looking. There's this place called Damanhur up near Turin—'

'There's no way we're going to Turin. It's virtually Switzerland.'

'The folks up there believe in time travel. Yeah babe,' she said, nodding ferociously. 'And then there's this place called Nomadelfia, north of Rome, where people all live together in households of thirty. Families are all mixed up in different houses and the groups change every three years so you keep having to form new bonds. They have their own TV station where they edit out all the sex and violence — *I know* — but they nix the advertising too. They say it breeds envy and unhappiness. And get this, they're all good Catholics.'

'Wowee.'

She cut her eyes at him and he turned back to the road. The GPS took them off the highway and beneath an underpass, emerging into something approaching, for this part of Italy at least, bucolic bliss. It was all olive trees — hundreds of years old if their thick, burrow-infested trunks were any indication, the sort no modern gymnast could mount in a single leap — and nice-looking houses set back from the road, freshly poured concrete drives and drug-lord gates.

Mack: 'Mille Fiori, the Thousand Flowers, the levitators, they're in San Marino.'

'San—'

'It's only forty-five minutes from Pietrarubbia. And kind of on the way to Fossombrone.'

'You're not suggesting—'

'I suggest nothing. I am merely sharing the fruits of my research. As an aside, now that I know what a bitch adulthood turned out to be, and how impossible it is to make new friends, the bugger of being stuck with the ones you've got, I can see the attraction of cults. But Mille Fiori have got some cool videos on their website. Their history is a little murky because they've used other names.'

'Like what?'

'Um. Manu Tangata was one.'

'Is that . . . Māori?'

'The founder's a Kiwi.'

'*Manu Tangata*? Like, bird people?'

'I think it was more of a reference to the big-ass kites Māori used to make.'

'Hold on. So we're talking about a branch of a New Zealand cult?'

'No, it's only in San Marino.'

'Why San Marino?'

'Why indeed.'

'Well, I appreciate the research, but I can't get distracted right now. Even if we did the next week on fast forward, we'd get all our hotels and guides out of sync. It'd be a full-time job just making sure we had a bed for the night—'

'Preferably two beds.'

'—and not tipping Uffy off to the fact we're going rogue.'

'I don't think I was the one who mentioned going there.'

'Don't play that game with me.'

'What game?'

The seal of the road deteriorated and the fences and pretences of wealth dropped away. The weeds on the roadside began to thrive, creeping higher and higher until they reached the top of the Micra's windows. A flash of red amid the untamed grasses, another, and then an entire field of poppies — wild or planted with intent, Duncan couldn't say.

'What is this?' he asked, nodding at the stereo's display.

'You know. Tell me you know.'

'It sounds like you've lost your mind. Hootie and the Blowfish?'

'It'd actually be kinda great if you got offended because you thought I was throwing shade about your prang in the car park by playing something off their seminal album, *Cracked Rear View*—'

'Is this another Mack's Fact?'

'—but it's actually off their third album, *Musical Chairs*.'

'And you have actual fans?'

Mack started drumming with the pre-chorus of 'I will wait', letting Darius Rucker trundle through the lyrics, rhyming 'solace of' with 'promises'. 'Trust me,' she said, just as Rucker's bandmates chimed in, a Greek chorus of whitebread journeymen, 'you and I will be singing along to this song at the top of our lungs by the end of this trip.'

'Right.'

'It's the perfect song, if you leave your pretensions at the door.'

'Expecting more from four minutes of my life than some easy bar-room chantalong underpinned by a factory-preset organ, if that's pretentious, then . . . What's the newest album you've listened to?'

'I keep tabs.'

Ten minutes from Martina Franca the landscape changed, became gently undulating. Flashes of large white cones set back from the road.

'You see those?' Duncan asked.

'What are they, babe? Like, grain storage or something?'

Another four cones appeared on the horizon. These ones were painted white only on the top half, left as bare stone beneath, all attached to a single whitewashed building.

'A house?' Mack said.

'There's more.'

And there were. They were everywhere, these cones. It was the stuff of postcards.

'Google them,' he said.

'Um.'

'Try, *Cone houses Martina Franca*.'

'They aren't on your itinerary? Oh, wow,' she said, looking at her phone. 'You're a Google savant.'

'What are they?'

'*Trulli*. "A traditional Apulian dry stone hut with a conical roof."'

'You know what I'm going to ask now, right?'

'Hold on.' She scrolled down. 'The golden age of *trulli* was the nineteenth century.'

'Hence the absence of— Hold on.' He reached into his pocket and passed her the itinerary. 'Where are we staying tonight?'

'What day is it? Friday.'

'Saturday.'

'B&B Trullo "Il Mirtillo". Romantic.'

'So long as Uffy hasn't cancelled our reservation.'

'Are we going there now?'

'Lunch first. A look around the centre. Then to the convent, which is on the outskirts, I think.'

'Then our love nest?'

'Can we not put on an act for the proprietor?'

'Who's acting?'

Duncan looked at her. 'You are. Constantly.'

'Maybe you should make another film about me. Like you used to.'

'Maybe,' he said, which they both knew meant: *No.*

MANSPREADING

The church of Saint Anthony the Capuchin was five minutes from the centre of Martina Franca, down the hill, past a dozen more *trulli* — some pristine, others almost indistinguishable from rubble — and down Strada Cappuccini, which was nothing more than a country lane flanked by dry stone walls and further narrowed by power poles, weeds sprung from beds of pine needles and the unruly trees themselves. The road opened up and the church appeared — its stone face faintly red in the early afternoon sun. A bell tower perched on its right shoulder. To the left, the facade of the church ran into another, less ornate building, its whitewash flaking. The convent, he guessed.

'It's funny how they build here,' he said. 'Like they don't have space, even when they do.'

'Maybe. But I don't think urban manspreading, like you see back home, is all that great either.'

'True.'

They had their choice of parking spaces. He could see no other vehicles, no pedestrians, just buildings, trees, pavement, as if he'd rolled on to a studio lot two days before the shoot began.

'Why do I get the feeling,' Mack said, 'this film will not pass the Bechdel Test?'

'Huh?'

'Tell me you know what the Bechdel Test is.'

'Yeah, of course. You just—'

'Two female characters talk about something other than a man.'

'I know what it is. I didn't know what film you were referring to.'

'Oh sure,' Mack said. 'I guess *Curio Bay* flunked it too. Flunked it hard.'

'Uh-huh.'

'But I meant *Giuseppe*. You know, the reason we're here. It sounds like another sausage fest.'

'I mean Motta won't just manufacture characters to tick a box. Giuseppe lived in convents. He swore a vow of chastity—'

'Maybe that's where his powers came from? All that pent-up spunk.'

'The only women in his life were his mother and his sister, and his sister adds nothing to the plot. I can't even remember her name.'

'Charming. Bet there'll be no people of colour either, right?'

Duncan shrugged.

'Well, at least it'll pass the Bechamel Test. Thoroughly white and cheesy and bad for you.'

'There should be a Bechdel Test for parents,' he said. 'You've got to have a conversation with each other about something other than your kid or the list of chores you have because you have a kid.'

'How would you and Kari go?'

'Oh, we'd flunk it, for sure.'

'And yet?'

'What?'

'Nothing,' she said, unlocking her phone. 'What would I know?'

He grabbed his satchel and camera from the back seat. 'You coming?' he asked.

'I'll join you in a tick,' she said, not looking up.

'More levitation research?'

'Only scratching the surface, babe.'

He was one minute early for his two o'clock with Father

Iandolo. The wooden double door to the convent was shut, so he poked his head inside the church first, in case that's where his host was hiding.

The church was small. A dozen rows of pews, dominated by an ornate wooden altarpiece with inset paintings, the largest of which showed the Holy Virgin ascending with the help of the Heavenly Father in a swirl of golden mist at the very top of the altar, his right hand held out like a puppeteer.

What *was* Giuseppe's sister's name? A minute ago he knew the mother's, but now that had gone too. Felice Desa, that was the father's name. Google: Happy Desa. The fool who guaranteed his friends' dodgy loans, did the family in, then promptly disappeared from the story. Maybe Duncan had already played his part in the movie of Zeb's life. Perhaps it was the scene in the park before his departure. Zeb, unmoved, a waist-high statue of some stoic philosopher.

Voiceover: *It was then I knew I'd outgrown the park and my father. My place was elsewhere.*

Back outside one half of the double door to the convent was now ajar. Mack was still inside the Micra, still scrolling. There was no intercom or ringer next to the door, so Duncan slipped through. A short passage led into a courtyard. He stepped into the light. Looked up at the birdshit-streaked corrugated-plastic sheeting that capped the space, the A/C units bracketed next to the second-storey windows, the sleeping spotlights. Through a series of arches in front of him and to his right he could see doors, openings for other passages, but no signs. In the centre of the courtyard a spindly conifer lolled in its hexagonal planter. He wanted to call it a monkey puzzle tree, but that didn't sound right, not here. There was a butter churn — no, a tiny olive press — and more plants pushed back against the walls. Tired pot plants. A bonsai. Maybe the other tree *could* be a monkey puzzle? To his right, two vending machines: one for bottled water and cans of soda, the other for hot drinks, with a picture of a woman wearing a one-piece swimsuit and a come-hither look. Did this place even belong to the Capuchins? Maybe the convent was somewhere else?

He coughed, letting the sound rattle around the empty space. No movement.

'Hello?' he called, then regretted not trying some Italian first. It was afternoon, so *Buongiorno* was no good. *Buona sera* was good evening. He got out his phone.

'*Buon pomeriggio?*' he said, sounding so foreign he was begging to be mistaken for an American again. He buried his phone in his satchel. Felt like an intruder. Turned and went back outside.

He sat on the hood of the Micra. Got out the itinerary.

'That was quick,' Mack said through the windscreen.

'It's like—' In his search for a simile, he recalled the empty mansion of his flying dreams, the many-roomed house of Gianluca's belief, then swallowed it. 'I'm gonna try ringing.'

His call went unanswered, even by voicemail.

He got back in the car.

'What do I do?'

'We're in the right place?'

'Yep.' He held up the itinerary. Beneath the address and the contact details for Father Iandolo, Uffy had written:

Important things:
- ★ *St Joseph's cell (home from August 1620 to April 1621), accessible through the cloister. Dimensions. Light. Adjacencies.*
- ★ *Dining area/kitchen as it might have been 1620/21 — for demonstrations of SJC's clumsiness; scene where SJC dismissed from order.*
- ★ *The grange — surrounding farmland worked by friars. Trees, livestock, buildings 1620–21.*
- ★ *Interior of church — get Iandolo to identify any elements that remain from SJC's time. NB: wooden altars/cabinetry from 1700s, facade 1698.*

'You were gone for a bit,' Mack said.

'The church is open. And I got into this courtyard inside what I think is the convent.' Was that the 'cloister' Uffy mentioned? He wished Gianluca was with them. He looked up 'cloister' on his phone: *a covered walk, open gallery or open arcade running along the walls of a building*.

'I think I know where Giuseppe's cell is. But it's weird. I feel like I'm trespassing. I'm going to go look around the other side, check out "the grange",' he said, making air quotes.

'I'll stay here and keep lookout for your expert.'

Duncan tried the phone number again, kept it ringing as he got out of the car and walked around the eastern side of the church. There was a small building, storage of some kind. What looked like a pizza oven, perhaps an incinerator. Beyond a small concrete lip: ivy, fig trees, the obligatory olives, pines and a half-dozen *trulli* cones that struck him for the first time as breast-like. *In Bed with Madonna*-era bras, at least.

'Fuck,' he said into his dial-toning phone, and disconnected the call.

Back inside the church, he had no idea what was four hundred years old and what was a more recent obfuscation. He imagined Father Iandolo's quarters next door, the walls lined with dusty volumes, framed reproductions, rolls of architectural plans.

'Babe!'

Mack was standing at the entrance to the church, her left side lit by sun. Another figure stood beside her, more out of the church than in.

'*Signore Iandolo?*' Duncan asked as he approached.

'No no no,' the old man said, backing out of the church, and drawing Duncan and Mack with him. Should he have addressed him as Padre?

Out in the light, it was clear this man was no padre. He wore brown slacks and a short-sleeved shirt. His chin pointed up, as if in denial about the snakes crawling over his feet — except, Duncan realised, it wasn't snakes he was avoiding but the flaming skull on Mack's t-shirt. Also, probably, the exposed slice of midriff.

'He doesn't speak English,' she said, oblivious. 'But he's the first person I've seen.'

'*Dov'è Padre Iandolo?*' Duncan asked.

'*Lontano,*' the man said.

'*I-an-do-lo,*' Duncan repeated.

'*Lon-tano,*' the man said, pointing back down the road.

'*Lontano,*' Mack said into her phone. 'He's saying, "Away".'

'Not here?' Duncan said, pointing at the pavement.

'*È in Taranto.*'

'*Taranto?*'

'*Sì.*'

'Fuuuudge.'

'Where's Taranto?' Mack asked in sidebar.

'It's not here, is it?'

'Babe.'

Duncan bent at the knees until his eyes were level with the man, turned him by the shoulders so Mack's t-shirt was out of his eyeline. 'Is there anyone else I can talk to about this church? *San Giuseppe da Copertino?*'

The man's eyes widened. Duncan wasn't sure if he was spooked by the barrage of English or the name of the Italian saint.

'No, sorry,' he said, holding up his hands as if asking not to be shot.

Duncan puffed out his cheeks, exhaled. '*Grazie,*' he said.

'Sorry,' Mack said to the man, and shrugged.

'We can go in there?' Duncan asked, pointing at the convent door.

The man pushed up his bottom lip, flapped his hands in a gesture of ignorance or exasperation and walked off.

'Mack, come with me.'

'You need a wingwoman?'

'I guess.'

They went back through to the covered courtyard.

'Whoa,' she said. 'This is kinda shitty.'

'Giuseppe's cell is accessible through the cloister,' Duncan said, heading through the first arch on the right. The first door was glass. No light came from within the room. He knocked. Tried the handle. Pressed his head to the glass.

Door after door: nothing.

On the other side of the courtyard, opposite the entrance, they found a restroom. At least that was unlocked.

'This reminds me of one of those mods of *Half-Life*,' Mack said, 'where they removed all the weapons and NPCs so there's nothing to shoot with or kill. All atmosphere, no action.' She pointed toward a unisex cubicle. 'I'll scout this one for you.'

Duncan tried Father Iandolo's number again. He wasn't sure if it was a landline or a mobile. He listened for ringing from the locked rooms or a second-storey window, heard only the flushing of a toilet.

Mack returned. 'You know what's missing here? The grail quest. Like, we can keep on pixel hunting through every church, move on to the next level, and the next, but where's the golden key that will save the kingdom? What's the end game?'

'I guess that Motta gives me another job.'

'Yes, but what are you trading with him for this next job? A memory stick? I don't think so, babe. You follow your itinerary, do your job, that's the bare minimum. You get a handshake and maybe a thank-you card from his assistant—'

'I doubt that.'

'And Motta walks away feeling like he gave you a shot, and you're left standing there like, *What'd I miss?* You missed the golden key, babe.'

Duncan, exasperated: 'This isn't a video game.'

She shrugged, unconvinced.

'So what, then? What should I be doing?'

'What if the key is inside you?'

'Stop it.'

'No, I mean, what if the thing holding you back is you don't believe in any of it. Levitation, God, your own talent.'

'One thing at a time, eh?'

'Exactly.'

'If you mention San Marino again I'm going to leave you to do your own walk of shame.'

'Just watch this one video.'

'I'm fine. Things are under control.' He stepped out into the courtyard and raised his eyes to the shuttered windows. 'A little help wouldn't go amiss. But the last thing I need is a side quest. I'm not the hero, Mack. Not this time.'

After an hour Duncan had all the photos and measurements he could manage without getting inside any of the locked doors of the convent. Maybe all the friars were on a field trip. Maybe they were crouched in the corners of the locked and darkened rooms, smirking. Maybe Uffy had downgraded his Martina Franca guide the way she'd downgraded his rental car — downgraded all the way to nothing.

'We done?' Mack asked when he returned to the car.

'For now. Let's go check into the B&B. I'll come back later, maybe. Perhaps I can get hold of Uffy, or Iandolo will pick up his friggin' phone.'

'Love nest, here we come.'

Duncan read out the address for Trullo 'Il Mirtillo' and his phone led them back the way they'd come.

Rounding the first bend, two cyclists appeared, a man and a woman, one behind the other. Saddlebags either side of their rear wheels. Tourists. What had brought them here, of all the places in Italy? Perhaps they were fellow pilgrims, following in the footprints of the levitating saint. There was room enough for the Micra and the cyclists to pass, even allowing for the overgrowth, power poles and the small silver dumpster hard up against the wall in the distance, but a white car came around the bend at pace, slid to its left to pass the cyclists — had the driver not seen the Micra? Or, worse, had he seen them and over-estimated his ability to thread the needle? Duncan was forced to pull as far right as he could, gritting his teeth and jamming the brakes, but there was a thunk and a clatter — a sound like one of those terrible NFL collisions that sends a wide receiver's helmet flying, and for a split second everyone thinks his head has flown with it — and the feeling as much as the sound of the passenger side being flayed by a power pole and the tyres searching for traction on the pine needles as they lurched toward the small but positively lethal dumpster. The Micra was starting to fishtail, he could feel it. And he felt the jolt again, the arrival of another fully formed scene, like the death of Giuseppe that had appeared unbidden while staring at Frank Motta's business card in Sforza's. Only this time Duncan didn't have time to unfold the scene of people tearing apart the church at Pietrarubbia — he could do that later, if they survived. Perhaps this scene arrived in lieu of his life flashing before his eyes, because the car had decided to pivot around him so that it led with the driver's side door. Only, no, it was going to roll. The Micra was going to roll and the roof would buckle like a foil swan full of leftovers, and they'd be scattered across the road, sweet and sour and sumptuously fucked.

The Micra didn't roll. Its fishtail ended with the car perpendicular to the road a few feet from the dumpster, which was on wheels anyway — hitting it might not have been the end of the world. But the clattering sound, the flaying. He looked at Mack. Bottom lip engulfed by her mouth. Both hands still clutching the grab handle above her door. There was no wing mirror on that side, just the stub of one. A black claw.

The cyclists.

He looked through Mack's window, beyond the place where the wing mirror had been, back down the lane toward the church. The

148

man and the woman had both come to a stop before the next bend, each with one foot on a pedal, one on the ground, necks twisted to look at Duncan, Mack, the Micra.

The white car was nowhere to be seen. What kind of car had it been? Something compact. A Golf or a Clio. Or was it lower, sleeker? A white 911?

Duncan released his seatbelt and turned to Mack. 'This is where I say something witty and brash and we laugh and get to move on with our lives.'

'It wasn't your fault,' she said, robotic. 'That fucking guy. Did you see him?'

'Not really. I mean, are you sure it was even a guy?'

'It was. It had to be. We should go back there. He's probably in the confessional now. We're just one more thing at the bottom of his list.'

'But, just go for it, right? Fill your boots?'

She drew in a deep, disappointed breath. 'Not now.'

The male cyclist, still wearing his helmet, appeared in Mack's window. Duncan lowered it.

'Are you okay?' the man asked. German, or Austrian, or Swiss. An echo of the couple in *Curio Bay*. Another cosmic down-trou.

'A little shaken,' Duncan said.

'That fucking guy,' Mack said, looking straight ahead. A small gap in the stone wall had been bridged by wire mesh. The field beyond was all dry grass and a solitary tree for shade.

'We have had many close shaves,' said the man. 'But it is a very beautiful country, with a great heritage in cycling, so—' He trailed off.

'You stay safe,' Duncan said, surprise beginning to register: that he was the calm one. The words kept coming. 'Are you going to the church of Saint Anthony?'

The woman appeared, her hair dropping from her helmet in two yellowy braids. She nudged her partner out of frame and held up two pieces of debris.

'These do not look so bad,' she said.

She turned the mirror around. The glass was shattered into maybe twenty pieces, but all of them still sat in the thin black frame.

Duncan reached out, took the mirror. He turned it upside down, shook. Nothing fell out. The glass was covered with milky spots. He licked his finger and rubbed away a couple of these spots, held the mirror back as if taking a selfie. He could recognise himself, his half-assed beard welcoming the grey, his eyes hidden behind gas-station sunglasses. He lifted his shades and looked into the woman's eyes.

'And the other thing?' he asked.

'The shell, I think?'

He got out of the car and went around to where the cyclists stood. He had expected to see a deep gouge running along the passenger and rear doors, but the silver frame looked more like crumpled foil. It was still silver for the most part, though there was a band of tiny white lines, like the filaments of a feather, where the impact had begun. He ran his hands down them.

'I will try this door,' the male cyclist said, and opened the rear door with apparent ease.

'Huh,' Duncan said, surprised. He looked in at Mack, but she was staring straight ahead. He tried her door. After the initial release of the handle he needed to give it a second tug, but it opened.

'You want to get out?' he asked her.

'I'm good,' she said, reaching for the door without looking, and pulling it shut.

The female cyclist handed Duncan the rear casing of the wing mirror. It was silver on the outside, black inside. It seemed complete, still had little plastic tabs sticking out — two at the top, two at the bottom — but it was an irregular shape and took a few goes to get back in place. The satisfaction when it clicked in. It was like seeing the perfect shot as you drove to the set. Like inserting his wankbank tape into the VCR the moment his parents' car was out of sight.

The man took the fragmented mirror from the roof of the car and set about inserting it into the bracket. Another orgasmic clunk.

'Not too bad, I think,' the man said.

'It's incredible. We hit that post pretty hard.'

'Is your friend okay?' the woman asked. 'Are you okay?'

Mack nodded.

'She can't drive,' Duncan said.

'We cannot either,' the woman said, putting her arm around her partner.

'Thanks for your help. Are you staying in Martina Franca tonight? Maybe we could buy you both a drink?'

'Now we are going to Locorotondo,' the man said, 'then stopping in Alberobello for the night.'

'Oh. Well. Go well.'

'And you.'

'Look after her,' the woman said, nodding at Mack.

'I will.'

Duncan went back round to his side, got in his seat, fastened his belt.

'It's so weird how cars just crumple on contact,' he said. 'The paint is hardly scratched.'

'Lucky,' Mack said.

'We have full coverage, so.'

'Right.'

'She was pretty concerned about you.'

'I'm fine. She should worry about you?'

'Me? I'm not the catatonic one.'

'Babe, *I'm* processing it. I haven't become a completely different person. *Stay safe? Go well?*'

'I'm just—'

'Forget it,' she said, picking up Duncan's phone, which still showed the route to their bed and breakfast.

Duncan turned the ignition, the engine started, and he brought the car around to face Martina Franca again.

PIETRARUBBIA

They have come to this valley from the towns and villages of Montefeltro and San Marino, from cities like Cesena in the north, Fano and Pesaro on the coast of the Adriatic, places, all of them, with more commerce, more people, more life than this valley, but fewer miracles.

Some have been carried on backs or wheeled in carts to be blessed by the padre's curative powers. For cataracts to be dissolved. A club foot unfurled. A debilitating pelt of boils not unlike Giuseppe's own childhood infirmity to acquiesce.

Most, however, have come under their own propulsion, ablebodied, in high spirits but for a nameless lack that, in quiet moments, can cast them into splenetic fits. Bowls of soup tossed against walls. The muzzles of barking dogs gripped tight long beyond the time of whimpering. This lack, this dryness, Giuseppe has also known, though he has well and truly transcended it now.

They have come, drawn by the promise of wonders, to this valley. The abandoned castle and deconsecrated church perched on an outcrop of rock hold no interest for them. They are not tourists.

They have come for as long as it will take. They have built huts along the road to the Capuchin convent. They have opened inns for the half-hearted who hope to catch a glimpse of the famous friar while on their way somewhere east or west.

He has been here not yet three months.

It is autumn. The trees look tired and the summer chorus of birdsong has been reduced to the occasional friendless call, just as the valley comes to life with pilgrims seeking the man who can ascend toward the heavens.

Even so, the concourse of people to see Giuseppe had been many times larger in Assisi, with its latent mass of believers, its perennial influx of pilgrims, its ready-made inns and comfortable Roman roads. Concerned, Pope Innocent X finally asked that Giuseppe be removed. Take him somewhere: in the mountains, perhaps. Shield him. Preserve his sanctity. At first, Giuseppe was loath to leave Assisi, which held the tomb of Saint Francis, whom he called his Father, and his companion, Lodovico, who was still very much alive. The Father Inquisitor of Perugia could not move the tomb of Saint Francis, but the written order said nothing about Lodovico. On hearing that his companion would make the journey too, Giuseppe kissed the feet of his superior and leapt into the waiting litter, lashed between two mules, that would carry him he knew not where.

The journey across the Apennines had been treacherous. Lodovico was frequently in tears as he walked behind the litter, seeing it and its precious cargo totter on the edge of this ravine or that. Rocks fell across their path. Mules lost footing. But Giuseppe's heart remained tranquil, his eyes dry, his mouth slit open in smiling wonder at the Highest Father's creation.

The new residents of Pietrarubbia have heard this story and contributed to its embellishment. The hat, mantle and breviary Giuseppe left behind in Assisi, such was his rush to obey the will of his superior. The girl in a house wherein they sheltered, her soaring fever quelled by Giuseppe's prayer. The lame stonemason who walked away cured. The thieves who beset the small travelling party but were undone by Giuseppe's scrutiny of hearts, his speaking truth where there had been so little for so long.

It is 1653. Rembrandt is painting *Aristotle contemplating a*

153

bust of Homer. The last teams of workmen and elephants are putting their final weeks of labour into the Taj Mahal. Cromwell has expelled the Rump Parliament and the Barebones is sitting in its place. Pascal, not yet distracted by religion, is working on many practical things, including readying his *Treatise on the Equilibrium of Liquids* for publication, wherein he says, 'All these examples show that a fine thread of water can balance a heavy weight,' before going on to demonstrate the cause of this multi-plied force. In this world, at this time, as in all times, there are pockets of enquiry, pockets of brilliance, unfaltering faith, crazed credulity and supreme artistry, just as there are great oceans of hard-headedness, kindness and covetousness, all overswept with waves of grief and joy.

These people in this valley of the reddish rocks can wait no more. The Mass is being performed in the church. It's him, they say, passing this knowledge down the line. Father Giuseppe is saying Mass.

The small church is already full when they arrive. Who are they, these blessed pilgrims, these grafting sons of whores? How did they get here so quickly? Someone has bolted the doors from the inside. Those left outside can hear singing, a lone high voice unacquainted with tune. A pained castrato? A madman? No, they whisper. Giuseppe.

Giuseppe.

Soon he will shriek like a gull struck with a sharp-edged stone and ascend above the altar. They claw at each other to peer through the crevice between the wooden doors. They climb over the wall to the olive grove that abuts the church, looking for other openings, weaknesses. They climb on the shoulders of others; form groaning, cursing, human ladders to reach the roof. Those who make it up do not thrust a hand over the ledge to pull up a fellow Christian. They are attacking the roof tiles to permit a bird's-eye view of the Mass. Below, they are scratching at the mortar of the church's walls with sticks, boot heels, fingernails;

rooting at the dirt as if to burrow beneath and through to the sight they seek.

They have come to this valley and they can wait no more. They have been about this world for so long and merely heard of ecstasy. They have fucked and punched and shat and puked, and they want instead to see a man take flight and, at last, give credence to the gut that says such a force exists and refute the other hissed whisper that says this shitty little life will not be followed.

ZERO G

'There've been a few hiccups.'

'Like what?' Kari asked.

'Like the dude who was supposed to show me around the convent that San Giuseppe got kicked out of wasn't there. No one was. Like—' Duncan stopped. Zeb was sitting on his mother's lap, a distant look on his face. Neither of them needed to know about the accident that afternoon. It was hardly an accident. Purely cosmetic. He was considering not reporting it until they got to Rome, lest they lose time waiting for repairs or a replacement. The Micra still ran fine. They were fine. 'Small things,' he said. 'It's all good. I've had a couple bursts of inspiration. I'll just call Uffy after this.'

'Good. You should. It's not your fault if people aren't there.'

He looked up at the conical ceiling. There was a fireplace at one end of the room. It felt like he was inside a kiln. Or a crematorium. But it was quaint. He could see how Northern Europeans, like those cyclists, might lap it up.

'And you say he's been good? Have you been a good boy, Zebbie?'

'He's been fine. I mean, he's woken at five every morning, but—'

'Are you eating lots?'

'He's doing all right.'

'Would you like Daddy to bring you anything back from Italy?'

Silence.

'How about you, Kar?'

'How's Mack? She a help or hindrance?'

'Both, I guess.' The bed and breakfast was a little out of Martina Franca but Mack had walked back to town to find food. She could be gone one hour or five. 'Gianluca, my guide in Copertino, took us to this restaurant last night. We had so much food.'

'Good. Make the most of it.' Kari winced as she readjusted Zeb on her lap. The boy started to chew his bottom lip.

'I should probably go,' Duncan said. 'Try get through to Ms Golinko.'

'Say bye bye to Daddy.'

'Bye buddy. Have a good day with your friends.'

'Bye.'

'Bye.'

He tried calling Uffy. It was Saturday, but she didn't strike him as the kind of person who observed weekends.

He got her voicemail.

Good for you, he thought. Work–life balance.

But also: Fuck.

'Hi Uffy, Duncan Blake here. One thing. The guy we were supposed to meet at the Capuchin convent in Martina Franca, Father Iandolo, he wasn't there. I think he was in Taranto today. Any updates on this? I did all I could without him. Maybe you could let me know if he's been in touch with you and we need to hang around tomorrow morning before we go to' — he looked down at the itinerary, tried to sound as she might — 'Montescaglioso, Matera and Altamura. You've got my number.'

He'd been considering going back to the convent that evening, but after leaving his message he figured it was better to wait until morning. Or skip it altogether. How much more could Iandolo really give him? The elements he felt surest about — the death of Giuseppe and his saying Mass in Pietrarubbia — occurred in places he'd not even been yet. How important was his input to the possible scenes of a young Giuseppe Desa on the outskirts of Martina Franca, spilling soup and burning bread, anyway? You could even start the movie with the door to the convent being shut in his face, his departure from Martina Franca and his walk of shame back to Copertino. Tell the story of the birth in the stable, the bed-ridden child, the witless student in flashback — if at all. Start with motion. At his lowest point. One of his lowest points. The film could be a string of lows — expulsion from the Capuchins and reproach at home, being called out by a jealous friar and sent before the Inquisition in Naples, his spiritual dryness in Assisi — culminating in his ascension to a more permanent state of bliss.

A redemption story.

Woe upon woe upon woe, and then . . . *Whoa!*

Was it right to try and bend the script to fit his location-scouting successes and hide his failures?

The next day would be different. Giuseppe hadn't lived in Montescaglioso, Matera or Altamura, though he'd probably visited all three when he was paraded around Puglia by an ambitious Minister Provincial in the mid-1630s. Uffy had explained how these towns had well-preserved buildings from Giuseppe's time. How the council in Altamura offered big subsidies for film and TV productions. He was to maintain the pretence that *Giuseppe* could still be shot in Italy in order to get access to the best locations, and shoot as much footage as possible so that the convent cells and dining halls could be reproduced by Motta's crew halfway around the world.

While he was on an admin kick, he emailed his old agent, Tanner Burge:

I see CURIO BAY is on Netflix here in Italy (here doing a favour for Frank Motta). Anything else you got to tell me?

Name-dropping Motta, making a play for his useless fucking agent to take him back, made him feel like he hadn't showered in days.

He hadn't eaten since lunchtime.

He wasn't hungry.

He was tired.

Again.

They were lucky to be alive. Him and Mack. The Micra hadn't rolled or ploughed into the dumpster, but it could have. They could have clipped one of the cyclists. A run of images: the woman with the braids splattered against the jagged stone wall; Mack being launched through the windscreen, a temporary torpedo; the guy in the white car, saying Hail Marys, fingering a rosary, being absolved, getting back into his car, which flickers, as if he's just respawned, except his invincibility is not temporary. He can go on driving like that, causing carnage, because he can't die. Not really. And then he, Duncan Blake, was in the air. This wasn't the empty mansion. He was inside the same room at the B&B, floating up inside the Trullo cone, tucking his knees to his chest, going foetal to fit as the roof closed in. He was awake. And levitating. Only it was a dream. It had to be. He let go of his knees, reached out and touched a grey rectangular stone. The contact pushed him in the opposite direction. The back of his head struck another stone. Zero gravity. *Apollo 11.* He was maybe eight feet above the queen-sized bed, the one he was supposed to share with Mack, separated by a ridge of pillows and two decades of zero chemistry. The B&B had two suites. He'd learned from the proprietor, a bald guy barely into his thirties named Bruno, that Uffy had originally booked both. One for her and one for Motta. But she'd cancelled the second. Why wouldn't she? She didn't know about Mack. And he didn't expect Echo Park to cover her costs. He wished he'd asked permission and been denied. That he was doing this alone. But he hadn't. He wasn't. They'd expected this would happen. It was fine. Everything was fine fine fine.

The door opened and Duncan's face was embedded in the mattress, as if he really had fallen from the top of the Trullo ceiling.

'Duncan?'

The lights were still on. He'd fallen asleep with the lights on.

'What were you doing?'

'I fell asleep.'

Mack had plastic bags in each hand, towers of white cardboard boxes in each bag. She was red faced, flustered. The walk plus the dumbass leather coat. He thought of sneaking out in the middle of the night, tossing it in a river like a sack of kittens.

'You weren't, like, jumping on the bed? Or, y'know, floating, just a bit?'

'I was dreaming. I can thrash about.'

'You reckon?'

'What'd you buy?'

'I found this amazing bakery. Cleaned it out. You like cannoli?'

'I don't feel like anything sweet.'

'Here's the receipt.'

'For what?'

'To claim back from Echo Park. Expenses.'

'Why would I spend *seventy-four* euros at a bakery?'

'Gratuities, for your host.'

'You gonna offer him some?'

'I might as well, if you're not eating.'

'I'm not, thanks.'

'I'm doing my best not to take it personal, babe' she said. 'To put this down to something glandular.'

'What?'

'You can't stay awake past nine. You're grumpy as fuck. You're a zombie.'

'It's not you, okay?'

'I don't care what it is. Can we just have fun? I could really use some fun. Tomorrow, can we take advantage of this trip we're on?'

Duncan thought about everything on the itinerary. He thought about blowing Motta away with his ideas for shots, his insights into character and place.

Mack must've seen his eyes glaze over. She picked up the plastic bags. 'I'm going to see Bruno.'

SCRUTINY OF HEARTS

Uffy Golinko didn't call.

Father Iandolo never answered his phone.

It was the weekend.

They each deserved a pass.

He cursed them relentlessly.

After checking out of 'Il Mirtillo', Duncan put on Midlake's album, *The Courage of Others*, and they drove back past the scene of their near-miss for one last visit to the Capuchins of Martina Franca. Duncan went into the courtyard of the convent, called out, clutched his right arm as if having a heart attack, cursed Iandolo for old time's sake and returned to the car.

'Strike two?' Mack said.

Duncan grunted and turned the ignition.

'So,' Mack said, 'about last night, when I came back into the room and you were floating?'

'No. Just stop.'

'Why are you doing Motta's bidding? Don't you think there's something in all of this for you to explore? What you need is to make another movie. Your *own* movie.'

'And you need to stop auditioning for the role of my life coach.'

'Maybe we can swap roles. You be the one who tries and I'll be the little bitch.'

'I think someone needs a hug.'

Mack folded her arms and they drove past yesterday's skid marks and the untouched dumpster, then headed toward the coast.

It was an hour and a half to Montescaglioso, where they needed to check out two convents: a lot of highway driving, which gave him time to unclench his jaw. Midlake's album, its feudal imagery and textured, flute-laden sound, helped lift Duncan's spirits. If he squinted he could banish the highway and the boxy buildings and picture Giuseppe walking from parish to parish with the Minister Provincial who pushed and cajoled the young simpleton to go into ecstasy. To awe the villagers to the point they wrote songs about the flying friar.

Giuseppe volava!

The album ended as they bore away from the coast and shot north. The crumpled right-hand side of the Micra didn't seem to affect its aerodynamics.

Mack: 'Can I have my DJ privileges back, please?'

'What are you going to play?'

'Something we both know. I'm generous like that.'

'Not more nineties.'

'Okay babe.'

Thirty seconds later the car filled with the dramatic drum intro to Electric Light Orchestra's 'Don't bring me down'.

Away from the coast, the landscape was lumpy without being hilly. The two main crops: wheat and solar panels. A windmill sprouted every couple of miles, though the turbines refused to budge.

The Romantics, 'Talking in your sleep'

The Records, 'Starry eyes'

Cheap Trick, 'If you want my love'

She was fucking with him again. Trying to lure him into one of her little scenes. To ask if she had feelings for him. Or open up about his flying dreams. He wouldn't know for sure until he went for the bait, but he wasn't going to. He kept his lips pursed, his eyes on the road, though he let them flick every now and then to the cubist rendering of the view in Mack's wing mirror. He was certain now that he wasn't going to tell anyone about the damage until Rome. The lost time, yes, but also the red flags it might raise back in LA.

Insurance claims already? That's it, call him back.

The car handled fine. The doors all opened. The windows worked. He could see behind him well enough.

The land rose up before them like a ripple in a pond, frozen in time. The ridge was capped with basking houses.

Montescaglioso.

'Nice,' Mack said.

The gradient of the road increased to the point Duncan had to change all the way down to first gear. The picturesque buildings dissolved and left in their place monstrous seventies apartment blocks.

'Not so nice.'

Once they'd reached the top of the hill, the GPS guided them through the town, which did its best to obscure any views of the plains below with buildings so brutish and abraded it was as if they weren't nearly four hundred metres above sea level but squatting in the intertidal zone and everything got ravaged twice daily by the harsh, corroding forces of the ocean.

They turned on to a lane with slick cobblestones. It was like driving on the floor of a basilica — the slipperiness, the squeal, the mortified onlookers. Ahead of them: a small piazza and another Capuchin church and convent, except there were cars parked all over the piazza. Duncan found a gap and slotted the Micra in.

'You're getting better at this,' Mack said.

'Now that I've lowered your expectations.'

'Pretty much.'

'You coming in?'

'I might go for a walk.'

Duncan went to try the church door. Bolted shut. It was 10.30 a.m. The door to the convent was only a couple of yards

to the right — the church couldn't have been that big inside —
but that was locked too. There was an intercom, so he pushed
it, unfolding the itinerary as he waited for a response. He didn't
have a contact for this convent. Uffy had only included one
bullet point:

Possible source of alternative material for Capuchin scenes.

Alternative material would be good, the way things had
gone in Martina Franca — he allowed a chuckle at how both
he and San Giuseppe had failed there — but there was little he
could do if no one opened the fucking door. He stepped out
from under the terracotta awning that shaded the entrance
to look for movement in any of the upper windows. Maybe it
was a Capuchin thing, not answering phones or opening doors.
He was pretty sure they didn't take a vow of silence — they were
a branch of Franciscans after all, and hadn't Saint Francis tried
to chart a new path for his followers, one more connected with
the community than sequestering themselves off to illuminate
manuscripts and make liqueur?

His phone vibrated. Mack? No. A text message from Uffy. It
must've been well after midnight in LA.

You're not making a hash of things, are you Duncan?

That was it. He'd tried to sound collected on her voicemail. To
make it clear Father Iandolo and her itinerary were the ones letting
him down. Maybe that was why she'd waited until after he'd have
left Martina Franca to bite back. Well, screw her then. He wasn't
just out to hitch himself to the Motta-train now. He also wanted
to uncouple Uffy. Two birds, one amazing lookbook/presentation/
fireside chat — he still hadn't nailed that part down — with the
Great and Powerful Motta.

He shot some exteriors, energised by the thought that each
shot of rusted spouting or dusty, stained-glass martyrs could be
the one that makes Motta's mouth drop open, his feet leave the
floor. Then he set off to find Mack. She hadn't made it far. About
a hundred yards down the street she stood in front of a concrete-

block wall that came almost to her chin. In her white trainers she was probably his height again. She was fitter, though. Could run rings around him.

As Duncan got closer he saw the view, framed vertically by two buildings and horizontally by the top of the wall and a powerline. From where he stood, slightly uphill from Mack, the shot was half sky and half earth; the earth a mixture of forest and pasture, with tiny buildings visible only if you tried to find them. He took a photo and shouted, 'Nice view.'

She turned, rubbed her eyes as if she couldn't believe Duncan was there. 'No luck?'

'Next!'

Back inside the Micra, he handed her his phone. 'Read this text I got from Uffy.'

'I thought you guys didn't get on?'

'We don't, obviously.' He took his phone back.

'If that's not good-natured ribbing, babe, it's flagrant flirting.'

'What? No way. You don't even know her.'

'What would I know, right?' She turned to look out her window. 'She wants me to fail. She thinks I'm a threat to her.'

She turned back to him. 'And are you?'

'No. I mean, we might ultimately want similar things. But I'm the one who has already made a film.'

'So you get a free pass to keep on making them? White male privilege alert!'

'Earlier this morning you were yelling at me to make another movie. Now you're telling me to sit down and let a sister have a turn?'

'Babe.'

'Don't *Babe* me. Travelling with you is like having the entire Twittersphere in the passenger seat. Any opportunity to pile on and *wham.*'

Mack made a show of biting her tongue.

He unfolded the itinerary as if it was a handkerchief he was about to lay over an unsightly stain. 'We need to go to *Abbazia Di San Michele Arcangelo.*'

'Yes, sir. Say it once more with feeling,' Mack said, holding out her phone to detect Duncan's voice.

★

The abbey was at the northern edge of Montescaglioso. As they approached, it seemed the town had at last given up its game of keep-away with the view.

'Maybe it's a form of portion control,' Duncan said.

'Huh?'

'With the view.'

'Okay.'

'Sorry, I forget sometimes you can't read my thoughts.'

'Or can I?'

'They say Giuseppe could. Although they called it *Scrutiny of Hearts* in his day.'

The only space available near the abbey was a parallel park between a green three-wheeled Gorilla car and a white panel van. The shattered wing mirror slowed him down, but the fact he'd already smashed the car up lowered the stakes. He completed the manoeuvre and pulled back the handbrake.

'Gimme your phone for a sec,' Mack said.

'Why?'

She snatched it anyway, then held it out for him to unlock with his fingerprint. He obliged.

'Just watch this video,' she said, typing. 'It'll only take two minutes.' She handed back his phone.

White text on a black background: *Why Levitation?*

'You might wonder,' a male voice began, the New Zealand accent and the influence of *whaikōrero* — Māori oratory — evident in the first three words and the loaded pause, 'why bother with such a phenomenon as levitation. So extreme, so rare.'

The screen was awash with light and lens flare, as if J.J. Abrams was trying to depict the afterlife.

'Your cult?'

'Just watch it.'

He put his phone to sleep and said, in his disappointed-parent voice, 'What would I have to gain from screwing with the itinerary just to spend a day with a bunch of hippies who think they can fly?'

Mack folded her arms.

'This location-scouting gig,' he continued, 'is a means to an end. I'm just trying not to stuff anything up so that I get fed something else. I'm prepared to live on scraps for a while, work my way back up—'

'Ingratiate yourself.'

'—and hopefully learn something along the way about how to make a big film that still has a heart and a brain.'

'Why does it need to be a big film?'

'Why does everything I say get picked apart?'

'Babe, I am genuinely trying to help. Maybe we could have a conversation, you know, like two friends or something. I swear I saw you six feet off the ground when I came in the room last night. If anyone should be looking for the truth, it should be you. What does your heart say, Duncan? What does your brain even say?'

'"Don't listen to her."'

'No, seriously. Take a minute to commune with yourself—'

'You visit a couple of cultish websites and suddenly you're this guru?'

'I spoke to Bruno. I spoke to Gianluca. To his sister. You know, people who live here. Who know stuff. Gah!' She had to lean her shoulder into the door to make it come free. 'You think I'm hard work. That I need to be managed.' She turned back to face him. '*Ameliorated*. But being with you. It's draining. I came here for the absolute opposite. To be recharged. You haven't even asked—' She stopped herself. Took a giant breath. 'I'm constantly fighting

167

this massive bummer, babe.' She climbed out of the car. 'Kari was right.'

Duncan leaned across the passenger seat. The door slammed inches from his face. 'What'd Kari say?' he shouted. He pushed himself up, turned the key in the ignition so he could lower the passenger window, and shouted, 'When did you even talk to her?'

She kept walking, slightly hunched, as if her shoulders had been permanently moulded by the weight of her stupid leather coat.

Duncan knocked the back of his head against the headrest once, twice. Looked into Mack's wing mirror, its spidery view of the road behind him.

DEMOLITION MAN

The entrance to the Abbey of Saint Michael the Archangel was wide open and — Duncan almost fell to the floor — it had a reception area with a desk and a real, live person seated behind it.

'Hello!' he said.

The woman wore a white blouse and had tied a thin blue scarf around her neck. She looked like an air hostess, or someone whose youthful ambition to be an air hostess had been thwarted by her plainness and the shallowness and rampant sexism of the era.

'*Buongiorno*,' she said, her face contorting as she prepared to switch to English. 'We have an exhibition through here —' she gestured to her right — 'and the rest of the complex is also open to explore.'

'Do you have a map?'

'No, sorry. But there is a scale model in the first room of the exhibition.'

'Fantastic.' He considered telling her that he was from Echo Park, laying on the story about this being a genuine location-scouting mission and the possibility of a full Hollywood production bearing down on this place, but it didn't seem necessary. He could always come back and ask questions, get her to show him inside any of the locked cells.

He headed for the scale model but became distracted by a table of two dozen clay figures in the next room. Each statuette was about the height of a Coke bottle and depicted a different monastic order.

The *Cassinesi*, completely shrouded in black, holding an open Bible.

The *Certosini*, all in white with a black cord around the waist, clutching a crucifix.

The *Frati Minori*, Giuseppe's mob, with tonsured head, brown robe, white cord and a wooden walking stick.

And the elusive *Cappuccini*, standing next to the brother from the Order of Frati Minori. It was like a game of spot the difference. Their robes were slightly different colours, the Capuchin's more reddish, but that could have been down to variation at the hands of the artist — a slightly different clay or the heat at which it was cured. The Capuchin didn't have the tonsure. Instead of a walking stick he had a brown bag sitting behind his left hip, the strap cutting a heraldic bend across his chest.

On the walls he found boards teeming with information in both Italian and English about all the different orders. He read about the Order of the Friars Minor and the Capuchins, took photos of everything else in case he needed a SparkNotes version of The Knights Templar or the Dominicans. It felt good to be back in the world of San Giuseppe. No Thousand Flowers. No Second Wave — those blighted trust-fund babies, global teens and murderous young adults were footnotes at best. They'd never get their own exhibition.

But what had Mack said? *Kari was right.* About what? Being with him was *draining*. A *massive bummer*. When had those two spoken? Did Mack ring Kari once a month, just as she rang him? They'd never met in person but that meant next to nothing. Everyone knew someone who'd met their future spouse online. But a female friend from high school striking up a friendship with your wife just to talk about you? What a complicated way to flunk the Bechdel Test. Perhaps Kari hadn't trusted Duncan; thought his story of the platonic female friend who locked herself in her bedroom for two years after high school was too far-fetched to be believed. Weren't all those Japanese shut-ins, the *hikikomori*, dudes?

He Googled *Female hikikomori*.

324,000 results.

Support groups emerge to help female recluses | Japan Times Oct 19, 2016

Any other girls/women here? Resources about and for female . . . Reddit

Why are there gender differences in hikikomori? — Quora

He didn't click any of the links. Seeing them was enough. Mack's withdrawal from the world had coincided with his leaving town to go to university. He heard about it through friends, then his mother when he returned home between first and second semesters: Mack's locked herself in her bedroom and refuses to come out.

She had a computer and a PS2, ordered new games every week based on the packages left on the MacKinnons' front porch, but didn't respond to his emails. Truth was, it was easy to forget about her when he was back in Dunedin. He had other friends, people into film, someone new to tug his heartstrings in every tutorial.

'You think I'm hard work,' she'd said just now. 'That I need to be managed. *Ameliorated.*' Was that her word or Kari's?

He sighed, began to walk back through the exhibits, past the reception. The thwarted hostess looked up, her smile broadening when he turned toward the courtyard of the abbey rather than leaving the complex without exploring further, as many tourists must've done. Tourists? He was alone. The abbey was abandoned. No, not abandoned. It was well maintained, looked after by the hostess and whatever heritage outfit she represented. But the Benedictine monks who'd called it home now lived somewhere else, had ceded their complex to information boards and clay figurines.

There was a well in the centre of the courtyard and some

kind of fount or basin closer to the back that the sparrows had claimed for their own. The holiest sparrows in Christendom. The courtyard was surrounded by four long corridors — *cloisters* — that remained cool even as the sun exerted itself in the sky. All the doors off the cloisters were shut, some of them boarded or bricked up, allowing only glimpses through cracks of the state of the cells. Some rooms were filled with rubble, some with filing cabinets, blackboards, lawnmower parts, spools of wire; all of them surely cooler than the cloister, even more removed from the world outside. Cells in every sense.

He walked through a passage at the end of the first corridor and found himself in a second courtyard. It was probably the same dimensions as the first but felt smaller. The grass had sprung daisies and dandelions; the well was cracked; the black stains either side of the downpipes were wider, darker. But this was good. A before and after. Two courtyards for the price of one. Standing in the shaded cloister, it didn't take much to imagine the place as it had been in the 1600s. Remove the brass guttering, the red fire hoses, the structural bracing. Add a padre or two. In a pinch, this could stand in for anywhere in Giuseppe's back catalogue. And weren't they in a pinch? Wasn't 1621 a long, long time ago? Wasn't *Giuseppe* doomed to bomb at the box office? Maybe it would go straight to streaming. There were questions, tons of them, but standing in that place, nothing felt insurmountable.

He saw something then, or felt it, knew it. Perhaps it was like the moment Motta had under the waterfall in Hawaii when he first saw how to turn Giuseppe's life into film. What Duncan saw was a workaround, or a *work-with*, for all the locked doors and holidaying friars. A way to film everywhere, the bits you could. Do it on location with a guerrilla crew, a couple of actors, bring it all together in the editing room: the gonzo camera work, the close-ups of faces, floating feet, rapid, relentless cutting as if it was one long music video, one of those snowboarding films you find playing in bars a day's drive from the snow, big air and talking heads.

172

A callback to Motta's *French Inhaler*, to Duncan's own work with the family Palmcorder and what came later, when the snippets of Tara James were not enough.

His wankbank tape.

His first foray into self-stimulating cinema had stalled when his nerve failed and he couldn't cross the line into full-blown creepazoid country. Couldn't film through Tara's bedroom window, or from the bushes as the high school girls got ready for soccer practice. He was already wracked with guilt over masturbating, those first few months. Felt like a dirty little boy and maybe it was just a passing phase. But, if so, why was the pull so great?

And then, as if answering his prayer, a new stock of stimulation had arrived courtesy of his father. He had taped a late showing of *Demolition Man* on the only cable movie channel they had in New Zealand back then. It was a good movie for a preteen, just violent and dark enough that he felt better watching it alone one Saturday afternoon while his parents and sister were otherwise occupied. He hadn't seen *Rambo* or *Rocky* yet, but he totally got Sly Stallone as the brutish fish-out-of-water in a sanitised future, baffled by the mystery of the three sea shells, dying to transfer fluids with Sandra Bullock. And then they do have sex, only it's via headsets! And the movie's climax? Where Wesley Snipes is frozen with liquid nitrogen, his head kicked off and smashed to smithereens? Great stuff. But the real magic came after the final credits. Duncan had left the video running while he went and made a sandwich — he would never be comfortable with a quiet room — and when he came back the next programme was playing. It was *Playboy After Dark*, a thirty-minute magazine show that played after midnight on the movie channel. He'd heard other boys at school mention it. Now here it was. A gift from the machine. He wasn't alone in the house, so he quickly stopped it playing and hit rewind. When the tape reached its clunky conclusion, he removed it and placed it back in the cabinet. There was no way he'd be caught watching *Playboy*

After Dark, however innocently. So he'd put it off until the next time he was home alone.

His wait lasted until the following weekend. His sister was at a friend's and his folks were following the advice of his mother's latest self-help book, heading to the coast for a picnic and some couple time. In the intervening week Duncan had become convinced the recording would stop after the opening credits of the second programme. His father would have set the VCR to record for two hours, enough to get *Demolition Man* without the hassle of setting specific start and stop times. It was all a big tease. A tut-tut from the unimpressed universe. A lesson — was there any worse word in the teenage lexicon? But as soon as his parents' car had pulled out of the driveway, the tape was in the machine and fast-forwarding to the end of the movie, just to make sure. *Playboy After Dark* started with a preview of the episode: something about strippers in San Francisco, a skit about a sick man and a nurse, a music video with a naked saxophone player. In twenty seconds Duncan saw more breasts than he'd seen his entire life. And, to his surprise, the show kept playing, and playing, until its own credits rolled. He was too jacked on adrenaline to absorb much of the content — there'd be time for that. But he had it, half an hour of soft porn. A moving-pictures *Playboy* his parents knew nothing about.

His next action was not to rewind and watch it again but to eject the video and try to find more. Surely his father had made this same mistake before. (It never occurred to him that it could have been intentional.) He cycled through ten movies he suspected had been recorded from the late-night slot, found one more episode of *Playboy After Dark* in its entirety and two partials. He moved these cassettes to the back of the cabinet so they wouldn't be overwritten and started scheming ways to extend his collection.

Over the coming weeks he suggested a number of late-night movies that his parents might like to watch later or store for posterity and repeat viewing. When they agreed, he'd casually offer to set the VCR up to tape the movie (and an episode of *Playboy After Dark*). In this way, he had four full episodes by the end of the month, but began to arouse the suspicion of his parents. *Why this sudden interest in movies?*

'Films,' he'd corrected. 'And it's not sudden. I want to be a filmmaker. You know that.'

His mother said she wished he would let them watch the little movies he made with his father's camera.

They were just for practice, he said.

It would not be the last time he used filmmaking as a cover for deviancy. Not that masturbating over soft porn was that deviant. It could even seem quaint when viewed from the future Duncan had been thrust into — a reverse Sly Stallone, where fluid transfer really did seem too difficult and hey, what's this? A lifetime's worth of hard-core action ready to be called forth on your phone as soon as you close the bathroom door? But back then the masturbation and the stimulation were secondary to, or at least shared top-billing with, the forethought and secrecy. There he was, asserting his own agency — he just chose to do so by hoarding moving images. And, because this was his most fervent secret, it came to define him for a time. He spent more time at school, or playing games on the family PC, or listening to CDs (Smashing Pumpkins, Beck, NOFX) on his bedroom stereo, or shooting hoops on his driveway. But so did everyone else. This, he felt, was his alone. In a way, it ruined TV for him. He couldn't watch without being on the lookout for scenes, images, that deserved preservation and repeat viewing. He started watching TV — alone, always alone — with one of the *After Dark* cassettes in the VCR, his hand poised over the record button should Gillian Anderson take off her coat or Kari Wuhrer get possessed by another sex-crazed alien on *Sliders*. (He thought of Wuhrer, for the first time in years, when he was introduced to his Kari, Kari Sedlak, an exchange student from the States, at a Film Society event in Dunedin. She had her hair cut in a similar bob to Wuhrer's, a decade out of fashion but sexy as hell because of it.) He was careful to record an episode of *NBA Action* over the first half hour of the tape and compulsively checked how close the new snippets he was recording were coming to the start of *Playboy After Dark*.

In this way, over the space of a year, maybe more, he created his first hour-long montage of titillation. Less flesh than on the *Playboy* show, but somehow more exciting. Jamie Lee Curtis performing a striptease in *True Lies*. Mia Sara topless in *Time Cop*. Michelle Pfeiffer's Catwoman, Tia Carrere rocking out, Nicole Eggert baywatching. But not as rapidly and efficiently cut together as that. Sometimes the recording came in late, catching a glimpse of a lifeguard leaving Mitch Buchanan's office. Other times he'd pushed record on instinct, and thirty seconds of travel-show stock footage — vibrant local markets, a heron flying over a river at dusk — would pass before the presenter, in bikini top and sarong, would stand with her arms out wide on a golden-sanded beach and welcome the viewers to Thailand.

The heat went out of this hobby when his parents separated. It was as if his guilt had found its vessel. It was his fault they were getting divorced. His actions, his deviancy. His mother, oblivious to the change in her son, mentioned his interest in film to his high school English teacher at a parent–teacher conference. As if it wasn't awkward enough already: his no longer amicable parents either side of him; his teacher, Mr Mears, trying to find nice ways to say Duncan was a non-entity in class. But Mears latched on to the film thing and Duncan, despite himself, developed a genuine interest. He found a way to harness his magpie instinct for arresting images, his idiosyncratic editing, to make things for other people to watch. Mack was at school by then, had become a friend and was taken along on the ride, until she left for university and she decided to stay in her bedroom.

Occasionally he still reacted to TV as if he was in the midst of creating his wankbank tape. The biggest trigger: nineties stars in the midst of PG-13 movies — Jennifer Aniston stripping in

We're the Millers, Elle Macpherson in a re-run of *Sirens*. These moments filled him with regret. But, of course, there was someone else out there now, recording and sharing it on YouTube or Mr Skin. That was the difference. There was now a community around private titillation. Teens were getting it handed to them in a search-engine result.

Jennifer Lawrence looking hot compilation. Click.

Same went for all the great films he read about in books and magazines but didn't get to see until well into his twenties. It was all there for them now.

Watch Tsarkovsky's Stalker free. Click.

Wild Strawberries. Click.

Death Rides a Horse. Click

Try as he might, Duncan could not go back and watch *The Hidden Fortress* on an iPad when he was fourteen and bored. Instead, he was stuck with *Demolition Man* and *Playboy After Dark*. There were already filmmakers emerging who'd had this other education.

The Next Generation.

Fucking hell.

He could only look into their work and reflect. Who had it better, these Millennials or his Cuspers with one foot in the analog, another in the digital? One thing he did know: watching limitless free porn, as hard core and disturbing as your tastes will take you, was less rewarding than staking out titillation, capturing it and reliving the moments with or without your dick in your hand.

THE WHEEL AND THE TELESCOPE

Mack wasn't waiting by the car when Duncan emerged from the abbey. He'd been gone an hour and a half, had many things he wanted to discuss, or at least say in her presence, air out, test — the way you toss a coin to learn the outcome you really wanted. Plus, they needed to get moving, still had to see Matera, find their lodging in Altamura — another bed and breakfast, the possibility of another shared room — and explore a few churches before day's end.

He got into the driver's seat, honked the horn. Again he had that Wild West feeling. The eyes behind the shutters. He pictured the sheriff in the saloon, hitching up his belt, his holster, knocking back one last shot of whiskey, taking his favourite whore in his arms, dipping her back and laying a thick, handlebar smooch on her half-open mouth.

He checked the time on his phone and realised he could call her. Honking the horn? How analog.

'Hey,' Mack answered, a space where the 'babe' ought to be.

'Time to go.'

'Gimme five.'

'Where are you?'

'Eating. Have you eaten? Do you eat?'

'It's not even midday.'

'I'll get a doggy bag.'

'Woof,' he said, flat and undoglike.

The call ended and he surveyed his open apps, the many ways in which he could while away his wait. YouTube still offered that cult's video. It might help soften Mack up if he could at least say he'd returned to it.

He pushed play.

'Simply put,' continued the disembodied voice of what must have been Mille Fiori's Kiwi founder, 'the extreme expression of a phenomenon is the most interesting. And the most revealing.' Duncan began to detect the rumble of an audience between each phrase. So this was a recording of a talk, then, some recruitment drive, to which the image of the blinding corona and its slow-whirling hexagonal flares had been added. 'If you want to understand the scope and nature of the English language, look to my mate Bill. Bill Shakespeare. To fathom the nature of evil: study the Holocaust. The wheel, hmm, that'll tell us something about technology, but the Hubble telescope will take us much further.'

On screen, the silhouette of a person had emerged, arms outstretched. Duncan expected the figure to lift off the floor like that, with all the distortions a TV magician might use, but the glare reduced as the camera began to move steadily to the left in a passable dolly shot that revealed the light source was a large window and the person was standing in a bare room with wooden floors.

'We train our curiosity on levitation,' the voice continued, the background rumble gone, 'to learn more about human capacities. The latent power and *outreach* of the human mind. To understand the empirical roots of a range of religious beliefs. To confront the strange godlike power of our subliminal minds.'

Duncan could see now that the person on screen was a woman. She wore a tight sleeveless top and figure-hugging jeans. Her feet were bare. Her eyes were closed, her face impassive, as if meditating through her own crucifixion.

'Might flying dreams indicate a secret affinity between our subliminal minds and the ability to defy gravity? What does quantum mechanics tell us about the so-called laws of nature? Might our dreams and all the documented cases of ecstatic levitation across a range of cultures and religions point toward our evolutionary future?' The cult leader stepped into frame. He wore a short-sleeved shirt and slacks. Must've been in his fifties, but his thick black hair still hadn't got the memo that it was time to add some grey. His forearms were sailor-thick and covered in the same black hair. He looked like the kind of guy Duncan's mum might have dated the first couple of years after her divorce. The treasurer of an alpine club. A keen fisherman. 'And how might we use this knowledge, not to transcend this planet, but to improve life upon it?'

The woman's eyes flicked open. She stared down the lens. Her full body was in frame, but he could still see her bottom lip move beneath her top teeth and the corners of her mouth arch as if she should not have signposted the effort she was about to exert. Her eyes rolled upward and her body followed, her bare feet lifting off the floorboards, two, three, four feet into the air. Her head passed out of frame, her chest, all amid lighting suddenly ordinary and commonplace. The room so bare and unremarkable, it looked more *Funniest Home Videos* than stage magic or blockbuster VFX.

The cult leader stood to one side, regarding the levitator with his hands in his pockets.

The lower half of the woman hung in frame for a couple more seconds, then it cut to black.

'You might ask: Why levitation? We ask: Why ever not?'

SASSI

Matera was only half an hour away. Between corkscrewing out of one town and into the outskirts of another, there was no time for Duncan to decode what the levitation video made him feel and slip it into idle chatter, or to build up to a confrontation about Mack's contact with Kari.

It was Mack who broke the silence. 'Your hands are shaking.'

He looked at his hands resting on the wheel, both visibly still.

'They were. When you changed gears. Do you feel it too?'

'What?'

'Like this place is going to give you an anaphylactic shock.'

'A bee sting for the eyes.'

'Totally.'

'What a day to leave your EpiPen in your other yoga pants.'

'Is that an EpiPen in your yoga pants,' she said, and tapped the ash of her invisible Groucho Marx cigar over the gearstick, 'or are you just pleased to see me?'

The outskirts of Matera featured the same ugly 1970s conniptions as Montescaglioso, only multiplied, expanded. Each complex had more floors than the last, more skew-whiff satellite dishes, more sheets, towels and stonewashed jeans flung over balconies to dry. The buildings grew larger still. Office blocks, he guessed, full of paperwork and crushed souls.

'The thing is,' he said, 'this place is supposed to be amazing.'

'Here?'

'Like, UNESCO World Heritage Site amazing. The *Ben-Hur* remake and the new *Wonder Woman* were filmed here. *The Passion of the Christ*. Even some of *More Than a Miracle*, which featured our mate San Giuseppe.'

'No way.'

The GPS was taking them to a parking area near the entrance to the old town. They came to a large roundabout, its centre filled with freshly mown grass to taunt the patients in the high-rise hospital that overlooked it.

'I'm starting to see the attraction of making this film of Motta's,' she said. 'Wiping all this modern rubbish off the map.'

'One giant green screen.'

'You could probably do that, you know.'

'What?'

'Augmented reality. Put on your goggles and anything built before 1621 is blotted out. For the mass market, give it five, ten years.'

'Is that a good thing?'

'Who's to say?'

Duncan thought about Twitter, Facebook. How people complained what echo chambers they'd become, blamed them for election results, extremism, the needlessly happy.

'What are your mission objectives here, Sergeant?' Mack asked.

'Basically walk around the old town, soak up the atmosphere. Visit two churches. In and out in ninety minutes. You want to join me?'

'Are you asking me out, Duncan Blake?'

'If you're good, I'll buy you a gelato.'

★

They leaned, elbows on the stone wall, gelato cups in hand, looking over the scrubby canyon that carved through the Sassi, Matera's filmset-worthy, UNESCO-listed old town. Stracciatella for Duncan. Chocolate of a deep, thoroughbred brown for Mack.

'So Matera,' he said.

'Matera,' she said. 'This is what I'm talking about.'

'What?'

'Don't you feel it?'

'What?'

'Open your mouth and let me spoon-feed you this wisdom.' She looked at him, really did expect him to open his mouth. She loaded up her tiny plastic shovel with gelato. He closed his eyes, opened his mouth.

'In-spired,' she said, as if it was two words.

He closed his mouth over the spoon, held the gelato back with his teeth, the roof of his mouth, his tongue, as she pulled the spoon back through his lips.

'The wine talking, maybe?' he said, opening his eyes, looking across to the man-made caves, ancient churches and dwellings that pocked the other side of the canyon. He still hadn't told her he'd finished watching the cult's video. The longer he left it, the less important it seemed.

'We had one glass.'

'Altamura awaits.'

'Fuck Altamura. It sounds like a concert overrun with Hell's Angels. I like it here.'

'The gravy train waits for no one. You can crash at the B&B.'

'I don't want to crash — in any sense of the word. Come on. Look at this place. Talk about a bait and switch. All that modern rubbish on the way in. And here. Here, I keep expecting to see someone writhing on a cross around the next corner.'

'That's been done.' He lifted his camera, removed the lens cap, framed Mack with the Jerusalem-ish jumble of old Matera behind. Click. He turned the screen around to her. 'Classic Facebook photo. Make 'em die of envy back home.'

'But have you spoken to anyone here? I bet the entire cast and crew of *Wonder Woman* never spoke to a single local about what it was like to live here, which can't be that different from what it was like to have lived three hundred and whatever years ago.'

'Back at that last place, at the Benedictine abbey, which was more like a museum now, I asked the woman there what she thought about San Giuseppe da Copertino.'

'And?'

'At first I thought it was a language thing. I was probably mangling the pronunciation. And I'd switched to Italian mid-sentence. But she was lost. She got me to write my question down on a piece of paper, so I wrote, *San Giuseppe da Copertino, do you believe he could do everything the books say he could?*

'That grammar has *me* in knots.'

'I know, but she said, "Everything?" as if she didn't know *anything*, so I said, "Levitation", and mimed rising up. I even rolled out some Italian, "*Giuseppe volava?*" I learnt that in Copertino. Nothing. Total blank. This woman had no idea who he was.'

Mack nodded, scooped up the last of her gelato. 'And what did you learn from this exchange?'

'I don't know, but I suspect you have the perfect gaming metaphor.'

'No, seriously. You think this means talking to locals is a waste of time, don't you? Well, I think that exchange is worth more than every photo you've taken so far.' She levelled her finger accusingly at the lens cap of the XC, which was back to hanging from his neck.

He straightened, grew a couple of inches, asked: 'How often do you and Kari talk?'

She pushed the rim of her gelato cup together and folded the corners in as if she was changing a diaper. 'She was the one who sent the friend request.'

'So she just bitches about me, is that it? How I'm a— a massive bummer, right?'

'No. Hardly.' She placed the folded cup on the wall, looked out across the gully. 'I mean, she *was* curious about me and you. Can you blame her? I had quite the online presence, even then. And what was it Gianluca said? You are not very forthcoming. Even with your wife, babe. So she took it into her own hands. But that was ages ago. Water under the bridge.'

'How long?'

She shrugged. 'Couple of years.'

'What do you talk about now then, if it's not me?'

'For someone with the benefit of growing up with a sister and a female best friend, you are so clueless about women. We're friends. We talk. It's like the chats you and I have, except I don't feel like I'm drawing blood. We don't need to diarise anything, don't need an agenda.'

It was Duncan's turn to put his hands on the wall, pretend to be transfixed by the man-made caves. 'Do you talk about porn?'

'Not much.'

'Do you tell her what I tell you?'

'For starters, I'm not your shrink, Duncan. There's no doctor–patient privilege here. But no, I try not to land you in it. And it's not all about you, all right? Jesus. You are the topic of conversation maybe five percent of the time.'

'Have you told her about our accident yesterday?'

'No. Have you?'

'How did you know to call me that morning, after my blunder with the Chromecast? Did Kari talk to you?'

She looked him square in the eyes.

'Fuck,' he said. 'And what about this? Did she want you to come with me?'

'That's not the whole—'

'Why did you even keep it a secret from me? That you guys were best buds?'

'I don't know. It started out a little cloak and dagger. Kari thought you'd be upset, like she didn't trust you.'

'She didn't!'

'She might have trusted you, but what about me? She was doing her due diligence on *me*. Seeing if she needed to worry about *me*.'

'And does she? Do I? Why are you here? Because the only options still standing are a) to spy on me for my wife or b) to pull the final thread and be there to watch as my life unravels completely. This trip, my career, my marriage.' He looked up. 'Have you spoken to Zeb?'

'Why is that important?'

'It is. To me.'

'Once or twice. She Skypes me at night, mostly, when you're at that fucking restaurant. She's lonely, babe. Sometimes Zeb's still up. He's a cool kid.'

'He's—' His index finger was in her face. He retracted it, turned away. 'Fuck!' he screamed out across the valley. Half a dozen pigeons pushed off from unseen roosts beneath him and flapped into the sunlight.

He swung back to face her. 'Is there even a gap between tournaments right now, or was that a lie too?'

'You may be slow, babe, but you get there in the end.'

ABOUT US

He found Mack asleep on one of the two queen-sized beds in their room in Altamura. He'd returned from staking out three churches and a piazza menaced by a family of reintroduced falcons. There was at least an hour left before the sun set. He looked for something to graunch. The curtains were open, the window thrust up for a non-existent breeze. He went back downstairs, to the stash of individually packaged *cornetti* in reception, and found that the proprietors, an impossibly young couple, had added a tray of homemade pizza cut into rectangles in the two minutes since he was last there. He looked up at the CCTV camera. On cue, the door to the couple's apartment opened. The guy, Silvano, emerged.

'Please,' he said, gesturing at the pizza. 'Freshly made.'

'Thank you,' Duncan said, taking a napkin and a slice, suddenly starving.

'You are a filmmaker?' Silvano said. 'I Googled you.'

Stunned out of his hunger, Duncan lowered the pizza from his lips. How many other hosts had Googled him? Maybe it was only the young ones. One thing he knew: no one had yet turned him away because of his connection to Second Wave. Gullible sorts might fear he'd blow up their place and reclaim it for Mother Earth. But Silvano, Duncan thought, was too young to garble the wisdom of the internet in such a paranoid, self-centred, Boomerish way.

'I am,' Duncan said.

'Are you here for work?'

'You could say that.'

'I'm sorry, I have not watched your movie yet, but we will tonight.'

'You don't have to.'

'It sounds interesting.'

'Maybe.' He took a bite of the pizza. The base was already a little soggy, the cheese vulcanising, but there was something in the sauce, some herb, that pushed an involuntary *Mmm* from his lips.

Silvano smiled. 'Can I ask what your new project is?'

'How old are you?'

'Sorry?'

'How old are you? You seem quite young to have your own B&B with— How many rooms are in this place?'

'Five.'

'Five rooms!'

'I am twenty-eight. Joanna is twenty-four.'

'You are married?'

'Two years.'

'And this place?'

'We had a spare room in our apartment which we began renting through Airbnb. We bought this place at the end of last year. Well, the bank, mostly. But the two of us, uh, I'm sorry, my English is not so good.'

'It's great. You should hear my Italian.'

'Thank you.'

'The two of you did up this place?' Duncan offered. 'Remodelled?'

'Precisely.'

Duncan smiled. He'd never said the word 'Precisely' in that way — he wasn't a detective in a Sherlock Holmes knock-off. But it pleased him to hear it from Silvano, to think there were alternative universes where all the English Duncan had forsaken found a home, free of irony or menial imitation.

'Tell me,' he said, 'do you go to church here?'

Silvano looked worried, as if he'd misheard.

'Are you religious?' Duncan asked.

'I have not been to church since my wedding.'

'That's fine. Me neither. I mean, I've been inside of a lot of churches the last few days, but only for work. Do you know San Giuseppe da Copertino? Saint Joseph of Copertino?'

'Um.'

'Patron saint of aviators, astronauts and students?'

'*Allora*. Um.'

'He could levitate. Lift off the ground, you know, like this.' Duncan raised his arms out, tiptoed back to the stairs, stepped up one, then another, pretended to float. He stayed like that and took a bite of pizza.

Silvano laughed.

'He levitated a lot,' Duncan said through his mouthful, 'so they say. The books. The people in books.'

'The church likes that sort of thing.'

'Yes and no. I mean, this was back in the 1600s, during the Counter-Reformation.' He stepped back down to Silvano's level, could feel another Schmaltzy Uncle riff coming on, as if his host was some helpless Lawson type and he was the expert on San Giuseppe — a *believer* — but the train kept rolling. 'The Inquisition was all guns blazing on heresy, witchcraft. Same guys that went after Galileo. Rome was worried about anything that pushed the Bible further down the pecking order, that might make them look ridiculous in the eyes of the monarchs of Europe who might swing Protestant, or *had* swung but could just as easily be persuaded to swing back. San Giuseppe, he would go into raptures just about any time he said Mass. That was problematic. Better to keep that showbiz razzle-dazzle under wraps, only use it when you need to pull out all the stops, like they did with Giuseppe and Prince Casimir, who later became King of Poland. But most of the time, better to hide him in the mountains. That's why we're heading up to Pietrarubbia and Fossombrone. You know those places?'

Silvano was smiling broadly — the kind of smile Zeb had as he watched some brightly coloured cartoon before he went all in on *Aladdin* — but shook his head.

'Sorry,' Duncan said. 'I got carried away.'

'No, please.'

'Listen, I'd better go check on my friend. Do you mind if I take a slice for her?'

'Please.'

'And don't feel like you have to watch my movie.'

'Okay.'

Duncan wasn't sure how to take this 'Okay'. Had Silvano been waiting for an out? His host had now sat down at his desk and was typing something into his computer, relieved of any duty to watch Duncan's misunderstood masterpiece, his massive cherry-popping face-plant.

Back in the room, Mack was sitting up, rubbing the back of her head. From where Duncan stood, he could see right through the large opening of her t-shirt sleeve to her grey sports bra.

'Pizza from Silvano?' He held out the slice.

'Bloody legend.'

'Me or Silvano.'

'Silvano, of course.'

'But I levitated for him. May have had a little help from the staircase, but still. Thought you'd be proud.'

'Oh babe, you know I am.' She chomped down on the pizza, spoke through her mouthful. 'This is amazing. Cold pizza, gamer heaven. Do I detect anchovies?'

'Maybe.'

'Hey, sorry about before. In Matera. And talking to Kari behind your back, I guess.'

'I don't like having the rug pulled, is all. Silver lining: I get to grill you about Kari. No doctor–patient privilege, right?'

'What about the Sisterhood?'

'Of the travelling yoga pants?'

'So we're good? Day Two is officially in the books?'

'For me it's Day Four, but yeah.'

Her phone vibrated and she looked at the screen. 'I haven't told Gianluca about our accident.'

'Why would you?'

'We've been messaging. He asked how you were with the driving.'

'Okay, then why *wouldn't* you tell him about the accident? I'll never see that guy again.'

'His son? Ah.' She folded the soiled napkin in half and half again.

'What?'

'You'd left by then.'

'What? His son died in a car accident? I figured it was something, you know, congenital.'

Mack stood, began to walk toward the rubbish bin. 'Tough wee man. Spent his last three months in hospital before . . .'

'God.'

'Or not, as the case may be.' She was standing at the open window, the curtains billowing either side of her in a new breeze.

Duncan could feel another *Interstellar* discombobulation coming on, the elastic band pulling him back through Gianluca's downsizable house, back into his puddle of gloop. He tried fighting it, scrabbling for something — a door frame, a candlestick, any handhold or keepsake that'd thwart the surge of premature grief. He hadn't lost his son. But he *had* flown to the other side of the world. He *was* missing two weeks of Zeb's life for the sake of this mission upon which the fate of the planet did not rest in the slightest.

'I keep having these dreams,' he said. The curtains dropped. All was still. 'Where I'm flying.'

Mack turned, smiling. 'At least your subconscious is taking this job seriously.'

'I mean, I feel like I used to have these dreams all the time when I was a kid. But I'd forgotten them. My subconscious had misplaced the script. But now they're back.'

'Flying how?'

'Like swimming, sort of. As if the air is suddenly thick and I'm just that bit lighter than it and I can breaststroke through the rooms of this empty mansion.'

Mack returned to the bed, folded her legs yoga-style.

'But everyone has flying dreams,' he said. 'Don't they? Don't you?'

'Sure, I guess. But this is like when you were a kid, how? Like the dream is some kind of serial and these are different episodes?'

'Mm.'

'So the roots must be in your childhood.'

'I'm not asking you to analyse my dreams.'

'I know.'

'It's not a mystery to be solved.'

'I know.'

'I'm just sharing.'

'I *know*.'

'Then?'

'Last night, when I came back from the bakery, were you—?'

'Yup. Dreaming that dream.'

She got up on to her knees. 'Did you ever watch *My Secret Identity*?'

'Doesn't ring a bell.'

'Sure you did. You must've. A young Jerry O'Connell lives next door to this mad scientist and gets superpowers. I think he got hit by some ray gun his neighbour was developing.'

'Was he kind of bald, the neighbour?'

'Yeah, I think so.'

'I think I do remember that.' He took a seat on the edge of the bed.

Mack continued talking over his shoulder.

'And young Jerry, whatever his character's name was, could fly.

Except it was like you describe. He just kind of floated in the air. I don't remember him breaststroking, but I do remember he used aerosol cans to move around, like a capsule docking to a space station.'

'That's right!'

She reached over to her phone. 'Here,' she said, crawling closer to where he sat, 'check this out.' She boosted the volume. A theme tune, something about it being more than a dream come true. And there was Jerry O'Connell in baggy red pyjamas and the last of his baby fat, three feet off the mattress, grappling with mustard-yellow bedsheets. Then he was upright, fanning his hands, but slowly floating up and up until he bumped his head on a light fitting. Cut to him looking up from a comic book, mouth agape. *Pippi Boccaperta*.

'There's the ray,' she said. 'Huh, the neighbour wasn't bald. Look at that head of hair. Ooh, ooh, aerosols.'

Jerry O'Connell, bare chested, was taking off thanks to two cans of air freshener.

O'Connell must've been fourteen or fifteen when this was made. How old was Duncan when he'd seen it? When had his dreams begun? Had this show started these dreams or mutated the dream-flying he'd already been doing?

'Marsha Moreau,' Mack said, reading the credit for the dark-haired girl, the apparent love interest. 'Where is *she* now? You right there, Duncan?'

'I'm just— It's a bummer that all this thinking about a levitating saint, and this is what my subconscious dredges up. Like all I've got to go on, all my raw materials, are from bad American kids' shows.'

'I think it was Canadian.' She pressed her finger to the screen, hesitating a moment before scrolling down to the comments. The second thread was dedicated to people jumping on someone who claimed the show represented an *old fashioned America that would never return*. 'Yep, Canadian.'

'Scroll down a bit more.'

'Is that ever a good idea?'

'Please?'

She reached the fourth comment thread and stopped.

> *This show is the reason i cant fly fast in my*
> *dreams :(lol*
> *JuseBeats • 3 years ago*

> *holy shit! you just made me realize that. this*
> *show ruined everything!*
> *Dimitri's Photography • 2 years ago*

The two of them spent the rest of the evening tunnelling into the internet, each on their own phone, changing position now and then, watching clips from *My Secret Identity*, taking their phones with them when they needed to pee, figuring out when the show was made (1988–91), how old that made Jerry O'Connell in the pilot (14), what happened to Marsha Moreau (KNOWN FOR: *MY SECRET IDENTITY* — ERIN CLEMENTS; *DEAD RINGERS* — RAFFAELA; *BABAR* — ADDITIONAL VOICES), what David Cronenberg was working on now — on and on, adjacent and alone, until Duncan found himself on Mille Fiori's website.

He'd expected a page of daisy-chain and hemp-shirt-wearing hippies rocking on to their tiptoes with screwed-up eyes, but the landing page — black background, floral logo with 'English' and 'Italiano' beneath — looked slick, commercial, as if maybe it was an online florist. To look at the bottom half of the logo you would think it was simply three concentric circles, white lines against the black, but in the upper half the lines jagged to form three points. Three petals. Without knowing the name of the community, he might have read the image as a stylised flame, or a crown, or perhaps a chubbier Bart Simpson. On closer inspection, the logo was made by two interlinking loops, a single teardrop and a more complex shape with a twist in the middle that formed the outer and inner tracks of the lower section. As he mentally pulled the two loops apart, he found the top of the more complex shape formed an M, the Roman numeral for one thousand — though maybe he was doing what cultish-types were wont to do: finding meanings where there had only been ambiguity.

He pressed 'English' and a menu appeared. He selected 'About Us' and was presented with three videos. The first kicked off with an image of an undulating patchwork of pastures and crops, the foreground bowed in, thanks to the use of a fisheye lens. The video panned to the right and began to zoom in. The sun was setting out of frame, casting the hills beyond the fields as silhouettes. White text dissolved in to announce 'WELCOME TO MILLE FIORI'. Through Duncan's earbuds, the voiceover began, a woman's voice this time, at home in both English and Italian:

'Located in the Most Serene Republic of San Marino, in the municipality, or *castello*, of Domagnano, in the plains below Mount Titano, you will find the growing community of *Mille Fiori*, or The Thousand Flowers, living in harmony with the local Sammarinese while pursuing better ways.'

As she spoke, the Ken Burns effect was put through its paces, enlivening photos of what must have been the castle on Mount Titano, a hundred or so people in brightly coloured t-shirts standing on a street with their heads cocked up to the photographer, a field of wildflowers, a prematurely grey-haired woman in a floral tunic and loose linen pants shaking hands with a hunched-over old man in a fusty brown suit. The woman reminded Duncan of his mother-in-law, Teresa. The way her outfit exuded joy and comfort to such a degree it was, in fact, a production. A counterweight to other consumerist sins. Although this grey-haired woman was not harking back to her hippie childhood. She was living it.

He shot a glance at Mack, who looked up.

'What are *you* watching?' she asked.

'Nothing.'

She got up to look over his shoulder. 'Hello!'

He shrugged, ripping the jack from his phone and removing his earbuds.

'Mille Fiori,' the voiceover continued, now broadcast to the hotel room, with a rhythm somewhere between overwrought political speech and amateur hypnotist, 'is an open and fluid collection of experts and enthusiasts in various scientific, theological, artistic and fantastical fields, all of us united by the pursuit of evidence. Evidence that human capacities are greater than the predominant twenty-first-century rational, materialist world view would have you believe. We are open to all. We welcome all. We invite you to explore our website, our videos and other resources.'

The logo appeared.

'Total cult,' Duncan said.

'That was only the first one, right? Keep going.'

'It's really bad, though. I mean, that video was put together by someone who's seen way too many induction videos. I feel like any second they're going to drop a six-step guide to coping with grief.'

'You don't have to critique it as a piece of cinema, babe. Keep. Going.'

The second video was called 'The history of Mille Fiori', and explained how the community had 'grown organically' since the mid-2000s 'as people were attracted to the goals and aspirations of James Alby-Cooper'. So that was the name of the guy in the 'Why Levitation?' video. There was no photo of Alby-Cooper to accompany the utterance of his name in this video, however. A deliberate ploy, no doubt, to keep him enigmatic.

The aloof mystic.

The shadowy founder.

And it was working. At least, Duncan was reminded of his initial curiosity about how a New Zealander had founded a cult in San Marino. Perhaps that was the story here. He wasn't being asked to mangle Uffy's itinerary to watch some airheads try to levitate; his next project had landed in his lap: a guerrilla documentary about Alby-Cooper. A day or two of footage, an interview with the man, the connection between subject and filmmaker, vehicle and tenor — that could be something to build around.

It could also come to nothing.

And there wasn't a day or two to spare.

One thing was clear: he didn't have thoughts like this back in LA. If he said no to this opportunity, when would he feel this internal chest tornado again?

But a cult? Really?

Beyond the reference to Alby-Cooper, the video was light on historical information, instead lapsing back into the idiom of a recruiting video: the loaded pronouns, the smiling faces, the utter lack of specifics.

'We are a community built on questioning, but also the pursuit of evidence.'

Pah!

'Many come to us with an open mind, thanks to experiences they have had, but we also welcome sceptics.'

Just you wait!

The third video, 'The Three Esses of Mille Fiori', was voiced by the same woman as the other two, but the tone was different, the language more garbled, as if it was the result of a poor machine translation.

'Life as a flower is supported by three pillars or, as we call them, "The Three Esses". The first is *Svago*, or "fun", "play", "sport".' A sudden explosion of images — people in fancy dress, people covered in mud, a group of musicians jamming on what looked like lutes, a tennis court with dozens of racket-wielding players either side of the net, and a barrage of other shots he couldn't compute — as if a stack of Polaroids had been thrown in his face. 'Through levity, we come closer.'

Closer to what? he thought.

'The second "s" is *Stendere*, which means "to reach" or "to spread".' A cycle of postcard-style images of supposed cult members in front of the Eiffel Tower and the Pyramids of Giza, on the edge of the Grand Canyon. 'By this,' the narrator continued, 'we mean extending our reach to others through initiatives such as our public workshops, but also remaining connected with life as it is led by those who have different goals to ourselves.

'The final "s" is *Sollevare* or "to lift", "to raise up".' The image of the cult members at the Grand Canyon came alive, the crowd stepping back to isolate one member, perhaps the same woman from the 'Why Levitation?' video. 'By exploring the ways in which we might lift ourselves, mentally, spiritually and physically, we hope to catalyse a positive upheaval for all of humanity.' The woman raised herself up and out beyond the lip of the canyon and hung in space.

There could have been a crane above her.

Any number of explanations.

The screen went black and that same logo appeared, the mash-up of a tulip and a bullseye.

'Boom,' Mack said from over his shoulder.

'The VFX were okay on that last one, I have to admit.'

'Mm-hm.'

'It's nuts though. They're all nuts.'

'And your quest isn't? Helping someone make a movie about a dude you don't believe could fly? Thinking that'll get you anywhere.'

'Maybe. So what?'

'Maybe you're holding on tight to the wrong rope.'

'Maybe.' He shrugged and the conversation petered out. It was late, they were both exhausted. But he didn't turn the lamp off beside him. He navigated through the rest of the content on the cult's website: a text version of 'The Three Esses', clips from visiting Sammarinese and Italian TV shows, a page dedicated to free public workshops with titles like 'Woodwork, heartwork, mindwork' and 'Foundations in weightlessness', phrases that made Duncan's skin contract around his skeleton as if he was being vacuum-packed.

He entered 'levitation' in the search box and found a single page, an orphan, unlinked to any other page and not featured on the site's navigation menu, with the 'Why Levitation?' video from YouTube. He put his earbuds back in and hit play again.

'You might ask: Why levitation? We ask: Why ever not?'

FUCK NAPLES

It was 10 p.m. in LA, but the absence of Zeb on the screen when Kari answered his Skype call still crushed him like a Porsche 911 hurtling over an empty soda can.

'How is he?' he asked.

'He's— I'm doing all right.'

'You getting cuddles?'

'Cuddles is something I am getting.'

'Clingy, huh?'

'And you?'

'No cuddling here.'

'I mean, you know—'

'Yeah, we, uh, it's all going swimmingly.'

'Swimmingly?'

'Precisely.'

'Duncan?'

'Uh-huh?'

'Everything all right?'

'Yes,' he said. 'Honestly. Sorry.' He'd begun to feel the build-up of Consequences Deferred as a pain behind his eyes. The things awaiting him when he made it to Rome and his location-scouting failures were laid bare to Motta. And then LA: the thing with the Chromecast and Kari secretly being best buds with Mack. Those two were connected, of course. Kari knew more than she was letting on, always had. But all he said was, 'I just thought you'd still be up. It's a big day ahead — *Napoli*! — and I wanted to check in. It's okay that I miss you, isn't it?'

'Of course. I like when you say it.'

'I miss you.'

'More.'

'I *miss* you.'

'Where's Mack?'

'Breakfast. Do you want to talk to her?'

'Nah.' He half-expected Kari's hand to shoot to the back of her head, begin ruffling, as if the tic was transmitted through friendship, but she was unmoved. Perhaps even forewarned.

'So, about that thing,' he said. 'The thing with the Chromecast.'

'Mm.' Kari leaned in. Her features filled the screen, became inscrutable, and another sequence from the life of San Giuseppe was zapped down into his brain from whatever alien craft was out there in the stratosphere, doling out inspiration at inopportune times. Like the other bursts, he saw it all — Giuseppe flagellating himself in his cell in Assisi, the trip to Rome, and the vision that broke his years of spiritual dryness — and trusted himself enough to suppress it so he could deal with Kari and then return to find this sequence as vivid and complete as when it first arrived.

'That was,' he said with great effort, as if hauling the words from a swamp, 'you know. There's no excuse. And—'

'Okay. It's okay. I mean, you're on my mom's shit list.'

'Yeah.'

'Look,' she said, leaning back, 'this isn't the best medium for this. Or the best time. You keep doing your thing for Motta, knock it out of the park, and we'll talk about your porn addiction when you get home.'

'It's not a—'

'Whatever it is.'

'Fine. I want that.'

'Fine. Good.'

'I miss you.'

'Yeah, you do.'

'And?'

'And I await your triumphant return.'

Mack returned to the room with *cornetti*, a large bottle of diet Coke and two miscellaneous items slowly turning the napkins in which they were bundled transparent. 'Fuck I love those guys.'

'Silvano and, uh—'

'Joanna.'

'I wasn't sure at first, but they're nice, eh?'

'So nice.'

'Hey Mack?'

'Yeah, babe?'

'Let's do it.'

'Do what, babe?'

'San Marino. Your cult.'

'*My* cult?'

'We'll skip Naples, take the autostrada up to Assisi today.'

'What about Naples?'

'Fuck Naples. There's only two places on the itinerary. San Lorenzo Maggiore and San Gregorio Armeno. We don't have any guides booked. I doubt anything looks like it did in the 1630s. We'd be better off looking in a library. If we need to go, we can do it after Rome. I can do it on my own dime, if necessary.' He didn't add that if Naples was really important the scene would come to him as another jolt.

'What brought this on?'

'Naples is, like, crazy for driving. I tried looking where to park. Like, maybe we could take the train in? But it was a logistical nightmare.'

'All this because you don't wanna drive in Naples?'

'I mean, it's a factor. But it's also an opportunity. You were right. I need to be able to offer Motta something extra, something unexpected. I'll make a little film of it, just for him. Life with the levitators. He won't care if I whiff on a couple churches. Uffy will, for sure. She'll try and use it against me. But maybe if we build up our accident to help explain missing Naples. Maybe we needed to take a day for repairs.'

'Or delayed shell shock.'

'Or repairs.'

'But this'll put us ahead of schedule, won't it?'

'That's where you come in. You're the Uffy to my Motta.'

'Bitch, why? Because I got a ponytail?'

'Because I have a driver's licence. It's about six hours to Assisi, that's if we take the toll roads. Plenty of time for the person in the passenger seat to make some phone calls.'

'But you know admin is not my forte. And, if such a thing is possible, my Italian is worse than yours.'

'You wanna meet the levitators, you gotta put your shoulder to the wheel.'

'This isn't my idea. You can't blame me if things go pear shaped.'

'I won't blame you.'

'So we're leaving now? For Assisi? And then San Marino, just like that—?' She clicked her fingers.

'Assisi, Pietrarubbia and *then* San Marino. Two nights, max.'

'Okay! I'll stop with the questions. God, it's good to see some passion and decisiveness.'

'Maybe you'll need to change my headstone?'

'Maybe.'

ASSISI

The only light in Giuseppe's cell comes from a small window. The only furniture: a pallet bed and a wooden cupboard.

We see him open the cupboard, shelve a book, remove a lash.

We hear leather striking the flesh of his shoulders, his back, but we see him hunched over his cupboard, forcing it into service as a writing desk.

Another book is shelved, a sponge removed.

Giuseppe kneels, reaches back to dab at self-inflicted wounds.

A restless night on his Spartan bed.

Soup and a hunk of bread sit atop the cupboard. He rips the bread in two, pushes the soup away until it falls to the floor.

Another letter composed to the sounds of flagellation.

The lash being returned to the cupboard.

A remnant of bread still sits atop the cupboard. A terracotta shard from his bowl rests on the floor.

Another letter.

A book returned.

Giuseppe on his knees, in prayer, in pain.

A cockroach scuttles across the top of the cupboard.

Giuseppe donning his hair shirt.

Wiping a tear from his cheek with the sleeve of his habit.

Writing a letter.

Sweeping crumbs from the cupboard, grumbling.

The swathe of light from the window moves slowly across the room to the sound of leather on flesh, quill scratches, inkwell clonks, fingers creasing paper.

The letters, the lash, the lamentations now cycle faster and faster until there is a knock at the door.

The saint, hunched over another letter, does not respond.

The door creaks.

'Father Giuseppe?' This confrere is perhaps a decade older than the saint, but well fed, rounded.

'If you have come to tell me of the death of one cardinal or another, do not torture me so. You know I haven't had a vision or any other kind of blessing since Palm Sunday.'

'I have no such news, my friend. Might you be in the midst of another request to return to Grottella?'

Giuseppe looks up for the first time, regards the man angrily.

'It is one thing, Brother Lodovico, for the custos to treat me with haughtiness and then contempt. To call me a hypocrite. For my confessor, that envious worm, to mock me openly. But to have tasted ecstasy and now have it withheld? How many years have we been in Assisi, so close to the *Poverello*? It is too much to be so near and yet feel at such a remove. If it is weakness to wish to return to Grottella, where I was not treated as a criminal and my ecstasies occurred daily, then I am weak a hundred times over.'

'Do I disturb your writing often, Father?'

'Thankfully not.'

'And thus might it be I have a reason to intrude now?'

'What is it?'

'You and I will take another journey?'

'Grottella?'

'No. The Father General has requested your presence in the Eternal City.'

'A welcome change, nonetheless. When do we leave?'

'We will be there for Lent.'

'No sooner? What did the Order say? Did it mention my letters?'

'No,' Lodovico says, 'but it does mention The Polish Prince—'

'I believe you mean Jesuit novice.'

'Your advice to Prince Casimir did not fall on barren ground. It merely required time to take root.'

'He will renounce his orders? Fulfil the destiny God has planned for him?'

'Perhaps. He requests another audience with you.'

'In Rome?'

'In Rome.' Lodovico nods and takes the saint's hands in his.

Lodovico and Giuseppe are on foot, leading two donkeys laden with provisions.

It is raining, the trail reduced to mud.

Now the sun is beating down. Giuseppe shakes the upturned canteen and the last drop of water falls to the earth.

The two friars and their donkeys reach the crest of a hill, and there is Rome, ten thousand wisps of smoke rising, mingling as one miasma above the decaying walls and arches, the resplendent dome of Saint Peter's.

The saint begins to chuckle.

'A welcome sound after so long an absence,' says his companion.

'Brother Lodovico,' says Giuseppe, 'I foresee that we will have to return to Assisi.'

Lodovico's shoulders drop. The lead for the donkey falls from his hand. Then he looks up, eyes filled with hope. 'A vision? You have seen it thus?'

Giuseppe nods. 'I await our return with glee. Even the scrape my pate shall receive from the ceiling of the basilica will be as nectar to my soul. And there I am,' he says, as if Lodovico can see what he sees in the smoke above Saint Peter's, 'begging the forgiveness of Saint Francis for ever wanting to leave.'

SIGN OF THE TIMES

Duncan selected one of his playlists to begin the trip to Assisi, as Mack would be on admin duties. Sharon Van Etten, Father John Misty, Destroyer — music from this century that could be played at an ambient volume. By the time they reached the on-ramp to Autostrada A14, Mack had sorted that night's accommodation and was on to Pietrarubbia. They blatted for three hours on the two- and three-lane Diamond League macadam motorway. The roading upgrade was like moving from a monastic cell to the cardinal's summer villa. Duncan was able to edge the volume up for Arboretum, Nadia Reid, Camp Cope. The Micra cruised at 120 kilometres an hour; locals passed them as if they weren't even moving. To their right, the banded, two-tone Adriatic: a dainty Tiffany blue nearest the shore and, stretching out to the horizon, the deep purplish-blue eyeshadow favoured by more than one of Duncan's primary school teachers. To their left — at first unseen, then a frame-filling, snowcapped presence — the Apennines. There was comfort in this mountain range, the sight of snow when it was approaching eighty-five degrees outside: an echo, perhaps, of the Southern Alps rising up from the Canterbury Plains as he drove home for Christmas, the shifts with one parent, then the other, sometimes pairing up with his sister, sometimes swapping places with her, as if they'd also divorced and couldn't possibly dine together without stabbing a fork into the rimu table and storming off to the woodshed.

After completing her rejig of Uffy's itinerary for Assisi and Pietrarubbia, Mack moved on to Mille Fiori.

'I'm emailing their comms person.'

'They have a comms person? What will you say?'

'That an award-winning filmmaker is interested in observing life in their community and learning more about their beliefs and practices.'

'Hm.'

'That's all true. I think they'll bite.'

'You gonna mention Motta? *Giuseppe*?'

'No. Should I?'

'No. Shouldn't we have emailed them before we committed to this?'

'Uh, yeah! But seeing as you only decided this morning that you'd rather do anything than drive in Naples—'

'I think maybe that whole *My Secret Identity* thing bummed me out. Like, I can't be angry about you and Kari being BFFs. Give me a week and I'll think it's great. But those dreams were my only real connection to Giuseppe, the saint and the film, and to have it laid out like that. That it's so . . . Typical. So mass produced.'

'So you're okay with that angle?' Mack asked.

'For the email to Mille Fiori? Like I'm Louis Theroux or something?'

'I'll give them a link to your IMDb profile, so don't literally pretend to be Louis Theroux. You do you. But maybe don't mention it might be for Motta's eyes only. They seem pretty keen on coverage.'

'Okay, but why would we give them only three days' notice?'

'I wasn't going to mention that. If they say, "Yes, come on up," then great. If they say, "Yeah, nah, we're too busy," then maybe we play the pathetic card. *But we've come so far!*' she said in a Droopy Dog voice. 'But trust me, they'll bite.'

★

They pulled into a service area north of Pescara to refuel the Micra, relieve their bladders, grab panini. The tables inside the Autogrill were all taken, so they returned outside with their sandwiches wrapped in greaseproof paper and walked along the line of vaping, texting teenagers perched on the low window ledge until they found a spot. E-cigarettes were popular with a certain set in LA, but it was on a different level in Italy. This was a nation, after all, that saw no difference between real and electronic votive candles.

Forget about the delivery mechanism; focus on the fumes, the chemical/spiritual kick.

They understood metaphor, Italians. Americans got so caught up on the vehicle — the flag, the anthem, the artillery — and so often forgot the tenor. And Duncan? Neither Italian nor American, he sat somewhere in the Pacific Ocean. Adrift. No vehicle, no fumes, no kick, but enough dumb pronouncements to sink an oil tanker.

He turned to look back inside the Autogrill. A group of teens had gathered beneath a TV screen that had been tuned to MTV Music. Maybe there was some breaking news. Another 9/11. He got up, walked as if in a trance toward the automatic doors, and re-entered the Autogrill. He could still hear music. There were no tears. The people waiting to order their food remained in line. The servers kept serving. Only the ten or so teenagers were transfixed by the screen. A localised disturbance caused by a music video. Duncan recognised the song — he'd heard it a couple times back in LA, and in almost every restaurant and cafe since arriving in Italy — but he hadn't yet seen the video.

On screen, Harry Styles was stranded on a barren, windblown coast in an oversized cashmere coat, skinny jeans and leather boots with a stacked heel. He sang his falsetto lines over the slow piano, holding his hand out to catch the breeze. Then came the wonky, ascending peel, echoing the blast-off in Bowie's 'Space oddity', and Styles stepped on to a mossy rock and launched himself into the air — Major Tom with no need of a tin can.

'Fuck,' Duncan said.

No one turned to look at him.

Harry Styles was floating over the slate-grey water, his flight clearly wire-assisted, but it was pleasing to see such an analogue form of deception, which meant it was no deception at all.

The song was in full symphonic swing now, the video cutting back and forth between a grounded Styles mouthing the lyrics and a miniature version being pulled across the sky by an unseen helicopter, though it could just have well been the heavenly puppeteer from the altar in Martina Franca. The same Almighty that yo-yoed Giuseppe in that godly mash-up of gift and grievance, prize and punishment.

'They're bloody everywhere,' Mack said at his shoulder. She took a bite of her panini, let the rest slide back into its wrapper and began folding.

'Huh?'

'Levitators. Floating Joe. Hovering Harry. Our friends in San Marino, from whom I just got a reply.'

Duncan stepped back from the teens, who were still transfixed by 'Sign of the times'. 'Already? And?'

'They'd love for Duncan Blake and his trusty assistant, Mack MacKinnon, to visit.'

He bundled her outside. 'What if they Google you?'

'When was the last time *you* Googled me?'

He looked at her and she at him. The silence broke her first. 'If they Google me, babe, they'll learn that, in addition to being too good a friend to an administratively challenged filmmaker, I'm also an influential broadcaster with two hundred and eighty thousand Twitter followers. The best lies, my friend, are true.'

'The best ones?'

They began to edge toward the Micra.

Mack: 'They'll put us up for two nights. We might even get separate rooms.'

'Just like that?'

'Just. Like. That.'

Duncan, turning the ignition: 'I guess this is where I say, thank you.'

'That'd be a start.'

'And after thank you?'

'Follow me on Twitter.'

'I already do.'

She narrowed her eyes, disbelieving. If he wasn't driving he would've got out his phone. He was sure he did follow her, though the longer he went without checking, the more doubt began to settle like snowflakes, one or two and then too many to count, blotting out his certainty.

After another hour on the autostrada they exited near Civitanova Marche, paid the toll — €27.10, which seemed steep, but they'd escaped the south, its failures and embarrassments, its no-shows and know-nothings, so maybe it was a bargain — and began heading inland on a *superstrada*. The highway was one notch down from the toll roads but must've cost a bomb to construct, as it went *through* the Apennines rather than over them thanks to a series of one- and two-kilometre-long *gallerie*, each with separate tunnels for east- and west-bound traffic. It was hard to tell where they were or how much longer the mountains would last, but at some point after Duncan had become accustomed to the gentle incline of the tunnels they entered a cascade of even longer, descending *gallerie*. Each time, the entrance and the exit dropped from view, leaving just the curved roof of the tunnel and a state dangerously close to vertigo. The lights zipping by in some jury-rigged seventies sci-fi warp drive effect. Ears and butt cheeks occupied by the rhythmic throb of the tyres over the frequent section joins. But every time Duncan felt like he was losing it — when it was as if they were a pebble being tipped out of a bottle and had no agency left — the *galleria* ended and he had five, ten, fifteen seconds of daylight, time to admire a stand of beech or an ancient chestnut, before plunging into the next wormhole.

Mack's phone told them to drive past the first exit marked 'Assisi', and the second. They took the third, which quickly became a narrow road with no centreline and almost no verge before the crops began — grapevines, dark-leaved vegetables — but it was clear they were headed in the right direction, as before them stood Assisi, the old town having melted halfway down the hill, leaving a green-fringed and potentially derelict tower at its apex. The town seemed to run from right to left, everything pointing to, and terminating at, the massive Sacro Convento, its rectangular form offset by the string of arches that formed each level, as if a cloistered courtyard had been flipped inside out, and, above that, the Basilica of St Francis.

The road ahead threaded through two postcard-perfect oaks. Duncan pulled over on the shoulder created by hundreds of like-minded tourist-photographers. Wheat, ripe for harvest to Duncan's uneducated eye, shimmered either side of the road. He imagined friars walking down the hill to tend these crops three and half centuries earlier, then flying back to the Sacred Convent à la Harry Styles when the day was done.

Photos taken, the GPS guided them up the hill until their path merged with a larger road dominated by orange buses. The buses diverted a short time later to be squared away in their freshly paved parking plaza, while Mack's phone urged the Micra on towards the Sacred Convent, then around and through an arched portal, and up a narrow street of souvenir shops and *gelaterie*.

'This can't be right,' Duncan said.

'You're fine. There's another car ahead of us. A buffer.'

Their buffer disappeared over a crest, and Duncan had to bring the Micra to a complete stop to let a quartet of nuns break ranks and press themselves against stone walls to allow the Micra through. Their expressions changed from tolerant to merciless when they saw its crumpled passenger side.

Duncan: 'We should have parked by the buses.'

'It's another four hundred metres to our hotel. I'm not lugging my bags that far uphill. Besides, they're all either tourists or pilgrims. Drive like you belong and you will.'

'Tell me how this is better than Naples.'

'It's actually quaint as a four-letter word, babe.'

'This hotel. Is it the same one Uffy booked?'

'No, that place looked so dull. It was also fully booked for tonight. So we're staying at, get this, a complex that specialises in religious conferences and meditation. *Cittadella Ospitalità*. It's got a Christian observatory chocka with reference material. There'll be lots of people to talk to.'

'If we can get there.'

'Look, it's getting more road-y.' Now, instead of shops and giddy nuns, it was apartments, parked cars and recycling bins.

'When we get to this hotel, or whatever it is, let's never leave.'

'Been there, done that,' Mack said.

An invitation to talk about her time as a shut-in. *Take it!*

But he was driving, at least two manoeuvres from that heavenly pin showing up on the map on Mack's phone. The device in his head didn't have the free RAM to run all the scenarios and walk it back to the best response.

'Your bedroom?' he managed, and cursed the dim-witted way it came out. He turned left into another alley.

'Forget it, babe. It was a bad joke.'

'No,' he said. 'I mean, I'm interested.'

He took another turn. Cittadella Ospitalità was ahead of them now, according to the phone.

'That's it,' she said. 'Where the flags are. Good job, Mr Blake.'

'Mack?'

'I said, forget it.'

DEUS EX

Was he responsible for Mack's stint as a shut-in? He'd always felt
some of the blame was his. If he had to pinpoint just what he'd
done, he'd guess the school ball in their final year of high school.
The New Zealand version of prom took place during winter, just
over the halfway point in the year, well clear of exams but long
enough into classes that the senior students could tap into well-
stocked reservoirs of premature nostalgia, change anxiety and last-
chance hysteria. Maybe she had expected them to go together —
just two friends who kept their genitals to themselves, seeking to
stave off the more profound embarrassments of not going at all, or
rejection, or accepting the overtures of someone you didn't fancy
and having to string them along until that period in the slow dance
where it's clear they want to kiss you and you must feign a sudden
thirst and disappear into the night. But he had asked his neighbour
Deedee James, Tara's younger sister, who was a year below them,
and she had said yes. Mack didn't know about his thing for Tara,
who by then had moved away for university, or about the contact
high he now got from the sister who had transformed over summer
from a grubby little kid into a Tara clone. If not Tara 2.0, then at
least Tara-Lite. He liked that she looked up to him. With a girl from
his year, he'd seem inexperienced, dorky. He knew Deedee had had
a crush on him at some point, maybe still did, but his window to
capitalise on this would be brief. So he took the leap, landed it, had

a fantastic month of hand holding, corsage purchasing, suit renting and generally acting like the guy Deedee thought he was. Maybe he was this guy, or could be full time. They went to movies. He bought her popcorn, peanut M&Ms, kissed her during *Star Wars Episode II*, moved to second base in the back of *Eight Legged Freaks*, told himself he didn't go further because she was younger and he was a gentleman. At the ball, they kissed some more during slow dances and on the bench seats behind Mr Mears, who was making a big show of policing the punchbowl from would-be spikers but in hindsight had to have known what his favourite movie buff and the buff's ingénue were up to.

Mack didn't go to the ball but she was at Carl Amon's after party.

'Hey, Mack,' he said, one arm around Deedee, the other brandishing the hip flask of bourbon he'd retrieved from the bushes near school. 'I didn't know you were coming.'

'That so, babe?'

'Maybe I forgot.'

'Deedee,' she said, smiling at his date.

'Hi,' Deedee said. She knew Mack. Had watched over their shoulders as the two best friends played *Deus Ex*. But she was no longer the annoying neighbour kid with spaghetti sauce on her chin.

Mack leaned in close to Deedee's ear to whisper something, then left.

'What'd she say to you?' he asked.

'She just, like, breathed into my ear.'

'Gross.'

'I guess.' Deedee tilted her head as if to tip Mack's ethanol-rich breath back out, but when Duncan looked up he saw Olly Price, hands on hips, smiling at his date.

Half an hour later, his window with Deedee had closed, Olly's had opened and the volume of his hip flask was found wanting. After a brief search, he requisitioned a half-empty bottle of Wild

Turkey from a wall cabinet that looked off limits but wasn't locked. 'Moral hazard?' he said to the room, as if he'd been asked a question in Economics, a subject he hadn't taken for a couple of years but still received grillings about from Ms Kinney in the occasional dream. No one took any notice of him.

He found Mack in a bedroom playing *Tony Hawk's Pro Skater 2*. Five other kids, all male, were watching in awe as she linked flip and grab tricks with grinds and flatland manuals. Each new element added a multiplier to the score.

x10, x11, x12

Duncan went to the rack of games beside the TV. 'Why are you playing this when Carl's got *Tony Hawk 3*?'

'He's got *Tony Hawk 4*, too,' said Carl Amon himself, holding up the case for the game.

'Shit, didn't see you there.'

'It just came out,' Carl said, and waggled the case.

'And so?' Duncan said, lightly pinching Mack's triceps.

x20, x21, x22

'I like the soundtrack,' she said over the shouty chorus of Powerman 5000's 'When worlds collide'. 'It relaxes me.'

'Eric Koston?' Duncan asked, taking a stab at which skater she was using.

'*Psh*,' she said. 'Steve Caballero.'

The time counter was flashing *0:00* in red but Mack's trick sequence was still alive.

x28, x28.5, x29

Duncan looked at the others, who were leaning forward, their jaws tight, eyes bugged. He knew Carl, of course, and recognised the other four, but faintly, as if he'd stumbled into his school's twenty-year reunion, had lost their names and notorieties in the course of his stunning rise to fame, fortune and infinite pussy.

x33, x34, x34.5

'To the end of high school,' he said, and swigged from the bottle. It burned but he kept the sensation to himself.

'Shut up, dude,' someone said. Not Carl. Definitely not Mack.

'She can do this in her sleep,' Duncan said.

x37, x38

'Grind?' another voice said.

'Multiple scorgasms?'

'Turning tricks?'

He turned back to them, expecting snivelling Dick Dastardly expressions, but their faces were blank, if still bug-eyed. It was force of habit, unconscious. This recourse to sex. This retreat from intercourse.

x40, x41, x42

She was right there. And they were saying these things. The best self-defence is a bad offence.

x43, x44

And he was right there too.

x45, x46

But Deedee and Olly. They were elsewhere.

The song ended. The whiny guitar and rim clicks of Papa Roach's 'Blood brothers' began.

x46.5

x47

Mack's skater landed a trick, slid to a stop, lifted his board up, and stood there panting while the seven-figure trick score fed into the run score in the top left-hand corner of the screen.

'What happened?' one of the nameless virgins asked, almost in tears.

'The song,' she said. 'I was hoping for Lagwagon.'

'Faaaar,' exclaimed another.

'That game is ruined for me now,' a third said. 'That *franchise*.' He stood and straightened his bow-tie.

'Where'd you get the drink?' Carl asked.

Mack selected a new level and started another impossible string of tricks to the sound of Bad Religion.

'Hey, Duncan, I'm talking to you.'

'This?' he said. 'Olly Price gave it to me.'

'Give it here, man.'

Duncan took another swig. 'What about one for the champ?' He wiped the mouth of the bottle with the shimmering viscose lining of his rented jacket, hung it down in front of Mack's face. To his surprise, she hit pause, grabbed the bottle, drank, passed it to Carl, and went back to her game.

'Fuck you guys,' Carl said, and left the room.

'Fuck Olly Price,' Duncan corrected. 'I hear it's all the rage.'

Mack's new score continued to mount. The band of gawkers began to slip away for refills or reprieve from Duncan's drunken maundering until it was just the three of them: him, Mack and Steve Caballero.

'You wanna play?' she asked, mid-run, eyes fixed to the screen.

'Olly fucking Price.'

'I'll take that as a no.'

'I'm gonna die a virgin, aren't I?'

The next morning he felt every blood vessel in his forehead, couldn't remember how he got home. At school on Monday people kept telling him how drunk he'd been, as if it was a badge of honour. No one mentioned Deedee James, not to his face. Maybe it never registered that they'd been an item. Had no one seen them pashing behind the punchbowl?

Mack didn't mention Deedee, his inebriation or her talent at an overtaken console's skateboarding game. They talked about other things: schoolwork, *Age of Empires*, which classmates were going to which universities. She still called him 'babe', agreed to let him film another of her monologues to round out his latest film. They still hung out at his dad's place on weekends, as schedules allowed — Mack being her typical unfiltered self, grilling Blake Senior about parenthood, thwarted ambition and divorce — until Duncan moved down to Dunedin and she didn't go anywhere.

DAY FOR NIGHT

He made the early morning walk alone, back through the heart of Assisi and the glorified footpaths he'd guided the Micra up the afternoon before. He was on his way to the Basilica of Saint Francis for the tour Mack had managed to move forward by two days but that she herself would not attend.

Late yesterday he'd walked up to the Rocca Minore, a small, abandoned castle at the eastern point of the city walls. He'd taken the mandatory shots of the sun setting through the small olive grove in the lee of the ancient wall, that same submerging sun backlighting the equally abandoned Rocca Maggiore. As a filmmaker all you have to tell a story are sight and sound, the visuals limited to what can be caught on camera and shown on a screen somewhere between the size of a business card and the side of a building. But sunsets are one occasion when cameras put human optics to shame. Through the XC's display, Assisi at dusk was a feast of chilling blue and fiery orange, silhouettes and lens flare, until he started thinking of adders in the long grass, hidden hypodermics, and muggers crouched like gargoyles atop the crumbling wall, and he bumbled back to the street-lit cobblestones. Had he always been so neurotic? Such a chickenshit? No way. He'd been fearless. He'd made his own feature film without financing and taken it to festivals on three continents. Then he became a father and Second Wave broke and Hollywood sucked him in. Maybe he should have been more scared? More cautious? Maybe he finally understood responsibility?

He came now to the barricades that signalled the start of queuing for the Basilica of Saint Francis. It must've been too early for the average pilgrim, because the two military guards let him amble past their checkpoint without breaking stride. He walked along the colonnade, which was how this covered walkway was described on Uffy's itinerary though he'd have used his new favourite word, *cloister*, then on past a barefooted, hunchbacked beggar and the emphatically closed door to the Sacred Convent to a spot a few yards from the entrance to the basilica. A man in a black polo shirt was handing out audioguides and headphones. Duncan was glad he wouldn't need to rely on a canned voice through a cheap headset. His tour, according to Uffy, was to be led by a Franciscan friar who lived at the convent. He stood back from the tourists fumbling with their audioguides, and eyed the door to the convent from where he guessed his guide would emerge.

'Excuse me,' the man in the black polo called out. 'Are you Duncan Blake?' He held up his clipboard, pointed at a page.

'Uh, that's me.'

'You are my number ten.' He didn't sound Italian. He could have been from Spain, or Mexico, or East LA.

'Pardon?'

The other tourists parted. Duncan stepped forward. The embroidered logo on the man's shirt was a dense heraldic shield atop crossed keys. He worked either for the city or the church.

'You're the last one on the list for the first tour of the day.' The man held out an audioguide.

'Ten people?' Duncan asked, letting another penny drop. 'You don't offer personalised tours, do you?'

'Our guides are English-speaking friars and sisters who have an intimate knowledge of Assisi and the basilica. They can answer any question you have. And with groups of no more than ten, you will be free to ask.'

'And this?' Duncan said, finally taking the audioguide.

'Supplementary information. Only if you want it.'

'Okay,' he said, and pictured himself bending over to let Uffy spank him once more. *He sent you to Italy, man!* WHACK! *You're going to play tourist* — WHACK! *and you're going to like it* — WHACK! *and tell Frank when you see him how grateful you are* — WHACK! *A no talent bum* — WHACK! *sent tripping around Italy on his dime.* WHACK!

'Sorry,' he said, conscious now of the number of eyes on him. 'I didn't book this myself.'

'That's fine, sir,' the guy said in his serene, hospitality voice, the kind insiders knew meant he was sticking pins in a mental voodoo doll. 'Just a reminder that no photographs are permitted within the basilica.' He nodded at the XC in Duncan's hand. 'But you'll have a great time. Look, here comes Father Nilton now.'

Behind the approaching friar, through the open door, Duncan caught a brief glimpse of people inside the convent.

No photos? Did Uffy know this? There was still a lot he could capture: the itinerary's list of important dimensions, light readings, and his own list of impressions and potential scenes to block out *in situ*.

'My group!' Father Nilton said, as if they were grunts and he a drill sergeant. He was short but broad shouldered, the kind of build for which a friar's habit does no favours. His face was ruddy, his hair thick and black like a plastic figurine's. Filipino? Peruvian? When did friars stop with the tonsuring? 'My group, we will go into the Lower Basilica first.' He waved for them to follow. Walked as quickly as he spoke. Duncan jogged to reach his side.

'Will we go into the convent?' he asked.

'There?' The friar indicated behind him without turning to look. 'Why would you want to go in there?'

'To see where San Giuseppe da Copertino lived for fourteen years,' he said, thinking of Giuseppe writing his letters pleading to be sent back to Grottella. 'Or at least the small apartment that was set up next to the Chapter Room,' he said, reciting now from Uffy's itinerary, 'where memories of that time are still preserved.'

Father Nilton stopped, stood on tip-toe to grab Duncan's upper arm. Smiling broadly, squeezing Duncan's bicep, he said, 'You will be the troublemaker in my group, I see.'

Those within earshot laughed.

The friar took them inside, let everyone's eyes tip up in wonder, then bundled them to one side of the entrance and began talking in one hushed tumble. 'My name is Father Nilton and I am from Bolivia and I have lived in Assisi for six years.' He held up that many digits. 'This is a living, breathing church. This Lower Basilica was begun in 1228, immediately after Saint Francis was canonised, and completed just two years later. From then until now, every day people come inside to pray, for Mass, to reconnect with the saint, with God, there are many weddings, but none this morning, lucky for you, so please be respectful by being silent, and when you can't be silent, be whispering. No photos or video are allowed but at the end of the tour there is a gift shop where you can buy all the photos you'd ever hope to have taken, but in focus —' he smiled a stagey smile — 'so you are free to experience this holy place in the moment and not worry about shutter speeds or selfies. We will shortly go down into the tomb of Saint Francis, but follow me and I will tell you about the two most important artists: Cimabue and Giotto.'

Throughout this preamble Duncan was casting his eyes around the church, which was unlike anything he'd seen. The ceiling was low, giving the space the cave-like feel of the restaurant in Copertino, except instead of exposed brick, every inch of wall and ceiling was painted, every arch and cornice had its own playful frieze, every other surface teemed with figures, all leaning this way and that with the curvature of the space, and backed either by gold leaf — given texture by slow centuries of decay — or that same deep, nocturnal eyeshadow he'd seen yesterday in the Adriatic as it touched the horizon. This blue stood in for the earthly sky and the heavens, but this was no daytime blue, this was some other way of seeing colours. Like the old filmmakers' trick of day for night, this blue stood in for the eternity of black, or white — whatever end of the colour spectrum your spirituality took you. He recalled the tunnels from yesterday, the sensory overload. Here was another tunnel, the arched ceiling, the riot of decoration that seemed a greater prompt for seizures than any *Power Rangers* battle scene. Was this how Giuseppe felt in every church? Overcome. Over-extended. Was this the sudden rush of critical errors that brings forth the blue screen of death? That shuts down consciousness while the body writhes or rises?

'It's something, huh?' said a man with the skull of a bighorn sheep on his belt buckle.

'It sure is,' Duncan said.

'Come on.' The man jerked his head in the direction of the others. 'I get the impression Father Nelson don't appreciate stragglers.'

Duncan didn't correct his new friend. Maybe he was the one who'd heard wrong. Nelson or Nilton. When you hear hooves, think horses, not zebra.

Their guide was explaining Cimabue's style with reference to the painting of the Virgin Mary and Saint Francis on the transept wall. How it was painted in 1280 and was probably the nearest likeness of the saint. How the static style contrasted with the livelier frescos of Giotto.

'According to Giorgio Vasari,' Father Nilton said, 'Cimabue was the one who discovered Giotto when he was a shepherd boy drawing pictures of his sheep on a rock. Cimabue took him on as an apprentice on the spot. You will see shortly how far Giotto surpassed his teacher, but spare a thought for Cimabue. This image —' he fluttered his hand back toward the Virgin and the Saint — 'was the best anyone had seen in its time, though *its time* was soon eclipsed.' Like Motta and me, thought Duncan, at once a bitter quip and a trying on of renewed hopefulness. Maybe the film he'd make in San Marino would set him back into orbit. 'Unlike many,' Nilton continued, 'Cimabue lived to see this eclipse. Vasari tells the story of the time Cimabue left his workshop and Giotto chose to paint a fly on the nose of a figure. When the master returned, he tried several times to brush off the fly before he realised his mistake and that he was no longer the master.'

'What would this place have looked like in the 1600s?' Duncan asked, careful to whisper.

'Come, troublemaker,' Father Nilton, said, manhandling him again, 'I will give you all the dates, but Giotto awaits.'

The group crossed into the right transept, and Nilton directed their attention to a fresco of the crucifixion on the ceiling. He pointed out the despair on the faces of the *serafini*, the way one tore at its cheeks, another ripped open its tunic.

Duncan moved closer to the man with the bighorn belt buckle. 'I don't think the good Father likes to deviate from his script.'

'Mm-hm,' the man said, and rocked on to his tip-toes to better see the guide.

They spent another five minutes being led around the basilica before they reached the entrance to the crypt. No matter how much Duncan had pestered, every time he mentioned Giuseppe that smile returned to Father Nilton's face, and he'd turned and led the group to the next painting. Now he was delivering his spiel about not talking at all down there, the story of Brother Elias hiding the body of the saint for its protection in 1320, how it remained hidden until 1818. He promised to explain the life of the saint using the fresco cycle somewhere else, barely whispering now, taking his first steps down into the crypt.

Duncan was one of the last to descend and did so in silence, thinking of the stories of Giuseppe sneaking into the basilica at night to pray before the image of the Virgin that reminded him of the one at Grottella, then slipping down into the crypt to hang with the venerated body of Saint Francis. How did this gel with the fact Francis's resting place remained hidden for another hundred and fifty years? Perhaps Giuseppe had felt his forebear's presence, pressed his head to the floor of the nave — how would this play on screen? Perhaps Duncan had misread, or misremembered, the histories, or had misheard Father Nilton. His passage into the crypt was slow, held up by those ahead of him, all of them either too old or too religious to descend at a reasonable pace. He'd seen images of Giuseppe's crypt in Osimo, the saint supine in his glass coffin, a black-robed Snow White, arms folded across his chest, hands and face covered with silver. But he saw now that Francis was entombed in stone at the centre of the room, his octagonal resting place surrounded by iron latticework.

The tour group filed around the tomb, though there was little to see, little to feel, until Duncan got around the back and almost stumbled over a friar in a pristine black habit who was kneeling on a small lip of stone. The man's hands grasped the latticework like two of those arcade strength testers, his forehead pressed to another band of iron. The soles of his sandals were suspended in space like the polished white feet of the statue of Giuseppe outside Santa Maria della Grottella. The people in front of Duncan had respectfully kept moving, as if such— what? Emotion? Devotion? As if whatever was on display here was somehow shameful, unspeakable, like a wreck on the side of the highway. One mustn't rubberneck with true believers.

But the friar was mumbling to himself.

Duncan stood there, maybe two feet away, listening first for the language, then the words. He got out his phone to record whatever it was that was happening.

The bighorn man and his wife edged past Duncan now, the woman with an admonishing shake of her head, but he stayed there, listening, recording, though the mumbling had stopped, or at least dropped from his audible range. In time, the friar pushed back from the iron, placed his sandals back on the marble floor, crossed himself and ambled around to the staircase. Duncan hadn't seen his face. Could only imagine the red indent the iron had left on his forehead. He slipped his phone back in his pocket, stepped forward, touched where the man's head had rested. It was hot. Not red hot, as the iron remained the same near-black as the rest of the lattice, but it stung. He moved both hands to the vertical bands the friar had been holding, clamped his palms around them, felt the searing pain. The burn of this heavenly cattle brand. He squeezed his eyes tight, tried to open himself up to a voice, *the* voice, any voice, any vision, but the pain was ebbing, the heat gone out of the iron.

His sneakers hadn't left the ground.

He moved swiftly up the steps, hoping to catch the friar, but was received instead by Father Nilton. Mr and Mrs Bighorn stood to one side. 'My group has asked that you do not accompany them to the Upper Basilica. You are free to explore it yourself, and the Cloister of Sixtus the Fourth.'

'Hold on, I've paid for this.'

'Two euros,' said Mrs Bighorn.

'Is that all?' Duncan said, chastened.

Stay in line, little tourist. WHACK!

'God bless,' the Father said. He bobbed his head and ushered the Bighorns toward where the rest of the group was waiting.

THE BATON

'That place was amazing,' Mack said, keying her order into the vending machine. They were in the public lounge at the Cittadella Ospitalità, which was deserted but for them.

'I got kicked off my tour before I even figured out what they meant by Lower and Upper Basilica. I thought it was just, you know, H-shaped or something.'

The machine sputtered Mack's ginseng cappuccino into a flimsy plastic cup.

'But,' she said, 'they fucking built another church on top of the first. Double-decker basilica. That was so badass. Your turn.' She removed her drink from the receptacle of the machine. 'You got kicked off your tour?'

'There were nine others on it, so it's not as bad as if it'd been a one-on-one.'

'That'd be an achievement.'

'Probably need your TOÄD t-shirt to pull that off.' He pointed to her cup. 'Can I try that?'

'It's coffee.'

'I know.'

'You don't drink coffee.'

'I know, but I keep seeing *ginseng caffé* everywhere. I'm curious.'

Mack shrugged, passed him the cup and narrowed her eyes.

'Motta doesn't drink coffee,' he said. 'Says if you don't have the energy to get through a day without caffeine you're in the wrong job.' He took a sip, could hardly taste the coffee. 'Warm fluff with a hint of . . . Chinatown?'

'Keep it. I'll get another.'

He swallowed the rest in a single gulp, not enjoying it but not hating it either. 'It was probably a blessing, getting kicked off. As a lone wolf I could snap photos with my phone without getting snapped myself. Then I came back here and asked the guy at reception what he knew about Giuseppe. I figured: he works at this religious retreat, right, they've got this massive library, he can point me in the right direction. But he said, "Who?" I'm like, "San Giuseppe da Copertino? He only lived in Assisi for fourteen years!" And he's like, "No." And I'm like, "What do you mean, No?" And he's like, "I think you're wrong. He was from down south. He never lived here."'

'Sunday School standards must be slipping. He did live here though, eh?'

'Yes!'

'Is it the guy on reception now, babe?' She pointed through the wall.

'I think so,' he said.

'I'll ask him.'

'No.' He reached out to stop her, but she danced away from his hand. 'What's the point?'

She stopped, hands on hips, sneakers pressed together. 'Either there were some serious crossed wires or dude needs to learn.' She moved one foot back, about to run for it, then tilted her head to the side. 'I didn't see any Giuseppes in the icon stores,' she said. 'It was like, eighty percent Francis, maybe fifteen percent Jesus and Mary mopped up the rest.'

Duncan swept forward and put his arm around her, as if she was a frazzled server on her first shift, and guided her back toward the vending machine. 'You saw that one fresco of Francis levitating in the Upper Basilica? It was just about the only scene not featured on a postcard. Maybe levitation and everything else Giuseppe did, is *said* to have done, is too fantastic. Too challenging.'

'Didn't Saint Francis have stigmata?'

'And he fucking spoke to birds.' He laughed, and let her peel loose and sit on one of the couches. He slumped down next to her. 'Are we in the midst of a Dan Brown conspiracy of the modern world to suppress the miraculous deeds of a simple southern friar?'

'Conspiracy theories are the refuge of the disempowered.'

'Hey, I can handle passing on the baton. You ladies, be my guest.'

'You'd need to find another assistant?'

'Mine wasn't really working out.'

'Bitch, I got you on that tour this morning. I bet Uffy wouldn't be zero from four.'

'It's not that bad.'

'Okay, so maybe you got what you needed in Copertino?'

'Yeah. I mean, his sanctuary was closed for repairs but that wasn't a big deal.'

'And then we went to Martina Franca and got stood up.'

'And nearly killed.'

'And nearly killed. Then, oh man, my memory is shot.'

'Well, we did okay in Montescaglioso, Matera and Altamura, but that was kind of just shooting coverage. Giuseppe never lived in those places.'

'Which brings us to you getting kicked off your tour here.'

'Don't forget us skipping Naples.'

'You know what? I did. So maybe you're one from four. You still suck at this.'

'I do, I do.'

'But you seem, I don't know, okay with it? More okay?'

'The more I see, the more I know this film can only work if Motta doesn't even try for historical realism. I mean, you've got to give set designers something to go on. But the best scene in Assisi is probably Giuseppe sneaking into Saint Francis's crypt at night, though that'd require him digging through solid rock because no one at the time knew exactly where Francis's body was hidden.'

'Does have a *Shawshank* vibe.'

'You got plans tonight?' he asked.

'I saw this cute place on the edge of the Piazza del Comune.'

'Sounds nice. I think I'll stay here. Get started on pulling a lookbook together. Something I can show Motta on a tablet in Rome. Do my best to paper over the massive cracks in my location scouting.'

Mack crumpled her cup and tossed it in the silver receptacle. 'Don't forget about the flowers.'

'Huh?'

'Mille Fiori.'

'Yeah, but Giuseppe comes first. I was thinking we bug out early tomorrow. Maybe seven-thirty? So we get to Pietrarubbia around ten.'

'You're the boss, babe.'

Duncan's stomach grumbled. They both heard it, both laughed. 'Maybe I should eat something.'

'You think? Come on, let's go to this restaurant. We can be efficient.'

They were not efficient. They were seated on the edge of the al fresco area, a perfect spot for people-watching. The truffle and sausage lasagne was a revelation. Each carafe of the house red was going to be the last until the next appeared. Each glass loosed a little more of what Duncan had decided to withhold. The detail of his flying dream in Martina Franca; the fact he wasn't in his usual mansion, was doing it there inside the *trullo* cone. His thoughts about filming in San Marino; how Mack might need to shoot some scenes so he could be on screen. The story of the friar in the crypt of Saint Francis; the burns on Duncan's palms from clutching the latticework.

Waiting for their desserts, Duncan's phone began to ring.

A WhatsApp call.

From Vilma Vegas.

Just voice, no video.

'Hello?'

'How's my favourite inside man?'

Mack: 'Who is it?'

'A friend,' he replied.

Vilma: 'Who are you talking to, D?'

'A friend.'

Vilma: 'I thought I told you to fuck your wife, Duncan Blake.'

He turned away from Mack, looking out to the piazza. 'Don't worry. My wife knows I'm here with this friend. They talk.'

'Sounds twisted.'

'It's not. Not very anyway. It could be worse, that's how I'm looking at it.'

'How's it going? The location scouting. I'm dying of curiosity.'

He was struggling to read her voice. He barely knew her, was a decade older. It'd been more than a day since her last levitation theory. When he thought about his incident with the Chromecast, he no longer saw Vilma rummaging through a bag of sex toys, just the aftermath: Kari beating on the door, the bathroom full of steam. He had been on the path to recovery. Not for a porn addiction. But a budding infatuation? Perhaps.

'D?' Vilma said, 'You there?'

'Yeah, sorry. I'm outside. And a little tanked.'

'Good. You could stand to loosen up a notch or six.'

He laughed.

'Just tell me you're doing good,' she said.

'I'm doing good.'

'Okay, I lied. You need to tell me a little more than that. Where are you?'

'Assisi. The Basilica of Saint Francis is actually two churches stacked one on the other. And the insides? Bananas!'

'Have you heard from Motta?'

'Since I left LA? No.'

'But you're seeing him again, right?'

'He's meeting me in Rome, after he's seen the Pope. In, like, a week?'

'Well, you wow him then, all right? I'm getting tired of the food-service industry. And I'm not getting any younger.'

'Write something.' He stood and eased through the gap between two of the wrought-iron barriers that separated diners from the piazza, mouthed his apologies to Mack and signalled with his free hand he'd be back in two minutes.

Vilma: 'Again with the writing.'

'Look, Vilma, honestly, I don't know if this is going to pan out for me. Even if I'm not drowning, I certainly don't have any life preservers to toss.'

'If I sent you something, would you read it?'

'Yes! Do that.'

'Save it for the plane, though, okay, D? Don't get distracted. Read it only after you're done with Motta. After you've wowed him. I know you'll wow him. But yeah, maybe I'll send you something for the flight back.'

'I'd like that.'

'It's not just the wine talking, is it? You don't sound tanked.'

'I'd better get back to it, then. Total commitment to the role.'

'Huh?'

'Send me something, Vilma Vegas.'

'Okay.'

'Duncan Blake, out.'

Her splutter of embarrassment was audible even as he pulled the phone from his ear to end the call.

Back at the table: a fresh carafe of wine. Mack had both dessert plates in front of her. There was a small scoop from her panna cotta, and she was carving into his slice of rocciata Assisana, a rolled dough filled with apples, raisins and pine nuts.

'Sorry, she said. 'Turns out I wanted more of this. The piece I had this afternoon: mmm.' She took a bite.

'Be my guest.' He refilled his wine glass.

She put her elbow on the table, twirled her dessert fork in the air. 'You gonna tell me about your friend?'

'From work. Sforza's.'

'Not the chicky with the Little Bird? In the porno?'

He'd forgotten he'd told her about this. Which was odd. Her M.O. was to relentlessly mock him about such things, never let him forget. But then she'd probably talked it out with Kari. Maybe there was no backlog of consequences waiting for him back home. Maybe it was like the way his mother stopped texting and emailing him and now just went through Kari instead. Because he was bad at replying. And wasn't great at empathising. Kari wasn't either, but she knew how to fake it, could live with the consequences of pretending to care. Maybe Kari needed her own Kari, had found it in Mack, which meant he was free to float in space, with only an umbilical cord, thin as three pieces of dental floss plaited together, keeping him attached to the shuttle. Those threads:

Vestigial chemistry.

Financial necessity.

Zeb.

Without them, he would be jettisoned. Maybe that's how Zeb felt now. An alien tethered to his parents' craft. Mildly curious about what his umbilical cord was made of, but more interested in the constellations that rose and fell behind the whiteness of the ship.

He looked at Mack, felt his way back to her question about Vilma, necked his glass of wine and stretched his vino-stained lips into a toothy smile.

'The very same,' he said, and reached for the carafe.

SISTER SILVER SHOES

They did not leave bright and early the next morning. Duncan barely checked out before the 11 a.m. cut-off, then waited almost half an hour under the eye of the Giuseppe-denier at reception for Mack to join him. Getting out of Assisi was no simple task. His hangover made every tight corner a skull-scraper. All corners were tight. Google Maps kept insisting he drive through the barricades of the basilica. The armed guards suggested this was a bad idea. They tried switching phones but encountered the same problem. Tried heading the wrong way down a short but unmistakably one-way street to shunt Maps on to a different path out of the town, got stuck, copped the castigations of the locals, turned around and gunned it through the first arch that looked like it might be part of the old fortifications and — *oh, the relief!* — found themselves on a country lane shaded by oaks. The map on Duncan's phone swirled as if it was about to plunge down the plughole, only to stop and proclaim Pietrarubbia lay two hours and twenty-four minutes dead ahead.

They listened to another of Mack's nostalgia-laden playlists — Eurythmics, Fine Young Cannibals, Tears for Fears. They were happy enough to zone out, as if they were in the back of a parent's sedan listening to an FM station in 1990, until Mack groaned, pushed herself hard up against her seat and asked, 'You fly again last night?'

'I'm not sure. Maybe.'

'I had this great playlist planned for you. Now I can't remember anything except, well. Hold on.' She tinkered with her phone and two forceful piano chords sounded.

'What is this?'

Mack raised her eyebrows.

Joey Scarbury started singing about his disbelief at being on top of the world.

'The theme from *Greatest American Hero*?'

'Brackets "Believe it or not", close brackets.'

'Believe it or not, but I can't walk on air. I have a recurring dream, is all.'

'And you're not American.'

'Right.'

'But apart from that?'

'This just reminds me of *Seinfeld*,' he said. 'George Costanza's answering-machine message? *Believe it or not, George isn't at home.*'

'I tell you, babe, we'll be singing Hootie by Rome.'

Pietrarubbia wasn't one town but a collection of small settlements near the base of Mount Carpenga. First stop: Ponte Cappuccini, which had a couple of low-rise apartment buildings, one restaurant, a clothing shop, a convenience store, and a tourist information centre for the national park that bisected the village. In short, it looked nothing like his vision of Pietrarubbia while the Micra was hurtling toward that dumpster in Martina Franca.

When Duncan tried to enter the information centre, he found it opened only on Monday and Tuesday mornings. It was Wednesday. 'Typical,' he said aloud, trying to channel Gianluca's ambivalence. As the name of the village suggested, there was also a Capuchin church and convent about a hundred yards back from the main road. This was where the veracity of his vision would be tested. Was it truly a vision, or pure fiction concocted by his over-stressed brain? There was no contact for this site visit on Uffy's itinerary, no specified time for their arrival, just a to-do list of photos and measurements to capture: the room where Giuseppe lived for three months before he was moved again; the interior and exterior of Chiesa di San Lazzaro, the one the locals tore apart hoping to catch a glimpse of the ecstatic friar.

The parking area out front of San Lazzaro felt like a narrow arena, the way the crushed stone surface sat lower than the road and was bound on the other sides by the church and two long rock walls. There were two other cars parked there, both compact like the Micra, though neither looked in any way scarred or scathed. But the church, its proportions, the slate roof, it all felt right. It sent a shiver down Duncan's back. As he and Mack approached, the crunch of each footfall resounded. As if they were Christians being marched out into an arena to await the lions. But this wasn't ancient Rome and he was no believer. He was an emissary from Hollywood walking on this overgrown *bocce* court, stopping occasionally to take a photo. He thought about the location scout for *Cartel*, the one who'd been shot to death in some Mexican alley. In the wrong place at the wrong time, the XC slung around his neck right now was enough to get snuffed. Nosiness could be fatal. But again this was no crime-riddled slum. Chill. *Chill.*

There was movement to his left, just above the wall. Branches stirred. Something cracked. He saw a four-legged form, the same sandy white as the ground beneath his frozen feet.

A goat. Just a goat.

'Jesus,' Mack said, as if she too had been on edge.

The beast regarded her, then Duncan, as if it was his turn to speak. Another goat leaped on to the wall nearer the road, its horns and beard longer, its underside mottled black. Duncan's thoughts skipped satyrs, went straight to Satan. The Satan of

Giuseppe's roadside encounters. *Malatasca*, Giuseppe had called him. Google couldn't translate *Malatasca* but splitting it into two words yielded: *bad pocket*. In a world without Google, without David Attenborough or Charles Darwin, Duncan could maybe see himself believing in bad omens.

Flying men.

The Antichrist.

The rustling behind the wall continued. The snapping branches. More goats, no doubt, but they were mute: no bleats or Wilhelm screams here. Birds, though. He could hear them chirping now. The kind of birds that had been released in New Zealand to make the Europeans feel more at home and had now been there so long, generation upon generation before Duncan hit the scene, they made *him* feel suddenly at home and centred in this Italian hamlet.

'Let's head inside,' he said.

The main entry was visible through the middle arch. The door was off its lower hinge and propped awkwardly against the wall. A string of sleeping fairy lights passed above the lintel. The sound of singing came from within.

Inside, an old man knelt in the second row. Blue shirt and waistcoat, the kind of beige moisture-wicking material Duncan associated with cameramen. Beyond the rail and the crimson rope sat four nuns, two on either side, their backs to him, only the white shoulders of their blouses poking out from behind their black habits. They weren't singing so much as chanting. A pipe-organ quality to their voices, as if they had necks the length of giraffes, extension ladders, waterslides. One voice was louder than the others, a higher pitch, hardly human at all, more like the squealing of brakes or an angle grinder gnawing at a sheet of aluminium, only pleasant, as if it had sailed west through Bad and Uncomfortable and reached the other coast of Joyous. The man was following along with some kind of hymn book, chiming in — lower, unsophisticated — whenever he caught the thread of their chanting.

Duncan kept his camera on his lap, let his head tilt back to the white scalloped ceiling.

The chanting stopped. One of the nuns stood, walked a few steps, and turned to face her sisters and the man from the village. She did not raise her eyes to the back, to Duncan and Mack. Mid-twenties, glasses. She read her passage quietly, went back to her seat, silver sneakers flashing as she walked.

More chanting.

A new hymn, human voices this time, harmonies. Duncan recognised the word *Hallelujah*, which unlocked a stream of thoughts about Vilma Vegas, Kari, Zeb, and the thief Gazeem who is swallowed by the Cave of Wonders. How long would this service last? Should he get up, survey the exterior more, come back when they were done? He felt Mack's hand working its way into his, taking advantage of his inattention. He allowed her fingers to interlock with his, for them to sit there as if this was amazing for both of them — because maybe it was, like: MAYBE? — until the singing stopped and three of the four nuns left through a door in the back wall and the one with the silver shoes was left to stand before the old man and the unacknowledged visitors to say a prayer.

Duncan let his hand go slack, pulled it free to scratch his head. 'She knows we're here, right?'

'Oh yeah,' Mack whispered.

The oldest nun returned with what Duncan guessed were communion wafers. The old man went forward to receive his. The nun held out the wafer for him, her chin high, eyeing Duncan down. He stood, eager to bolt, felt Mack's hand grabbing for his again, wanting him to wait, but he pulled her with him, back into the dumbfounding light of day.

'Babe,' she said. 'What was that?'

'I can't receive communion. I wouldn't know what to do.'

'Okay. Me neither. But she looked like she'd guide us through?'

'Who? Boss Nun? She looked like she wanted to rap my knuckles with a ruler.'

'Babe. She looked *sweet*. Better than that sour-puss with the spaceman shoes.'

'She was just shy.'

'Surly, more like. But you *are* going to talk to them, right?'

Half an hour later he'd scouted the exterior and had no choice but to push the intercom buzzer beside the door to the convent. He scanned the noticeboard while he waited: leaflets encouraging people to pray for Padre Pio and to buy the nuns' biscotti, marmalade and candles. A stone plaque dedicated to Giuseppe Garibaldi was affixed to the back of one of the portico's pillars. But there was nothing, as far as he could see, for San Giuseppe da Copertino.

'*Pronto*,' someone said through the intercom.

'Uh, hi, *buongiorno*, uh— *buon pomeriggio*. Sorry, do you speak English?'

'*Un momento*,' the voice said, and the door to the convent clicked open.

'Should we go in?' Mack asked.

'No, wait.'

She pushed the door open further. 'Oh, hello,' she said.

Duncan came closer and caught a glimpse of white hem vanishing down the hall.

'I don't have the plague,' Mack called, then turned back to Duncan. 'She ran away!'

'I'm telling you,' he said, not telling her anything.

A minute later Boss Nun and Silver Shoes appeared, the younger nun in front of the older as if cuffed and being led to a squad car.

'She will talk you,' Boss Nun said. 'Good English.'

'*Grazie mille*,' Duncan said. 'We are researching the life of San Giuseppe.'

Boss Nun clasped her hands together and rocked them back and forth — a gesture of good luck, but for Silver Shoes or for them?

'Come inside, please,' the younger nun said, looking down at Duncan's sneakers.

She led them around a bend, down a long, dimly lit corridor and outside again, only now they were on the other side of the convent wall. They stood on a concrete deck, bare but for a blue pedal car that was too small even for Zeb.

'Are there kids here?' he asked.

'No,' she said, looking a little childish herself. She was a head shorter than him, her hair completely hidden beneath her veil.

There were three goats in the garden. Plastic sheeting was peeling back from the large polytunnel. The rest of the garden was peppered with bamboo stakes, but there were no beanstalks or sunflowers, just clumps of grass.

She saw him looking at the surroundings, bowed her head. 'I would like to look after this garden,' she said with just the faintest accent, each word its own crisp island, her pace held in check by humility, 'but I have other duties.'

'It's fine. My name is Duncan, and this is Mack.' The nun stiffened, as if Mack was no name for a girl. 'As I said before, we are researching the life of San Giuseppe.'

She brought both hands up to her glasses, apparently still caught on their names. She pressed the pink metallic arms with her fingertips, winced and asked, 'Garibaldi?'

'No,' Duncan said in a voice he often used with Zeb, back when his son was more boisterous. A voice for explaining The Facts of Life, which always boiled down to You Can't Because I Say You Can't. 'Giuseppe Desa,' he said. 'Saint Joseph of Copertino. He was sent here, to Pietrarubbia, in 1653.'

'Really?' the nun said, still playing catch-up.

'I'm sorry,' Mack said, 'we didn't get your name.'

'You can call me Sister Francesca.'

'Dumb question, but you're not Capuchins, are you?'

Sister Francesca brought her hand to her mouth to catch her laugh.

240

'But this was a Capuchin convent once, right?' Duncan asked.

'Yes. That is a thing I know. It was built in fifteen-something, I think. Garibaldi came here in 1849 —' she pointed to the earth with her thumb and index finger pressed together — 'on the way to San Marino, after being defeated by the Austrians, or maybe the French, in Rome.'

'You know quite a bit about the wrong Giuseppe,' Duncan said, smiling.

'I have heard of your San Giuseppe. But I did not know he stayed here. I am still quite new, and this order has only been here eight years. We have three sisters now in San Marino, too.'

'San Marino,' Mack said, her eyes widening. 'Have you been?'

'No.'

'Have you heard of Mille Fiori?'

'One thousand flowers? Is it a book?'

'Never mind,' Duncan said, which earned him an elbow from Mack.

'Sister Teodora,' Francesca said, 'she is one of the three in San Marino. She was on television recently, when Sister Maria Celeste visited the Republic. I could show it to you, on the computer.'

Duncan: 'You have a computer?'

'One. We share it. We are encouraged to email our families once a week. It is cheaper than posting a letter.'

Mack had her phone out, was already Googling. 'Is this her?' she asked, turning the screen around.'

'Yes,' Sister Francesca said, her hand over her mouth again.

Mack started the video playing. Sister Francesca looked at Mack, then Duncan, and saw they were lost. 'She's explaining how the Franciscan friars left the convent and now the Sisters of Eucharistic Adoration, which is a new foundation within the Order of the Adorers of the Sacrament, have moved in. How, in addition to prayer, they enrich the old town of San Marino with art and singing the liturgy, and also playing medieval instruments and making candy, biscuits and jam.'

'I saw that you sell stuff here,' Duncan said.

'Are you interested? I can get Sister Mar—'

'In a moment,' Mack said, holding out her palms as if to calm a skittish horse.

'I could ask her about San Giuseppe for you. She is bound to know.'

'The singing was beautiful,' Mack said.

'Thank you, I will get Sister Maria Celeste now.' She slipped between Mack and Duncan and into the convent.

'She's worse than you at taking compliments,' Mack said. 'There's something weird about her.'

'Francesca? She's a Millennial nun. That's weird right there.'

'No,' she said. 'It's just— Ah, I don't know.'

'All right.'

They waited on the deck for another five minutes, Duncan taking photos and zooming in on the XC's display to check for spying eyes in windows, Mack turning a pinecone back and forth with her foot, until Sister Francesca came and led them back through the hall.

'Sister Maria Celeste says this was his room.' She gestured for them to enter. Duncan obliged, but Mack seemed happy to peer in from the hall. 'She is ashamed of her English, that is why she is not here.' There was a simple bed, a cabinet with two gold monstrances atop, a wooden chair and a single-cushioned prayer bench. It was hard to picture Giuseppe using anything with a cushion. The painting on the wall of Giuseppe floating beside the Virgin Mary was another contemporary addition. 'I never knew why no one slept here until now,' Sister Francesca said.

'He was only here for three months.' Duncan took photos as he spoke. 'Word got out that he was here and people started tearing up the church for the chance to see him say Mass.'

'No?' Sister Francesca said. 'Really? I can't imagine anything like that happening here.'

'They wanted to see him levitate,' he said. '*Giuseppe volava.*'

'Here?'

'Here, Assisi, Fossombrone, Rome.' He got out his laser distance measure and notebook.

'And yet there is no plaque for this Giuseppe,' she said, letting herself smile without covering her mouth.

'Precisely,' Duncan said, aiming his beam at the far wall.

'And you will make a film about him?'

'A film?' Duncan looked at Mack for confirmation they had not mentioned a film. He remembered saying they were researching the life of the saint, but it could have been for a book or a TV show or a family tree.

Sister Francesca's fingertips were pressed once more to the arms of her glasses, as if that would keep her head from exploding. 'The measurements?' she said slowly. 'The sisters and I, we saw you taking many photos of the outside.' So he had been watched. 'I thought maybe you would like to film here? Maybe I am wrong. It would make a good story, people tearing up the church to see San Giuseppe, like you say.'

'I'm working for someone else,' he said. 'It's Frank Motta, actually. Do you know him?'

Sister Francesca gave an unconvincing shake of the head. Was it piety? A language thing?

'What did you do before you came here?' Mack asked from the doorway.

'I'm sorry, but I have prayers—' She made for the door, but Mack didn't budge.

'What made you come here?'

'My faith.' The nun tried to smile.

'But here? You and the two Giuseppes. People come here to hide, or be hidden, don't they?'

'Garibaldi was just passing through. His wife was sick.'

Mack waved this off. 'You know what I mean.'

Sister Francesca dropped both hands to her sides, her arms stiff as rifles. 'I must ask you to leave.'

'Mack,' Duncan said, hurriedly taking a light reading. She stepped into the room, as if she might explain herself, but instead stood shoulder to shoulder with Duncan, saying with her posture she'd have to be removed by force. Sister Francesca had her hand wrapped around the doorjamb to shepherd them out.

'Would it be possible to see—' Duncan began, but Sister Francesca was shaking her head, using her free hand to waft stale air from Giuseppe's cell into the hall.

'Your English is excellent,' Mack said.

The nun turned to face the hall, her cheeks flushed.

'I'm so sorry,' Duncan said. 'We're leaving now. Come on, Mack.'

'Babe.'

As they were bustled down the hall by Sister Francesca, one nun appeared, then another, a quiet commotion capped by Boss Nun/Sister Maria Celeste stepping out and blocking the exit, arms folded across her chest. She waited until Duncan, Mack and their escort were within inches before firing off some hushed Italian. Sister Francesca responded with her own unparsable defence.

Another fine mess they found themselves in. Duncan glowered at Mack, but she was focused on the nuns. Sister Maria Celeste had Sister Francesca by the shoulders, turned her and, with the help of two more nuns, was guiding her, still talking, away from the guests.

Duncan pushed down the handle of the front door.

'*Ci dispiace*,' one of the other nuns said, and fluttered her hands, letting them know that Duncan was right and they really should leave.

Sister Francesca was yelling now, in what sounded like a mix of Italian and Spanish. The two nuns were restraining her, but she leaned to one side to see Duncan and Mack one last time.

'They are kicking me out!'

Duncan lowered his eyes. 'Come on,' he said.

'I didn't mean to—' Mack said, but followed him.

Outside, only the Micra was left in the car park. No goats. No snipers. Just those familiar birds chirping their familiar tune, followed by the sound of something, a vase or the glass of a picture frame, breaking inside the convent.

Duncan stopped halfway to the car. 'What was that even about?'

'I got a vibe.'

'That she had run away to become a nun? No shit. Isn't that the origin story of every nun in the history of the world? I wanted to see the kitchen. Where they ate. Plug some of the holes left by my failure in Martina Franca.'

'She wasn't Italian.'

'And? Maybe they didn't have a convent where she was from. Not everyone's mum is happy for them to camp out in their bedroom for two years while they sort themselves out.'

He expected Mack to curse, turn the conversation back on him — his stifled career, his shortcomings as a husband — but she nodded and said, 'True.' She fixed her eyes on his and repeated, 'True. But did you see how she was looking at you?'

'Don't start.'

'How'd she know you were making a film?'

'She explained that.'

'Did she?'

'Come on.'

She put her hands on her thighs and gave a throttled scream. 'Okay, fine. I've got other things on my mind, babe. Maybe I could have handled that better.'

'Yeah. But she did just flip. You must've been the last straw, if they really are kicking her out. Come on. It's fine. We've heard enough about the wrong Giuseppe for one day.'

245

LOOKBOOK

Kari wanted to Skype. The call alert showed on both his laptop and his cellphone, a sudden bombardment. It wasn't scheduled. There'd been no preliminary text message. He'd been immersed, at long last, in his lookbook. He would've started sooner but for domestic intrigues, moreish house wines and his insatiable appetite for sleep. But now, tonight, he'd made a start. More than a start. He'd put in two solid hours. Had settled on a form. He was in the process of inserting images and feeling better about what he'd accomplished over the last seven days.

Despite the locked doors and premature exits, he'd captured the textures of church walls, the woodgrain of confessional booths, the harsh light of Salento and the cloud-diffused shimmer of the mountain towns. Rather than seeming myopic, amassing a stack of stillborn glamour shots of resting bouquets and shoeboxed stilettoes you'd expect from an overpriced wedding photographer, his images had movement. There was story in their DNA. Something as simple as adding the back of Mack's head into a shot could lift it from a tourist snap to something cinematic. A kind of storyboard for place. It was good he was doing this now. He could do more of what was working in Fossombrone and Osimo. It was also encouraging to see the number of notes he had for each location. Not just dimensions, but opinions, feelings. He had something to contribute. It might not be what Motta was looking

246

for, but if he was smart — if he alluded to the vagueness of his brief, the lack of a script, the short notice he'd received — if he could muzzle Uffy Golinko — if he was standing beside Motta as he swiped from page to page, providing commentary, adding the right depth at the right time—

Well, then, he just might impress the master.

But this call from Kari. It was either bad news or no news, though no news meant he was on her mind, was missed. After all these years. Which must count as good news.

He took the call on his phone.

'Hi?'

'Hey.'

He placed his laptop on the small table wedged between his single bed and the double Mack was sprawled on to watch some gamer streaming on Twitch.

'What's up?' he said.

'It's nothing.' Kari had headphones on, lipstick. His earbuds were still plugged into his laptop and he felt strange about getting them, as if the two of them had secrets from Mack. If anything, Mack probably knew more than he did. 'Just seeing if you were still up.'

'You at work?'

'Yeah. What you up to?'

'Been working on my lookbook for Motta.'

'Good.'

'I miss you,' he said, meaning it, but also hoping to prompt Mack to get up and go for a walk.

'How's Mack?'

'Hey, Kari,' Mack said, double Duncan's volume, but not moving or pausing the stream on her phone.

'You good?'

'I'm good.'

Duncan turned his phone so they could see each other. Maybe he should be the one to go for a walk.

Kari: 'I saw there was another article.'

Mack, still not looking up: 'Article is being generous.'

'Have you and Duncan had your talk?'

Silence.

'You two!'

'Okay,' he said, turning the phone back on him, 'I'm still getting my head around the fact you two are, what— Friends? So, guess what? I'm lost.'

'Google her,' Kari said. 'Check out her mentions. She needs you.'

'I don't—' Mack began.

'You two are as bad as each other.'

'Tomorrow we're going to a cult that believes in levitation,' Duncan said. 'It was Mack's idea.'

'I only—'

'Shit, I'm getting another call,' Kari said. 'Look. You've got a week left. I thought this would help you both. Don't prove me wrong.'

She ended the call.

Mack was on her side, her back to Duncan, staring at her phone as if locked in its tractor beam.

Fine, he thought, and opened Twitter. He *did* follow Mack.

Her only posts from the last week were photos of *pasticcerie* window displays. He searched for 'Mack MacKinnon' to see what others were saying about her and maybe turn up the article Kari had mentioned. Maybe she'd been overlooked for an award or passed over for some commentating gig. What he found instead was a torrent of abuse. Photoshopped images of Super Mario and Luigi double-teaming a girl with Mack's superimposed face. Rape threats. Death threats. He half expected this, and even the other half wasn't *that* surprised. He scrolled down, alighting only on the surface of tweets that compared her appearance to a range of animals, a bowel movement, a scrunched Oreo packet. Tweets comparing her voice to feedback, a crying toddler, someone chewing with their mouth open. Bad puns about salami, focaccia, breadsticks, macaroni, stinky cheese and the Dolmio grin. And, oddly, every five or six tweets made mention of her father, who hadn't been on the scene in high-school days. Mack never talked about him. But now people were saying what a deadbeat/kiddyfiddler/snowflake he was, or admitting to his murder.

All of these messages had come within the last half hour.

He scrolled some more, hoping for the article that might explain it, his stomach churning now, a lancing pain above his right eye. It was infinitely worse than the trickle of abuse he got when Second Wave started using *Curio Bay* without permission or the faceless crowing when he got booted from *Fury's Reach* — but still, on one level at least, he was not surprised. The hotel room was spinning and he might even hurl, but he had known this was a thing that happened and had shut it out of his mind.

'Mack?'

She didn't turn.

'How'd this start?' He stood. Over her shoulder he saw she had his laptop and was scrolling through his lookbook. Hadn't he locked the screen? When had he last hit save?

'This is looking good,' she said.

'Hey, um?' he said.

She sat up. Turned to him. 'Sorry.' She handed him back his laptop, parting so freely with the work he had felt so good about ten minutes ago — ten seconds ago — that he couldn't bring himself to look at the screen, just pressed CTRL+S and slammed the lid shut.

'Why didn't you tell me you were getting this kind of flak?'

'You asked how it started. Did it ever start? I mean, there've always been dicks, babe. It certainly started before I met you. Maybe not online. But notes were passed. Graffiti in the bathrooms.'

'Was that why you didn't leave your room? After high school?'

'No. I mean, not really. But also maybe yes, it could've been a factor.'

'Is it something to do with your job?'

She shrugged. 'I'm on a leave of absence. I'm still getting paid, so: silver lining, right? It —' she winced — 'it ramps up from time to time. This month has been—' She turned her hand over, as if she'd concealed the perfect word in her palm, but didn't finish her sentence.

'Why? I mean, did you do anything different?'

'I just did what I always do. I was myself. I did some great broadcasts. But sometimes my having a vagina gets too much for them.'

'They're just trolls.'

'They are just trolls. And? One of them, or a group, I don't even know, they decided to doxx me. Somehow they found out about my dad. How I hadn't seen him since I was ten. I'd tried to find him at various times, using the internet of course. That's how it started, me not leaving my room. Someone told my mum she'd seen him in Auckland. This was the middle of our last year at high school. It kinda threw me. Well, you know what happened in those final exams.'

Did he? He felt his version of the last fifteen years begin to crumble. He wanted to ask about the school ball. Him and Deedee James. But she was on a roll.

'I wasn't thinking about university. I just wanted to track my dad down. As soon as school was done, I committed myself to it. Got online and promised I wouldn't log off till I had an answer. I thought it might take a week. After a month, I still hadn't found him but I'd become accustomed. I wasn't agoraphobic. I was claustrophilic. I loved being enclosed in my room, my mind, my quest. Clearly I didn't cover my tracks. Anyway, this year 4Chan found out and went to town. All these conspiracy theories about what he did, why he left. Deep fakes with my face and his face as I remember it — I'm telling you, the trail went cold soon after my parents split and Mum and I moved away.'

'Fuck. Why didn't you—? I mean, you say *I'm* not forthcoming?'

'I just wanted to not think about it. For two weeks. I came here to get away from it.'

'And have you?'

'I don't want to hijack your thing, babe.'

'You haven't. You won't.' He got on to her bed like a supplicant, his knees pressed against her thigh. He put a hand on her shoulder, gently, but she folded into him, a reversal of that first hug in the dining room of the Hotel Grottella. He felt he'd grown, was now made for this moment, physically if not mentally. Words were called for, though. Instead he saw Giuseppe being led across a Neapolitan courtyard to stand before the Inquisition, and the fifteen hundred frames either side of this moment. He let out a groan, a mix of pleasure, chagrin and the desire to, just for ten fucking seconds, obliterate himself, and said, 'You are brave, you know that, right? It's not just a show. It's not just talk. It's not. It's not.'

'Thing is, though,' she said into his chest, 'they found him. They found my dad. Or at least what happened to him.'

'He's dead?'

She gave the slightest nod. 'All that time I spent searching. Two years I didn't leave my room. I thought the internet would take me everywhere I needed to go. But he was already dead. And they found out. Death certificate and everything. They found out, babe, not me. Not me.'

NAPOLI

Giuseppe, Lodovico and his confessor, Father Diego Galasso, are walking the final miles to Napoli after more than a month on the road. Despite the reason for the journey, the accusations which Giuseppe must face, the three men are in high spirits. To their right: the best-defended and largest port in the Spanish Empire, embroiled in what hindsight will deem a golden age. To their left: Vesuvio, enjoying a seventh year of rest after its most recent destructive burst. They pass palaces and Spanish villas, hectic markets and churches that dwarf anything Giuseppe has seen in his circuits of Puglia.

They enter the friary of San Lorenzo Maggiore at the centre of the metropolis. Galasso announces their presence. A pack of friar-brutes descend on Giuseppe and part him from his companions.

High spirits: squashed!

They lock Giuseppe in a room.

No food. No water.

No messages until the next morning, which history will record as 25 November 1638, when he is dragged out of his cell and across the courtyard. On one side: one of the brutes from yesterday, a man of perhaps fifty who smells of the sea and brims with its pugnacity. On the other: a young friar who does not lay a hand on him.

'Think upon that other saint,' the young friar says, 'who grew tired of preaching the true Gospel to those who would not listen, and turned to the mouth of the Marecchia and preached to the fish instead.'

'Other saint?' Giuseppe asks.

The young friar, his smooth skin radiant in the morning sun, continues. 'The fish did gather and the heretics did follow.'

'Brother Giuseppe?' Lodovico calls from a doorway.

Giuseppe raises his hand to greet his friend, turns back to the young friar, but he is gone.

Giuseppe is brought before the court. Chief among them, Antonio Ricciullo, former ambassador to Rome and Bishop of Belcastro. Giuseppe has been subjected to stories about this man ever since that painful letter arrived from Rome. How he styles himself Inquisitor-general and has condemned three clerics for functioning without priest's orders, and had them strangled and burnt in public. A fourth was strangled in private.

Would he be given a choice?

As the court creaks into motion, following processes as mysterious as the Mass had once seemed, Giuseppe thinks about that other Antonio, the saint of Padua with the blessed tongue who preached to the fishes. But what were the people before him now: the fish or the heretics? Neither. He mustn't think such things about his superiors.

He bows his head and dares not raise it.

During a break in proceedings, without a single question having been put to him, and without him looking up, Giuseppe asks the brute, still affixed to his side — as if he would run away, as if he had not travelled two hundred and fifty miles on foot to face the Inquisition — who the other friar was.

'What friar?'

'The one on my left as we crossed the courtyard. Young. Handsome.'

'There was no such person.'

Lodovico will later confirm he saw no one but the brute. That Giuseppe was indeed granted a vision of San Antonio of Padua ahead of his great trial.

When Monsignor Ricciullo finally addresses Giuseppe, he asks him to recount the facts of his life. Where he was born. Where he first entered the Order. When he was examined, and by whom. To test his suitability as a priest he is asked to read from the breviary, and is then sent away, back to his cell, though there is food and a little water this time.

Two days pass before he is called before the court once more. Ricciullo summarises the accusations of Monsignor Giuseppe Palamolla, Vicar Apostolate of a vacant diocese, present in Giovinazzo when Giuseppe and the Father Provincial of Puglia, Antonio of San Mauro Forte, visited a second time.

'It is said that you stirred up such enthusiasm with your first visit that members of both the nobility and the clergy requested your return. Is that correct?'

'That is my understanding.'

'And what happened when you celebrated Mass before the Blessed Sacrament in the cathedral at Giovinazzo?'

'I do not remember what happened to me. There was a large crowd of people. As in all such places, my superior directed me to go among the people. I went reluctantly.'

'Reluctantly?'

'I did not wish to commence the tour but was bound by obedience. Because I am weak, however, at every stop I asked the Father Provincial that it might be the last.'

'And yet you persisted for more than a year?'

'Under obedience, yes. I came to see the tour as a means of mortification sent by God himself. Even so, I was continually praying that God would free me of it.'

'These are not the words of a man acting as a Messiah,' says the man to the left of Ricciullo.

'Words will not settle this,' Ricciullo says. 'Not words alone.

Padre Giuseppe, would you be so kind as to celebrate Mass for us, that we might judge you on your deeds and not rely on words that any pauper could muster?'

Giuseppe agrees. Indeed, his heart alights at the thought of celebrating Mass for the first time in over a week.

But another two days pass in his cell with no indication of when he will be called upon.

★

It is daybreak when Ricciullo commands the man outside Giuseppe's cell to let him in.

There is no light in the room. Ricciullo curses the prisoner for his sloth. He asks the guard to bring him a candle. While he waits, the sound of mumbled prayer finds his ears. It is coming from within the cell. Not from against a wall, where he presumes the pallet is positioned, but from the very centre. The prayer clarifies. The accused, Giuseppe Desa, is asking Our Lady to withhold her blessings from him that he might celebrate the Mass in its entirety without any external show of his internal ecstasy.

Ricciullo considers announcing his presence, getting Desa to turn and walk into the light of the passageway, but the guard arrives with a candle before he can summon his voice.

He takes the flame and steps into the room, which takes on an orange-brown glow that intensifies around the habit of the man kneeling in prayer five feet off the ground in the centre of the room.

The Inquisitor does not find his voice. He steps back, out of the room, slams the door and instructs the guard to get Desa ready to say Mass in the church of San Gregorio Armeno.

★

Ricciullo and the other inquisitors occupy the first row of pews, but they are joined by others. Officials of the court, and too many nuns for his liking. But he holds his peace.

Desa's Mass passes without miracle.

'What are we to make of this?' one of the officials asks Ricciullo.

'I say it gives credence to the charge that he cannot fly without contraptions,' remarks another.

Giuseppe cannot hear this. He is facing the altar, saying, 'Oh, Blessed Virgin, thank you, thank you,' over and over again. His heart is in flame, his feet off the ground before he knows what is happening. His ascent takes him almost to the top of the altar.

Ricciullo turns to see the nuns have all taken to their feet. The young and foolish among them are already making their way down the aisle.

No, they are not all young.

The nuns have stormed the sanctuary and are leaping to take hold of Giuseppe's habit, so that they may tear off a piece for themselves.

The Inquisitor folds one hand over the other, stands and walks back up the aisle.

FLOWERS

Google Maps had said it would take 55 minutes to reach Mille Fiori HQ, but they crossed beneath the road-spanning sign that welcomed them to San Marino so quickly Duncan half expected last night's hotel would still be visible in the rear-view mirror. The Most Serene Republic and its kookiest inhabitants had felt much further off — in time and space and relevance — though it now seemed likely Duncan had already spied San Marino and captured its castle-topped mountain in one or more of the panoramas he'd taken from the ruins and crags around Pietrarubbia the day before.

He and Mack had hardly spoken all morning, drained from the night before and careful not to disturb their fitful calm. He could have handled it better last night. Should've cottoned on sooner. But he couldn't kick the thought that she must have confided in Gianluca that night in Copertino, and maybe other hosts: Bruno, Silvano and Joanna, the Giuseppe-denier on the desk in Assisi. So he kept to himself, though at some stage they'd need to talk about filming in Mille Fiori. What Mack could and couldn't say. How they'd capture sound. What to do if they were separated. They should have covered this well in advance, but now here they were, another country.

Aside from the welcome sign, there was little else in the way of fanfare. The first few villages beyond the border were sleepy affairs — the houses perhaps a little newer or better maintained than their

Italian neighbours but otherwise unremarkable. As the main road approached the base of Mount Titano upon which San Marino's historic centre nestled, the number of lanes doubled and the locals really put the foot down, which, in turn, made Duncan hunch his shoulders and tighten his grip on the wheel. It was the suddenness of the change, each and every time, from one kind of driving to the next. The fact one minute you could be stuck inside an Ancient Roman one-way system and the next be on an oak-shaded road, little wider than a footpath, with a tractor coming your way. And the speed at which you were expected to adapt. To always be at the redline of safety or else get taken up the bumper by an impatient local who would rather die in a head-on collision than putter along behind you.

Gas stations, bridal salons and car dealerships flashed either side of the *de facto* motorway as they left the base of the mountain. A fashion boutique. A McDonalds. They hadn't been part of anything so disposably modern since leaving the A14 and the Adriatic, the Autogrill, Harry Styles and the vaping, gaping teens three days ago.

Five minutes later they were back down to two lanes, bus stops and apartment blocks. The green patches between the buildings grew longer, gave way to pasture and unknowable crops. It was like driving through the model town his grandfather began after his retirement, and which grew a little each year until it had a bit of everything: one farm, one zoo, one school, one shopping mall, one skyscraper, one tram, one airport and one mini Cape Canaveral, all squeezed on to what was once the dining-room table.

Although Duncan had seen shots of Mille Fiori on its website, he still imagined some sort of compound. An entire abandoned village resuscitated by newcomers eager to buttress themselves from, as the narrator of those videos put it, 'the predominant twenty-first century rational, materialist world view'. But there was no gate or privet hedge, no century-old stone buildings. With 300 metres left until their destination, according to Duncan's phone, the Micra crested a hill and entered another small settlement with the standard row of colour-coded dumpsters for the villagers' recyclables and the board plastered with notices about concerts and energy conservation. The buildings with their smooth walls of reinforced concrete — either large homes or small apartment blocks, it was hard to say — were placed at generous intervals, products of modern sprawl rather than the crush of antiquity. And then they were through the other side and flanked again by farmland, the Republic's eastern border somewhere ahead of them. Drive too far, he thought, and they might topple off his grandfather's table.

Duncan looked back at his phone, which insisted they'd driven past their destination.

Mack shrugged.

He pulled over, re-entered the address of Mille Fiori HQ and was told it lay 150 metres back in the direction they'd come.

After backtracking, they found the public front of Mille Fiori was located on the ground floor of a four-storey building that also housed a pizzeria, an accountancy firm and some apartments. The cult's office resembled a tourist information centre — the smiling woman in canary yellow behind a blue counter, the racks of brochures and the liberal sprinkling of the tulip/target logo — except no self-respecting information centre in this part of the world would be open seven days, as this place announced it was.

'We going in, babe?' Mack asked.

'Hold on,' he said, zipping up his gear bag. 'We need to talk about sound.' He had an external microphone connected to the top of the XC which was good enough for the vibe-capturing work he'd been doing in churches and piazzas but would struggle with dialogue once people got more than six feet from the camera. He'd also brought along his own portable digital audio recorder, a relic from *Curio Bay* days. He held it out for Mack. 'Keep that on you. Don't mess with the settings. Just hit "record" and "stop" when I say. Actually—' He took it back, pressed record, returned it to her. 'Just leave it running. Hold it in your hand, not in your pocket. But don't hold it out like a microphone or anything, you'll put people off. I'll also record audio on my phone, if need be. What? We're not going to be able to light anything properly. People will understand. But crappy audio? No way. Battle lost.'

'People? I thought this was just for Motta.'

'It could be. But let's not limit ourselves.' He stepped back, fired up the XC and pointed it at Mack. 'Tell me what's happening.'

'What's happening is you seem panicked.'

'Say, "We're here in San Marino and are about to go into the Mille Fiori headquarters for the first time."'

'You say it.'

'You're in frame.'

'How's my hair look?'

Duncan lowered the camera, noticed the woman behind the counter watching them through the glass. She waggled the fingers of one hand in greeting. It was all looser than he would have liked, this plan. He may have been happy to let Mack improvise back in high school, so long as he was behind the camera and controlled the edit. But together, live, in a cult made up of people who were at best stultifyingly earnest, and at worst psychologically unstable? No: worst-case scenario was their night ending with the two of them tied to a giant firework, James Alby-Whatshisname coming up to them in a big wooden witchdoctor's mask, a burning taper in his hand, the taper being brought down to the tip of a comically long fuse that, once consumed, would send them 'levitating' up to unsurvivable heights, the latest dual sacrifice to a bloodthirsty sky god.

'I'm going in,' Mack said.

Duncan was still rolling. Had he caught the counter woman's finger-waggle? Perhaps it would play like a mockumentary: the joke on him, his pretensions and ignorance. Motta would never begin something so loose. Uffy or no Uffy. But here he was, fumbling for content. For the possibility of saying something with other people's words, their faces, the way they hold a pen or swat a fly.

'Now, you'd be Mack,' the woman was saying. 'And Mr Blake, I take it?' She was in her early twenties. Short hair, dark roots showing through the blonde, a little like Charlize Theron a few years/a dozen movies ago, which is to say Duncan thought of seducing her, or at least began to fixate, reflexively, on the fruits of a successful seduction. He felt the muscles in his face tauten, his spine lengthen, but kept the camera held out in front of him.

'Is it all right if I film from the get-go?' he asked.

'Why not? We've been expecting you,' she said, eyes wide, bright and down the barrel of the camera. She wore no name badge, just a small pin on her blouse. That logo again. 'We always welcome interested souls. And a famous filmmaker? Well,' she said.

'I wouldn't say "famous",' he said, trying to decide if she was from the States or Canada; how someone so normal, so exceptional, could wind up here.

'We had a showing of your last film up at The Nursery the other night. It was a big hit.'

'The Nursery? Like, for little kids?' He thought about what would happen if Zeb watched *Curio Bay*. How much further into his shell he had left to withdraw. How the sight of tourists being shot through the antihero's scope, the sea turning red, would shunt him the rest of the way.

'No, that's what we call our— I guess you would call it a community centre? Our hub? But we are into the floral theme, you may have noticed. Like, my flower name is Trumpet Honeysuckle,' she said, an ironic, rah-rah quality to her voice to let them know she was aware how ridiculous it sounded, 'but you can call me Honey.'

'Not Trump?' Mack asked, and Honey gave two short shakes of the head. 'Does everyone take a flower name?' Mack was holding the audio recorder against her hip, so casual he couldn't tell if she'd forgotten about it or was trying to conceal it. She'd chosen, at least, to rest it on the same side as she'd knotted her white t-shirt so there was little chance her clothing would rustle or obscure the dual mics.

'I mean, it's pretty new for us,' Honey said. 'Like, it only caught on last year. It's all in the spirit of *svago*, you know, playfulness? When we started calling ourselves The Thousand Flowers, it was only a matter of time before some bright spark started calling herself Tiger Lily. Except, there is no Tiger Lily. Heck, I can't remember who was first. It's like a meme, you know?'

'Oh, we know memes,' Mack said. 'Must be harder for the guys, though? Flower names?'

'Not really. It's probably easier, in a way. All the good flower names are either so old lady or so Walt Disney. Rose, Hyacinth, Iris, Daisy, Violet, Buttercup. *Gawd*, I can't stop myself. Whereas for guys it's easier to have some fun. Like, I'm sure you'll meet Cush, our fitness flower, which is actually short for Cushion Spurge.'

Duncan caught a laugh early, let it writhe inside his abdomen.

'And, like, there are so many good ones,' Honey continued. 'Boneset, he's just the sweetest guy, always in his lab coat. Goatsbeard, who, you guessed it, has a gnarly beard. And Black-eyed Susan, which is some kind of sunflower, I think, but it's also the name of just the butchest guy, which is why it's funny.'

Mack, smiling, turned to Duncan, expecting him to talk. Man, did they need some structure!

'What about James,' he asked, careful not to blow out the microphone, 'your founder?'

'He endorses it. Like, he's totally down with The Three Esses. Any way to lighten the tone. But he was the toughest to pin a flower name on. He couldn't find anything he liked, which was just the biggest invitation for it to become this group bonding activity, you know? Like, everyone was on Wikipedia, searching for names. Jack-in-the-pulpit, Clary Sage, I remember those were suggestions. It went on for days until he just put his hands up and announced that his new name would be — get this — Gas Plant. Like, oh my gosh. He can be such a dad sometimes. Mostly, we just call him GP.'

Duncan gave a weak smile and panned to Mack, who appeared lost in contemplation and might at any second announce she would henceforth be known as Pear Blossom.

'But what am I doing?' Honey said, picking up some pieces of paper and moving out from behind the counter. 'You probably have way more interesting things on your mind than silly old nicknames. We have some paperwork here for you, not too much boring legal stuff. We use a standard location release if you're happy with that. I imagine you have your own personal release forms you want to use, but if we use the ones our lawyer is happy with, it would be easier maybe? This here's your *draft* itinerary. Ms MacKinnon,' she said in a lower voice, 'we were going to email it through, but we figured it might seem presumptuous — we really are an open book — so what we'll do instead is bring you through to the meeting room we've got back here, which doesn't have a flowery name yet, by the way — if you have a good idea, we'd be glad to hear it — and I'll get Tansy and Red — that's short for Red Valerian, he just loves *Game of Thrones* — who will be your buddies for your stay. You can sort it out with those two. What you wanna do. What you wanna see. That page is just to show you one possibility. Okay? Okay, follow me.'

'I was emailing with Gypsy?' Mack asked her as they walked.

'Yes, you were. Gypsophila. She's in the studio this morning. She does the voiceovers for our videos, which I'm sure you've seen. We've pencilled her in for tomorrow afternoon. Once you've had a chance to get your bearings, experience what we're about without feeling like we're putting on a show. But she is keen to meet you both and discuss your project when the time is right.'

'Will we get a chance to talk to —' Duncan paused, cycling through names— 'GP?'

'Oh, sure. This isn't like North Korea or whatever. I mean,

we do have nuclear warheads, but.' She made a *psssh* sound and punched Mack's upper arm. 'GP's around, he's accessible. He's got some business to attend to this morning, but he's excited to see you both. We don't get many Kiwis coming through. It's not an interest thing. We're getting some good cut-through with our Facebook videos at the moment, but it's really hard to convert looks and likes into foot traffic all the way up here, when you lot are all the way down there.'

'You seem pretty up with the analytics?' Mack said.

'Not just a pretty face,' Honey said sweetly, though the image that flashed in Duncan's head was of her putting Mack into a headlock. 'Some people here just have one job, but most of us can float, no pun intended. We get to know a little about a lot. See how the sausage is made, as GP likes to say.'

She led them down the hall.

'Are you one of the younger ones?' Duncan asked.

Honey stopped outside the meeting room, looked up toward the flickering hallway light. 'I might be. I mean, there are some kids here, families. But among those who work? I guess. It's never really come up. It's not like age is a good proxy for the kind of wisdom we're pursuing, you know. Maybe if you were a thousand years old, that'd be something. But basically everyone alive today was raised within the same narrow frame of reference, with certain inalienable truths, which, I'm sure you're aware, are not so inalienable.'

'Like levitation?'

'Exactly.' She gestured for Duncan and Mack to enter the room, which contained an oval table and four chairs that looked like they'd been salvaged from the trash of the accountants upstairs. Nothing on the walls. No external windows. Perhaps it was Honey's invitation to name the room, but Duncan was reminded of the ice-cream container his mother used to store dahlia bulbs over winter.

'Will we see someone actually levitate?' Duncan asked.

Honey delivered a bad-news smile. 'It just so happens our three *fioritura*, the ones who can levitate at will, are right now on *stendere* missions. Outreach. But, like a flower bursting into blossom, it can happen all of a sudden. Wouldn't that be something, to see someone lift off for the first time? And on that note—' Honey spun and disappeared down the hall.

Duncan stopped recording. Took his tripod from his bag and began setting it up in the corner of the room.

Mack picked up the stack of papers and straightened them against the tabletop.

Duncan walked behind her and pulled the door to, revealing a poster tacked on its reverse. An image of a bewigged Isaac Newton, above which it said, in white lettering, *DID YOU KNOW?* And beneath: *Before Isaac Newton invented gravity in 1869, people could fly.*

'This is so cool,' Mack said.

'You can put the Zoom on the table.'

'The what?'

'The thing you're holding. The audio recorder.'

'Did you hear how flippant she was about floating? She can fricken fly, that girl.'

'Her? No way.'

'Oh, so what other reason would you have to be totally gaga over her?'

'What? Her? Me? I was filming.' He went back around to the camera. The lighting was terrible. The angles all wrong. He'd have to sit on someone's lap if all four of them were to be in frame. He got his phone out of his pocket.

'You looking up Trumpet Honeysuckle on Pornhub?'

'Stop it. I thought you liked her.'

'I said *this* —' she gestured around the room, and presumably what lay beyond it — 'was cool. Lil Miss Float Like a Butterfly, Sting Like a Bee? I'm reserving judgement.'

'We should talk about last night.'

'Babe, we really don't have to.'

'Maybe not now. But whenever you want, I'm here.'

She was still for a moment, her cheeks reddening, as if she might cry, but then she rolled her eyes from left to right as if following the path of a rainbow across the sky. 'So they've watched *Curio Bay*? That's cool.'

'Netflix, huh? Tanner, my agent —' he rapped the knuckles of one hand on the tabletop — 'ex-agent, still hasn't come back to me about that. Like, he must've licensed it to them, in some territories at least, last year.'

'*Cha-ching*. Pizza's on you.'

'Where are we sleeping? Do they have guestrooms? Do we pay?'

'Settle, Gretel. Separate rooms is all I know. They said they'd look after us. We only gave them three days' notice, remember.'

He scanned the release forms Honey had left. They looked fine. Better than fine. Granted him perpetual rights. Gave him final edit. Asked only that he include their logo and an acknowledgement in any finished work.

If they had something to hide, they would do it in plain sight.

He moved on to the itinerary. 'Nice to be consulted for once,' he said.

The door eased open and a clean-shaven head poked in. 'Did someone call for a consultation?' He wore a black t-shirt for the band Týr which showed a red-eyed woman holding a skull as if it was a crystal ball. Duncan thought of Mack's TOÄD the Wet Sprocket tee, but also his premonition of witchdoctors and skyrockets.

'Let me guess,' Mack said, 'Red Valerian?'

'Hiya.' He rubbed his scalp and sat down. 'You can call me Red.'

'Norwegian?'

'Danish, actually.'

'You okay that I'm filming?' Duncan mouthed, but Red didn't seem to respond.

'Like Nikolaj Coster-Waldau,' Mack said, which was not a question. She, too, was into *Game of Thrones*.

'And Pilou Asbæk.'

'Stop it!' Mack shouted. Duncan tried not to look like he had no idea who that was. 'You guys are killing it.'

'I come from Zealand, actually. Maybe you call it Old Zealand?'

'Get out!'

'I'm serious. I mean, nearly half of Denmark live on that island, so I'm not that special.' He turned to Duncan. 'I liked your film, by the way.' He smiled, lips and teeth parted. A smile so fake it could have been ripped straight from the video for Soundgarden's 'Black hole sun'.

'Thanks. Do you mind being filmed?'

'Go for it.' Red leaned back in his chair and shouted, 'Tansy!' through the open door.

Ten seconds later a dark-haired woman appeared, short of breath. Her jeans looked a couple years too tight and yet, as she composed herself, she hitched them up, like a gunfighter or perhaps a clown, as if they were two sizes too large.

'*Buongiorno*,' she said.

One goggle-eyed greeting and he could tell: if she wasn't a former school teacher, she must've raised a dozen kids, which meant everyone she met from here on out was a kid in her eyes too.

'I was wondering when we'd see our first Italian,' Mack said.

'No. *Sono Sammarinese*,' she said, slow, like a pharmacist handing over a heady prescription. 'I was born one kilometre that way.'

'Duncan and Mack,' Red said, pointing at them in turn.

'Yes, I know. The producer and his assistant. Mack MacKinnon. What kind of a name is Mack?' she asked.

'It's short for Felicity,' Duncan said.

Mack glared at him, then turned to Tansy. 'A local? How long have you been with Mille Fiori?'

'I'm rolling now, okay?' Duncan interjected, pointing to the camera in the corner of the room.

'*Tre anni*,' Tansy said, holding up three fingers, then swivelled the hand, '*più o meno. Com'è il tuo Italiano? Capisci tutto?*' She looked at Mack, then Duncan.

'*Un po*',' Duncan said, demonstrating the extent of his Italian with the minuscule gap between his thumb and forefinger.

'*Va bene*,' she said, then turned to Red. '*E com'è il tuo Italiano?*'

'*Ancora molto male*,' he replied, looking down at the table.

'We will talk in English then,' Tansy said, miming wiping dirt off her hands, 'for Red's benefit. *Va bene?*'

'Thank you,' Mack said, sweet enough that this time the image was of Mack putting this woman — half her height and nearly twice her age — into a headlock.

SERENITÀ

Honey's draft itinerary had allotted a full hour for its own disassembly and reconstruction, but there was nothing Duncan or Mack could fault. They would check out The Nursery first, meet some newcomers to the community — *fresh flowers*, as if they could be called anything else — then have lunch at its cafeteria before spending the afternoon at The Green House, which was neither green nor a single house but a collection of buildings now owned by Mille Fiori to accommodate their experiments into the depths of human capability and the limitations of Newtonian physics. Beds had been offered in a dozen different houses and apartments, and they were both happy to leave it open, see who they met during the day and what kind of experience they'd like on the 'homestay' portion of their visit. Some alone time with James 'Gas Plant' Alby-Cooper was pencilled in for the morning of day two before rounding back to The Green House for some more show and tell, a debrief with Gypsy, the comms person and Voice of Mille Fiori, and a group dinner at the pizzeria.

'Well,' Red said, 'if that all sounds fine, maybe we just head straight to The Nursery now then?'

'Will Honey be joining us?' Duncan asked, careful to be out of range of Mack's elbows.

'Honey?' Tansy asked. 'She is on the reception today.'

'Oh drat,' Mack said.

The Nursery sat on a rise behind the main road through the village. According to Tansy, the whole area had been generously landscaped in the eighties by the municipality responding to the population boom in San Marino after the Second World War and preparing for further growth that didn't hit until the flowers began to blow in on the four winds. Tansy was proud of the work in recent years, a collaboration between the government, the villagers and Mille Fiori. The fresh plantings, a new blacktop and LED floodlights for the basketball court, the children's playground with its collection of scaled-up wooden toys: a shimmying snake with seats on its back, a delivery truck, a bi-plane. The kind of place Zeb would've liked — might still like, if you could pry him away from whatever screen held him. If he could just forget himself long enough to make believe he was a pilot, a delivery man, a passenger on the Rainbow Serpent as it carved out the hills and rivers of a new land.

The main building was a not-so-old brick church that had been converted into a kind of meeting hall/movie theatre/ping-pong stadium. Most of the workshops Mille Fiori put on for the people of the village — and curious types from further afield — took place inside. Posters at the entrance announced 'Verbal Remedies: The healing power of words' for that evening. A group of fresh flowers were busy inside, clearing away tables and benches to make space for an informal meditation group. Tansy clapped her hands. Work stopped. She made the introductions. None of these newest members of Mille Fiori could have been much past twenty-five. Their floral names — Snapdragon, Evergreen Candytuft, Sea Thrift — made them sound more like My Little Ponies than future Thought Leaders or Nobel Laureates. They seemed particularly keen to discuss the film they'd seen two nights ago, Duncan's film, but Tansy was quick to intercede.

'Non abbiamo tempo. Mr Blake is only here for two days. And you all have duties to perform.'

'It's fine,' Duncan said. 'Maybe we could have a Q&A session?' He turned to Mack, raised his eyebrows. 'Maybe tomorrow afternoon?' He began unfolding his Mille Fiori itinerary. 'I probably don't need so long with Gypsy. Maybe we could have it here, if there's nothing on?'

'I'm not sure if that—'

'C'mon, Tansy,' one of the ponies protested.

'Yeah,' said another.

She folded her arms. 'We will see.'

After watching the group meditate for thirty seconds, Duncan lowered his camera and whispered, 'What's next?'

Tansy led them outside. Red took Mack one way around the building, while he and Tansy went the other.

The old Divide and Conquer trick.

The manicured landscape dropped away and the two of them came to a stop. Yellow and red wildflowers jostled with seeding grasses just beyond the path. Duncan got on to one knee to take a photo through the grass.

'Have you been to *La Città*?' Tansy gestured at Monte Titano, the castles on its three peaks. A dark crown resting on the countryside.

'No,' he replied, standing. He snapped a shot of the mountain. 'We came straight here from Pietrarubbia.'

'*Lo vedo*,' she said, her eyes locked on to his.

'We're tight for time on this trip. But we might come back.'

'*Certo, per filmare*. To film.'

'You got it,' he said.

'Strange that you would leave it so late to make contact? What was it, three days ago? You were already in Europe, yes?'

'We were,' he said, thinking this was why they had separated him and Mack. That for all their open doors and hospitality, there was something sinister here. A thing they would guard fiercely. A thing Duncan shouldn't give two hoots about.

She smiled, a thin line of white visible through the part in her lips. 'We are a little different to your last film, no?'

'I guess.'

Tansy hitched her pants again. 'And may I ask what else you are doing on this trip?'

'Research. The project is a little vague right now. This trip is about narrowing it down.'

'Closing off possibilities,' she said.

'Yeah, I guess.'

'Well, do not close yourself off *completamente*. Not yet.'

'I won't. It's a shame about the *fioritura* all being away, but I'm really interested to see what people are up to in The Green House.'

Tansy broke eye contact at last, looked down at her watch, a tiny face on a delicate gold band. 'For some people, even seeing is not believing.'

'But surely if something's real, if levitation is possible, why would anyone turn the other way?'

'*Questa* camera,' she said, cupping her hand beneath the lens in a way he couldn't help but read as sexual, then bringing her eyes up to his, 'it can act as a barrier. You put it to your eye and your guard goes up. You are not really here. Not really in the moment. You are thinking about *il pubblico*, people who are not really there, do not exist in any real sense.'

'You lot seem pretty happy to get coverage.'

'A TV crew is one thing. *Un mezzo per raggiungere un fine*. But you and your friend, you are different.'

It was too late to film this moment. Impossible now to raise the XC and point it in her face after what she'd just said. But he managed to lift his phone from his pocket, set it recording the audio, and slip it back in without Tansy noticing. He could see himself describing this scene to camera in a couple of hours. Having her words verbatim would help.

'Different, how?' he asked.

'You asked why anyone would turn away from the truth, even if they could see it with their own eyes. GP talks about this in terms of risk and reward, but he was *un uomo d'affari*. A businessman.

Me? I was a history teacher, so I will talk about history. Did you know this Republic was founded in the year 301? It has survived a great many things in that time. The improbability of its survival can be seen in the fate of other small sovereign states. In 1797, the threat was Napoleon's army. But one of the Regents, a man named Antonio Onofri, befriended that little man and managed to get a guarantee that our *serenità*, our independence, would be protected. Napoleon even offered to extend the territory of San Marino so that we might have access to the sea, a port. How wonderful! But the Regents, in their wisdom, refused the offer. And history says they were proven correct. When Napoleon was overthrown, all annexed land was returned to its prior owners, often with interest. San Marino could have been wiped from the map. But it persists, small and static, its only glory its smallness, its longevity. Individuals think the same way. They do not want to overextend themselves, physically or emotionally, and certainly not— ah! *Come si chiama? Come si dice "psichicamente" in inglese?'*

'Psychologically?'

'Psychically. Can you say that?'

'I think so.'

'It is not what happens inside the brain, but the way the mind can act outside of its biological form.'

He thought about Mrs Pandy from the plane. It was as if he'd stumbled into her voyage of discovery by mistake. Not just the wrong story but the wrong genre. He'd need to be careful not to wind up in the arms of a shirtless Italian stud muffin.

'People,' Tansy continued, 'do not want to overextend themselves in these ways because they do not believe the potential gains are worth it. *We've survived this long without a seaport. I've survived this long without the ability to hover just about the ground.* People fear that reaching for this new ability will fire back on them and they will never be as comfortable as they are right now.'

'So you think the Regents should have accepted Napoleon's offer? Taken temporary glory over long-term comfort?'

'I think countries, borders, these are not important. What a thing for a historian to say, but—' She mimed throwing something into the air with both hands. 'I have come to see that the best move is always the one that lifts the most people upward. Were you a socialist once upon a time?'

The question caught him off guard, left him only with honesty to fall back on. 'My wife more so than me.'

'Okay, but you will know what happens when people buy houses and start having kids and all the best ideas become a little harder to fight for. *Certo*, if it worked out perfectly, if we had a workers' paradise, then it'd be worth it. But when has anything ever gone to plan? If you elect the next Bernie Sanders, who is to say he will not make a mess like Chávez did in Venezuela? Then your house is worth less than your mortgage and your kids are losers. Losers.'

'Okay.'

'Come,' she said, leading him along the path that looked as if it might spiral back down to the village. 'You have a daughter, yes?'

'A son.'

'Ah, *si*. I thought you said a daughter.'

He couldn't remember mentioning his family at all. Eager to change the subject, he asked if she knew anything about San Giuseppe da Copertino.

'Ah, so that is why you were in Pietrarubbia?'

'You know that story?'

'Of course.'

'And what do you think of him? What they said he could do?'

'If there was not a kernel of truth to those stories, I would not be here. And, I suspect, neither would you.'

'Well—'

'Was it God, though? Is that your question? I was raised a Catholic. I still wear this.' She slowed her pace, lifted a slender crucifix out from the neck of her blouse. 'The older I get, the harder I must work to not rule anything out. You will see what I mean.'

THE LENS CAP

'And I said, "James Alby-Cooper, you have finally won me over".'
Tansy knocked her soup spoon against the side of her bowl as
if about to proclaim a toast, but it seemed she was finally done
speaking. They were seated at two long tables inside The Nursery,
which had transitioned back to a dining hall. Red and Mack were
to Duncan's left, sharing an aside. Tansy, oblivious to their school-
kid antics, sat opposite, with Honey — a pleasant, canary-yellow
surprise — seated next to her. The other half of the table was filled
out with fresh flowers, while the table behind was occupied by Mille
Fiori members Duncan hadn't yet met — presumably scientists,
theologians, artists and fantasists from The Green House.

He'd set up the XC on its tripod so that a wide-angle shot would
capture three-quarters of his table, doubting he'd capture anything
of value but recording it all the same.

'This is good,' he said to Honey, holding up a spoonful of
what he would have called minestrone, though Tansy had given it
another name.

'The first fifty times, yeah.' Honey smiled. It was a good smile.
Knowing yet warm. He hoped the camera had caught it. 'Those
two seem to have hit it off.' She nodded at Mack and Red.

'Mm.'

'Don't worry, we're not out to trick anyone, though sometimes
we might seem a little over-zealous. It's just we do have a steep hill

to climb with most people. Are you familiar with what the research is saying about cognitive bias?

'Not exactly.'

Tansy leaned back in her seat as Honey launched into her pitch. 'People reject science, good science, all the time, and it's not due to ignorance or stupidity. We all do it. We hold facts that support our opinions in higher regard than those that don't. People who dismiss climate change see it as coming from a political or social slant when they slant the other way. Anti-vaxxers see a bigger conspiracy behind a simple inoculation. That's one of the reasons why GP is trying to chart a path for us through the middle ground. We're not political. We're not religious — though if we were, it would help us financially. You could bet we'd already have a community in the US if we met the requirements of section 501(c)(3) of the Internal Revenue Code. We're not liberal or conservative, at least not with capital letters. If we believe in anything, it's the Enlightenment ideal of the use and celebration of reason, unfettered by any pre-existing world view. I mean, the Enlightenment got us partway. It kind of looks like a dead end about now, but we lost the thread. Didn't we, Tansy? She's my history teacher. You can't just call something you don't like Fake News. That shouldn't stand in a truly rational society. The rational thing, when you see someone levitate with your own eyes, isn't to call it Fake News. It's to look for the wires, the jet pack, the smoke and mirrors. You test your hypotheses. That's why you're here, right? And if the feat still stands after all that scrutiny, the rational world ceases to be the exclusively material world but one in which greater possibilities exist.'

'Babe,' Mack said, 'you had him at "Hello".'

He wasn't sure when she and Red had stopped their tête-à-tête and started listening to Honey. He cricked his neck. 'I'm yet to see someone levitate with my own eyes,' he said, charting his own middle path between scepticism and credulity, deadly serious and deadpan.

'We may just be able to help you there.'

'I thought you said all the people who could were on outreach missions?'

'There were. They are. But Water Lily is on her way back. She might be here in time for the party tomorrow.'

'Party?'

'Dinner at the pizzeria, whatever. Anything after five o'clock with more than three people I call a party. *Svago*, yeah? It's all about your mindset.'

'Fun,' Duncan said, and lifted his bowl to get the last of his soup on to his spoon.

'You can have seconds,' Tansy said.

'You can have mine,' Honey said, pushing her near-full bowl away from her. 'I should get back to the front desk.'

'No, no. I'm fine.' He didn't want her to leave. She would look great on screen, and however much her words might be boilerplate for all potential recruits, she delivered them expertly. It'd make compelling viewing. It was compelling. He considered telling her about Sforza's: the utter devastation its free meals must have wrought upon his internal organs; the sadness of its patrons; the limits of the contemporary materialist, rational-when-it-suits world view laid bare — but the other conversations dropped away and all that could be heard was a single set of footsteps, joined a moment later by bench seats scraping the wooden floor as people strained to see the man in khaki shorts and a maroon polo shirt who was approaching the serving area.

'Any left for me?' he asked the dining hall, accustomed to an audience, maybe even expecting one.

'GP,' Honey whispered.

'I thought we wouldn't—'

She shrugged, though her face said, *Lucky you*.

James Alby-Cooper ladled soup into his blue plastic bowl and took a seat at the end of their table, just in frame, a random flower between him and Mack. No chance for Duncan to say anything to the Big Cheese, though he could observe him well enough. The pixie glint in his eye. The two deep creases that formed either side of his mouth like scare quotes when he smiled. Without a doubt: the guy from the video.

You might ask: Why levitation? We ask: Why ever not?

Red stood. 'Mack, uh, and Duncan,' he added hastily, bending to catch his eye, 'this is the one and only Gas Plant.'

'In the foliage,' he said. 'Sorry, that was really bad. You two are the filmmakers, right?'

'What tipped you off?' Mack said, straight to camera.

'Oh, you know, heightened something or other.'

It was disarming to hear another New Zealand accent. Both Duncan's and Mack's had been sanded down by their time away, but Alby-Cooper sounded as if he'd just come from a marae or a milking shed. Yet there was something stagey about his sudden appearance, the fact that Honey and the rest had set them up to believe they wouldn't see their leader until Day Two. Maybe the accent, too, was part of the facade.

Alby-Cooper had stepped behind some fresh flowers and was offering his hand for Duncan to shake. A gormless smile and a slow, deliberate blink let Duncan know he was amused by how long he'd been left waiting.

Duncan: 'Honey said you had something else on today?'

'I did. Finished early. Bit peckish.' He slunk back to his seat, then said, more to the table than to him or Mack, 'And of course, any chance to say hi to a couple of Kiwis.'

'Tansy was just telling us how you convinced her to join,' Mack said.

'Nearly killed me,' he said, getting some laughs.

'And what about you, Red?' Mack asked, turning to her buddy. 'How'd you wash up here?'

'The internet.'

'Tim Berners-Lee has a lot to answer for.'

The two of them laughed, but they'd already lost the rest of the table.

Alby-Cooper's phone began to vibrate in his pocket. He excused himself and walked over to the entrance.

'I had a twin who died,' Red said, as if this was also a joke. He looked first at Mack, then at Duncan. 'She and I were not close. I always thought she was crazy. Like, always. Others only saw it after she got into the drugs, began to waste away. But she'd always been looking for something. There was this time our father took a home movie of our birthday party, we were turning four or five, but he forgot to take off the *linsedæksel*. Do you say "lens cap"? Yes? Okay, so you can hear everything that is going on, our mother bringing in our *kagemanden*, cakes in the shape of, for me, a boy, for Rikke a girl, and our parents and grandparents singing the birthday song, but the screen is completely black for five minutes until my father realises his mistake.' Red put his hand on Duncan's forearm. 'Maybe there's a film that does this, is always black? I don't know. But Rikke, she loved this movie. She would watch it all the time, just the black part. It annoyed my father. He felt she was taunting him. Reminding him of his mistake. I asked her why she was always watching that stupid movie, and she said there was more to see on the back of the lens cap than in the entire world. Crazy, right? I thought so.'

Duncan was finding it harder to stay still in his seat. The way Tansy and Red had both keyed in on camera analogies, it seemed so tailored, so fake. If only they knew the way to draw him in was to talk about local saints or regressing pre-schoolers. Minute by minute his opinion of this place, these people, changed. They were surprisingly sane. They were batshit crazy. It was a well-oiled machine. It felt sloppy, half-hearted, unstable.

'And then,' Red continued, 'twenty years later, she died. Overdose. We didn't know where she was, hadn't heard from her for months, didn't find out she was dead until three weeks later. But the day she died, I went blind. Literally blind. For no apparent reason. I spent three weeks being checked by doctors and specialists and just freaking out. And then the police came to my

279

parents' house and told them about Rikke, and my parents came to my apartment, which I didn't leave unless it was to visit another doctor, and they told me. When? I asked. How long has she been dead? Three weeks, they told me. She was the one who placed my lens cap on. I don't mean like from the afterlife, as a ghost or a curse. I mean there was some connection between us. How could there not be? Even though we never saw eye to eye, were so different, we had begun to exist in the same instant. When she died, when her energy left her body, where did it go?' He tapped his temple. 'Just a sliver. Enough to last me three weeks and one day. And it was in those last twenty-four hours with my lens cap on that I finally understood Rikke. There is more. There is.' He bobbed his head up and down.

Alby-Cooper returned, making *Sorry* gestures with his hands and shoulders.

'*Send mig din skål*,' Tansy said, her hand held out.

Red passed her his bowl and she stood to collect more.

'She likes to speak Danish,' Red whispered, 'to make me feel bad about my Italian.'

'And does it?' Mack asked.

'*Un po*',' he said, mimicking Duncan's thumb and forefinger gesture from earlier that morning. 'But her pronunciation is very bad. I see her using Google Translate sometimes, when she thinks I'm not looking.'

'Sly.'

Duncan considered getting up to talk to Alby-Cooper, maybe suggesting a short interview that afternoon. But the improbable guru was looking down at his phone. Any contact, especially this early on, would be better filmed tighter in on the man's face, capturing every twitch or hesitation.

'Where do you live?' Mack asked Red.

'I have a small apartment. I did my time in the dorm here, but I'm pretty focused on my work these days.'

'Which is?'

'Inner work, mostly. Though I still help out in the labs from time to time.'

Duncan got up and loomed over the fresh flower that sat between Alby-Cooper and Mack, though she didn't get the hint.

'Me, I'm mostly interested in the levitating,' Duncan said.

'Of course,' Alby-Cooper said. 'The Green House—'

'He has a recurring dream where he flies,' Mack said.

'Really?' Red said. 'You should talk to Periwinkle. He's the dream dude.'

'Yes, Perry can help,' Alby-Cooper said. 'You may be closer than you think.'

'Closer to what?'

'Blossoming.' Tansy had returned from the kitchen. 'A *fioritura*.'

Alby-Cooper's phone vibrated again and he made to answer the call. Duncan reached out and caught his arm. 'Can I interview you this afternoon?'

Alby-Cooper gave him another of his gormless smiles and nodded, put the phone to his ear, said, '*Pronto*,' and slipped away toward the exit.

STREGONERIA

It was divide and conquer again at The Green House. Tansy claimed it was to minimise disruption — some of the rooms were on the small side — but surely two separate visitors were more distracting than one set. Still, Duncan didn't object. Having fewer voices, fewer places to point the camera, would make his life easier. And maybe Tansy would put the hard sell on him again, feel around for that vein of weakness she'd sought in him outside The Nursery, only this time he'd get it all on camera.

The Green House complex comprised four separate buildings that had been converted into a downbeat Silicon Valley-style campus. There was a large communal space with pool tables and bean bags; half a dozen fully kitted-out laboratories with names like 'Bioprocess Engineering' and 'Gravitational Harmonics'; and an array of offices and meeting rooms stuffed with new computers, tablets and data projectors that made the Spartan decor of the unnamed room at the Visitors' Centre stand out all the more.

That line about minimising disruption was shown false each time Tansy opened a door and loudly introduced him to whoever was in the room, though these people really did seem preoccupied. As if they *were* on the verge of decoding the secret of levitation. He kept expecting to bump into Mack around each corner, but their respective passages through the maze of pseudo-scientific inquiry must have been carefully mapped and choreographed to avoid such collisions. The only time it was clear Mack had preceded him was in the cringily named Dream Laboratory. There were six people in lab coats, though Duncan could tell right away they were in fact five acolytes and one high priest: a short man in his late fifties with wavy hair. He was the last to look up, but almost sprinted to greet him when he did.

'Ah, Mr Blake,' he said, an Italian rhythm to his speech, 'the frequent flyer.' He took Duncan's hand between both of his and held it, cupped, without moving, for several seconds.

'*Si chiama* Periwinkle,' Tansy said.

'*Va bene*,' the man said, releasing Duncan's hand. 'Call me Perry, if you like.'

'Nice to meet you, Perry.'

'*Parimenti.*'

'I'll just—' Duncan said, splaying the legs of his tripod and positioning the camera.

'We will stand here,' Perry said, his back stiff, helping Duncan with his focus. He was handsome, in a vain, spits-in-the-face-of-Father-Time kind of way. One of those charismatic little men who manage to avoid outward bitterness and draw strength from the way others must lean in to talk to them.

'*Bene?* Now, come, we have many questions for you, the man who flies in dreams. Yes, yes, your friend has told us all about you and your secret identity.'

'*My Secret Identity*,' corrected one of the acolytes, a young woman with another strong Italian accent and her nails painted black. 'We have been watching an episode.' She turned the tablet the group had been huddled around to reveal Jerry O'Connell paused mid-flight. 'I think you call it "The Pilot"? A play on words, no?'

Duncan could only laugh. 'So you know where it comes from, the dream? My dreams.'

'Not at all,' Perry said. 'The subconscious takes only what it needs. It drapes the skin of living memories over structures of its own design.' The acolytes pushed back their shoulders, jazzed by his words. 'Déjà vu, precognitive dreams, flying dreams — these may be moments when the iceberg of psi abilities breaches the surface. What better territory to stake out and study? You, my new friend, from a very young age have been doing the work that we do here in this community. But while we must labour awake, you accomplish as much while asleep.'

'When did you first have a flying dream?' a male acolyte asked, stylus and tablet poised to capture his notes.

'I don't remember.'

'Roughly?' Perry said.

'Five or six, maybe.'

'And you are where in these dreams? Always in the same place?'

'Lately, yes.'

'Describe this place.'

'It's an empty house.'

'Big? Small? In what way is it empty?'

Through this process the group extracted what they wanted from him. At one point Perry asked if he had children, and whether he knew what Zeb's dreamlife entailed.

'I wouldn't know. He hardly talks these days.'

'But he can talk, correct?' the woman with the black fingernails asked.

'Yeah, he's not slow, by any measure. It's just a phase.'

'And is he a good sleeper?'

'I don't really see where this is going. Any of it.'

'*Scusa*,' Perry said, '*mi dispiace molto!* Some of us believe that there may be a gene, or genes, that predispose people to certain abilities. Your dreams may be a marker of these abilities. And we are curious if your son shares any of the markers.'

'What abilities?'

Perry brought his thumb and forefinger together slowly, as if squeezing the question down until it disappeared. 'Your son has never slept well,' he said, 'correct?'

Duncan gave a *What do you want me to say?* shrug.

'I'm sorry,' Perry said at last. 'You did not expect the Inquisition today, I am sure. However, you are coming to the workshop tomorrow, no?'

Duncan looked at Tansy, who nodded.

'You have given us much to work on already. And we believe you will get much out of it. *Tanto, tanto.* You may be closer to Giuseppe than you think.' The man winked.

It was the first time anyone in that lab had mentioned the saint.

The last stop on The Green House tour was the large, book-brimming office Tansy shared with a tall slender man in a loose brown cardigan — Duncan couldn't kick the image of the guy knitting the thing himself.

'Clem,' the man said, shaking Duncan's hand, 'short for Clematis, the Virgin's Bower.' His voice, the cardigan, the back-pedalling hairline — all that was needed to complete the impression of an ineffectual English vicar was the clerical collar.

'Duncan is interested in one of your saints,' Tansy said.

'Really?'

Clem straightened to his full height, which must've been at least six foot eight.

Duncan was rolling. He still held the camera, not sure what was coming, which made it hard to know where to place the tripod. Despite Tansy's warning about putting up his guard, he had to capture everything. He'd fallen back into wankbank mode. Even before he'd set foot in Mille Fiori, before this half-assed, possibly fake documentary, he'd had his finger poised over the record button, hoping for something good, something to return to later.

'*Quel ragazzo di Copertino*,' Tansy said, her hands in her pockets.

'Giuseppe Maria Desa? Of course. He's very well known. And quite revered in America.'

'I'm from New Zealand, originally,' Duncan said.

'The best of us are,' Clem said.

'You too?'

'Oh, no, I only meant GP. Without him, where would we be?'

'Me? *Giusto qui*,' Tansy said, smiling. 'I'd be here, all right, but I wouldn't be where I am up here.' She tapped her temple.

'Were you a priest?' Duncan asked Clem.

'I went some way down that path, yes.'

'And you obviously believe that Giuseppe flew?'

'Unreservedly.'

'On what grounds?' Duncan asked. He was enjoying himself. It was like a tea-table exchange in a Merchant Ivory production.

'Even Giuseppe's inquisitors didn't doubt that he flew. What they worried about was where the power was coming from. Was it the good guy —' he pointed up — 'or the bad one?' He pointed down. 'That, and did he have the right attitude? Was he really doing it to foment revolt? Was he an agent of change?'

Clem stepped over to a shelf and pulled down two large ring-binders. 'This is the record of Giuseppe Desa's beatification from the 1750s.' He plonked the binders down on a desk between them and began to turn the yellowed pages with care. They can't have been the original church documents, but the text had all been copied out by hand. 'You're welcome to have a read.'

'I've read Pastrovicchi, in English. And Parisciani. My Latin is not so flash.'

'I see. Fair enough.' Clem closed the first binder and returned it to the shelf.

Duncan looked at the shelves on Tansy's side of the shared space. Her books tended to be slimmer and had less gilt lettering on their spines. Amateur histories, perhaps.

'*Stregoneria*. Witch craft,' she said, making it two distinct words.

'Witchcraft?' Duncan turned to Clem, who nodded. There'd been nothing in the story of Tansy's slow conversion to Mille Fiori that suggested he was being led around by a fricken Wiccan.

'It's a fascinating subject,' Clem said. 'We cannot be closed minded. At the same time that Giuseppe Desa was flying by the grace of God, women were being burned at stakes for flying on broomsticks. What if there was truth to both? What if they were the same but society responded differently?'

'I'm pretty sure,' Duncan said, 'the whole witch thing was just a convenient way of getting rid of mouthy widows.'

Clem picked up the second binder from San Giuseppe's beatification, held it for a moment, considering. 'And where does this certainty come from?'

'Books. History. Science.'

'Your guard is up, Mr Blake,' Tansy said in a singsong way.

He grimaced, but knew enough now to be able to place the camera on its tripod and be confident he'd capture what he needed.

'Are you familiar,' Clem asked, 'with what the research is saying about cognitive bias?'

'I've had that spiel.'

'Great, well, in that case, hold this.' Clem passed him the binder. 'Heavy, no?'

'Just a bit.'

'Tansy, would you please do the honours?'

She hitched up her jeans and began to make theatrical movements with her fingers, mumbling something, not English, not Italian.

Duncan: 'Come on, guys. You know I'm still filming.'

Tansy's face was all concentration. Clem stuffed his hands into the pockets of his cardigan and said, 'Notice anything?'

'This isn't funny, you two.'

'The binder, Duncan. How does it feel?'

He looked down at the volume in his hands. Its weight barely registered.

'Lighter?' Clem offered.

Tansy's brow remained furrowed, her fingers cast toward the book.

'It's just some lame magic trick,' Duncan said.

'Tansy?' Clem said.

She stood upright, brought her hands to her side with a slap, and it was as if the binder had been dropped in Duncan's hands from a great height. It was all he could do to keep from sinking to the floor with it.

'It is certainly a trick,' Clem said. 'But magic? I guess that depends on your definition.'

'I'm not impressed by that,' Duncan said, and he meant it. He began to regret the time he'd wasted there already. The desire for content and the constant refrain to open his mind had left him susceptible. A dupe. He wasn't some teen runaway they could manipulate with word play and parlour tricks.

He wasn't.

Clem took the binder back, making a show of its weight. Duncan looked at his hands. They hurt, but fair enough. He'd aggravated the burns on his palms from Assisi. Burns from the iron lattice left searing by the devotion of the praying friar in the tomb of Saint Francis. Burns he'd told no one about but Mack. He looked at his palms, but nothing was visible. Perhaps he was still favouring them, though. Perhaps Tansy had noticed. Wasn't that how magicians worked? It was all set up while you queued to enter the theatre. The ushers scanned the crowd for potential marks, for vulnerabilities, fed messages backstage. The show was crafted around the audience.

He closed his fingers over each palm, forming careful, enraged fists.

RITZ

'I take it you have no other accommodation plans?' Tansy asked as they walked toward the Micra.

'Well—'

'*Quello*, you didn't make friends with anyone else, did you?'

Stay at Tansy's? She lived a little outside the village and her house might be worth checking out — he imagined prowling black cats and a shrine to Aleister Crowley — but his back was up. The binder thing, and now this presumption. Another apparent looseness that was, in fact, an act of misdirection. He wanted to see Mack, if even for five minutes. And he wanted to be far away from Tansy's teacherly gaze. The memory of her and Clem's shlock-and-awe routine.

'I'd like to stay with GP,' he said.

'That was not one of the options.'

'He said I could interview him this afternoon.'

'Did he?'

'It's important that I have time with him early on. My project,' he said, dashing off the word as if it wasn't the only piece of leverage he had, 'it relies on GP being a compelling figure. If I could observe him—'

'There's time set aside tomorrow morning.'

'Yeah, but that just feels a little—' he put his hands on his hips, cocked his head to the soon-setting sun — 'official.'

'I'll see what we can do.'

'And Mack?'

'She's staying at Red's. *He* has a spare room.'

'You assume or you know?'

'Confirmed,' she said, and waggled her phone.

'I'll need to see her. I've got the keys,' he said, nodding toward the Micra, now twenty yards off. 'Her stuff is in the boot. The trunk,' he corrected, as if even here, in a minor cult in a tiny republic enveloped by a floundering Italy, his mother-in-law Teresa would hear him, take this betrayal of their rules of engagement as an invitation to undermine his marriage. As if she hadn't begun to already.

'Let me make a call,' Tansy said. 'Oh no,' she said, bringing her hands to her mouth. 'Your car. Someone has hit it.'

'It's fine. It's been like that for days.'

'How did it happen?'

'It's nothing,' he said. 'You should make that call.'

Ten minutes later Mack and Red rocked up to the Micra, all smiles.

'We're going to be neighbours!' Mack said, slapping Duncan on the shoulder blade.

'Huh?'

'GP's apartment is next to mine,' Red said.

'You didn't know?' Mack said.

'I figured he had a mansion somewhere. Knee-high plush carpet, a bookshelf that revolves to reveal a stash of single malts, a pair of white tigers roaming free.'

'Like Siegfried and Roy?' Red asked.

'Aw,' Mack said, her bottom lip protruding, 'little Duncan wanted to be the Roy to GP's Siegfried.'

'It's not that,' he said.

'You're going to be so disappointed,' Red said. 'And there's a reason we call him Gas Plant.'

'Ha ha,' Duncan said flatly.

'So,' Tansy said, calling them to attention. 'I will be off then.' But she stayed there, making eye contact, as if waiting for a tip.

Duncan couldn't even muster a thank you. But when he said, 'You taking your broomstick?' he meant it as a light riposte, not the dagger that evidently plunged into the woman's heart.

'Duncan Blake!' Mack said.

'That came out wrong.'

Tansy stood there, stricken but perfectly still.

One beat.

Two.

Then she said, '*Va bene*,' as if he'd just stuck his hand up a corpse and started a ventriloquist routine. She began to walk down the sloping road, her shoulders stooped.

Red frowned at Duncan.

Mack shook her head.

Duncan: 'You know she studies witchcraft, right?'

'Yeah. And I met Clem.'

'Did they do the binder trick with you?'

'The binder trick?'

Red stepped away to take a call.

'Never mind,' Duncan said, bringing Mack around to the trunk. He opened it without reaching for the luggage. 'Are you all right?'

'Fine. A lot to process, but—'

'Did you tell anyone about my hands?' He held them, palms out.

'No. What about your hands?'

He retracted them. Told her to forget it.

'Babe, what binder trick?'

'How was the Dream Lab?' he asked.

'It's never nice to hear you are not exceptional in bed.'

'They interrogated you?'

'They asked me a few questions but soon lost interest. I'm a dud dreamer.'

He checked on Red — still on the phone, pacing slightly — and started lifting out their bags. 'But you told them about me.'

She nodded. 'I told them about your dreams. Should I not have? What'd they say?'

'All the work they do during the day I achieve asleep, or something like that. Flattery. It's a tactic.'

He slammed the trunk and extended the handles of their two roller suitcases.

Red, phone glued to his ear, led the way back to the building with the Visitors' Centre and the pizzeria on the ground floor. Duncan, Mack and the roar of their luggage fell in behind.

Mack: 'What a fucking shame it would be if they were right.'

'Huh?'

'What if you *were* preternaturally suited to levitation? All manner of telekinetic feats? *You*?'

'Promise I'd use my powers for good.'

'It's not a matter of "good" versus "evil", babe. It's a matter of "off" or "on". You'd never flick the switch.'

'What makes you so sure?'

She splayed the fingers of her left hand, ready to list the top five reasons.

'Forget I asked. I'm going to the workshop tomorrow. I'll open my mind.'

'It should've been open already.'

'It is. I mean, it's ajar. What do you think I missed, anyway?'

Mack shrugged, which could have meant *nothing* or that a new tirade was loading, but they had already passed between the Visitors' Centre and the pizzeria and come to a stairwell.

'No elevator,' Red said, his phone pressed to his chest, 'sorry.' He reached back, took the largest of Mack's bags and began up the clackety stairs.

Three flights up, Red ended his call, pocketed his phone and turned a door handle.

'This is GP's.'

'It wasn't locked?' Duncan asked.

'Our fearless leader will be here in about ten minutes.'

'Was that who—?'

'He said to make yourself at home.'

'And what will you two be up to?' he asked, sounding like the father in a teen comedy.

'Red's challenged me at *Call of Duty*,' Mack said, winking. Then she turned from him, hand worrying the back of her head, and proceeded down the hall with her latest victim.

Duncan stepped inside GP's digs. Graceland this was not. To his left, a kitchen with the cheapest kind of kitset cupboards. In front of him, a tiled living room with a square grey sofa, a thick-trunked ficus in too small a pot, and a 24-inch TV balanced on a stack of books. Two doors to his right: one to a mussed bedroom, the other a bathroom blurry with soap scum.

Total bachelor pad.

Was Mille Fiori just one man's post-divorce, mid-life crisis that had gotten out of hand? Maybe that was how all cults started. There *was* something Christ-like, perhaps Franciscan, about the barebones apartment. But maybe that was another trap. A front for his followers. Maybe he really did have a mansion somewhere. A discrete manservant to feed his tigers, press his satin PJs, shoot trespassers on sight.

Duncan left his bags near the door and went to inspect the sofa. It promised to fold out into a bed while performing neither of its functions well. He checked for WiFi. Went looking for a router and any sign of a password.

He didn't hear the apartment door open, just the rustle of plastic bags. He looked up to see GP/James Alby-Cooper holding two bags of groceries. 'Supplies!' He looked more frazzled than he had in The Nursery, like an actor who has finally made it backstage after delivering his last line. Duncan hurried to set his camera recording. 'Now, I'm sorry,' Alby-Cooper continued, 'but I've got to attend a board meeting tonight. Most nights, in fact.'

Secret mansion, Duncan thought.

'It's always one thing or the other. The heritage people. The tourist board. The chamber of commerce.'

'You're on all of those?'

'Not officially. But they like to hear from us. And we like to be . . . connected.'

'And "we" means "you"?'

'Every ship needs its figurehead.' He went from upbeat to exhausted, from the guru Gas Plant to the expat James Alby-Cooper, in the space of three seconds. 'People want me to be this guy. This magnet. They want us to be a cult. I've pushed back, but we get more done when I just go with it. And we're getting somewhere. You run a big enough electric current through any metal, you get a magnet.' He looked up, his eyes locked on the camera's lens, and the charge was gone.

Duncan: 'You're a long way from home.'

'San Marino has a lot going for it, but it's difficult in some respects. I'd need to live here thirty years before I could become a citizen. When I spoke to the Regents about setting up a community here, they were all for it, so long as we were somewhere on the outskirts. Somewhere in need of regeneration. They're all paranoid about losing territory. I guess it's been imprinted in their genes for generations: use it or lose it. We were able to set up where we are now, but it's been hard graft to be considered anything but a necessary evil. So we do our part for the wider Republic — historic preservation, cultural promotion, sport and leisure, civic pride, and on and on — and they bounce between celebrating and berating us. But for the most part we are tolerated.'

Alby-Cooper coughed into a balled-up fist and nudged the plastic bags on the kitchen counter. 'Look, I didn't know what you fancied, so I got a range of things. I'm not much of a cook myself. We're doing the pizza thing tomorrow, downstairs. It's bloody good. Anyway, take a look. I've got to freshen up.' Alby-Cooper disappeared into his bedroom without shutting the door and re-emerged seconds later topless, lupine, his entire torso covered in matted black hair.

'What time will you be back?' Duncan asked.

'Late. You'll be smashed, I'm sure. It's a lot to take in. That couch isn't too uncomfortable,' he lied. 'Feel free to crash whenever. I'll try not to wake you.'

'I'll get some work done. Maybe we can have a chat when you get back.'

'Yeah, maybe. WiFi password is on the fridge.' He slid into the bathroom.

The WiFi password wasn't on the fridge. Duncan got out his laptop, set himself up at the kitchen counter, slid the memory card from the XC into the laptop's port. As he waited for the files to appear, he saw his lookbook file on the desktop. Imagined it dragging its toe in the dust like the last kid to be picked up after a little league game. He'd taken a couple hours of video and maybe a hundred photos in his first day at Mille Fiori, but as far as he could see nothing had a place in his lookbook for Motta. He had a night ahead of him scouring his footage, looking for fishing line attached to the binder in Clem and Tansy's office, the acolytes covertly Googling 'Duncan Blake' and passing messages to Perry. And, once GP left, he should film the half-hearted squalor of the apartment. Say something to camera. But there was the perennial question:

So what?

Who'd want to spend time with a cult leader who lived like this? Top Ramen and Ritz Crackers. Nights spent at board meetings. Maybe that contrast would sound compelling in a pitch, but from where he sat the reality was one of frustration. Maybe he should devote his night to a real film, Motta's film, about a real person and his impossible miracles.

As soon as he got the WiFi password.

He looked at the kitchen cupboards and squinted as if that would activate his x-ray vision. Even if the walls were paper thin, there was no way he'd hear anything going on next door over the sound of the shower behind him. And didn't he have all night there on the sofa bed to wish he couldn't hear the goings-on at Red's? How could he sleep? The thought of having another flying dream, the knowledge that Perry and the acolytes would be there, inside the ballroom of his dream house — stretching tape measures, tablets held like clipboards — would put paid to any chance he'd nestle into the sofa bed. He would wait up, ambush Alby-Cooper on his return — presuming he did return — and get the good oil from him. Something to power him through the second day at Mille Fiori. He wasn't convinced by any of it, but his store of scepticism felt depleted too. Down to one bar. Flashing red.

What's left when the capacity for both belief and disbelief disappears?

Men in capes in front of green screens.

An old Italian town overwritten by an island of Amazons.

Hollywood in the Yucatán, in Seoul, in Wellington, and every corner where a boy's imagination used to be.

He looked at his watch. He'd already missed the chance to Skype with Zeb before he was deposited at daycare. He'd have to wait until two or three in the morning to catch him in that evening window already stuffed with dinner, bath, stories and bed. He could provide that night's story. Yes, he'd wait up for that.

He went back to the fridge, removed a large magnet in the shape of Monte Titano and found a small card with the WiFi password on it. 'This is not a metaphor,' he said aloud, the single red bar of his scepticism flickering.

As he settled back in behind his laptop, a notification popped on to his screen. At the same time, his phone vibrated in his pocket. A new email. A Google Alert. Mille Fiori had started publicising 'A Q&A with Hollywood producer Duncan Blake' at The Nursery at 4 p.m. the next day. Hollywood producer? The thing had been knocked up quickly. Maybe by Gypsy, the comms person he'd yet to meet, or some other lackey. Tansy's instructions would have been that infuriating mix of Italian and her perfect English. The person on the receiving end must've latched on to the first thing from his IMDb profile, the fact he was credited as a producer for *Fury's Reach*. That'd explain the picture of the Millennium Falcon on the flyer. Slapdash, approximate. That was Mille Fiori through and through. He would get them to take all this down after the event, keep his name free of cultish associations, but there was something pleasing about the event, the promise of it. The fact they'd seen *Curio Bay*. Everyone had said they liked it, which was what everyone always said, but within the context of a Q&A there'd be specifics. He could get a real read on their thoughts. Some filmmakers didn't like the current craze for Q&As — let the film speak for itself — but Duncan had come to miss being seated on stage, talking about himself, his work, as if it mattered. He was good at it. How could you not be? It was like being on *Mastermind* and your specialist subject was yourself.

Did anyone else have a Google Alert set up for 'Duncan Blake'? Tanner Burge, his former agent, was lazy enough to have kept it running. Uffy Golinko? If she saw this, she'd know he had gone off script. She would tell Motta, get him un-invited from the meeting in Rome next week. Would she? Even if this happened, there'd be solace in the fact Uffy had set up an alert for his name.

He Googled 'Uffy Golinko' to see what the web had said about his nemesis in the last seven days.

THE NAMES

Breakfast? My place or yours? read Mack's message. Duncan looked at his neglected bowl of Special K that had begun to break down into something even less appetising.

Yours? he replied.

Door is unlocked.

He'd been up since seven, trying to make sense of the material he'd shot when he was still half-asleep. James Alby-Cooper, fresh from a night of committee meetings and Sammarinese schmoozing, holding forth with an audience of one and his trusty XC.

—I made my money investing in server farms. Finding a bunker somewhere and filling it with floors and floors of servers reaching down into the earth. A lot of the people I worked with, the executives and the Silicon Valley phenoms who were just entering into their thirties with all those zeros in their bank accounts but their one good idea already spent, they started getting into survivalism. Prepping for Doomsday. Some of them were convinced society as we knew it was on the precipice, though they refused to consider what role they'd played in putting it there. Instead, they bought crossbows, started making their own pemmican, even tried drinking their own pee. I'm serious. Now I hear they're buying up land in New Zealand, their own idyllic bolt-hole for the apocalypse. Wrong way, brother. [laughs] The action's all up here. And up here [taps his temple]. Me? I went from investing in subterranean server farms to trying to build something from the ground up. I had some money at the start. What was left after my divorce and the trust funds I set up for Nick and Hannah, I put into Mille Fiori. No fallback plan for me. But it takes more. I knew it would. The Green House is already too small. The Nursery isn't fit for purpose. And we need another branch if we're to keep growing.

—Where would your next branch be?'

—Somewhere stateside, probably. They struggle to care about anything beyond their own borders. And for some reason the rest of us still give a damn about what happens within theirs. But we can't forget the basics. We need to be good hosts, in the here and now, if we are going to reach anything meaningful in the there and then.

Duncan folded the lid of his laptop, tucked it under his arm and went next door. Mack greeted him with a yawn. She wore a pair of loose-fitting pyjama bottoms and a t-shirt just large enough it could have been Red's.

'Good night last night?' Duncan asked.

'Meh.'

'Oh, really?'

'Turns out Red Valerian is a little bitch. Don't worry, babe, he's not here. I should have gone easier on him. But I thought he could handle me unfettered.'

'We're talking about *Call of Duty*, right?'

'Sadly, yes.'

She looked suddenly childish, diminished. Until that moment he'd been hoping nothing had happened between her and Red. She'd come to Italy to escape the worst of mankind, was vulnerable. To have her hooking up with a high-ranking member of a cult — the buddy they'd handpicked for her, no less — it would not end well. But then, seeing her like that, dejected, he had to concede he hadn't liked the idea of her sleeping with *anyone*. He loved her like a sister and, as such, brimmed with brotherly prudishness.

Mack opened the fridge. 'I beat him so bad,' she said, addressing the milk she lifted from the door, 'that he didn't have the nerve to put a move on me. I'm sick of being the slutty teacher, or step-mom, or whatever the metadata says is hot right now, just to convince a nice guy that yes, I too would enjoy a tumble tonight.'

She began opening cupboards. 'Looks like it's Special K or Special K.'

'Fine. Whatever.'

'What about you?' she asked. 'How was your night with Gas Plant?'

'It wasn't a total write-off.' He placed his laptop on the counter and lifted the screen. 'I've got forty-five minutes of him gas-bagging in the wee small hours on here.'

'Anything good?'

'Maybe, in the right context. I could've maybe led him more, but I had to fight through my usual state of exhaustion.'

'You never led me, back in high school. Maybe it's all about the edit again.'

'Or maybe we're wasting our time here.'

Mack shrugged, unwilling to slip back into the role of his provocateur. Fair enough. It was on him to keep this going, to pull his weight. 'When he came home,' Duncan said, 'he woke me from another one of my flying dreams.'

'Of course he did.'

'Although I didn't know it straight away. I'd planned to stay up, but fell asleep on the couch. I woke up when he got back home after midnight, and the memory of the dream only started to filter back into my consciousness while I was trying to convince Alby-Cooper to let me interview him. The empty mansion. The fruitless search. The tension in my pecs.' He stretched and felt the tenderness.

He stroked a palm.

It still smarted from the iron at the tomb of St Francis and Clem's aggravating binder.

Another psychosomatic niggle.

Another own goal.

He felt like a banged-up sedan in the latter stages of a demolition derby, though it wasn't other cars inflicting the damage but his own driver, the unruly mind that conjured visions of Giuseppe at moments of heightened stress and put him through such rigours in his dreams that he woke exhausted. Spending time in a cult was the last thing he should be doing. It was like dousing himself in kerosene and charging through a forest fire.

'So, can I watch a bit?' Mack asked, passing Duncan his cereal. 'Maybe I can tell you if you've got anything.'

I've always struggled with naming things. I let my wife choose the names for our kids. My companies had the most boring names. When I first got here, I liked the name Manu Tangata, but no one could say it right and I got sick of explaining. We went by La Serenissima for a while, you know, like how San Marino is 'The Most Serene Republic', which doesn't mean 'calm' so much as 'sovereign', and we're all about retaking sovereignty over our innate abilities in order to arrive at a state of, you know, serenity. But then the Bitcoin people started referring to their virtual community as La Serenissima too. Some of those guys are total jerks. We didn't need to be tarred with that same brush, let alone the havoc it was causing from an SEO perspective, which is important when you're trying to spread the word. It's not about getting people to follow me, James Alby-Cooper. Pfft. I'm no one. But the more committed people we have on our team, the more chance we have of moving the needle. So we had to change our name again.

Like *Giuseppe*, Duncan thought, a.k.a. *The Mystic*, a.k.a. *Tirami Sù*, a.k.a. *The man who could fly*, a.k.a. *Yonder flies your saint*. Maybe this cult leader and Motta weren't so different, though he suspected the filmmaker wouldn't warm to Alby-Cooper on screen, seeing too much of himself to be objective. And in person? Maybe they'd get along — perhaps too well. Maybe this is what worried Duncan: that the unmasking of the witchdoctor would reveal the ageing director to whom he'd hitched his wagon, the man who not only believed in telekinesis but claimed, in his weaker moments, he could wield that power to lift coffee mugs with his mind.

There was a period when I thought maybe our thing would be always changing our name. One day, up at The Nursery, I talked about letting a thousand flowers bloom, just like I'd done with other businesspeople around boardroom tables for decades, only this time we were searching for the secret of levitation rather than ways to lift stock prices or predict interest-rate movements. So the next name we used was The Thousand Flowers, *Mille Fiori*, kind of as a joke, but everyone went along with it. The flower names. The

Green House. The Nursery. Blossoming. I guess
there's no turning back now.

'I expected someone with a little more charisma,' Mack said,
nodding at the screen. 'I mean, he's not without charm, but he's
just so—'

'Kiwi?'

'It'd be easier to write him off if he was some suave American,
right? Some Tony Robbins clone.'

'He's like someone's dad, right?'

Mack ran her tongue across her top teeth.

'Sorry,' Duncan said.

'For what? Let me guess,' she said, picking up his bowl of cereal,
'you're not going to eat this?'

'Listen, Mack. If you want to talk about your dad, I'm here for
you. Totally.'

'Babe, you don't have to do this.' She emptied the contents of
his bowl into the trash.

'It's not— I know I'm useless. But this is me asking. I'm here.
I'm trying.'

Mack kept her back to him as she loaded the dishwasher. 'So
are you going to interview Gas Plant again this morning? Isn't that
what's on the agenda?'

'Mack,' he pleaded.

There was only the sound of James Alby-Cooper rabbiting on
about possible future streams of revenue and the tension of trying
to overturn the rational, materialist, capitalist machine while
playing by its rules.

Duncan closed the lid of his laptop and the cult leader's voice
cut off two seconds later.

Mack set the dishwasher going and turned to face him.

'That time we booked with Gas Plant,' he said, 'was on the
assumption I hadn't interviewed him prior. What do *you* want to
do before we're due at the Dream Lab?'

'Does GP know you're blowing him off?'

'It was his idea, actually. He's a busy guy.'

'I wouldn't mind some time just to chill. Alone.'

'Cool, sure, that's great. Do it while you can.'

'And you?'

'I'm not sure,' he lied, 'but I'll find something to keep me busy.'

SOLLEVARE

Trumpet Honeysuckle was not at reception when Duncan went downstairs.

'Any idea where Honey might be?' he asked the male flower behind the desk.

'No, but I could call her for you,' he said, sweeping his long bangs from off his forehead. Ten seconds later he passed Duncan his own cellphone that was dialling 'Honey Bunny Boo'.

'Yo Comfrey,' Honey answered.

'It's Duncan, actually. Duncan Blake.'

'Oh, right, hi!' she said. 'How was your sleepover with GP? Nothing's gone wrong, I hope.'

'No, everything's fine. I was wondering, if you weren't too busy, if I could see you. Film you. You said some interesting things at lunch—'

'Sure,' she said. 'Only, I'm on gardening duties right now. I look a mess. Do I have time to tidy myself up?'

'No. I mean, I think it would work really well to have you talking while pulling up weeds, or whatever it is you're doing.'

'That's exactly what we're doing. Are you sure?'

★

Honey and a band of five other flowers were working their way around the plantings below The Nursery. All of them wore pink gardening gloves and toted a white bucket, looking like members of a very camp community service detail. He took an establishing shot from fifty yards back, before anyone knew he was there. When he moved again, Honey looked up and shouted, 'Duncan!' She wiped her brow with her forearm, leaving a smudge above her right eye.

'This is perfect,' he said, coming to the edge of the path. 'You look perfect.'

'No.'

He set up the tripod, checked the light and started rolling. He took up a position just out of frame, midway between the tripod and where Honey stood among the rosemary and sage. He held out the sound recorder and asked, 'How did you find out about this place?'

'Oh, you know, same old story.' She stooped to pull out a clump of long grass.

'Which is?'

'I came here with my boyfriend. I stayed, he didn't.'

'But what made you come?'

'Everything they were saying, it struck a chord.' She smiled at Duncan, which would have lit up the viewfinder of the XC, but he needed her to open up. To say something passionate or incriminating.

He tried silence.

She stuffed another clump of grass in her bucket and stomped a white trainer down on the weeds to create more room. 'What'd you do to Tansy, by the way?'

'Why? What'd she say?'

'She's taking the day off.'

'Really?'

'She said you were really resistant, to the point of, um, she used an Italian word. Anyway, she reckons you're a lost cause and she doesn't want to risk damaging the work she's done on herself.'

'Seriously? I just made a joke about her being a witch. Because of the witchcraft.'

'It wouldn't have just been that.'

'She seemed so— I don't know. I guess I'm not good at reading people.'

'And what's your read on me?'

He laughed. 'I really don't know. To be honest, I came here hoping you'd get on a run like you did over lunch yesterday, but with the frame tighter on you. When you talk, people want to listen.'

'But you've interviewed GP, right? He's the compelling one.'

'Yeah, but it's not all about him, is it?' He was beginning to see what Alby-Cooper had been saying about people wanting him to be the magnet. To put it all on his shoulders. 'Why does it always have to be a middle-aged man?'

'It doesn't. But in this case—'

'So Mille Fiori is the exception to the rule?'

'If you want to talk about privilege,' Honey said, 'let's talk about privilege.' She stood up straighter and Duncan could feel the electricity prickle down his back. 'Another word for privilege might be comfort, right? It's pretty darn comfortable to be a rich white person within the narrow and fixed rational materialist view that is utterly, utterly dominant. I imagine it's even more comfortable if you're a man. If life is a game, you and GP have been playing it on EASY. Why would GP or you or me or Tansy fight against the gravity of the status quo when we're the ones who have the most to lose personally? Shouldn't it be the six-year-olds sewing on sequins in a Bangladeshi sweatshop and their poor heartbroken parents who are rising up? Because they have the most to gain and the least to lose, right? The irony is movements like this always start out drawing their members from the privileged, those who have the most to lose, because they are the only ones afforded the breathing room to consider so-called non-essential questions. The ones beyond, "Where will I sleep tonight?" and, "How will I feed myself and those who depend on me?" There's no vast conspiracy behind all this. It's human nature. We built this imperfect machine and most of us can't see it as such, can't even see it's man-made. We live such blinkered lives. When confronted, we cry out for the blinkers to be put back in place. Like a skittish racehorse that knows what the blinkers are, knows what they mean, but can't help calming down and proceeding into the stalls and running when the gates are opened and following the same track as all the other horses. But if we built this machine, this narrow view of what's possible and what's impossible, we can break it, and in its place erect something broader, grander and more generous.'

'Have you flown?'

'Mostly just in my dreams.'

'Mostly?'

She opened her mouth and held the tip of her tongue against her top teeth, as if she was about to say something beginning with L, but she just held her tongue there and stared off into the distance.

It took Duncan a moment to regain his composure. 'Are you in any videos?'

'No.'

'You know that video on your website, *Why Levitation?* Was that—'

'It's still up there?'

'Yeah. I mean, when I last looked. And YouTube—'

'It was supposed to be taken down.'

'Why?'

'Everything GP says is pretty much ripped straight from this essay by a guy called Michael Grosso.'

'That stuff about the wheel and the telescope?'

'Yeah, it was early on. You could say we were a little naïve. There are more videos in the works.'

'Who directs them?'

'You looking for a job?'

'Just curious.'

'It's a guy called Trillium. He's off in Eastern Europe with Mirabilis.'

'Who *can* fly, right?'

'You gotta earn a name like Mirabilis.'

Duncan thought of Giuseppe being dragged like a helium balloon around Puglia by Father Antonio of San Mauro Forte and all the trouble that brought down on him.

'How's their trip going?' he asked. 'I imagine it's more convincing in person than online.'

'People like you,' she said, smiling, 'Hollywood types and computer wizards, have seen to it that people are indifferent to flying men and women.'

Duncan's phone began to vibrate. Another Skype call from Kari. He motioned at the phone; Honey shrugged and went back to her weeding. He left the camera rolling and began walking down the slope as he answered the call. The video feed looked completely black. He shielded his screen from the sunlight and saw the barest outline of a face lit by the cellphone screen at that end.

'Hello? What time is it there?'

Silence.

'Kari?' Then he clicked. 'Zeb? What are you doing, mate? It must be midnight there! Is your mum with you? How'd you get her phone?' Duncan bit his lip, not wanting his son to end the call. 'Well, I'm in San Marino. It's pretty, um, pretty out there.'

Zeb's face was becoming clearer, the fact it was shrouded by a bedsheet. He wasn't going to say anything, Duncan could tell, but he didn't look as distant as he had while sat on Kari's lap for the last couple of calls. This wasn't an accident. He'd gotten hold of her phone and called his dad. He needed something. Something from his dad.

'I love you so much, bud. This call can be our little secret, if you want. I'll be home in a couple of days. Hey, how 'bout I show you where I am?' He switched to the phone's rear camera and began to pan, taking in the flowers in their pink gardening gloves, the playground, the basketball court, the road that ran through the village, The Green House complex, the houses and apartments.

'Okay, bud, I think you need to get some more sleep now, all right? I think about you all the time. I do. I'll call you again at dinner time, okay? But I'm going to hang up now so you get some sleep, yeah? All right, matey? Okay, Zeb? Yeah? Understand? Love you. Nun-night.'

He returned to the XC on its tripod. Honey had cribbed along the hillside to the point she'd left the frame. He lifted the tripod and repositioned it ten paces to the left. As soon as he stepped back from the camera, he saw it. Not another vision of Giuseppe. No, it was as if he had left his body and could see himself clearly for the first time in how long? He was being a creep. Had crossed that line. *Predatory*, that was the word. Five minutes ago he'd have tried to spin it: yes, there was an element of flirtation. *Pre-date* energy, perhaps, but not *predatory*. It was about what would play with an audience. But this scene might never have an audience of more than one. Like his Palmcorder efforts and his wankbank compilations. And even if it did, he was being led around by his cock. Was using filmmaking as a cover for deviancy. The only counter he had, the only currency to address this debt, was honesty.

'Sorry, that was my son,' he said. 'It's, like, midnight in LA. He must've sneaked into my wife's room and pinched her phone.'

'How old is he?'

He knew he shouldn't talk about Zeb. That he was breaking one of his own rules of engagement and playing right into their hands. But he said, 'Nearly four.'

'And he can call you all by himself?'

'It seems so. He— He doesn't talk much anymore. He's kind of gone back into his shell. Everyone says it's just a phase, but what if he hasn't changed at all? What if he was always like this, we just didn't see it? Seeing him just now, it reminded me of when we first tried moving him into a proper bed. He wouldn't cry out, he'd just get out of bed and walk into our room and stand there beside the bed, silent, till one of us noticed. Freaked me out every time. Like he was still asleep. Or possessed. His skin looked like bone china in the near dark. He still spoke to us during the day, seemed to cope with things, other people. But what if how he is now is the real him? This china figurine. I don't want to love him any less. I *can't* love him any less. But there's this feeling. Of knowing what it'd be like if it was just a phase, if he grew back out of it, back into his childhood, his happiness. And my heart bursts for this Zeb. And it breaks for the other one.'

'There's a lot I could say to that,' Honey said, plucking off her pink gloves, 'but maybe all I need to say is *grazie mille*? And I left a little something on there —' she nodded at the camera — 'just for you.'

STENDERE

'Proceed through to the next room,' Perry instructed.

'I feel stupid,' Duncan said.

'You're doing great. That's it.'

Duncan could hear the excitement of the twenty or so onlookers behind him. Mack was there, holding his camera, amid Perry's lab-coated acolytes and a few other familiar faces from his tour of The Green House. No Alby-Cooper or Honey. No Tansy or Clem. Red was there, but keeping his distance, at least until Duncan put on the VR headset. Thanks to the flat-screen to his right, everyone could see what he saw through the goggles: the blocky approximation of his dream mansion that one of the flowers had knocked up in a single sleepless night. To move, Duncan made the same breaststroke gestures as in his dreams. If he stopped moving, he floated into walls or bumped against the ceiling. It was an impressive feat of programming, yet he couldn't kick the feeling he was inside a Dire Straits music video rather than back in one of his flying dreams.

Perry: 'Describe what you feel.'

'I feel lost.'

'Good. Keep going.'

Duncan pushed through the air toward the next doorway. How big was this place? What was he looking for? He was looking for things to prove this was not his dream. Evidence that this was a rudimentary 3D environment, perhaps a mod of a VR game with all the identifying monsters removed. It was uncanny, though, to be playing a game of his dream that had felt like a game. He hadn't told anyone about that feeling. With Mack, it might well have come up a couple of nights ago, if *My Secret Identity* and Mille Fiori hadn't sidetracked them.

Perry: 'I'm going to ask you to close your eyes now—'

'Okay?'

'—and ask that you keep picturing the room in your mind. Can you see, in this picture in your mind, where the door to the next room is?'

'Yeah.'

'Pass through it.'

From the gasps behind him, it seemed he was heading there, was passing through, had made it. He could have been peeking of course. The headset formed a tight, real-world-eradicating seal around his eyes. But he hadn't peeked. He'd kept his eyes shut because *what the hell*, right? Why not breaststroke in front of these strangers and his own fucking camera as if he was inside one of his innocuous dreams? He'd already bared his soul to Honey and found, on the walk back to GP's apartment, that his camera had captured her lifting about six inches off the ground while he was distracted by Zeb's call. It could have been what street magicians called Balducci levitation, which relied on angles and body control to make it appear you'd lifted off the ground. Maybe she was making fun of him, in the spirit of *svago*. Or maybe it was legitimate. One small flight for a young woman. One giant lift-off for humanity.

Then there was the phone call from Uffy during lunch in which he agreed to take one for the team. It had just gone seven in the morning in New York, which meant however many times she repeated it was no big deal, something was up. She told him to expect a call from Emma Sisley, a journalist at *Variety*, when the sun finally rose in LA. The *Hollywood Reporter* was about to publish a piece — presumably another *Giuseppe* breadcrumb — that mentioned the notorious young director Duncan Blake was associated with the project and was now in Italy as part of pre-production. Uffy had offered Sisley exclusive access to Duncan, had given her his cellphone number, and would email him through some 'notes' for the interview in the next hour or so, though nothing had come through before he donned the VR goggles. He was being used as a diversion, that much was clear, but from what? He didn't know how he could get out of it without revealing to Uffy that he'd gone off-piste — was in a cult of levitating gardeners — and jeopardising any one-on-one time with Motta, which, despite his moment of clarity and self-loathing with Trumpet Honeysuckle that morning, was about the only rational way to salvage something from this entire exercise. So, yeah, he was in a bind and had decided to just roll over and take it, and this compliant mood had flowed through into the Dream Lab. But soon enough, he told himself, they'll be done with me and I'll be up in The Nursery for my Q&A, talking about *Curio Bay* and filmmaking and the evils of Hollywood.

'With your eyes still shut,' Perry said, 'tell me what you see.'

Murmurs behind him.

There must be something in this room, something on the screen.

He turned his head, eyes screwed tight, surveying the empty room, the one in his mind, waiting for his subconscious to plant something — another vibrating restaurant pager, his mother's silhouette through a floral shower curtain, a demon feasting on the innards of a fallow deer — but none of these inventions leapt from thoughts to become images present within his imagined room.

'There's nothing,' he said. 'An empty room.'

More murmurs. A better-designed experiment would get rid of the onlookers. Put him in soundproof headphones through which only Perry's voice would be piped.

'Okay. Can you see the next door?'

'Yes. It's in the same place as the last one.'

'Good. Continue on.'

He swam, thinking how the game's mechanics would work if his dream had preserved the use of aerosols, the original means of propulsion, if it all in fact began with *My Secret Identity*. The kit would have to be sensitive enough to detect the movements of his index finger, the angle at which he held his imagined canisters of air freshener.

Through the next doorway he moistened his lips to say once more that this room was empty, that every room would be empty, when he saw something in the far corner, crouched like the demon he'd half-conjured a minute ago. But it was a boy. It was Zeb. Duncan took a deep breath, held it, listening for murmurs from the crowd. Silence. He waited for Perry to say something. Remembered he could just open his eyes to see what they all saw. But Zeb was there, crouched in a plain blue t-shirt, his arms meth-addict skinny, his head bowed. The momentum from Duncan's last few strokes continued to edge him closer to his son, continued the zoom, art-house slow, telling him to steel himself for the moment of horror — the lizard-person eyes or the total lack of facial features. But his drift continued and Zeb remained crouched, bowed, normal.

'Duncan?'

'Uh huh?'

'What do you see?'

He opened his eyes. There was a dark box in the corner of the room. He must've seen the contrast through his eyelids and his subconscious had done the rest. He thought of every way these people could use this information against him, every reason he should be keeping Zeb out of this, but he said it anyway.

'My son. Crouched in the corner of the room. I see my son.'

SVAGO

'That's correct,' Duncan said into his phone. 'I'm here for two weeks. This is day nine.'

'Can you tell me a little about where you are now?' Emma Sisley of *Variety* asked.

'Sure,' he said, taking another step down the path that led around the back of The Nursery. Monte Titano and its towers came into view. 'I'm in a little place called Pietrarubbia,' he lied. 'It's where San Giuseppe da Copertino was sent after he got too popular in Assisi, which is beautiful, by the way. Just phenomenal. But he only lasted three months here. People started tearing up the church in the hope of seeing him say Mass and he had to be moved again.'

'Uh-huh,' Sisley said. 'What's it like working with Frank Motta?'

'It's a privilege,' he said, sticking to Uffy's emailed instructions. He could talk about being 'associated with' Motta or his 'incredible project'; could even talk about it as a 'collaboration', but he had to remain vague about when he'd begun working with Motta and what would happen next. 'Like so many people,' he continued, 'I've been curious about this project for so long. And to finally be associated with it: it's incredible. Such a privilege.'

'And Motta personally?'

Uffy's email: *If she asks anything about Motta, only talk about him in terms of his filmmaking.*

'He's a maestro, right? I mean, it's a privilege.'

For the second time that hour he felt like he needed a cold shower. It had taken him five long minutes to understand that the three dozen people seated in front of him for his Q&A had *not* seen and loved his film, *Curio Bay*, but instead were fans of John Lever's *Fury's Reach*. When he finally clicked, he'd tried explaining how he had very little to do with the finished product — that the producing credit was virtually meaningless — but they'd taken this for false modesty and continued probing.

Mack had just sat there. The biggest, dorkiest grin on her face.

And now here he was, running interference for Motta, playing up his artistry and the fact his passion project was kinda-sorta in pre-production, and lending whatever notoriety Duncan himself had left to distract from the maestro's latest indiscretion. He hadn't had time to search online yet, so he could only guess at the specifics. The disintegration of another marriage. The unpaid alimony to an earlier wife. A new love child with the same late-starting hairline, the same penetrating gaze.

When he got to the pizzeria, it was humming. The air was rich with the smells of burning oak, charred crusts, fresh basil and molten mozzarella. The place was not officially part of Mille Fiori, though both rejoiced in the other's existence. He set up his camera in the corner nearest to the seat Mack had saved for him at a rectangular table shared with a half-dozen flowers, all of them familiar from The Green House or the audience of his exasperating Q&A, though he couldn't see Tansy or Red or Trumpet Honeysuckle anywhere. Mack and two others already had pizzas in front of them.

He shouted into her ear, 'This makes me think we should've gone to Naples.'

'What?'

'The pizza,' he said. 'This is how they do it in *Napoli*.'

'Okay.' She cut a slice, folded it in two and took a bite.

'In Napoli, there was a scandal,' the flower opposite Duncan said. He'd introduced himself at the Q&A as Boneset before launching into the first of his three impossible questions. And now, it seemed, he'd staked Duncan out in the hopes of extracting more over dinner. He was maybe forty and sported the accidental beard of someone suddenly preoccupied with parapsychology. However hard he worked to present himself as a scientist — he was the only one in the pizzeria in a lab coat — Duncan couldn't shake the impression he'd recently ditched his IT job in Milan or Bologna and was still getting used to living away from his *mamma*. 'It was maybe five years ago,' Boneset continued. 'Pizzerias were burning the wood from coffins that had been dug up from the cemetery.'

'Jeez,' Duncan said.

'What happened?' Mack asked. 'With the scandal?'

'The investigation went nowhere. The Camorra were behind the cemetery raids. And the pizzerias employ so many people. People will forget anything that threatens the status quo. Plus,' he said, shrugging, 'it is the south.'

Mack took another bite and turned to Duncan. 'You don't regret skipping out on Naples for this, do you?' There was something searching in her voice, almost as if she was talking to herself. 'It makes sense,' she continued, well aware Boneset was hanging on every word, 'that this lot would like *Fury's Reach*. The concept, at least. Those people aboard a spaceship, originally crewed by their grandparents, that won't reach its destination until after they're long dead. The way it mashes up Big Purpose and Greater Good with Total Powerlessness. I always thought it was a metaphor for being a teenager, but this lot see themselves as the crew, don't they, babe?' Boneset was wincing, though Duncan couldn't tell if it was from the strain of following the conversation or its content. 'Like,' Mack said, 'they might not all get to fly themselves, but they can at least stoke the fusion reactor that keeps the place running until all of mankind gets their wings.'

Duncan sighed. 'This is where you say that L. Ron Hubbard wrote sci-fi, and five percent of people listed their religion as Jedi in the last census.'

'And,' Boneset added, 'the Church of All Worlds was based on a Robert Heinlein story.'

'Okay,' said Mack, 'I'll shut up then.'

Duncan: 'No. Sorry, I—'

A minor commotion. Chair legs dragging across the vinyl floor. Craning necks. Another James Alby-Cooper arrival. He walked between the tables, rubbing his hands together, and approached the counter. He shared a joke with the cashier, then swung around, surveying his flock until he locked in on Mack and Duncan. The almighty Gas Plant, he of the unremarkable bachelor pad and exhausted server-farm fortune, made eye contact with them each in turn and delivered a series of hand gestures that contained a greeting, an apology and some kind of instruction. He turned back to the young woman behind the counter. The music playing over the speakers began to fade out.

Duncan got up and stood behind the XC on its tripod. This seemed to please Alby-Cooper, though he let the smile drain from his face and lowered his eyes before he began to speak:

'Two weeks before my mother died, I saw her levitate in my back yard. Most of you have heard this story before, I know, but bear with me. It was the middle of the night. I don't know why I woke up, but I did, and I felt this incredible compulsion to look out my bedroom window, which was on the second floor.' Duncan thought of his first piece of filmmaking, the shot of Tara James, stupidly happy and unreachable on her trampoline, captured and preserved thanks to his father's Palmcorder. 'There must've been a light on in the kitchen beneath me,' Alby-Cooper continued, 'because there was a golden glow reaching out across the lawn and touching the outer leaves of our apple tree. I didn't notice her at first. I wasn't looking for anyone floating sixteen feet off the ground. But then I saw her feet, the damp patches on the soles of her white socks, dangling there, halfway between the house and the apple tree. She was facing away from me. Her arms held out.' He closed his eyes and modelled the pose. 'The hem of her nightgown rippled around her knees.' Alby-Cooper let his arms drop and opened his eyes. 'I was only six, but I knew enough then to feel panicked by what I saw. I let the curtain drop back down and lay flat on my bed till the morning came.

'I never mentioned what I saw to my mother, or anyone else, even after she passed. I pushed that memory so far down it began to feel like a dream. A childish flight of fancy. I thought the gnawing lack I felt was just the loss of my mother. I convinced myself it was that and that alone. I built myself the safest, most comfortable life I could, but the lack still ate away at me. I began to act rashly. I put my fortune at risk. I put my family at risk. I lost my family first. What I craved wasn't comfort, but mystery. And so, eventually, I let myself think about my mother up there in her nightgown on that damp evening in late summer. And my whole body tingled. Pleasure and pain. Electricity. There was something there. It was like a drug. So I cashed up and started on the journey that led me here. And even though I've now seen half a dozen more people levitate, not to mention the countless other feats you lot have been able to accomplish, I still get that tingle when I think about my mother. I live within that tingle. And I know it's right to do that. It's right to be here. To be doing this. And I'm thankful for each and every one of you.'

He ran his eyes across the tables. Slow. Deliberate. 'Many of you will know we have had two guests among us these last two days. Two special guests who come from the same place as I do. Aotearoa New Zealand, down there at the bottom of the world. Duncan Blake and Mack MacKinnon. Stand up, Mack.'

Mack stood. Duncan gave a feeble wave from behind the camera.

'*Nau mai, haere mai*,' Alby-Cooper said, his hands forming a steeple against his sternum. '*Benvenuto*. Welcome.' He scanned the faces of the others in the pizzeria. 'I say that now because I hope this is only the beginning, not the end. You're welcome to stay as long as you want and return as often as you need to make whatever film you want to make. They tell me your session this afternoon up at The Nursery was great. I'm sad I missed it.' He shifted his shoulders slightly, conscious of how he might be framed by the camera.

'I was hoping Water Lily would be back by now and you could see what a *fioritura* can do. But she's been delayed.' He consulted his phone. 'Give it another hour, maybe.'

'I'll believe it when I see it,' Duncan whispered to Mack.

'Will you?' she replied.

'You know, everyone comes here with their own reasons,' Alby-Cooper said. 'But there is something in common. We've all had some taste of the higher truth. Whether it be through lucid dreams, or standing witness to the feats of someone else, or doing it ourselves without really knowing how or why. It's not always about levitation. Some of us started on the path that led to Mille Fiori because we've experienced people being in two places at once, or moved things with our minds — any number of miracles that are only labelled as such because science has not caught up with these capacities. Our greatest capacity as humankind, the one that no one can dispute, is the ability to focus, for many to work as one. And if we do that on a global scale? What does that mean for economic systems? For the way we treat each other? If we unlock the psychokinetic potential of even five percent of the population, we'll probably eliminate all war. The alternative is the first psychokinetic war, which will also be the last. The final chapter of humankind. Like the cold war but everyone has their own nuclear football.' He lowered his head and brought his hand up to his forehead. 'This is not what I intended to say at all.' He smiled, at once the bumbling father of trust-fund collegians and the magnetic leader of a cult. 'Cush? I think you wanted to provide some entertainment, eh?'

Cushion Spurge, Mille Fiori's resident personal trainer, stood and walked over to the counter. He wore knee-length basketball shorts and an Adidas jumper zipped up to his chin, and was holding an acoustic guitar by the neck. He began to play. A generic, campfire strum that made it hard to place the song until he started singing. 'Mind games' by John Lennon, only mangled by Cush's strong accent and, perhaps, his imperfect grasp of the lyrics.

'Those' became 'Dhose'.

'Lifting' became 'lilting'.

'Karmic' became 'Comic' — which applied to the whole scene, Duncan thought as he left the camera running and returned to his seat. The fresh flowers from The Nursery with their eyes shut, their heads turning back and forth. The older members keeping stock still but seeming transported, too — caught up in this kumbaya moment — which explained why it was Duncan who first noticed the figure approaching the automatic doors to the pizzeria, and why it was he who stood when the glass parted and the nightmare figure entered, not wearing the wooden witchdoctor mask of his earlier vision but the kind of hooded gas mask that had vexed him once upon a time. Water Lily this was not. Others began to look, first at Duncan, then to the entrance, to this thing, this walking premonition, this Jim Henson Workshop dark angel with its arms held out in front of it, elbows locked, its silver shoes splayed in a shooter's pose, the shouted words muffled beyond comprehension by the gas mask. Duncan would later speculate why he didn't take cover, at least sit the fuck down, though in the moment he was busy cramming in thoughts about Kari and Zeb and the mess he'd leave them in. But the moment stretched — the shooter's hesitation lasted so long it couldn't just be the time-distorting adrenalin in Duncan's bloodstream — leaving time enough for Cushion Spurge to place his guitar on the floor without a sound, stalk the five or six paces to the doorway, and spear-tackle the intruder. And even then Duncan could not let loose the breath he'd held, because he was presented with another vision of Giuseppe, the perfect scene to cap his failure in Martina Franca.

He closed his eyes.

Let everything sink in.

Then Duncan stepped back to the tripod, brought the legs together, tucked it under his arm and took Mack's hand, raising her to her feet.

'C'mon,' he said, 'we're getting out of here.'

MARTINA FRANCA

Giuseppe is clearing breakfast dishes from the dining room. All the brothers have left but, unusually, the master of novices remains. It is no secret that Giuseppe has struggled with this task of late. As a sign of penance he has attached fragments of dropped plates and bowls to his robe, such that its hem is constantly brushing the ground, making another spill even more likely. And beneath his robe: the knee behind which the tumour appeared, as if overnight, signalling, he feared, the return of his childhood affliction. The tumour he attended to himself, cutting it out so completely there was little flesh left and no chance of him walking, let alone undertaking the labour required of a novice, for the better part of a month.

'Brother Stefano?' says the master of novices, for this is the name Giuseppe was given upon his arrival with the Capuchins.

'Yes, Father?'

'Sit with me a moment.'

'But Father—?'

'Put them down.' He nods at the dishes. 'Carefully. Good, now sit. Yes, there.' The master of novices grimaces and, though he lets his muscles slacken almost instantly, it seems to take many seconds for the skin of his face to reach a restful attitude. 'Brother Stefano, do you know why men go through the period of the novitiate?'

'To demonstrate their suitability for life within the Order?'

'And how long have you been with us?'

'Eight months, Father.'

'And what chance do you see of demonstrating your suitability for spiritual life or manual work in the next four months?'

'Father?'

'Giuseppe,' he says, meaning to continue but making the mistake of looking into the not-yet-eighteen-year-old's eyes and seeing that, despite his mental deficiencies, he has grasped the significance of hearing his birth name, just as San Stefano saw the men laying down their coats at the feet of Saul of Tarsus and knew that he was to be stoned. 'Giuseppe,' he repeats, letting his chest inflate, 'I must ask that you return to the world. Your health is frail, you are constantly distracted. Whether in garden or kitchen you are sure to wreak havoc and not one of your brothers has come to your defence. When I raise the question of your suitability, it is I who fall into the role of your defender. This is not how it must be. Your continued presence is a threat not only to our store of crockery, but to the novitiate period of your brothers and the harmonious operation of this entire convent.' The master of novices sighs and caresses his beard. 'There simply isn't enough cloth left to display the extent of your ineptitude, and thus I must ask for your habit and that you take your leave of us — today.'

Giuseppe will later describe this moment as if he was being asked to take his skin off with his habit. Indeed, since he has managed to lose most of the clothes he brought with him to Martina Franca, he takes his first steps away from the convent clad only in a wide-brimmed hat, a vest, and a pair of trousers with one leg cut off at the thigh to accommodate his still-bandaged wound. It is April 1621. He is at equal risk of too much or too little sun. He has no money. Nothing on his feet. He is leaving his first religious order without ever mastering the ecstasies he has known since his earliest memories. Even now, in the midst of this failure, he can feel the string that runs from the back of his tongue to his heart vibrating as if plucked with great violence. He can feel the Virgin's presence. He attributes to her the vision he sees: the image of Our Lady that was discovered in a cave near Copertino.

But there are other visions too. They come unbidden, uncontrolled. The young mystic is standing in the midday sun with a long walk ahead of him, but he is seeing the encounter with his uncle, Francesco Desa, in Avetrana two days hence, and the news that Giuseppe's father has died and that he is now, as his heir, liable for his debts and will be sent to prison if he falls into the hands of his creditors.

He sees his mother remove her shoe to beat him over the head upon his return to Copertino.

He sees another uncle, Gianni Donatus Caputo, the Provincial for Puglia and Poland, upbraiding him for his failure with the Capuchins and refusing to help.

He sees the priest in charge of building the sacristy at Grottella stepping forward after his uncle has left and offering to let him hide in the small attic of the church until his creditors relinquish their claim or his uncles relent.

This is what he sees as he resumes his lock-kneed bumble back to Copertino.

He does not know it will be six months in that attic cell as a *clandestino di Dio* before his sad fate and hidden virtues exert themselves on his uncles. Six months before he receives the habit of a tertiary and the immunity this grants him from secular law.

He does not know that he will face similar challenges with his new set of brothers, or that his ecstasies will begin to lift him to the heavens, or that he will be revered and reviled in almost equal measure until the final years of his life.

He does not know these things, though none of them will come as a surprise. Not in the least.

STRANGE TORPEDO

They arrived in Fossombrone in total darkness. A day early. No accommodation booked. No plan. It had taken only an hour to get there from San Marino's eastern edge. Google Maps had honed in on the nearby Convento Beato Benedetto, where San Giuseppe da Copertino had spent four comparatively uneventful years, and with a shrug (Duncan) and a nod (Mack) they continued on this route, out of the township, across an old bridge that spanned an unseen river, and up a narrow, winding lane untroubled by any light source but the headlamps of the Micra. On reaching their destination — a pin on the map on his phone, rather than any structure visible through the windscreen — they parked up, reclined their seatbacks and set about trying to sleep, which soon felt more like trying not to rock the car too much whenever one of them needed to change positions.

A couple of hours in, Mack ended the charade: 'That *was* Sister Francesca of the Silver Shoes, wasn't it?'

'Uh-huh.'

'*It's all your fault.*'

'What?'

'That's what she screamed.'

'No,' he said. 'There's no way you could have understood that.'

'What else could she have said before pointing the gun at me?'

'At you? That was a Second Wave outfit, Mack. The hooded gas mask. That's why she was hiding out. That's how she recognised me.'

'Looked more like what the zombie soldiers wear in *Paranoia* to me. Besides, I was the one who almost rumbled her. I'm the one who made her snap and got her kicked out of her convent.'

'We should have probably stuck around,' said Duncan. 'I mean, we could have helped the police, you know, piece things together.'

'I honestly don't think they would've called the police. That chicky was messed up. She probably already has a flower name and a bunk in The Nursery.'

'You reckon?'

'Babe, they put the moves on me. They sure as hell tried with you. You think a gas mask would put them off?'

'They put moves on you?'

'Amateurs,' she said, readjusting her weight in a way that somehow ended the conversation. But they didn't sleep after that either, or at least Duncan didn't. The certainty he'd felt in the pizzeria as Cush had tackled the would-be shooter — that it was Sister Francesca beneath that hood; that the Consequences Deferred from moving to Hollywood on the back of his Second Wave-induced infamy had finally come to a head — it all seemed less concrete now with time and distance between him and Mille Fiori. Did Sister Francesca — or whatever her real name was — really blame them for getting kicked out of the convent? Did she think they'd dob her in to the authorities? Was shooting one or both of them the solution to anything? And how had she tracked them down, anyway? They'd talked to her about San Marino, but the Republic wasn't *that* small. But — *oh yes* — the spiel about his Q&A on Mille Fiori's website. She must've Googled 'Duncan Blake' and the most recent result had led her right to him. Only, she hadn't made it in time for the Q&A. If she'd barged into The Nursery in the middle of his grilling about *Fury's Reach*, he might have welcomed a bullet between the eyes. But instead she'd arrived late.

And she didn't pull the trigger.

What if it wasn't her, but a flower pretending to be her? If, somehow, maybe during that Virtual Reality bullshit in the Dream Lab, they'd managed to tap his deepest anxieties and had staged the near-assassination to push him into their arms at last? It seemed far-fetched, but what wasn't? Flying friars? Telekinesis? Collaborating with Frank Motta? His and Mack's hasty retreat meant he'd never know about the shooter for sure. But maybe knowing was overrated. He guessed Mack would prefer not to know the truth about her father — certainly the way in which that truth was delivered. He thought about how to direct her through a conversation about this, one that didn't make it seem like he felt obliged. Maybe he just needed to train a camera on her and push record.

He was woken by the slamming of a car door. If it wasn't for the sensation of being woken, he would have said he hadn't slept a wink. But the sun was up and someone else was in the car park. Mack was awake too. In unison they pulled the levers to bring their seatbacks upright and saw that they hadn't even made it fully into the car park, but had spent the night on a grassy verge between tapering cedars. There was no sign of the owner of the car parked out front of the church. The activities of the convent were cloaked behind its brick facade and the long stone wall that stretched all the way back down the drive to the turnoff.

Mack: 'I'm famished, babe.'

'There's a box of Cipsters back there.'

She groaned. 'Any chance of a cooked breakfast?'

'This is another Capuchin convent.'

'Oh great. We've had so much success with them so far.'

Duncan leaned over his seat to the bags in the back, getting his things together for another tilt at location scouting. He hadn't watched back those final moments in Mille Fiori: Alby-Cooper's goodbye-welcome, Sister Francesca's entrance, Cush's tackle. Perhaps, if he'd been making a documentary about Second Wave, he might have captured its climax. Perhaps he could still make that film. Then again, the action might all have happened out of frame. Besides, they'd left all that behind and were back in the footsteps of Floating Joe.

The gravity of the status quo.

The comfort of the familiar.

'Banana?' he offered.

'Guess that'll have to do.'

They sat on the hood of the Micra, Mack eating the banana, Duncan checking if the journalist had filed her piece about him working with the maestro.

'Is it some kind of Lent?' she asked.

'What?'

'You not eating.'

'I eat.'

'When was the last time? We left before you'd even ordered any pizza last night.'

'I don't know. Lunch?'

'How are you not famished?'

He put his phone back in his pocket. 'Nothing yet.'

'What?'

'That interview I did yesterday. I'm running interference for Motta's latest scandal. But the article isn't up yet. Couldn't find anything about Motta either.'

'You know this will blow up in your face, right? If it's big, like, if Motta is marrying his step-daughter or ordered a hit on his ex-wife, your name and his will be linked. You didn't, like, act all gushy about him, did you?'

'I may have called him a maestro.'

'Fuck. You pleasure a monster, babe, it's gonna take more than a breath mint to cover the stench.'

'He's not a monster.'

'No, he's the *maestro*.'

'It might be nothing. Maybe there is no scandal to suppress. Maybe he's actually doing me a favour. Throwing me another bone to lift my profile. Maybe he's already got another job lined up for me.'

Or maybe this is just another false start for Motta's passion project, he thought. Maybe *Giuseppe* is about to be returned to the backburner. Maybe he'll be back at Sforza's this time next week. A grovelling call to Bill Gobbins and one sly reference to the *Variety* article and he could waltz back into the job.

They approached the convent on foot. It felt less enclosed than Pietrarubbia. More hilltop than arena. No satanic billy goats, just the convent buildings and trees and the thirty-foot-high iron cross that looked like it had been made out of red Meccano and, slowly, the view deepening with every step until they were at the base of the cross and could see the entire valley beneath them. The emerald Metauro snaking through the terracotta township. The tree-clad hill opposite them. The rolling plains and glinting solar farms. Just the hint of sea before the vanishing point.

Mack: 'I think I just jizzed in my pants.'

'Better than Matera?'

'Some gelato wouldn't go a miss, but, yeah. Someone should put this place in a movie.'

He stepped back to read the inscription on the pedestal that held the cross. He'd just typed the first line — Fvlget Crvcis Mysterivm — into his phone when Mack called him over to a waist-high concrete plinth with a red-flowering plant on top. Around her side, the face was marble and inscribed with what looked like a list of names.

'Lookee here,' she said, tapping the fourth line.

S. GIUSEPPE DA COPERTINO 1653–57

Duncan lifted the drooping foliage to reveal COLLE DEI SANTI inscribed in larger lettering.

Google: HILL OF SAINTS

From P. Lodovico Tenaglia 1536 through to P. Giuseppe Bocci 1974, it appeared that eight saints had spent time atop this hill, though Duncan's Giuseppe was the only one to stay more than a year. Of all the places in Giuseppe's life, this one had seemed the least eventful. He underwent no trials in Fossombrone; his faith appeared constant; his ecstasies were frequent without ever threatening to disrupt the seclusion he and his confreres enjoyed. His next and final destination, Osimo, at least saw his death — his remains were still on display in the crypt beneath the basilica that came to bear his name. But Fossombrone? No scene set here had presented itself to Duncan as a premonition, and there'd seemed little reason to jimmy this location into the movie of Giuseppe's life. Uffy's bullet points were cursory, suggesting that if anything from Fossombrone was ever going to be depicted it would be brief and possibly set to music. But being here, looking down from the belvedere to the bottleglass river, Duncan began to consider how you could set the entire picture on this hill of saints. A scene began to form slowly, a mix of workaday inspiration and deliberate construction, and he reached into his satchel for his notebook: the camera follows three friars as they walk the path up the hill, burdened by sacks of supplies, pausing at every Station of the Cross until they reach the top, at which point we zoom out and see that it was Giuseppe's perspective we had inhabited as he watched his brothers' laborious journey. A kind of premature omniscience. But this was Motta's signature shot, wasn't it? One character looking down on others from a great height. Or maybe it was just a rehash of the opening to *Aguirre: The Wrath of God*. Motta once called Werner Herzog a dangerous egotist. This was after Herzog claimed never to have seen one of Motta's films.

Duncan shut his notebook and returned it to his satchel.

A man and a woman walked past, coming within just a few feet of him. Duncan hadn't heard another vehicle, but it was there when he turned to inspect the car park: a white Audi with tinted windows. The man had a sweater tied around his waist, and his hand was slid into the back pocket of his partner's shorts. They stepped on to the small wall where the paving ended and the slope down to the valley floor began, then sat to admire the view.

'We should get inside the church,' he said to Mack, 'before it gets too crowded.'

Through the first door he found the usual church newsletters and copies of *Donare* magazines on a narrow table, only these were joined by stacks of glossy, palm-sized books on *Il Beato Benedetto da Urbino* and *San Giuseppe da Copertino*. This second book, published in Fossombrone in 2011, had the subtitle, *Il santo che sconcerta le consuetudini umane*.

Google: *The saint who disconcerts human habits*.

Mack had already gone through the next door and into the church proper, but there were also back issues of *Donare*, each with features on San Giuseppe, including an edition from 2006 which showed poor Joe on the cover being lifted/molested by a cast of uninterested angels. Duncan gathered up copies of everything and was stuffing them into his satchel when the couple from outside entered, smiling. The anteroom was hardly big enough for three people, but they stopped and stood there, tanned and toned, the kind of people who live their forties like they should've lived their twenties.

'*Buongiorno*,' the man said, clearly in his mother tongue.

'*Buongiorno*, Duncan parroted.

'*Anche tu sei in pellegrinaggio?*' the woman asked, bringing her plaited ponytail forward from behind her shoulder.

He knew *pellegrino* meant 'pilgrim' and guessed she was asking if he was on a pilgrimage. '*Più o meno*,' he said.

'*Anche noi! Non è bello qui?*'

Duncan smiled and nodded, hoping to edge into the church where talking would be frowned upon, but the man asked, 'Are you American?' in perfect English.

'I'm from New Zealand.'

'Is that your car out there?' The woman's English was equally flawless, and she contorted her hands and face to mimic the distorted passenger side of the Micra.

'She's a little banged up but she runs just fine.'

The man turned to his wife and mumbled something. She went back outside, still holding the door, and yelled in Italian.

'Did you come here because of San Giuseppe da Copertino?' Duncan asked the man.

'I'm a pilot.'

'*Dice che aspetterà fuori*,' the woman said, returning. 'Aurora, our daughter,' she explained to Duncan. 'Shall we go in?'

Duncan led the way. Mack was sitting in the frontmost pew, looking up at the altar.

'Your wife?' the woman asked. There were no clergy around to frown at her.

'We're just friends,' he said, leading them along the right edge of the church. 'Do you fly too?'

They came to a stop in front of a small statue of San Giuseppe behind a pane of glass. The pilot was behind them, inspecting the detailing on one of the confessional booths. The sculptor had depicted Giuseppe in the instant before he took flight, the toe of his right shoe still in contact with the wooden display box that probably once held a relic but now looked empty.

'Like him?' the woman asked, pointing at Giuseppe.

'No, I mean, like your husband. Airplanes?'

'Oh! Yes, well, I used to. Before Aurora.'

'*Do* you fly like him?' Duncan asked, now meaning the saint.

She smiled, interpreting the remark as flirtation rather than genuine enquiry. 'His head's too big, don't you think?'

'Giuseppe? Is it the halo?'

'Maybe you would get a big head too,' she said, 'if you could fly.'

Her husband joined them, nodded at the figure of the saint, and crossed himself.

'This is a long way from anywhere,' he said, 'but especially New Zealand.'

'I'm working on a movie.'

'About him?' He nodded at Giuseppe.

'It's not going so well. Maybe if my Italian was better.'

'We can help!' said the woman. 'I'm Maura, by the way, and this is Carlo.'

'Are you making friends, babe?' Mack asked, one hand on his shoulder and one on Maura's.

After another five minutes inside the church, Maura let loose a flood of fawning Italian over the intercom that not only got them inside the convent but gave them access to a range of resident Capuchins and every room they could ever want to see. Through his translators, Duncan asked about San Giuseppe, his life in Fossombrone and the modern occupants' opinions about his flights and ecstasies. They were all of a type, these friars — kind-eyed but dull. Like dairy cows, he thought, then scolded himself. They put a lot of thought into their responses, were proud of their convent's connection to the saint, but nothing they said or showed him was in the least cinematic. The only thing Duncan felt compelled to record in his notebook, besides the usual dimensions and light readings, was the story of a miracle attributed to a different saint, Aldebrando, a bishop who pre-dated the convent but had a cathedral dedicated to him down in the town. When he was old and bedridden, Aldebrando was brought a cooked partridge, but it was a fast day. Rather than send his servant away, the future saint prayed over the bird until it came to life and flew out through the window.

Even Mack had to admit, as they ate lunch with the rest of the convent — a watery bean casserole that Duncan couldn't be fussed with, even on an empty stomach — that maybe engaging with the locals wasn't all she'd expected. Maura and Carlo, on the other hand, seemed enthralled. It was as if they were using Duncan and Mack, gaining confidence, access and understanding thanks to *their* presence, rather than the other way around. From time to time Maura would duck outside to check on her daughter — Duncan imagined a sourpuss teen glued to a phone in the back seat of the Audi — but each time she returned fondling her braid in girlish anticipation of another theological grilling. When Duncan ran out of questions, Maura added her own. She seemed especially pleased when Duncan asked her or Carlo to fill the frame of photographs, even if it was always just the backs of their heads. In the end, he and Mack left their tanned translators with a particularly slow-blinking padre, claiming they were on a tight schedule and needed to scout the exterior.

Outside, Mack followed the sign for *Servici Igenici* and Duncan headed for the car. Halfway between the Audi and the Micra, a small girl was crouched over something, her back to him. As he moved closer, she shot her head around, then returned to her task just as suddenly. She looked Asian. Maybe five or six years old. No sign of her parents. Her hands were held out as if warming them over a fire. Only there was a black smudge where the fire should be.

A blackbird.

Long dead, if its stiff, torpedo posture was any indication.

The girl's hands pulsed inches above the bird.

He thought about Aldebrando's partridge.

He thought about *Matilda*, the scene where the little girl mind-flings a newt on to the evil schoolmistress.

He thought about Giuseppe bringing a flock of sheep back to life with these self-same movements.

He lifted the XC and took a photo, then another. The girl gave no indication she'd heard the shutter. Her eyes were screwed tight. She seemed to be emitting some kind of sound, not a hum, more like the sustained scream of someone deep inside her belly.

He switched to video mode.

'Aurora!' Maura yelled, still thirty yards away. '*Ti ho detto di stare lontano da quell'uccello!*'

'You're Aurora?' he said, for the girl's ears only.

She looked up at him — that ageless stare some kids possess — then stood, locked her thumbs into the waistband of her floral skirt and waited for her mother to arrive.

He brought the camera down, held it against his belly, but kept rolling.

Maura clamped a hand on the girl's shoulder.

'So this is Aurora?' he said, hoping to soften the scolding Maura was about to deliver.

She smiled, rediscovering her earlier cheer. 'We saved her from an orphanage.'

What an origin story.

'She's a little—' Maura rolled her hand over, never finishing her sentence.

THREE CALLS

A WhatsApp message from Vilma Vegas: 'Tell me what this means?' It was followed by a pasted link for the *Variety* article: 'Frank Motta gives *Curio Bay* director a lifeline after Hollywood false start (EXCLUSIVE)'.

Duncan replied, 'Meaning: Undetermined.'

Next thing, she was calling him.

'What do you mean, undetermined? That story read like you're doing more than just taking some photos for Motta. It also read like you're so far up his ass only your sneakers are showing, but I guess that's the game.'

'I had pretty clear direction from Motta's assistant.'

'But, I mean, this is good, right? You're part of the crew? You're "collaborating"?'

'I promise if there's ever the need for a jiu-jitsu expert—'

'Taekwondo, but yeah. Hey, um, did you get my script?'

'I did. At least, I've noted its presence in my inbox. I haven't opened it yet. Saving it for the plane trip home. That's what we agreed, right?'

'Yeah, sure.'

'Maybe I'll get to it sooner. I've got to finish my lookbook and pitch for when I see Motta in Rome the day after next. And I've got to *get* to Rome. I'm in Osimo now, just a couple hundred yards from the crypt of San Giuseppe. But I'm done gathering material.

Just got to knuckle down and knock it out.'

'You got this, D.'

'It's a lifeline, right?'

'You got this.'

It was Monday morning in LA and the beginning of his second evening in Osimo. He was staying in the hotel Uffy had booked, on a day she'd booked him in, in sync with the itinerary once again. Mack had wanted to splurge on a separate room, and he didn't stop her. The town had been an old Roman fortress, and their hotel perched between the outer wall and a natural escarpment. When he'd first pushed back the shutters to reveal the valley beyond his window, he could see how Motta would like it here. Nature and history both at arm's length.

He and Mack had spent all of their first day in Osimo together at the Basilica of San Giuseppe da Copertino, and he had the bounty from that visit now spread out on his hotel bed. A half-dozen glossy pamphlets on the saint, as well as books — entire books — that tackled (in Italian, but still) the theological bird's nest of Giuseppe's talents, his connection with Poland, and his parallels with Saint Francis of Assisi. There was even a short graphic novel called *Il Frate che Volava*.

Google: *The Friar Who Flew*.

As far as he could tell from the pictures and his minimal Italian, the story centred on Giuseppe's Inquisition in Naples — the whole thing was basically a storyboard for the one scene Duncan hadn't scouted in person. He'd just finished cobbling together a two-page spread for his lookbook using frames from the comic and photos of the churches of San Lorenzo Maggiore and San Gregorio Armeno from the internet. He couldn't say if it was good or bad that his Naples pages looked in keeping with the rest of his first-hand content.

The basilica and convent in Osimo had more riches in store than just books and pamphlets. He and Mack had been led around by Brother Otto, a close-cropped, bespectacled Austrian with excellent English. He'd studied philosophy and theology before saying yes to The Calling. Maybe it was his monastic attire but, like the brothers in Fossombrone, he seemed weighed down, slowed — physically and mentally — by the life he'd chosen.

The basilica itself was dominated by San Giuseppe in fresco rising above the altar and organ pipes to take his place on the ceiling of the apse as if he had just sprung from his hiding place. A jack-in-the-box that had sat coiled this whole time, waiting for Duncan. Then there was the wing of the convent dedicated to Giuseppe paraphernalia. Room after room of relics in glass display boxes: his tatty brown habit, his slippers and handkerchief, the more ornate vestments he wore to celebrate Mass, the wooden bowls he ate from, his chipped spoon, the letters he wrote, books he read, his rosary, casts in wax and silver of his death mask, and, of course, the real deal down in the crypt: his physical form in its final repose inside a glass coffin held aloft by two sculpted angels. Back upstairs, the poky timber cell in which the saint spent his final years was on display for pilgrims and location scouts, replete with the artwork Giuseppe chose as a reminder of the impermanence of earthly toil: a skull and crossbones against a black background, with a golden crown floating above it as a halo might. The skull was detailed, unnerving. It seemed to pop out from the unframed canvas, as if you could stick your finger inside the nasal cavity so long as a slender snake didn't slither out first.

'Maybe you *should* have been wearing your TOÄD t-shirt all along?' Duncan had said, but Mack had just wrapped her arms around his waist and pressed her head to the side of his arm, having seen something — or someone — else in that skull.

It was as if the tap that had been so difficult to budge until The Hill of Saints had now been opened right up and there was more Giuseppe pouring forth than one person could ever handle, but it was still not as pleasurable as the build-up might have suggested. The pane of glass between them and everything extended to Brother Otto's responses, his true feelings about the man who spent so much time in ecstasy within the same complex. What it would have been like with Gianluca at his side? Another student of theology, though one for whom this earthbound life could not so easily be dismissed.

È una gran tentazione non avere tentazioni.

It is a great temptation to have no temptation.

★

Five minutes after Duncan's call with Vilma, it was the turn of his old agent.

'I thought I told you about the deal with Netflix,' Tanner Burge said, no time for small talk, 'just a handful of territories, but still. Maybe I didn't. My bad. What are you working on now?'

'Hi Tanner, good to hear from you.'

'So—?'

'I take it you read the *Variety* piece? And then you got around to opening my email?'

'Listen, maybe I should have been more patient with you. I get that. But do you know how many people bounce back? I give my all for my clients, you know that—'

'Do I?'

'—but I can't do that for *everybody*.'

'So what am I now, Tanner? Somebody or everybody?'

'Are you repped by someone else, is that it? Someone must've looked at whatever you've signed with Motta, right?'

'No, I signed all that myself. No agent, no attorney. It felt good.'

'I don't have time if you're going to play hard to get, Duncan.'

'Who's playing?'

'I gotta say, even though you're being a pain in the behind, I like this new you.'

'I bet Echo Park treated you real good, Tanner, after you served me up on a platter. Another disposable sucker.'

'Hey, Dunk, c'mon man.'

'No, you come on. Be honest, just this once.'

'Fuck it. Sure, I knew Echo Park had a Plan B if you weren't knocking it out of the park. They saw it as a win-win. Maybe not for you, but you gotta bring your big-boy pants when you come to Hollywood, right? But you had a chance, however slim. You know deep down you never got control of the crew. The shoot was chaos. Getting the boot after Day Three, okay, that's harsh. They could have given you another week or two, maybe, but why burn money? You had your shot and you blew it. You're not the first and you won't be the last.'

'I'm sure you're right, but at least this is the last time I have to talk to you. Goodbye Tanner,' he said, and ended the call.

A couple of hours later, just as Duncan was weighing up another run-through of his presentation — he still had all of tomorrow in the car, that night and the next morning before his audience with the pope of cinema — his phone went off again. A Skype call from an unknown user. He answered it in video mode, but remained silent while waiting for the caller's video feed to appear. In that two-second gap he could hear— What? The clamour of a cafe? The disorder of a farm yard? And then Zeb's face appeared, tinted fuchsia, as if he had some tropical disease.

'Mate?! How did you—? Where are you calling from? Daycare?'

His son began to smile. He'd smiled more broadly, more mischievously, before entering his stoic phase, but nothing back then had pancaked Duncan like this slight curvature of the mouth and the widening of his eyes. He fought to swallow.

'Did someone help you? One of the teachers? No? Jesus, Zeb. You're a little whiz kid.'

Zeb had called yesterday as well. Duncan was at breakfast with Mack, working through a plate of sliced blood orange and a gritty cup of tea. But that was the middle of the night for Zeb. Another call using Kari's phone and Skype account. Duncan considered the 'how' of this latest call: getting access to one of the daycare centre's tablets, finding or downloading Skype, looking up his father and making the call all by himself. And the wider significance of this string of calls: the fact Zeb got something out of them. That he needed his father. Though what was it Zeb received? Duncan's incessant questioning? Or the inevitable, rambling update that followed? Maybe it was just seeing his face.

'Hey,' he said, 'I'll be back in time for dinner on Thursday. Are you in a tent?'

Zeb looked left and right, as if he might get up and walk away.

'No, it's fine. Stay where you are. I'll pretend that your teachers can't hear me. Do you think your mum knows you've been borrowing her phone yet? It's nice to have someone to talk to. I've got Mack with me, kind of, but we mostly just talk at each other, always have. I guess I'm talking at you now, but you keep calling, so—' Duncan sat down at the built-in desk, propped his phone against the wall and leaned his chin on his hands. 'I used to get Mack to talk and talk, back in high school, and I'd just film it all, never saying a word. I had this vision, you know, of what a filmmaker was. Of what reality was. Of truth. I can excuse myself for being young and stupid, I guess, but I still thought like that up until— Ah, I don't know. Oh, Zeb. You should come back out into the world. You won't spoil anything by participating. You'll enrich it. Do you see the way my face lights up when I realise it's you that's called me? I got a call from my old agent earlier. It felt so good to hang up on him. What's that? Did you say something? No? Must've been one of your friends, huh? Maybe they want to play with you? I love you, my little brainbox. You can teach me how to use all the technology when I get home, okay? No more Chromecasting for me.' There was the unmistakable sound of a zipper and Zeb's face lost its fuchsia tinge. He'd been discovered. 'Okay. You give the tablet back to whoever you pinched it from. Okay. I love you, champ. Okay, see you in a couple of days. Bye.'

STAY LOST

The odd thing wasn't that Mack was fifteen minutes late the next morning, or that she was wearing her long leather coat for the first time in at least a week — the man at reception had warned Duncan, in what may have been his own colourful idiom, that the sky was full of sheep and winter danced in summer too — but that she emerged through the automatic doors with just an apple in her hand. No luggage. No checkout fluster.

'What gives?' Duncan asked.

She bit the apple, one of those dark-red, top-heavy deals that look good in fruit baskets but aren't engineered for eating.

'I'm not ready to leave, babe,' she said through her mouthful.

'Clearly.'

'No, I mean—' She stopped to swallow. 'I'm not coming with you to Rome. I'm not ready to go back to work.'

'You're not going to go back to Mille Fiori, are you?'

'No, but maybe I'll go to Turin and check out the time travellers of Damanhur.' Another bite of apple.

'But what about your guarantee that we'd be singing along to Hootie and the Blowfish by the end of this trip?'

'I put a little something on your phone for the drive back.'

'Thanks,' he said, processing how long she must have been planning this non-departure, 'but it won't be the same without you.'

'You're damned straight it won't be.'

'I feel as if I've failed you. As if I've never been a good friend to you.'

She brought the apple to her mouth slowly, holding eye contact, took a bite. 'Maybe you should come see the time travellers too?'

'If I mess things up with Motta tomorrow, maybe I'll have to.'

'You still want it, huh?'

He hadn't told her about his call with Tanner Burge, the thrill of brushing him off, and how the urge to keep brushing, to scrape and scour the last of Hollywood off him, had only grown.

'Yeah, I do,' he said. 'I want to see where *Giuseppe* will take me.'

She cocked her head to the left, deciding whether to press him, then looked at the apple as if she had no memory of it. She tossed it high over her shoulder, like a bride with a bouquet, sending it off the escarpment and down into the valley below.

'Come here, you,' Duncan said, and wrapped Mack and her stupid coat in his arms.

'You look after Kari and Zeb, babe,' she said, voice muffled, possibly crying.

'I will.'

'And don't go endorsing any more terrorist groups.'

'I won't.'

'And don't just accept the first crappy script that gets thrown your way, no matter how many zeroes come with it.'

'I've learnt my lesson.'

'And I really do think you can fly. Or *could* fly, if you put your mind to it.'

They separated. Stood there, an arm's length apart.

'I saw you fall from the ceiling of that *trullo* cone in Martina Franca,' she said. 'And I saw enough at Mille Fiori to know it wasn't *all* bullshit. I mean, think of the odds stacked against your boy, Giuseppe. That the village idiot would become a saint. Smoke and mirrors will only get you so far.'

'If he hadn't had a penis, he would have been burnt at the stake.'

'But he flew, right? Don't you believe that now?'

'I don't know.'

'Come on. Babe, the sky won't fall if you just admit it.'

'I don't know!'

'If Motta finds you sitting on the fence tomorrow he's going to leave you there, you know that, right?'

'I have my pitch.'

'That's all you'll say? Okay, fine. You say you still want it? Cool. Best of luck to you.'

'Mack.'

'It's cool. I said, it's cool.'

'I'll give you a call tomorrow night, either way.'

'You'd better.'

'And come to LA sometime. It doesn't have to be for work.'

'We'll see.'

PLAYLIST

This is tomorrow — Brian Ferry
When tomorrow comes — Eurythmics
Desperately wanting — Better than Ezra
Do you sleep? — Lisa Loeb
Singing in my sleep — Semisonic
Fall down — Toad the Wet Sprocket
Always the last to know — Del Amitri
I will wait (live) — Hootie and the Blowfish
Into your arms — The Lemonheads
Saint Joe on the school bus — Marcy Playground
Objects in the rear view mirror may appear closer than they are —
    Meatloaf
Always crashing the same car — David Bowie
Big bang baby — Stone Temple Pilots
God shuffled His feet — Crash Test Dummies
One headlight — The Wallflowers
Turn me loose — Loverboy
If you could only see — Tonic
This mess we're in — PJ Harvey
I have loved me a man — Allison Durbin
Crazy — Seal
I will wait (acoustic) — Hootie and the Blowfish
Strange glue — Catatonia

La la land — Shihad
Wonderboy — Tenacious D
Seven wonders — Fleetwood Mac
Walk on the ocean — Toad the Wet Sprocket
Basket case — Green Day
Don't worry baby — Beach Boys
Since I left you — The Avalanches
Give me one reason — Tracy Chapman
It's alright (baby's coming back) — Eurythmics
This time tomorrow — The Kinks
In the meantime — Spacehog
I will wait — Hootie and the Blowfish

GRACE, TOO

Duncan's arrival in Rome that afternoon showed him how comfortable, relatively speaking, he had become driving in the more sedate Italian modes. Negotiating the first tight car park under the watchful kohl-rimmed eyes of the two clerks in Lecce and the near-death experience on leaving the convent at Martina Franca felt like ancient history. But there was no pretending the Micra didn't bear the scars. That he didn't have some explaining to do.

When he made it to the designated rental-car branch, just a couple of hundred yards from the walled gardens of the Vatican, he couldn't see anywhere special to park, so he found a space on the tree-lined avenue and went inside to tell the clerk. There was just the one guy behind the counter. His name badge said 'Basil' but he looked like a full-blooded, twenty-something Italian: the manicured facial hair, the burnt-sienna skin, the hint of *Vaffanculo* in every hand gesture.

'I've parked out on the street,' Duncan said.

'It is okay.'

'And she's a little banged up, I'm sorry to say.'

Basil seemed reluctant to leave the counter, as if he expected someone far more important to arrive any second, but he went out with Duncan to inspect the damage. He noted the crumpled bodywork and shattered mirror on a form, his expression never wavering from Business as Usual. He didn't ask any questions, just got Duncan to sign the form and thanked him for his custom.

'How much will it cost?' Duncan asked.

'You have full insurance,' Basil said, pained by his exposure to sunlight or his distance from an imminently ringing telephone.

'Yeah, but—?'

'Don't worry,' he said. He patted the air beside Duncan's arm and jogged back inside.

It seemed wrong to end the road trip like this. His and Mack's most dramatic vehicular incident reduced to paperwork and a shrug. To him alone on the pavement with his scuffed luggage. And what of that other near-miss: the attempt on his life by Sister Francesca? Nothing had come of that either. Google was silent about the attack. No email from Mille Fiori trying to weasel him back. Not a scratch on him. Maybe it was all the film noir he'd watched with Kari the year they met — their tender, tentative steps towards a relationship in the shadows cast by Edward G. Robinson, Lana Turner and Ida Lupino — or maybe it was the image of the real location scout, the one riddled with cartel bullets in a Mexican alley, that made him feel he might only have learned something — *really* learned something — if he had come to some harm.

A pinky finger snipped off with garden shears.

A busted eye socket.

A couple broken legs.

And then it hit him as he crossed the road to reach the narrow park in the median strip. No great epiphany, just another complete scene from the movie of the life of San Giuseppe da Copertino that existed only in his head and unfolded for him incomplete and in reverse. He had to take a seat as he processed this sudden download of images. The father fleeing his debtors. The mother giving birth to the future saint in an empty stable. The beginning of the *vita*. The end of the line for his inspiration.

He saw it then. What he'd present to Motta. More than these visions, he'd share what he believed. That Mille Fiori was on to something. That Giuseppe did some of the fantastical things they say he did. That there was bound to be exaggeration. Various groups and individuals who wanted to run a current through Giuseppe to make him into a magnet. But he *could* fly.

Okay, Italy. You've broken me. I yield. I believe.

'Do you mind if I smoke?' Duncan lifted his head from his hands to see Basil, still in uniform, holding an e-cigarette. 'This is where I usually smoke.'

It was odd to see him out here after he'd seemed so anxious away from the counter a couple of minutes ago. 'Sure,' Duncan said, scooting over on the park bench. 'Is anyone minding the counter for you?'

Basil sat down. 'It's okay,' he said, and took a pull from his e-cigarette and emitted an impossibly white plume of smoke.

'Watermelon?' Duncan asked.

'Strawberry.'

'Huh.'

'Are you okay, Mr Blake? Do you need directions?'

'No, I'm fine. I'm staying nearby. Is your name really Basil?'

He nodded while taking another drag.

'Not Basilico or Basilano or—'

'Just Basil.'

'Huh.'

'The damage was no problem. Many people—'

'It wasn't that. I was just thinking about a scene. For this movie I'm working on. For someone else. It's someone else's movie I'm working on.'

'I see.'

'I've got to pitch my ideas tomorrow. Only, the director probably isn't expecting ideas.' Duncan noticed his single-use friend get out his phone. 'Sorry, I'll shut up. You probably want peace and quiet.'

'You are working with Frank Motta?' Basil asked.

'How'd you—?'

Basil swivelled his phone. The *Variety* piece was clearly top of the pile when it came to 'Duncan Blake' search results that morning.

'I forget others have the same superpower as me.'

'I like his films.'

'How many have you seen?'

'All of them.'

'All of them?'

'I'm a filmmaker too.'

'I work in a restaurant back home. At least, I did. What sort of films do you make?'

'Short ones.'

'Best place to start. I sometimes wish I could start over again. Stay small. Maybe I'll have to. I'm going to blow it tomorrow.'

'Don't worry.'

'You say that, but—'

Basil stood, inhaled one last burst of vapour and held it, his chest puffed out, for three seconds, four, then let loose a swirling white haze.

The Hotel Pacific was ten minutes' walk further from the Vatican, though its chief selling point still seemed to be its proximity to the Pope. It certainly wasn't the Pacific theme which, besides a model ship in reception and the odd nautical photograph framed on the walls, was non-existent.

Was it possible to feel homesick for an ocean that covered a third of the Earth's surface? Answer: yes.

He wasn't sure if Motta was staying at the same hotel, or when he and Uffy were due to arrive. He sent her a text: '*Sono arrivato a Roma*. All checked in. Rental car relinquished. Are you here? Fancy a drink?'

She replied a minute later: 'Glad you made it. I had my doubts. Busy tonight. Make sure you're there early tomorrow. But bring a book. Gotta work around the Pope. Will try prime M for your bit, but can't control his mood.'

Can't control his mood. Duncan brooded over that phrase and its many possible meanings at dinner and through the hours of darkness he spent transcribing his visions of Giuseppe and completely overhauling his material for Motta. He was still thinking about it at breakfast the next morning in the narrow dining area — *Can't control his mood* — and as he followed the itinerary's penultimate set of instructions, negotiating clumps of tourists and security checks to get into the Vatican and through a series of courtyards and corridors to a kind of lobby where he was to wait.

Can't control his mood.

A short, suited man, well beyond retirement age, directed Duncan to sit in one of the half dozen red-upholstered, golden-framed chairs lined up against a wall. The man spoke into his headset like a Secret Service agent, and left.

Alone again. Unscathed. Clueless.

Duncan got up to inspect the water-cooler. It was all crystal and marble and gilt bronze — the Rolls Royce of water-coolers — only it had run out of disposable cups. He returned to his seat. The carpet was red with crimson diamonds that each contained four yellow dots. The kind of carpet that spoke of LUXURY and RESTRAINT, but also HIGH TRAFFIC AREA and SPILL RESISTANT. It felt like the liminal space at a multiplex, the bit after you hand over your ticket and before you enter your particular screening. The sort of place you could choose to spend all day, because no one in their right mind ever would. Anything of interest or necessity was through another door.

Can't control his mood.

The two most likely interpretations: 1) Motta was in an intractably bad mood, or 2) his moods were so changeable they could not be predicted or curtailed. And if it was 2), any number of things could nudge Motta into unreceptiveness. Being stood up by the Pope. Making some kind of faux pas or being on the receiving end of one — rumour had it Motta's less than fluent Italian was a sore spot. It could be a phone call from Hollywood, a bad night's sleep, a bunion, a stye or a tickling cough. To be at the mercy of these things and to be left waiting in the most godforsaken lobby in the Holy See did nothing for Duncan's nerves. Could Motta and the friggin' Pope really be on the other side of the wall? What could they possibly discuss? What would happen if he just burst in? Maybe that's where his harm was waiting for him. The other side of the wall.

He hadn't brought a book. All he had at the hotel were books about Giuseppe. The only ones he hadn't read, weren't sick of, were in Italian. It occurred to him he could download Vilma's script, which was waiting for him in his inbox, though there were no wall sockets near the row of seats and he didn't want to add running out of battery mid-presentation to the list of possible mood killers. He thought about ringing Kari, or Zeb, or Mack, but found reasons not to for each.

He needed to focus.

All he could focus on was a list of ways this would all come to naught, and the traffic, grime and disrepair outside the walls of the Vatican. The hordes of dazzled tourists oblivious to the fact the Emperor was long dead and in his place: pettiness and corruption and inattention. The sameness of the restaurant menus. The dogs as carefully chosen accessories. The primped girls with PYREX in white letters across their budding chests, when last he checked Pyrex was a brand of glassware — the measuring jugs and casserole dishes in his mother's cupboards. Everyone in Rome and beyond trying to live their best lives on the outside, leaving nothing beneath the surface, nothing to excavate, nothing to build upon, no chance of being lifted. The show had become the reality.

'We're not ready for you just yet,' Uffy said, her head poking out from the door nearest him. He hadn't even heard it open. The red frames of her glasses matched the carpet and the seats in the lobby, as if she'd been working up to this moment her whole life. Duncan looked down at his own outfit. White button-down, black Levi's fastened with his grandfather's belt, white sneakers. A thirty-two-year-old intern.

'Is the—?' He pointed inside and made reverent gestures with his hands and eyebrows.

'The Pope?' Uffy laughed. 'You haven't seen in here, have you?' She withdrew her head. Duncan got up and entered the room. It was about the size of a classroom but even less inviting. Bare walls. A tower of plastic stacking chairs in one corner. The only other furniture was a black cathode-ray monitor and VCR on a powder-coated mobile stand. He remembered Gas Plant's apartment and, for some reason, the moment when, carving into passionfruit after passionfruit in his childhood kitchen, he realised his parents would inevitably split up.

Two men, both dressed in tan cargo pants and grey polo shirts, and carrying a folding table, came in through a door in the opposite wall.

'You're not going to need that, are you?' Uffy asked, flicking her black bangs in the direction of the monitor.

'Oh, God no,' Duncan said, then checked if the men had caught his blasphemy. They were grimacing, but it was the grimace of two people engaged in a task they'd performed hundreds of times but had yet to master: in this case, unfolding the legs of the table so that they locked in place.

Uffy ran her index finger down one glossy column of the TV stand, momentarily lost in thought. 'When I get to Hell,' she said, loud and clear, as if she'd already tested the limits of the other men's English, 'I'm going to be forced to make presentations about things I know nothing about to a bunch of seven- and eight-year-olds on one of these monitors for the rest of eternity.'

'And these guys,' he said, 'will be down there unfolding that table.'

On cue, the older of the two men stepped back from the table and said, with just the flick of his fingers, *Fine, you do it.*

'Did it go all right?' he asked. 'With the Pope?'

Uffy shrugged.

'Does that mean the information is on a Need To Know basis or that it just went so-so?'

She narrowed her eyes. 'If you must know, I meant the first one, but the second one is also true.'

'Fuck.'

'Don't worry.'

'That's what Basil said.'

'Who's Basil?'

'A friend I made this morning.'

'Another friend? And male this time.'

'You know about Mack?'

'I didn't know her name, but thanks, I'll add that to the rap sheet.' She shook her head at Duncan's bewilderment. 'Did you think I wouldn't get emails every time one of your bookings was changed? Did you think I wouldn't check out what was going on? We let you have some rope, I mean, nothing was mission critical, but once we needed to— Well, you did the interview with *Variety*. Emma owed me one. But I had to make sure you hadn't gone completely Colonel Kurtz on us.'

Duncan straightened up. 'It's all in my presentation.'

'I'm sure it is.'

The younger guy succeeded in setting up the table but knew better than to say anything, and the two men left the room in silence.

'Listen,' Uffy said, 'I gotta go check on Frank. He's having some quiet time. Feel free to set up this place however you want. I don't imagine your thing will take that long?' She turned it into a question perhaps out of courtesy. She had just belittled the quest he'd been on and admitted to using him as a diversionary tactic to preserve the credibility of her master, but he liked this Uffy a lot more than the one he'd encountered in LA.

'What are you doing after this?' he asked. 'I'm not creeping on you, honest. I'm just curious. About you.'

'And Frank's latest predicament.'

'There's a predicament?' he said with mock sincerity.

'Hold that thought,' she said, and nipped away.

He pushed the table closer to a wall, set out three seats along one edge, and began unpacking his tablet and laptop. He tried to visualise a successful presentation. Him standing; Motta seated, enraptured by the images on the tablet in his hands; Uffy next to him, unable to contain how impressive it all was.

That's so good. Isn't that good, Frank?

The old man with the earpiece entered with a silver tray of water glasses.

'*Grazie*,' Duncan said.

'*Prego*,' the man replied like a proud grandparent, and left. Duncan felt his chest bloom from the simple exchange. He wasn't the same person as the one who'd landed in Brindisi. He'd brushed off Tanner Burge and been booted from his tour in Assisi. He'd walked into the middle of Mille Fiori and walked right back out. He might still have patching up to do with Kari and be completely unequipped to deal with whatever it was that Zeb was morphing into; he might still be the same flawed friend to Mack he'd always been; he might be no closer to knowing what his new cinematic project would be — but he had managed a two-word exchange in Italian after being in that country two whole weeks.

'You got this,' he said aloud, sounding less sarcastic in that empty room than he had intended.

That was when Frank Motta entered, dressed to the nines, like a courtier entering the parlour of a Renaissance Duke.

Motta took one look at the room, the folding table and the once-promising filmmaker in smart-casual attire, and heel-turned right back out of there.

THREE NAILS

A moment later Uffy returned, followed by Motta. In his wide neck-tie and black suit with glossy lapels, he looked shorter and wider than in LA, as if he'd been whack-a-moled in the intervening fortnight. He looked like someone else, but who?

'Blake,' he said, running the meat of his hand back across his glistening scalp, 'so good to see you.'

So, yeah, maybe Frank Motta had got his name wrong. Or maybe he was just calling him by his surname — wasn't that how *he* referred to Motta? Either way, Duncan didn't correct him, just put out his hand and received Motta's, which was lacquered in scalp sweat.

'This place is quite something,' Motta said, and jutted out his chin as if his tie was too tight.

'Sorry, Frank—' Uffy began.

'My parents had a passionfruit vine,' Duncan said, loud and clear and fast. An express train zipping through a station. 'We had some great crops. Then one year, when we cut into the fruit, each and every one was completely empty. It kind of feels like that in here, right?'

'Do I know passionfruit?' Motta asked Uffy.

'You've had passionfruit.'

'Like pomegranate, right?'

'They both have seeds—' Duncan offered.

'Persephone and Hades,' Motta said, looking at a wall. 'Madonna of the Pomegranate.' He turned to Duncan. 'That's Botticelli, right?'

'He said passionfruit, though,' Uffy said. He wished she'd just drop it.

Motta: 'As in Passion of the Christ, no doubt.'

Uffy was on her phone. 'The flower,' she read aloud, 'symbolises Christ's scourging, crowning with thorns, the three nails and five wounds.'

'And on that cheery note,' Duncan said, 'shall we talk about Giuseppe?'

Uffy: 'I tried telling them we needed better chairs, Frank.'

'It's fine. Reminds me of Sforza's, right, Blake?'

'Duncan,' Uffy corrected.

'Veal manicotti,' Motta said, 'and a diet Coke, huh?'

'Coming right up, sir,' Duncan said.

Motta frowned, as if weighing up whether Duncan really would go and get him a plate of pasta. The director lowered himself into the middle chair, slowly, like he might burst the seat of his pants. Duncan held out a chair for Uffy to sit, then walked around the front of the table and stood before them like some schlub auditioning for a talent show.

'You didn't give me a script,' he said, 'so I've taken some liberties. A *lot* of liberties. I'm going to give you more than you asked for, more than you could have dreamed of.' He picked up the tablet, set the first part of the presentation running, and held it for the others to see: a silent video from inside Santa Maria della Grottella. The light streaming in through the high windows. The space seeming massive but also insignificant, cramped. 'I've scouted the locations you asked me to. I've got the measurements, the photos, the video. But I've also dived deep into the story of San Giuseppe da Copertino, into the dilemma at its heart: did he fly and, if so, how? And what does that mean for the way we live our lives now? All of which has involved diving deep into my own beliefs, my own prejudices.'

He passed the tablet to Motta, and the video cut from Grottella to the *fioritura* from Mille Fiori's website, arms held out, scarecrow straight. Her feet left the ground and her head cut through the top of the frame. There was a congruence between the stark room on screen and the one in which they sat — something Duncan couldn't have planned and hadn't considered until it smacked him in the face. The skin on his back came alive, as if a shower of snowflakes was landing upon his bare flesh.

'I was a sceptic when I landed two weeks ago. A friend of mine, an amazing actress, we exchanged theories to explain away Giuseppe's levitations. There's no shortage of them. But taken one by one, none of them stack up against the possibility that levitation is real. That what I have considered to be the realm of the possible is too narrow. This past fortnight I've been in a car crash and possibly survived an assassination attempt, but it's the paraphysical questions I can't shake. Has my sanity been tested? I freely admit it has. Have I recovered fully? Absolutely not. Can you convince anyone of anything anymore? Not unless they already want to believe. But you can pull the rug out from under them. If your film can do to your audience a fraction of what this past fortnight has done to me, you should consider it a success.'

'Do you know what he said to me? Pope Francis?' Motta said, turning to Uffy. 'Right at the end? He said, "We must leave room for the Lord. For doubt, not certainties." What does that even mean?'

Uffy winced. Duncan reached over to swipe the screen and kick off a slideshow of images from Mille Fiori that would culminate in the video of Trumpet Honeysuckle levitating in her gardening gear. 'In San Marino, a stone's throw from Pietrarubbia and Fossombrone, there's a community that not only believes in levitation, not only has a handful of practitioners, one of whom you just saw, but they're working to unlock its secrets. The challenge with *Giuseppe* has always been to bridge that gap between the beliefs — the possibilities — of the seventeenth century, and the cynicism and apathy of our own time. But through Mille Fiori, this community of psychokinetic detectives, I learnt that there is no gap. That in each of us there is both the believer and the cynic. Doubt and certainty. The levitator and the couch potato.'

'How much does he know?' Motta asked Uffy.

'Him?' She nodded at Duncan.

'No,' Motta said, annoyed, 'the pontiff. About —' he coughed — 'Miss Delaware.'

'Nothing. How could he?'

'Why'd he keep going on about God never tiring of forgiving us? That it is man who tires of asking forgiveness?'

'It sounded to me like the kind of thing he'd say to everyone.'

'Did he say San Marino?' Motta turned back to Duncan. 'Did you say San Marino? You know the story of Darryl Zanuck renting the entire country, must've been in the late forties, to film *The Prince of Foxes*? They rented a whole country and yet they shot in black and white to save money — never a good sign. Orson Welles as Cesare Borgia. Stole the show, of course. It's a total bore whenever he's off screen. *The obvious solution*,' Motta began, apparently impersonating Welles in a film Duncan had never heard of, '*to the problems I am about to present to you might be an assassin's blade in the back of that gentle old man.*'

Duncan smiled and reached into his satchel to produce the pages he'd prepared last night. His prose descriptions of the scenes from his jolts of inspiration, beginning with Giuseppe's death and working back to his birth in a stable in Copertino.

'*Now there's the jewel.*' The director continued his reverie, though the distinction between true self and impersonation, remembered lines and actual intent, was dissolving. '*Imagine all that beauty wasted on a husband old enough to be her grandfather. Spring in the lap of winter. But you're the man to correct that.*'

'Your memory is better than mine,' Duncan said, hoping to segue to his visions of Giuseppe.

'What about *Black Magic*,' Motta said, 'you seen that? Orson Welles plays a hypnotist. Ed Small wanted to film it in Mexico, but turned out it was cheaper to shoot in Italy. How's that for irony? That was seventy years ago, mind you.' Once more he wiped his brow and the scalp beyond, and Duncan saw it, finally: who Motta looked like. It was Baron Greenback, the amphibious villain from the old cartoon *Danger Mouse*. The giant, sweating head. The non-existent neck. The too-tight suit.

'Which brings us back to the locations,' Uffy said.

'Of course, my dear,' Motta said, fiddling with a cufflink. 'We absolutely owe it to Blake here to hear him out.'

'It's Duncan,' he said. 'Duncan Blake.' Each word distinct. Decisive. And yet Motta's expression was that of a passenger standing on the platform as his train rushed by.

Uffy gestured for Duncan to continue.

He and Motta weren't so different. Motta couldn't conceive of a room in which he wasn't the centre of attention — would he ever be able to process the fact the Pope had only been humouring him? — just as Duncan couldn't help but make everything about himself. This location-scouting gig. The life of San Giuseppe. The machinations of Mille Fiori. And, until recently, his friendship with Mack. Perhaps being with him was like being with Baron Greenback. One slimy ball of ego in need of pampering. That same ego blundering over the tenderness of others. Or worse, filming it and splicing it up to feed his own hunger for control. His wankbank tape, his shorts of Mack talking, even — *yes, come on, admit it* — *Curio Bay*. The way he used filmmaking as a cover from the outset. 'Why this sudden interest in movies?' his mother had asked when he was trying to record another episode of *Playboy After Dark*. 'Films,' he'd said. 'And it's not sudden. I want to be a filmmaker. You know that.' That's what Motta was doing with *Giuseppe*. He'd long suspected it, but this time the thought fell into place with a satisfying clunk.

'Do you want to make this movie or not?' Duncan said.

Motta pulled at his collar and looked down at the tablet in his other hand. He pinched the screen and a digital contact sheet of photos from the places Giuseppe lived appeared.

'You've talked about it a lot over the last thirty years,' Duncan said. 'You've talked a lot about belief. But here's what I believe: you're never going to make a film about San Giuseppe. You're going to keep changing its name, keep hiring and firing people to make it look like something's happening, but you don't believe in it anymore. Maybe you did, under that waterfall in Hawaii, maybe even the first couple of times you tried to make it. But now? No way. I'm done fooling myself it's even possible. I don't even care what your latest indiscretion is. Well, I care on the level that I hope when it inevitably comes out that I can live with myself for being associated with you, for providing even the slightest cover for you. Like, please don't say it's cannibalism or anything to do with kids or—'

'Duncan?' Uffy said, though it seemed she was trying to shunt him back on track rather than shut him down completely.

Motta's eyes were still directed at the tablet as he swiped through Duncan's photos.

'Because if it's real, if there's a script for *Giuseppe* and it has funding and the crew are ready to roll in Mexico, then it's all here. Everything you need. You're welcome to it.'

'I can't see anything from Naples,' Motta said.

'Fuck Naples.'

'Duncan,' said Uffy.

'You want Naples?' Duncan flicked through the pages in his hands. 'Here's Naples,' he said, jabbing a finger at the start of the scene. 'Here's Giuseppe being manhandled through the courtyard of the friary. His vision of Saint Anthony of Padua. Here's the two flights that defeated Monsignor Ricciullo.' He laid the pages in two piles on the table. 'This is my vision. A collection of waterfall moments. If you're going to make this movie, fucking get on and make it. Stop hiding behind it. And if you're not, move aside.'

'Move aside? For you?' Motta removed his hands from Duncan's tablet and let it fall against the table with a slap. 'You little prick. You ungrateful little naïve fucking prick.'

'Frank,' Uffy said.

Motta stood and leaned over the table to eyeball Duncan. 'You call me a cannibal? That's a new one. I thought I'd heard 'em all. You get to where I am, people only ever try to drag you down. You string two hits together and there's no one left to lift you up. You have to do it on your own. You have to sacrifice everything to stay up. Up! I have sacrificed everything. I can't feel bad about the people who've seen the soles of my shoes.'

'But for what? What's your next project going to be, Frank? The well is dry, isn't it?'

'I've shaken more talented fucks off my pant leg than you've had boners. You're nothing. I'll shake you off and sleep like a baby tonight.'

'But will you dream? Cinema is the language of dreams, isn't that right, Frank? You wrote that once upon a time. You've said a lot of things over the years,' he said, gathering up the pages and his tablet from the foldout table and stuffing them under his arm. He was going home tomorrow. He'd see Kari and Zeb and wouldn't have to spend any more time away from them. What a relief! What a farce! 'But today,' he said, 'I'm going to have the last word. You can have your pant leg back. Any boner I had for this —' he cast his free hand around the barren room — 'it just fizzled out.'

COPERTINO

A man runs through the narrow streets. Sweat has darkened a T on the back of his shirt. Exhaustion has sapped his balance. He looks over his shoulder, granting the camera the briefest glimpse of his face, his expression, his despair. He keeps running, keeps glancing back until surprised by a building that has appeared in his path, and must cushion the impact with his hands. He stands there, palms pressed to the wall, and lets his head drop. He could be panting or sobbing. He pushes himself clear of the wall, snatches his hat from his head and uses it to wipe his brow before holding it against his chest. He looks skyward, then sets off once more.

Other people appear, poking their heads from windows or stepping toward him on the street, but he presses his index finger to his lips, stumbling on until he reaches a door.

We are inside the house now. A simple dwelling. One bed, one table, one heavily pregnant woman stirring one large pot. The door opens. The man enters in shadow.

'Franceschina,' he says, stepping forward, his hat pressed against his heart. 'They are coming for me.'

'Who?'

'My creditors. The soldiers they have enlisted.'

'What creditors, Felice? You have no need to borrow.'

Felice gives a piteous smile.

'You fool,' she says. 'I told you not to act as guarantor. And where are these so-called friends of yours now?'

He looks at the floor. 'Disappeared.'

'As you must.'

'Yes,' he says, 'I know that.' He reaches a hand out to touch her belly, but she strikes it away with the wooden spoon.

'Your foolishness and sentimentality have led you here. That I should marry such a man! My brothers were right.'

'Franceschina?'

She turns and begins gathering up pieces of clothing, a loaf of bread, the few coins that fall from a clay dish. She stuffs them all into a sack and hands it to her husband.

'It would be best if you do not try to contact us for some time.'

'Us? What about the baby?' He extends his hand again, quicker this time, and finds her belly before she can deflect him. The screen explodes with images so saturated with light they might be watermarks or after-images on the underside of eyelids:

The birth of a son.

A boy of maybe ten being carried in Franceschina's arms.

A young man in rags, mouth agape, being attacked by dogs.

A tonsured friar rising from the ground with his arms outstretched like the crucified Christ.

PART THREE

SEPTEMBER–OCTOBER 2019

THE MAN IN THE BROWN DRESS

Duncan was wrong. *Giuseppe* did get made. After his outburst in the Vatican, it's no surprise he played no further part in its creation. What is surprising: getting a call from Uffy Golinko after two years of virtual silence.

'You want tickets to the screening of *Giuseppe* at the DGA next month?'

'Uffy?'

'Hi,' she says. 'Do you?'

'I guess. How are you?'

They've hardly talked since that night in Rome. Back then Uffy had texted and told him to meet at a place called Bukowski's. It was furnished like the home of a rad, gin-drinking aunt. Green velvet couches. Book-lined walls. Vape fumes. An equal mix of Italian and English conversation. She'd thrown on a leather jacket with quilted sleeves, and her red-framed glasses were perched on the top of her head as if she didn't want to see too clearly the state Duncan was in. (He was already a couple of slick cocktails to the good.) Her face looked rounder without the glasses. Her eyes smaller, less dramatic.

'I should have worn my Sforza's name badge this morning,' he said. 'At least he'd have got my name right.'

'You know I was the one who told Frank who you were, right? That first time I went to Sforza's with him. He had no idea.' Duncan's face must've started melting, because Uffy added, 'Listen, Frank's not all bad. He's just built to make movies. He's good for little else.'

'When are you going to go out on your own?'

'It's complicated.'

'I'll bet it is. I worked for him for two weeks, I can't imagine what it's like after— how many years?'

'Did you really mean what you said this morning?'

'I said a lot of things.'

'Before you lost your wig. When you were talking about the levitators. That cult? It sounded like you believed in them.'

'I got caught up. In everything. The whirlwind.'

'And now?'

'If I was a stock exchange I'd have suspended trading. This helps,' he said. He took a sip from his tumbler and found there was only ice, a twist of orange peel and a maraschino cherry left.

'Nine years,' Uffy said, reaching across the coffee-ringed writing desk that had been repurposed as a bar table to pluck the cherry from his glass. 'That's how long I've been with Frank.'

'The skeletons you must know about!'

'There's not—' She bit down on the cherry. 'It's not how you imagine.'

'Come on. The history of film is the history of creeps. D.W. Griffith, Roman Polanski, Woody Allen, Frank Motta. You can tell me. I signed all those NDAs, remember?'

'You think that's the history of film?'

'Okay, maybe I used some selective editing there. But you can add me to the list. I'm waking up to how my approach to film comes from a deeply creepy place. And how Hollywood makes it all feel okay.'

She shook her head. 'What he said to you was true. It's hard to stay up so long when everyone's trying to bring you down. I mean, he's no angel, but—'

He pressed his palms flat and hard against the desk. 'Are you scared? To make that break? To make something yourself?'

'Must be my round,' she said, standing.

Later, through the blur of dry Martinis and Dorothy Parkers, he'd passed Uffy a memory stick. 'I believe that fulfils my contractual obligations.'

'You got the cult on here?'

'Gotta keep something back for me.'

'And those papers you were waving around this morning? Some scenes?'

'Na-uh.'

'Fine. But I'd be interested in reading them. I could give you notes.'

'That's what they all say.' He took another drink and tried to reconcile his conviction the film *Giuseppe* was a charade with the detail of Uffy's itinerary, her eagerness to see his pages. 'You guys really were going to do the road trip yourselves, weren't you?'

'Uh-huh.'

'Why? To give Echo Park something?'

Uffy kept her lips pressed together.

'And Frank really did need to stay back to work on the edits of, what is it?'

'*Folding the River.*'

'Any good?'

'It's of a piece with his recent work.'

'Leave him.'

'And I should take career advice from you because?'

'Because it's the gin-truth talking, not me.'

She sucked through her straw with her eyebrows lifted.

'With just a splash of vermouth-truth thrown in for good measure,' he said. 'Whose idea was it to send me? When Frank's fortnight in Italy fell through?'

'That was all Frank.'

'And you tried to stop him wasting my time?'

'I didn't think it was fair to get your hopes up.'

'Why didn't you just tell me? When you were taking me through the itinerary in such painstaking detail?'

'Where was the vermouth-truth then?' She smiled, swapped out her normal voice for a Facts of Life one. 'Your hopes were already up, Duncan. Who knew how you'd react. Besides, your stuff might still come in useful one day.' She held up his memory stick. 'If we have to go into production. We can't cry wolf for ever.'

'Leave him. Forget about Frank and make something yourself.'

'Funny,' she said, 'that's the same advice I was about to give you.'

★

A month after his return to LA, she'd called him. 'I went looking for you at Sforza's.'

'Unlucky.'

'I know.'

'I'm looking for work,' he said, 'if that's why you're calling?'

'I was hoping to unload over a Dorothy Parker. Don't worry, I've found another victim.'

Click.

That was the extent of their friendship — which is to say no friendship at all, but they weren't adversaries.

And now, with this latest call, she is offering him two tickets to the West Coast premiere of *Giuseppe* more than two years after his Italian road trip.

He accepts the offer.

She's going to email the tickets through, but he convinces her to meet up the night before the screening.

He has observed the progress of *Giuseppe* from a distance, through the old *Hollywood Reporter* and *Deadline* drip-feed, but can only guess at why it actually got made. Until five minutes ago he hardly cared. Forget about how he'd been used as a distraction:

371

he'd been genuinely busy, despite not sliding back into his job at Sforza's or any other kind of regular employment. He'd judged a short film competition in New Zealand, which had led to a string of other tasks he could carry out from LA, while playing the canny-uncle role on a couple of projects in the US. And then there was that other life. Family life. The one everyone must pretend doesn't exist if they want to get anywhere. He got sick of pretending. When he took Kari and Zeb back to New Zealand to visit his whānau that first Christmas after his Italian job, he wrote 'Stay at home dad' on his Customs card, which was true enough but, like Vilma calling herself a 'writer', it was also a form of wishful thinking.

And now, in the fall of 2019, what would Vilma be writing on her Customs card?

Was there space enough for 'Writer, Director, Producer, Actor'?

He'd read the script she sent him on his flight from Rome to LA, and now *Come Together* has almost wrapped filming. It's one of those three- to six-million-dollar jobs that not long ago might have languished on the festival circuit, if it ever got made at all, but in the age of streaming is now seen — by the algorithms, if not every last person in the industry — as low risk with the potential to catch fire. As well as writing and directing, Vilma plays the lead, also named Vilma Vegas, an aspiring actress who responds to a job ad for a 'sex therapy assistant'. The male impulse with such a story would have taken it into *American Pie* territory, where the aim is to land on the pinhead of a PG-13 rating to excuse the titillation of its audience and objectification of its cast. But Vilma steered right into the skid. The target was an R-rating and, once there, to expose the lunacy of the entire system.

'With everything else Vilma is subjected to,' she told him once, referring to the character, though the line between the two of them was deliberately blurred, 'the racism, sexism, the economic exploitation, the thing you want to protect the kids from is seeing her snatch?'

The script had made him squirm — for his prudishness and hypocrisy — as often as it made him howl with laughter.

He had not been popular in cattle class during that first read.

He is set to earn another producer credit on his IMDb profile for *Come Together*. It'll be token, like his *Fury's Reach* credit, though he feels okay about this one. He *has* helped. Not because he saw it as an alternative way to resurrect his career. It just felt good. It felt right. The way the phone calls he made actually led somewhere. How his praise of Vilma's script fed into an upward spiral of her enthusiasm and self-belief and the distance that took her in such a short space of time. It was something to behold.

He has kept away from the shoot, but she still rings him every night.

'I'm invited to a screening of *Giuseppe* at the DGA,' he tells her after her daily download.

'Shit! When?'

'Next month.'

'Has there been a trailer yet? There must've been. I've been so out of it.'

'Understandably. Are you getting your laptop?'

'Let's both watch it together now.'

'I'm not sure I want to.'

'Come on. Come on, come on.' He thinks, not for the first time, that it could be Mack on the other end of the line. That he must bring it out of people, this friendly antagonism. 'Yep, here it is,' she says. 'It was uploaded fourteen days ago. Can't be a good sign that neither of us knew.'

'Seven thousand views? Eesh.'

'So you've got it up? Come on, click play on three. One, two—'

'Vilma.'

'Three.'

The trailer opens with a man in silhouette, leaning on a doorway. The only music: a slow, menacing drum beat.

I am unworthy, a raspy, whispered voice begins. The man in the doorway is captured by a handheld shot, making the viewer feel as if they are really there, standing behind this man dressed in what appear to be rags. Giuseppe's departure from Martina Franca, perhaps?

I am unclean. I do not deserve God's grace or the Virgin's love.

Cut to the logos of Echo Park and two other production companies, then back to shots of friars falling to their knees with their eyes cast up, a scrum of frenzied villagers, a weeping nun.

I did not ask for this. I ask every day for it to stop.

The screen goes black again. A hum begins to build, like an approaching storm or a plague of locusts.

White text on black:

FROM
AWARD-WINNING DIRECTOR
FRANK MOTTA

Shots of a calvary being erected, swallows zipping around at dusk, a courtyard inundated with rain.

But it does not stop.

Back to the man leaning on the doorway. He steps away from the threshold. Away from the camera. He is barefoot.

The names of American actors appear on screen, none with any real box-office pull.

The man stops after fifteen or twenty paces, perfectly framed by the doorway. A classic Motta shot.

Why won't you believe me? he pleads in voiceover. *What will it take?*

More text against a black background:

AND INTRODUCING PIERFRANCO FICCO AS GIUSEPPE

The stormy soundfield cuts off. The man — Pierfranco/Giuseppe — rises into the air with arms outstretched and hovers there for three seconds.

Cut to black.

IN CINEMAS OCTOBER 21

'What'd you think?' Vilma asks.

He'd forgotten that she'd been watching it too, that she's still on the line. Nothing much had happened on screen, and yet he is unnerved. Maybe it was the lighting. They'd nailed the lighting. Or maybe it's being confronted with the story of Giuseppe again after believing he'd moved on.

He says, 'They nailed the lighting.'

'Is that all you got to say?'

'I don't know. What'd you think?'

'I think they'll struggle to break even, despite the undisputed star power of Gary Sinese.'

'Don't forget Neal McDonough.'

'But they made him a brunette. I hardly recognised him without his bleached hair. So you're gonna go, I take it?'

'To the screening? There's a Q&A with Motta afterward.'

'You should totally ask him something. You've got time to come up with *the* perfect question.'

'Nah. Someone else can take their shot. I have a feeling there'll be quite a queue.'

'You'll take Kari with you, right?'

'Sure,' he says. 'If we can find a babysitter.'

'I thought things were peachy between you two?'

'They are. But tell me, how much more do you have left to shoot?'

★

Zeb's in bed and Kari is on her way out for another meeting with her collaborator — *Book two won't write itself!* — when he finally has a chance to tell her about yesterday's phone call with Uffy and his invitation to the special screening of *Giuseppe*.

Kari: 'You should take Mack.'

'What about you?'

'Me? I can mind the fort for one night. Besides, she'll recognise the places. I won't.'

If Duncan's life was a movie, there would have been a single, concise, dramatic conversation with Kari upon his return from Italy. A chance for her to call him out for the Chromecast incident and the rest of the pornographic iceberg, for his self-centredness and his constant need of amelioration, for how she had to engineer time for him and Mack to really connect and he'd let her run off to another cult in her vulnerable state. But theirs isn't that kind of marriage — is any? Instead, these things brushed the surface in bad jokes or went unsaid in pregnant pauses. It lay beneath the increased affection between the two of them, the spark that made a simple cuddle seem worth the effort or no effort at all. His life wasn't a movie and he'd stopped acting like the director of it. Stopped expecting Kari to always be there, the hopeful starlet desperately clinging to her big chance. And she'd changed too. After years of growing out her hair, she reverted to the distracted student bob from university days. What worked for endless exams, waitressing and a permanent hangover also suited parenthood. There's something pleasing about this cycling back, as if she'd been trying to become someone else, had been sculling against the current and finally said, 'Fuck it.' It's sexy as hell. Way more than just a haircut. She still works her day job, making dull things beautiful, making rich people richer, but has illustrated a children's book about a plucky fennec fox written by one of her friends. The book is due to hit shelves before Christmas. Sketches of the big-eared heroine jostle for space on the refrigerator with the simple geometries of Zeb's houses and trucks.

'It'll come out on DVD eventually, won't it?' she says.

'DVD?'

'Or digital download or whatever. You know what I mean.'

'Mack won't come. She seems happy up in La Crosse.'

'You know as much as I do,' Kari says. She pecks him on his cheek, 'Gotta dash,' and goes out to her car.

Did Duncan ever suspect this illustrating sideline was cover for an affair? Of course. For a time. The more proof emerged of the project's existence, the more deviant it seemed. Hadn't he built a career in film as cover for his own voyeurism? No, whatever he's built, it isn't a career.

And Kari isn't him, thank God.

It is a daily battle to get over himself. A full-time job. Try writing that on a Customs card.

Occupation: Getting over myself.

He has come to terms with the fact his mother-in-law's estimation of him is permanently diminished and, possibly worse, nothing he does has any impact whatsoever on his father-in-law.

And Mack?

For the longest time he didn't even know where she was. He got an email from Red Valerian six weeks after his return to LA, ostensibly asking how they both were but mostly interested in Mack. Duncan's native scepticism told him not to reply. That, even though there were no apparent fishhooks in this email, it was part of a bigger plan. That the questions about his Mille Fiori film and his flying dreams and his son would come in later messages. So he replied with one line:

As far as I know, Mack is still in Italy. We parted ways shortly after leaving San Marino.

Red replied, asking to Skype. This set alarm bells ringing, but he agreed. It was thrilling to flirt with danger, only Red really was just interested in Mack. And it seemed to be for personal reasons. As if he was tempted to leave Mille Fiori to track her down. Though Duncan couldn't help and, as far as he knew, Red had stayed put.

He got an email from Mack that Christmas — a picture of her in a desert somewhere giving a thumbs-up and the words *I'm still alive, babe* — and another on his birthday — *I bought the villagers a goat and named it after you, old man* — but that was it until she arrived on Duncan's doorstep in the middle of 2018. She wore her long leather coat and a look that said, *Wait till you hear what I've been up to*.

After ditching him in Osimo, she had spent a month with the time travellers in Damanhur, then bounced from new-age commune to new-age commune, slowly tracking east through the Balkans, Turkey, Israel, India, the Philippines, Papua New Guinea and the Pacific Northwest, walking over hot coals and submerging in sensory-deprivation tubs, until reaching LA with a pitch for a video game based on her experiences.

'It's called *Destiny Manifest*. The player must travel from place to place, acquiring the special ability each cult, kibbutz or tribe focuses on — imperviousness to pain, mind reading, flight, time travel, resurrection — but with that same cringe-if-you-think-about-it, colonial-disaster-tourist feel of *Oregon Trail* and those old Sid Meier games. The player needs to be able to manifest these supranormal abilities for the boss battle to end all boss battles and stave off Armageddon.'

'Supranormal? It sounds— How much of this do you believe?'

She ruffled the back of her head, and he thought: she hasn't changed at all. Her look. Her way of talking. A year without contact, a year with Buddhists and barbarians, and she was back to her riffing ways before he could make her a cup of tea.

'Babe,' she said, 'the only thing I'm cynical about is the end.

GP was right about a lot of things, including that Doomsday preppers are the worst. Better to believe in positive evolution than aim to be the cockroach that survives mutual destruction. But I can't see how the game works without that looming prospect. It's *Save the Cat!*, right? That's why I'm here. I need a script consult.'

Kari's parents were visiting at the time, but Mack was happy to crash on the couch. 'The ability to sleep anywhere is one talent I *did* acquire in the last twelve months.' And he was happy for the distraction she provided. Teresa had begun to fixate on a couple of wistful remarks he'd made about New Zealand and recently confronted him about a non-existent plan to ditch LA and take her grandson half a world away.

Dwarf Star David just sat in the armchair, absorbed in his magazines.

To everyone's surprise, David proved the most help for Mack. 'The hard-won simplicity of board games,' he explained with hard-won simplicity. He helped her key in on what she wanted to do, which was offer a counter to the hyper-repetitive, quick-hit, thrill-packed battle royale games like *Fortnite* and *PUBG* that had come to dominate the landscape. A hundred players parachute on to a map and shoot each other up until there's one left standing. You die? Start a new game. You win? Start a new game.

'But what does any of it mean?' she'd said to David, who sat like a therapist, his index fingers pressed together against his philtrum, while Duncan sat at the dining table Googling what the indentation between your nose and upper lip was called. 'It's pure gaming — and I'm not saying it isn't hella fun, it is — but it's meaningless. At least *League of Legends* and *DoTA* tried to have backstories, mythologies, if you went looking. I want something that builds, something one person works away at over time, *without* competition. It's all on you. You're the only person in the world on this particular quest.'

'Is that really what people need?' Duncan asked. 'To be told they *are* the centre of the universe?'

'Hmm,' Mack said, not turning to look at him. 'Maybe the only avatars you can select are female?'

Together, David and Mack mapped out the journey the player would take using a *Risk* board. They talked incessantly about pacing. Duncan was there too. He helped, but not enough to win a writing credit through arbitration, if such a process exists for video games. He didn't look it up. He didn't care. He was glad to have Mack back from the clutches of the cultists, and away from the toxicity of the e-sports scene, at least for the time being.

When David and Teresa flew back to Wisconsin, Mack followed a week later. In short order, she attracted a small band of developers to work out of the Sedlaks' garage. Teresa brought them plates of cookies and sat cross-legged on the Turkish rug in team meetings. David never set foot in the garage.

'He's like a guru, babe,' she'd told Duncan over Skype. 'Sitting in his armchair. He won't talk to the younger ones. It's an honour to have an audience with him.'

'If this was your game, he'd be the final boss battle, right? The Yoda figure who reveals he was the antagonist all along. That he was just toying with you—'

'David?'

'—only, he's underestimated your abilities.'

'David?'

'If this was a game. For the twist.'

'That's some twist.'

'You can't see it?'

She leaned into her screen and shook her head as if to say, *Oh Duncan.*

★

With Kari off to work on book two, Duncan is left to his own devices. He sends Mack a text message: *Wanna Skype?*

Mack: *Maybe tomorrow?*

Duncan: *You want to come to the West Coast premiere of GIUSEPPE with me?*

Mack: *In LA?*

Duncan: *In LA.*

Mack: *When?*

Duncan: *Next month.*

Mack: *What about Kari?*

Duncan: *She said I should take you.*

Mack: *What about Zeb?*

Duncan: *Okay, I can take a hint.*

Mack: *No, seriously. He might like it? Plus, things are hectic here.*

★

He slides back into his routine of school pick-ups and drop-offs, of meals prepared and their aftermaths erased, of bedtime stories and broken sleep, of time alone spent on his playlist of *Destiny Manifest*-vibed songs for Mack (The Horrors, REO Speedwagon, Aldous Harding . . .) and hiking in Caballero and Coldwater canyons, O'Melveny and Wilacre parks, of *Caution: Rattlesnakes* signs and the spurious clatter of crickets, of faintly familiar faces from TV spots and billboards but no stone-cold celebs, all the while thinking about other places, other times. Such as? Well, this one in particular.

An autumn day in his twenties on the underside of the world. He'd wrapped the shoot for *Curio Bay* and was in the midst of the edit. It was looking good, better than he could have hoped. But he'd lost track of what day it was. He needed to get outside, change his focal length. He walked from his flat in North Dunedin down to the steamer basin, and followed the edge of the harbour along Portsmouth Drive before climbing up into the hilltop suburb of Waverly. There were large homes with balconies jutting in all directions, and smaller, squatter, brick affairs, but all were trained on the view of the harbour and the city he'd later come to think of as perfectly sized.

He came to a mid-century wonder with floor-to-ceiling windows on the upper level. From the footpath he could see the stained timber ceiling and a brass light fixture that spidered into small lampshades like white peace lilies.

The house was for sale. There was no indication of price on the sign out front. Nothing yet to stub out his daydreaming.

A car pulled up. A man in a blue suit got out and began to erect an Open Home flag. So, Duncan thought, it's Sunday.

'Sorry, mate,' the estate agent said, 'running a little late.'

'That's fine,' he said, and stuffed his hands in his pockets.

Inside, it was as if someone had stitched together fragments of every house he'd loved as a child: the exposed beams, the private courtyard off the master bedroom, the planter of mortared river stones, the gingko in the planter, the step-down living room, the red-brick feature wall with floating liquor cabinet, the pair of armchairs with their hind legs stretching back like a sprinter in the blocks. Each room glowed. All that glass. All that wood. The rimu floorboards upstairs. The cork tile in the basement conversion. The veneer on the walls. The coffee tables, the dressers and tiger-striped sideboard.

'I think that's teak,' said the agent, who must have seen Duncan run his fingers along the wood. 'She's something, isn't she?'

'Yep,' Duncan said.

'That view.'

Duncan nodded, took hold of the veneer slider that separated the living room from a smaller space, moved it back and forth as if testing its rollers, and let the door close in the agent's face. It was a kind of reading nook, this second room. The walls were covered with built-in bookshelves full of paperbacks, their spines creased and cracked, the titles and authors fading to nothing. Why wasn't anyone else at the open home? Why was it even on the market? How could anyone have this and move on to something else?

Back in the living room, the ceiling felt higher, more chapel-like. The view more expansive. A squadron of tiny Optimists, helmed by invisible children, slid away from the unseen yacht club at Vauxhall.

He thought about the protagonist of *Curio Bay* training his sight on one of the novice sailors.

It'd be quite a shot.

The holiday house down in the Catlins, the one featured in his movie, was of the same vintage, though designed with less flair. Preserved only by neglect.

I could buy this home, he thought. Maybe not today. But I'm finally getting somewhere with my filmmaking. Maybe this thing will take off?

The mates who'd helped him with the shoot had begun to regard him with a kind of awe. His old supervisor from university, to whom he'd shown a rough cut a couple of days earlier, had been rendered mute in person — *was it really that bad?* — but sent a long email the next day that began, 'I haven't stopped thinking about what you have created.'

The confidence he'd felt, in that moment, all those years ago, in that honey-toned room in Waverly, had not been misplaced. The finished film *had* found an audience. It *had* opened doors for him.

And he'd walked through.

As he tramps around Topanga and Solstice Canyon, ever conscious of the time and cellphone reception in case Zeb needs to be picked up early, he considers a different version of this story: him moving back to Dunedin, knocking on that door in Waverly and making the current owners an offer they can't refuse. But here he is, wearing out another pair of sneakers, relying on Kari's salary to pay the bills. Even if they had the money to up sticks and return to New Zealand, he can't do that to Zeb. His transition to school was rocky, but he now goes without complaint. His teachers aren't worried about him — which, in itself, might be cause for concern — and he doesn't seem to get bullied. Perhaps his classmates are too young to leave a lasting mark with their fists or their put-downs. Though Zeb refuses to write — something about the irreversibility of the act, even with pencil — he loves to read. He'll throw a hissy fit if a movie is turned off before the end of the credits. Reading that scroll of names and titles under his breath is a challenge of the highest order, an incantation of great power, though the meaning of the words must still be beyond him.

Background makeup supervisor
Dimmer tech
First assistant director: second unit
Second second assistant director
Greens foreman
Prop maker gang boss
Fabricator
Utility tech
ADR mixer
Rotoscoping artist
Render support
Image pipeline supervisor
Lead matchmove artist
Depth lead
Stunt rigger
Casting associate
Ager/dyer
Key assistant location manager
Orchestrator
Picture car dispatcher
Dialect coach
Animal wrangler

★

For his reunion with Uffy, he chooses the closest thing to Bukowski's in LA — the velvet sofas, the kitschy artwork — but finds the people there too theatrical. He can't remember the last time he went out at night. If Kari isn't out collaborating, the two of them just power through their parenting and crumple into each other to binge another show for which they are unfashionably late to the party. LA tonight is one big casting call. Everyone made up. Faking it. Totally committed to their roles. Only the cigarettes are real.

Uffy, though. She doesn't seem to mind.

'I've left Frank,' she says without prompting.

'About blimmin' time.'

'Only a handful of people know, so don't run your mouth. It's all planned out. By the time the *Reporter* breaks the story, there'll be nothing much to say. An amicable parting after a long and productive partnership. A desire to work on different projects.' She rolls her eyes.

She's changed her look, replacing the pin stripes with a floral print, and ditching the glasses completely.

'So what's next for you?' he asks.

'Oh,' she says, 'fifteen different things, you know how it is.'

'And *Giuseppe*? What does it look like? I mean, I've seen the trailer, but that's like judging how happy someone is by their Instagram.'

'I have a strict No Spoilers policy.'

'No kidding.'

'You and your plus-one will just have to find out tomorrow.'

'I was thinking of taking my son.'

She squints at him. 'How old is he?'

'Six. But a weird six.'

'It'd be a weird dad that would take a child to that movie.'

'Parenting is like backing a trailer,' he says. 'Do you drive?'

'I'm from New York.'

'What I mean is, your natural instincts, your adult logic, often it's better to do the opposite. Being a good person — generous,

385

patient — doesn't automatically make you a good parent. It might fuck up your kid. Set them up for a life of dissatisfaction.'

'So, you're a good person?'

'And bad people,' he says, ignoring the question, 'can make great parents if they channel their selfishness in the right way. Their cut-throat natures.'

'You writing a parenting book?'

'Just time on my hands.'

'Don't be modest. I heard about your thing with Miss Vegas.'

'It's her thing,' he says. 'I just helped her a little along the way. She needed a cheerleader more than a mentor.'

'Well, good for you.'

He says, 'I'm dabbling in new media,' succumbing to that self-promotional slipstream, his weaker nature. He doesn't want a job. *I just want to be liked.*

'Video games?'

He shrugs. 'Did Motta ever—? I mean, he made *Giuseppe* because of what happened after we were in Italy, right? The fall of Weinstein and what that started. Spacey, Ratner, fucking John Lever —' he pumps his fist— 'Louis C.K., Charlie Rose, Matt Lauer . . . He figured he was next and needed to finally make his religious flick. His selfless, commercially fraught *non mea culpa*, right?'

'It was an interesting time to have finance secured. To have actors attached. To have a clear vision for the look and feel of the picture, and set designers ready to go.'

'So you used my stuff?'

'No spoilers,' she says, and smiles. 'But,' she whispers, 'you really should have gotten an entertainment lawyer to read through the contract you signed.'

'The trailer had seven thousand views in its first fortnight. There'll be no residuals.'

'You want to know why *Giuseppe* got made? For starters, my daughter got sick.'

'Your daughter? How old—?'

'Twelve. She's twelve now. Some virus took her — *and me* — out of commission for a month. Just when #MeToo started blowing up. Frank panicked, I wasn't there to counsel him otherwise, and *Giuseppe* passed the point of no return. Turns out he can do the business side when he sets his mind to it.'

'I didn't know you even— Why did you let me blather on about parenting?'

'Years of practice.'

'But you're saying I'm right, aren't you. It is just one big, cynical, cinematic diversion?'

'I wouldn't say that.'

'What would you say?'

'No. Spoilers.'

★

Duncan sits next to Zeb, six rows back in the six-hundred-seat Theater One at the Directors Guild of America on Sunset Boulevard. *Giuseppe* opened with little fanfare in New York the night before. Nothing about that screening has made it into the Hollywood press, and the only tweets he's found are amusingly vague, calling Motta a 'master filmmaker', a 'safe pair of hands', an 'old head', or complaining about the rudeness of an usher or the poor lumbar support of the seats. Despite the promise of a Q&A with the director after tonight's screening, and the jumbo shrimp and thumbnail blinis in the lobby after that, there's still a good many empty seats. Perhaps because this is *exclusive*. For DGA members and their guests only. But Duncan isn't a DGA member. He still doesn't have the hours and, though Echo Park had made noises about helping him to join back in the days of *Fury's Reach*, it's no longer a pressing concern. No. It's thanks to Uffy they're there. How many others are mere seat-fillers? How many are getting paid to be here and how many are schmucks like him?

There's a gentle trickle of applause as Motta and his entourage file in to take their seats in the front row. So, he thinks, that's really all there is. Two hundred people max to see the maestro's passion project. But then the movie opens just as it had in Duncan's vision — Felice Desa being pursued by the camera through the streets of Copertino to be met by his wife's cold shoulder, the explosion of images when his hand touches her full-term belly — and he has to look around once more.

Is this some kind of joke? Will the people in the row behind him remove their masks and reapply their Mille Fiori pins, as if this was another Sister-Francesca-Wants-to-Kill-You-style headfuck? As if they know how hard he's been trying not to make everything about him. To take a back seat. And then this. How could he resist?

He can't.

It's irresistible.

The first two hundred seconds of screen time has played out just as he foresaw that afternoon in Rome outside Basil's rental-car office. Just as he'd described on those pages he typed up well past midnight at the Hotel Pacific and brandished in that depressing room in the Vatican.

Brandished but never relinquished.

He'd thrown the pages from the Ponte Sant'Angelo and watched until they hit the Tiber.

The file hadn't been on the memory stick he gave to Uffy.

There is no way anyone could have punked him to this degree.

So, then, maybe it's all just some massive fluke? A coincidence that can be explained away thanks to him mainlining Motta's oeuvre before landing his location-scouting gig. Of course he'd begin to see the story as Motta might. As Motta did.

On screen, Franceschina is stumbling into the stable to give birth. Both Duncan's version and Motta's neglect to reveal how Felice responds to his premonitions. His glimpses of the misery and otherness and ecstasy of his son. If he, Duncan Blake, had been granted such a slideshow of Zeb's life before he was born —

or even now: there was still so much ahead of him, so much that could go wrong — would he react with horror or joy?

Probably just confusion and disbelief.

Like now.

He squeezes his son's thigh. It's approaching Zeb's normal bedtime but he's engrossed. There *is* an *X-Men* vibe to it all. The premonitions. The imminent levitations. The suggestion that Giuseppe's gifts are powerful mutations inherited from his hapless father.

Premonitions.

That's the truth of it, isn't it? Those bolts of inspiration hadn't been inspiration at all but foresight. Somehow he'd seen snippets of this movie before it had been made. The same part of his brain that made him fly in his dreams had cast itself forward and retrieved chunks of Frank Motta's *Giuseppe*.

He feels it then, actually feels it as he pushes back in his cushy theatre seat: the rush of white blood cells, the body's cynics, up to his head to swamp the site of the infection. This idea that is beyond the bounds. This thought that cannot be permitted to take hold. For the sake of sanity. To maintain whatever shreds of security and respect and love he has left.

After two years of fooling himself that he has regained control.

Two years.

Franceschina is experiencing the first stabs of labour. Unlike the Nativity, there are no animals to bear witness. It's the middle of the day outside. The horses are out pulling ploughs or doing other horsey things. Maybe they've already been slaughtered for the table.

What would Mack say to this?

Duncan works his hand into Zeb's. The boy looks up at his father as if he's a stranger but — *small mercy* — doesn't withdraw his hand.

The camera pulls in close on Franceschina's face. The sweat cascading down her brow. The way her top lip arches, as if she'll deliver a cutting one-liner or a curse. But there is no one there to hear it.

It's strange watching another Motta film again after his moratorium. There's a kind of beauty in every shot that is both geometric and tactical. Every frame has been agonised over, though it now feels to Duncan this beauty comes at the expense of the humanity of the character. Franceschina is but an object, perfectly lit. Her pain, her heavy breathing, are an element of sound design. Hardly the sort of thing that might inoculate Motta from the avalanche of #MeToo takedowns. But the final product doesn't seem to matter. Either the sheer fact of its production has done the job — there he is in the front row at the DGA — or it was unnecessary. Maybe there really is no truth to the rumours. The one case of smoke without fire. But it's hard to believe, even with Uffy vouching for him. Which explains the empty seats. The presumption of innocence is so June 2017. And even if he is squeaky clean — which, again, *really*? — Uffy has every right to enact their amicable split. Motta is no longer 'bank'. This vain, sweating, froggish, self-involved man. If he isn't cancer, he's a rattling cough in a hospital waiting room. He's had a good run. A great run. But this film about a simple Italian boy with supernatural abilities, be they granted by a biblical God or one operating at the level of DNA, might even be his last.

After the beauty and horror of Franceschina's solitary labour, Motta cuts to her carrying Giuseppe, aged nine or ten, afflicted with his debilitating tumour, to the hermit in Galatone. The sun is harsh. The landscape flat and dry. The olive trees have been planted by digital-effects artists, but the average viewer — even the average Salentino — would buy that this is actually shot in the heel of Italy. The hermit receives Giuseppe in front of a small church, the one Duncan captured on his second day with Gianluca. It's another VFX job, his stills painted over whatever ply and two-by-four job the crew erected down in Mexico to cast the right shadows. The symbolism is clear: they are doing this outside because the act is not sanctioned by the Church. The pouring of oil from a lamp that burned before an image of the Madonna is too close to paganism or sorcery.

But it works.

In this version of the story, at least.

Motta's *Giuseppe* proceeds to replicate all of Duncan's visions: the novice's eviction from Martina Franca, his trial in Naples, his spiritual dryness in Assisi and his own premonition on the verge of Rome that signalled the return of his charisms, the villagers tearing apart the church in Pietrarubbia and his death in Osimo. When Duncan wrote his visions down, that night in the Hotel Pacific, he became aware for the first time how Giuseppe was not presented as the village idiot. Far from the bumbler of Edward Dmytryk's *The Reluctant Saint*, his Giuseppe spoke in the same high formal mode as the other characters. His innate intelligence had been kept in check by his childhood infirmity, but he was no laughing stock. He had dignity. He could not be dismissed.

As Zeb dutifully reads the credits aloud, Duncan tries to make sense of what he's seen. All up, his premonitions, his pages, accounted for only about fifteen minutes of run-time, but the first two were enough. More than déjà vu. More than a string of epileptic episodes fucking with his temporal lobe, planting false memories. Yes, his brain is on the edge of chaos, but whose isn't? He is not special, but this experience is. It's outside the bounds of what is thought possible, but only because those bounds are too narrow. In Italy he'd softened toward all things telekinetic. Thought it had broken him. But rather than a dam breaking, it was like the first tear in the pocket of a new pair of jeans. The kind you think: Oh great. First time I wear these things and they're already falling apart. But then the pocket doesn't tear anymore and the jeans last forever. Back in LA he'd tried to levitate a handful of times, in his bathroom and on the edge of canyons, but nothing had happened. He was able to turn his back on all of it, put these thoughts in a shoebox labelled *Claptrap* and slide it under his bed.

He hasn't had a flying dream since. He hasn't touched the footage he shot in Mille Fiori. He's treated Mack's supranormal game as a piece of fiction. The little tear in him hasn't grown, but it is still there. And now— What? Is this his version of seeing his mother levitate on the back lawn in the middle of the night? What will following this thought, *believing* in it, require him to give up?

When the houselights finally come up, it's as if they're all inside the belly of a whale. The bright white ribs of the lights. The deep red of the seats and the curtain that has come across the screen. Two armchairs have appeared on stage, separated by a low table furnished with two glasses of water. Motta sits in one chair, his right leg crossed over his left knee, exposing a candy-striped sock. He's back to his low-key dapper self, not the primped palooka he'd been for his audience with the Pope, but Duncan can't un-see the Baron Greenback in him. Perched on the edge of the other chair is Fiona Ebbett, director of a couple of Sundance darlings and a documentary series for Amazon Prime on the Green Christian movement in the UK.

'A spot of housekeeping first,' Ebbett says, her accent pleasingly regional, though Duncan can't say which region. 'As regulars will know, this talk will be recorded for the DGA's podcast. There'll be time for two or three questions from the floor at the end, which may or may not make the podcast. And with that said, let's give another show of our gratitude and awe for the work of this fine director, one of the finest, seated to my right.'

An obliging round of applause.

'What a fantastic crowd, isn't it, Frank? We've all packed in here today to watch your latest film, *Giuseppe*, and it'd be fair to say this one was a long time coming?'

'Yes, that would be fair,' Motta says, steepling his fingers and launching into a standard retelling of the genesis of *Giuseppe*: the waterfall in Hawaii, the stories from his Nonna and Sunday School and the fact these normal-looking, God-fearing, workaday people believed in levitation, his looking into it more and more and finding it harder and harder to dismiss, and the challenges of getting a script that met his expectations.

Ebbett's a decent chair, letting Motta run as long as he has momentum, interjecting whenever he begins to flag, steering the conversation elsewhere, though it never goes beyond Motta's comfort zone. Any discussion of future projects seems verboten. And his personal life? Forget about it.

Zeb is trying hard to follow what's being said, but it looks as if his forehead is holding back a considerable weight. A weight that might come down like a garage door at any moment.

But they need to stay. To see this through.

After twenty-five minutes, Ebbett has the houselights brought up and invites questions from the audience. No one moves.

Duncan remembers Vilma telling him he should ask Motta something. That he had time to come up with the perfect question. Time he's squandered walking canyon trails and pining for Dunedin.

'We have a roving mic,' Ebbett says. 'Don't be shy.'

He'd been so sure that Motta had a rotten core, that it was only a matter of time. That it was time for conflict. For comeuppance. For truth. But no one is calling for the mic. Maybe it is all smoke, no fire. All of it. Maybe that's the problem. He's been put through the wringer by this film and Motta probably doesn't believe in any of it.

È una gran tentazione non avere tentazioni.

It is a great temptation to have no temptation.

Duncan pats Zeb on the shoulder and stands.

A runner with an orange t-shirt over a white business shirt delivers a wireless mic. Motta makes a visor with his hand to block the stage lights.

'Hi Frank,' Duncan says. 'Congratulations on finally making this film, which I know you've wanted to make for a long, long time. My question is: now that you've scratched the itch, what next?'

Fiona Ebbett mouths her thanks.

Motta's hands are wrapped around the armrests, one butt cheek lifted off the seat, his eyes cast down at the front row. After a beat, he raises his head and says, 'Blake Duncan, everybody. He did some great work on the locations for this film.' If this is supposed to elicit a round of applause, another diversion, it doesn't work.

'Or,' Duncan says, 'did this picture scratch the itch at all? Was the itch *ever* real?'

'Those are some great questions,' Motta says, still readjusting himself as if someone has tipped a lunchbox of salamanders on to the stage.

The silence builds. Ebbett doesn't look like she's about to break it. Everyone wants to know.

'Look, if this is about the credits, maybe there was an oversight. I don't know.'

'It's not about the credits, Frank. It's about the itch. Belief. Levitation. Telekinesis.'

Motta smiles. Manic. Cornered.

'What do you want me to say? Of course the itch was real. What San Giuseppe da Copertino did, what he represents, is absolutely real. It's indisputable to me. Indisputable. I believe profoundly in the capacity of the human individual. In contrast to that, I do not believe any collection of humans has the ability to manage a deception on the scale of what we see in the evidence for San Giuseppe's acts. There's no conspiracy. It's hard enough to make a two-hour picture hang together with a team of two hundred. But I know words are cheap. I deal in images. But I believe. More than that: I know.' It looks as if he might snap the armrests off of his chair. 'I don't know what else I could do to—'

Motta stills. His back straightens.

He leans forward, takes the coffee table with both hands and pulls it in front of him, something prim about his movements, like a white-gloved butler following his master's orders or a female server placing a high chair beside an ogling father. 'I guess there's this,' he says, and refills his glass with water, his lapel mic picking up the sound. Otherwise, the theatre is silent as a tomb. Motta pushes the sleeves of his blazer midway up his forearms and holds his hands either side of the glass. There's no way Duncan could have predicted his question would lead to this. He was scratching his own itch but has knocked the scab off something bigger.

Back when Motta tried this on the *Late Show with David Letterman*, one Tuesday in November 1995, it was about now that Letterman put his finger to his ear and followed his producer's call to cut short the interview and go to a commercial. But Ebbett has no earpiece. Uffy Golinko, he senses, is not about to intercede from the front row either.

Still standing, Duncan surveys the faces behind him. The older crowd, the ones who'd presumably seen Motta's third and final appearance on *Letterman*, begin to mutter to their plus-ones. The younger tribe, the ADs and the seat-fillers, are the next to twig.

Zeb has climbed on to his seat to better see what Motta is attempting. On his face: that ageless stare.

Poor, well-meaning Fiona Ebbett, however, seems completely lost.

Motta's hands begin to shake from the strain, but he persists in his attempt to lift a glass of water with his mind.

Ten seconds, fifteen.

He winces as a bead of sweat runs down the side of his nose, but his hands don't leave the airspace around the glass.

Twenty seconds, twenty-five.

The glass remains fixed to the table.

Like the blackbird on the gravel outside the convent in Fossombrone.

Like a fully conscious Duncan, alone in his bathroom with the shower running, whenever he tries to lift off like Jerry O'Connell in *My Secret Identity*.

The glass doesn't move.

Motta withdraws his hands as if suddenly scalded and collapses into his chair.

Duncan nods his thanks, lifts the mic to his lips one last time and says, 'Nice knowing you, Frank.'

★

'He's asleep?' Kari asks when Duncan edges into the living room.

'Not yet, but he should drift off.'

'He's gonna be a wreck tomorrow.'

'Yeah. How's book two coming along?'

'Meh.'

'That bad?'

She pulls a face that says she knows what's about to come out of her mouth is ridiculous. 'It's starting to feel like a job.'

'That's normal.'

'I know.'

'It'll pass. Normal never lasts long.'

From the hall: the sound of Zeb stirring. They both stop to listen.

If he is ever going to tell Kari about his premonitions, if he is going to pick up this thread and follow it properly, it's now.

'Did he like it?' she asks, her bare arms crossed as if fighting a chill.

'Zeb? He seemed to.'

'And you?'

'Hold on,' he says, raising a finger to his ear. Zeb is saying something. 'I'll just—'

'He's probably just talking to himself.'

'I'll check,' he says, and slips back into the hall.

Kari's right. Zeb is talking to himself. The kind of soothing burble he's done off and on since he started talking. Duncan is about to pull back when the trance-like rhythm strikes him. At first he thinks his son is repeating the credits for some movie, possibly even *Giuseppe*. Maybe he has a photographic memory — yet another well-guarded secret.

Duncan leans against the doorjamb.

No. It's not credits he's repeating.

Kari appears beside him and finds her way beneath his arm, in search of warmth. The two of them stand there in the faintest light, listening to their son.

The sun is a moon on fire. The moon is the earth gone cold. The stars are the dust on fire and blown by the wind in the night. The air is the water gone thin. The water is the blood of the earth. The clouds are the faces of heaven. The ladder to heaven is invisible. The man in the brown dress knows where it is. The man in the brown dress can climb it. The man in the brown dress stays up there for hours. He makes people happy but he is not. He makes people angry but he is not. I am not happy or sad or angry. I am the earth gone cold. I am the dust on fire but too far to touch. I climb the ladder in my room but the ceiling stops me. I climb the ladder behind my classroom but the bell stops me. I am the man in the brown dress in jeans and a t-shirt and shoes without laces. School shoes have laces and ticks. A school is a place of ticking and the gaps where ticks should be. The man in the brown dress couldn't close his mouth. The man in the brown dress broke the dishes. The man in the brown dress made friends with a donkey. A donkey is a horse turned cranky. A horse is a cow made fast. A cow is a mother that shares. The man in the brown dress knows the future. The man in the brown dress can heal you. The man in the brown dress is a face in the clouds. The man in the brown dress is too far to touch. The sun is a moon on fire. The moon is the earth gone cold. The stars are the dust on fire and blown by the wind in the night—

ACKNOWLEDGEMENTS

This book is dedicated to the memory of Gord Downie.

I broke the back of this book while the Robert Burns Fellow at the University of Otago in 2017, fuelled by the financial support of the fellowship, the collegiality of the English and Linguistics Department, and the bookish buzz of the southernmost City of Literature. Tēnā rawa atu koutou.

Thanks also to the New Zealand Ministry of Education and the Italian Ministero dell'Istruzione, dell'Università e della Ricerca for the opportunity to present on safety and innovation in Rome in May 2017, after which I was able (at my cost, naturally) to carry out my own location scouting.

As Trumpet Honeysuckle later admits, James Alby-Cooper's speech in the chapter 'The Wheel and the Telescope' borrows heavily from Michael Grosso's essay, 'Why Levitation' (*Rhine Magazine*, October 2013). I began this book before Grosso's *The Man Who Could Fly: St Joseph of Copertino and the Mystery of Levitation* (Rowman & Littlefield, 2015) was published, but it became a touchstone for a certain kind of thinking present in the book.

Final and biggest thanks to Marisa, Lia and Caio. I can't wait to see where you'll take me next.

The Mannequin Makers is at turns a gothic tale of a father's obsession, a castaway story worthy of a *Boy's Own* adventure and a thorny remembrance of past tragedies.

Colton Kemp is stunned when he sees the first mannequin of his new rival. Rocked by the sudden death of his wife and inspired by a travelling vaudeville company, Kemp decides to raise his children to be living mannequins. What follows is a tale of art and deception, strength and folly, love and transgression, that ranges from small town New Zealand to the graving docks of the River Clyde and an inhospitable rock in the Southern Ocean to Sydney's northern beaches.

A startlingly original collection of short stories that was winner of the 2011 Commonwealth Writers' Prize for Best First Book.

A son worries he is becoming too perfect a copy of his father. The co-owner of a weight-loss camp for teens finds himself running the black market in chocolate bars. A man starts melting and nothing can stop it, not even poetry. This terrific collection of stories moves from the serious and realistic to the humorous and outlandish, each story copying an element from the previous piece in a kind of evolutionary chain. Amid pigeons with a taste for cigarette ash, a rash of moa sightings, and the identity crisis of an imaginary friend, the characters in these eighteen entertaining stories look for ways to reconnect with people and the world around them, even if that means befriending a robber wielding an iguana.